Line of Sight

Also by Claire Askew

All the Hidden Truths
What You Pay For
Cover Your Tracks
A Matter of Time
The Dead Don't Speak

CLAIRE ASKEW

Line of Sight

HODDER &
STOUGHTON

First published in Great Britain in 2024 by Hodder & Stoughton Limited
An Hachette UK company

The authorised representative in the EEA is Hachette Ireland, 8 Castlecourt
Centre, Dublin 15, D15 XTP3, Ireland (email: info@hbgi.ie)

1

A CIP catalogue record for this title is available from the British Library

Hardback ISBN 9781529348354
Trade Paperback ISBN 9781529348361
ebook ISBN 9781529348385

Typeset in Plantin Light by Manipal Technologies Limited

Printed and bound in Great Britain by Clays Ltd, Elcograf S.p.A.

Hodder & Stoughton policy is to use papers that are natural, renewable
and recyclable products and made from wood grown in sustainable forests.
The logging and manufacturing processes are expected to conform
to the environmental regulations of the country of origin.

Hodder & Stoughton Limited
Carmelite House
50 Victoria Embankment
London EC4Y 0DZ

www.hodder.co.uk

In memory of Lorna MacDougall,
who helped make me the woman I am.

Prologue
Bee, 2010

The first time it happened, I thought it was just a dream. A weird dream like any other, though it shook me awake at 3.32am, my heart spluttering. I know it was 3.32am because I sat up in bed, put on the light, and recorded it in my dream journal: Thursday 20 May 2010, 3.32am. I wrote:

It was night, and I was standing in someone's back garden. Not somewhere I'd been before, not familiar. The house was a little white bungalow, and the garden was a long, narrow lawn with huge trees at the bottom. Leylandii that had grown out of control. I stood in the deep shadow of those trees, looking at the house. There was a main road beyond it, and I saw a lit-up N49 bus go by, empty. I walked up the garden to the back door of the bungalow, and let myself in. It was dark inside, but the moon shone into the window, and I could see in the gloom that this was the kitchen. It was very old-fashioned, 1960s style: chipped Formica units with rail handles; a black-and-white linoleum floor, like in the old Flash ads. I had a horrible feeling, standing there: this house was a bad place, something bad was happening in it. I wanted to leave, but instead I walked through the kitchen and into the utility room, tacked on to one side.

I knew things about this house, as though I'd lived there. I knew that there was a loose edge to the linoleum – that same black-and-white linoleum – just under the lip of the washing machine. I knew that if you lifted that flap, it would pull back a whole section, revealing the bare boards underneath. I knew that once I did that, I'd reveal a trapdoor set into the floor. I knew that if I looked in one of the cupboards, I'd find a short pole I could use to lever the trapdoor open. I knew that it had been designed this way, so that when it was closed and the lino laid over it, the floor was completely flush: no sign at all that anything was under there. That this house had a secret room, and the secret room was where the bad feeling lived.

I did it: I levered the trapdoor open, and though I didn't want to, stepped down into the hole. There were wooden stairs that creaked loudly, and I felt afraid that I'd wake whoever lived in this house, and they'd come and shut me up in this secret place. There was no moonlight now: just a pitch-black space that felt close, and smelled like concrete dust and human sweat. When my feet met the floor, I could feel through the soles of my shoes that it was bare earth, and cold. And then I realised there was something down there with me – some sort of animal. I couldn't see it, but I could hear it breathing. Then, as if it sensed I was there, it started to cry out – these horrible, anguished cries, almost like a human baby. I turned to get back to the stairs, to get out, but I couldn't find them in the dark. Above my head, the trapdoor slammed shut. I woke up, panicked and thrashing.

Just a dream, I told myself, and gradually forgot the shabby kitchen, the secret room, the high, thin cries in the darkness. Just a dream, until the *Edinburgh Evening News* report, two months later. *Missing toddler Rosie Cole found alive and well in Mountcastle neighbour's cellar.* The same horrible feeling from the dream returned as I pinned the paper to the kitchen table with my forearms, put my face close, and read. The missing three-year-old had been hidden in a makeshift room in the basement of a house just a few doors down from her own. The house was a white 1960s bungalow in the suburb of Mountcastle; the paper had printed a photo of it, police tape billowing from the front garden fence. The skyline above the bungalow's roof was ragged with unchecked leylandii. Mountcastle: I googled it. The 49 was the only bus that passed directly through. A fifty-five-year-old man, the paper said, had been arrested in connection with Rosie's disappearance. She'd been missing since Wednesday 19 May.

The article kept the details scant, but I knew. The walls of the cellar were concrete, but the floor was earth. She'd been cold. There was no window, and no light, save whatever light the man brought down – a torch, perhaps, or a lantern. From where she lay on that dirt floor, Rosie could hear him moving around, the joists above her head shifting as he walked. The scrape of the lever in the trapdoor. The creak of the stairs. She was hungry, and hurt, and the man was strange and frightening. She cried at first, but then she stopped crying, because no one ever came.

Alive and well, the article said, and every time I thought of that phrase, my teeth set on edge. I'd dreamed of Rosie on her first night in that place, before there was even a formal missing persons report. She'd been held there a further two months. I didn't want to think of how she'd suffered, but I knew: the horrible feeling ached in my bones like flu. If I'd only told someone. But who? The police? Who'd have believed me? It was a dream, they'd have said. It was only a dream.

I.

Birch, Monday 10 January

'How's the physio going?'

DI Helen Birch had been attending counselling for almost six months now, and she'd never known her therapist, Dr Jane Ryan, to be anything other than perfect. She kept her hair cropped short, but it never seemed to need a trim. She never lost her notes or misremembered anything – she always seemed to be a step ahead of Birch at every turn. And yet, Dr Jane hadn't taken her Christmas cards down yet. Birch was finding it extremely distracting.

'I'm sorry?'

Dr Jane repeated herself. 'How's the physio going? You've walked in here with just a stick. When I saw you before the holidays, you were still on the crutches. Looks like you're making great progress.'

Birch touched the curved handle of the cane she'd leaned against her chair, as though checking it hadn't somehow disappeared. 'I should probably 'fess up to the fact that I did that myself,' she said. 'I haven't been back to physio since before Christmas. That last time, we talked about how I was getting to the point where I could switch to just a stick, and honestly, I was so ready to be finished with those damn crutches. So, one day over the holiday, I just did it.' She touched the walking stick again, hearing her own voice softening. 'This was my mum's – she needed it, towards the end of her life. I don't know why I kept it. Maybe because it was something I knew she'd touched, interacted with a lot, before she died. Anyway, I'm glad I have it now. Though it's not exactly trendy.'

Dr Jane smiled. 'As long as it's doing its job,' she said, 'that's the main thing. Your pain's okay?'

Birch shrugged. 'As okay as it ever is. I'm still managing it fine.'

'And the nightmares?'

Birch flinched at this, and realised Dr Jane had noticed. She wished she'd never said anything about the nightmares.

'There's a part of me,' she said, 'that wishes I'd never said anything about the nightmares.' It had taken her six months, but she'd come to learn that, as a general rule, it was a good idea to just say the thing she was thinking. Dr Jane usually knew, whether she said it or not, so she may as well say it.

'Why's that?'

Birch couldn't stop looking at the Christmas cards. Were they from clients? She hadn't sent one to Dr Jane. She wasn't sure if it was appropriate or not.

'I don't know. Because it's to be expected, isn't it? I was shot, that's a traumatic event. Aren't the nightmares just my subconscious working through it? I've been thinking, maybe they're good for me. Maybe I need to have them. Maybe they're actually a sign that I'm dealing with it.'

Dr Jane cocked her head. 'Dreams can certainly serve a purpose,' she said. 'But when you first mentioned the nightmares to me, you suggested that they were becoming quite life-limiting. They were affecting your sleep, and, by extension, your concentration. Obviously, it's completely up to you what we talk about here – but I definitely think there's value in discussing anything that's limiting your life. Seeing if we can't get a bit of a better handle on that.'

Birch stepped out into the street, dazzled by the bright, crisp day. She always felt a little unusual after a therapy session: generally, she needed at least half an hour for her brain to stop whirring and return to its normal programming. She was enjoying being off the crutches, but also missed them, and she thought about the times she'd heard amputees talk about missing their absent limbs. The crutches' presence had become so familiar to her that now – still walking at a hobble, but far less encumbered than she had been – she felt oddly light without them. The pain in her hip – where the shotgun blast had shattered the bone – was a low, constant hum, but the hum was that little bit quieter with every day that passed. Soon, Birch hoped, she'd be able to drive her car again. Of all the things she'd missed in the months since the shooting, it was driving alone – with something good on the radio and the windows down – that she yearned for the most.

'You mentioned,' Dr Jane had said, 'that some of the night-mares were recurring.'

'A few of them, yes. One, in particular.'

'Would you feel okay telling me about it? About that one dream in particular?'

Birch had taken a deep breath to indicate that yes, she'd be fine to tell the story, but then she'd paused, unsure how to begin.

'You don't have to give any specific details,' Dr Jane urged. 'Just tell me what feels most pressing.'

Birch nodded. 'It's a dream about work,' she said. 'That's how it starts. I'm at work, sitting at my desk. Everything seems to be normal, mundane. But then something changes.'

'Something literally changes? Or it's more of a feeling?'

'It's a feeling,' Birch replied. 'Suddenly I feel a real sense of … threat? But perhaps threat isn't the right word.

Foreboding, maybe. Like, nothing's wrong in the moment, but I know that something bad is about to happen, and I know there's nothing I can do about it. Then the room begins to fill with water.'

Dr Jane blinked. Whatever she'd been expecting, it wasn't that. 'There's a flood?'

Birch cocked her head to one side. 'Sometimes,' she said. 'But it depends. Some nights, I dream that I notice a wet patch on the office floor, and it spreads and gets bigger and bigger, until the whole room starts to flood. Or I look up and see there's a drip coming from the ceiling, and what starts as a trickle turns into a gush, and then a torrent.'

'But other times it's not like that?'

'No.' Birch was beginning to feel boring – the way you do when you get so far into describing a dream you've had, and you realise that the details that feel fascinating to you are not, in fact, interesting to whoever's listening to you. But Dr Jane was asking, so she had to go on. 'Sometimes, it's like that scene in *The Shining*. You know, where the lift opens, and all the blood spills out? Sometimes the water is like that. It comes crashing in through the office door, and there's no way out.'

'That sounds pretty frightening.'

Birch nodded. 'The frightening thing about it,' she said, 'is the not being able to get out part. When the flood begins gradually, I cross the room and try to open the office door, but it's locked. I can see my colleagues outside in the bull-pen, going about their business as if nothing's happening. The water gets up to my knees, and I can see it's up to their knees as well – they're being flooded out, too – but it's like they haven't noticed. And I shout at them and bang on the door, and no one hears me. No one comes to let me out.'

'You feel powerless.'

'Yes.'

'What about the times when the water comes suddenly, from outside the room? Where are your colleagues then?'

Birch looked down at the floor. She felt almost embarrassed about the way her subconscious was behaving. 'I know this is exceptionally weird,' she said, 'but in that version of the dream, I somehow know that they're all dead. They've all already drowned.'

Dr Jane nodded, but didn't speak. After a moment's silence, she looked down at the screen of her iPad, and tapped in a note.

'How's that,' Birch had said then, trying to laugh, 'for a conversation stopper?'

Birch walked slowly through the streets of Stockbridge, taking her time. She had a little buzz on, as if she'd drunk a strong beer on an empty stomach. She'd come to like therapy, but still found it uncanny: sometimes, after a session, she was left feeling as though Dr Jane had in fact opened her skull and literally poked around in her thoughts. She stopped in front of the Bethany Christian Trust shop, and peered into the window. They always had a selection of interesting things to look at: today there was an old printer's tray full of wooden letters neatly arranged in their slots, along with an ugly silver lustre teapot that reminded Birch of going to her granny's house when she was wee. There was also a plastic storage box full of mismatched Christmas baubles, a sheet of foolscap stuck to the front of it on which hand-drawn bubble writing read 'January Sale Bargain Box!!! 10 for £1!!!!' The charity shop called to her – she wanted to go in and loiter among the 50p paperbacks and baskets of scarves.

'I never go in those shops,' she heard a familiar voice say, as clear in her head as if her dead mother were standing right beside her. 'They're full of clothes other people have died in.'

Birch grinned. After a final brief glance at the lustre teapot – so shiny that her own face grimaced back at her from its convex surface – she wandered on.

'Do you think it means,' she'd asked Dr Jane, 'that I want all my colleagues dead? Do you think I ought to be on some sort of list?'

She was joking, but could hear the subtle trill of anxiety somewhere in her own voice. She'd never had a dream recur this persistently before. It was disturbing to be sent the same cryptic message night after night, but not be able to understand the code. It felt a little like the time that Charlie had reappeared: her missing brother's return was foretold by a series of crank phone calls, which came at fifteen-minute intervals throughout the day. Someone trying to tell her something, and Birch clueless as to what it might be.

Dr Jane had laughed at the joke, thankfully.

'Do *you* think it's that? You know that if you're having homicidal thoughts, I'm obliged to report it.'

They'd laughed together. Birch liked it when she could make Dr Jane laugh, though she'd never have said that out loud to anyone.

'No,' she said. 'I don't wish my colleagues dead. Apart from anything else, when I'm in the dream, that's part of the horror. I'm not *happy* about them being washed away by the flood, I'm terrified.'

Dr Jane let the laughter fade, and they sat in silence again.

'In the slow version of the dream,' she said, eventually, 'what happens when the water gets over your head?'

Birch hung a right on to Raeburn Place, one of her favourite streets in Edinburgh. Her colleague, DS Amy Kato, lived here, in a tiny, immaculate flat. The street was full of coffee roasters, wine bars and artisan cheese shops. Because the hip young things who lived here valued *authenticity*, there was also an old-fashioned greengrocer's, an old-fashioned hardware store, a florist with a beautiful window display, and a post office with cheery staff who knew everyone. The place was full of happy dogs in little tartan coats. Walking through Stockbridge was like walking through one of the Shirley Hughes storybooks of Birch's childhood.

She stopped outside the narrow Mexican gift shop with its hammered tin hearts and strings of tiny ceramic chilli peppers. It was cold out, so the door was closed, but Birch could still smell the incense burning inside. On the window, someone had drawn the words 'Human Kind: Be Both' in looping coloured chalk pen. Inside, the shop glittered like a jewellery box, and Birch had to peel herself away and carry on along the frigid pavement.

'I wake up,' she'd said, 'and then that's it, I'm awake. Sometimes it's 2am, sometimes it's 5am, but every time, I wake up with my heart hammering like I've run up ten flights of stairs. There's no getting back to sleep after that.'

Dr Jane had entered another note on the iPad. The room was quiet enough that Birch could hear the soft patter of the therapist's fingertips against the glass.

'And you've had this dream … how many times, would you say?'

'In one form or another? I'd say dozens. Enough times that I've stopped counting.'

Dr Jane hadn't looked up from the screen. 'And you think it's as a result of the shooting, that you're having these nightmares?'

'Yes.'

Dr Jane met Birch's eye, and held her gaze. 'Even though the content of the dream has nothing to do with Operation Kendall, or what happened?'

Birch had been working on this for six months: working to be okay with the sustained eye contact that seemed to be part of Dr Jane's therapeutic style. She'd learned somewhere – in some dim and distant past piece of training – that people's eyes automatically move to the left if they're remembering something, but to the right if they're making something up. Over the course of these months, she'd noticed with horror that it was true: whenever she tried to fib or fudge an answer, her eyes moved rightwards, towards the door in the corner of the room, the exit she could lunge for if things got too uncomfortable. She'd realised she was looking at it in that moment, and flicked her eyes away – too late. Dr Jane must surely have seen.

'I don't know,' Birch had lied, 'what other explanation there could be.'

The shops had petered out now, and with nothing much else interesting to look at, Birch focused on her steps, maintaining the studied walk that caused the least amount of pain in her hip. She stopped at the junction where East Fettes Avenue became Comely Bank Avenue, and stared up the hill at the neatly stacked tenements, their identical bay windows and black iron railings. She couldn't deny it any longer: it was time to go to work. Her Fettes Avenue office was only five minutes away. These were the last few days of her phased return: next week, the compressed days would become full days, no doubt with overtime piling up from the off, diligently entered in the spreadsheet, never to be claimed back.

'Promise me,' Anjan had said, sitting her down a few weeks before Christmas, the morning of her first phased-return half-day, 'you won't overdo it. Promise me things won't go back to the way they were before.'

Birch had scoffed at him, as he must have known she would: Anjan Chaudhry was renowned for being first into the office and last out of the courtroom, for poring over casefiles on the weekends and pulling all-nighters before a major judgement.

'In my line of work,' he'd say, 'it's expected. It starts in law school and it never, ever stops.'

You think my line of work is any different? She'd said it plenty of times in the past, but didn't see the point, just lately. It was a fight they'd had enough times to know that neither one could win, so they'd stopped trying. Anjan could no longer understand her loyalty to the job. That job, he'd say, had landed her in hospital with a gunshot wound. The job that had seen her, while still in recovery, left to fight off a violent criminal without back-up, setting her physio treatment back to zero. How could she be loyal to DCI McLeod, who had caused every part of her present predicament? Anjan repeatedly demanded an answer. Birch couldn't admit to him, or anyone – not even Dr Jane – that lately, she was struggling to understand it, too.

'It won't,' she'd said, that morning, enjoying the gentle weight of Anjan's hands on her shoulders, as though he were trying to stop her from floating away. 'I promise.'

Her eyes had shifted rightwards then, too.

Bee, 1977

I didn't know the old man wasn't real. I heard other children talk about their grandfathers – indeed, sometimes their grandfathers turned up to collect them at the school gates – so I assumed that he was mine. He looked like those other men: his head was bald, and there were lines around his eyes that made his face seem kind. He looked, I thought, like a tortoise. His clothes were strange, but I'd been taught not to stare or make comments about people who were different.

We lived in what would once have been a fancy Edinburgh residence, though it was shabby by the time we owned it, and only became shabbier as a result of us moving in. It was a detached townhouse: I slept in what my mother called the servants' quarters: a wee narrow room with a sink, up its own twisty staircase under the roof. Rain trickled in under the slates and made large brown blooms on the ceiling. In really bad weather, the blooms let down their own little raindrops: I thought they were indoor clouds, because the plaster swelled and puffed them out like the fluffy clouds of cartoons. My mother showed me how to put down pans to catch the drips, and I'd lie awake listening to the weird, flat xylophone music they made.

My father was meant to fix the house. He seemed to make a lot of noise – hammering, drilling, swearing at things – but nothing ever really improved. A section of the living room ceiling was held up by scaffolding poles, following the ill-advised demolition of an internal wall. My mother gave me sock yarn, which I strung between the struts, and turned into a washing line for my dolls' clothes. At Christmas, we looped tinsel around those poles. No one ever came to visit that house.

Late one afternoon, at the tea table, I asked, 'Where does my grandpa sleep?'

My mother looked at my father, who would have been behind an evening newspaper, though I don't remember clearly. I wasn't looking at him.

'Your grandpa?' my mother asked.

'Yes. Where does he sleep?'

My father still didn't speak.

My mother leaned over the table towards me. 'Sweetheart,' she said, 'why are you asking that?'

I wasn't accustomed to my questions being answered with other questions. Often, when I asked things, I'd be told, 'Because,' or, 'You'll understand when you're older.' I'd begun to learn that when my father said, 'I don't know, ask your mother,' it wasn't because he didn't actually know. Nevertheless, I considered my mother the fount of all knowledge, and couldn't understand her evasiveness.

'He says goodnight to me every night,' I replied, 'after I've gone to bed. Where does he go, after that? Does he have his own house?'

My mother's eyelashes were fluttering. 'Your daddy says goodnight to you every night,' she said. 'Are you asking where Daddy sleeps?'

I remember putting my hand firmly on the table then, because it made my mother jump. I'd never managed to do that before. I recall that I felt quite grown-up.

'No,' I said, as though speaking to an idiot. 'I mean my grandpa. He's different from Daddy. I know he's different from Daddy.'

At this point, my father must have emerged from behind his newspaper, because he said, very clearly, and without emotion, 'Kid, both your grandpas are dead.'

There was a pause, during which I probably looked to my mother for confirmation. I was old enough to understand the word *dead*, in the sense that I knew it meant that someone had gone away, permanently.

'Long dead,' my father added. 'And good riddance to the pair of them.'

I imagine my mother must have given him a look.

'So ... if he's not my grandpa, then who is he?'

I wonder if this panicked my mother. I wasn't worried, myself: I was still young enough to believe that grown-ups had logical explanations for absolutely everything, even if they sometimes kept those explanations to themselves.

'Who, darling?'

I didn't know why she was acting this way.

'The old man,' I said. 'The one who comes to say good-night to me every night.'

My father must have thrown his paper down on the table, because I remember the rattle of cutlery, of cups jumping in their saucers.

'What?'

I remember my eyes boggling at the pair of them – did they really not know about the old man?

'There's an old man,' I said. I spoke slowly. For the first time, I thought perhaps my parents were not as smart and sensible as I had always assumed. 'He comes to my room every night, after I've had my bath and Mummy has tucked me in and Daddy has said goodnight. He comes to say goodnight, too.'

'Beatrice,' my mother said, and for the first time since the conversation began, I felt a spike of worry. My parents only ever called me by my full name when I was in trouble. 'You're telling me an old man – a stranger – comes into this house at night? How does he get in?'

'Through the door.'

My father was shaking his head. I could hear his breath moving faster, which meant he was getting angry. I *was* in trouble.

'Impossible,' he said. 'That's impossible. Sheila, you surely can't *believe* this? This house creaks like a bloody sinking ship. There's no way someone could get up those stairs without us hearing them.'

This quietened me. I'd never noticed it before, but now my father mentioned it, I realised that no, oddly, the old man never made any noise – yet the floor of my room was an assault course of squeaks and cracks. I never dared put even a toe on those floorboards after bedtime, because I knew my parents would realise I was still awake.

My father rounded on me.

'She's making it up, the wee devil. She's lying.'

I was old enough to know that lying was very wrong, and punishable – in school, at least – by a ruler to the knuckles.

'I'm not, Daddy,' I said. 'I promise, I'm not lying.'

I was getting worried now. I didn't want the ruler on my knuckles, nor did I want any other form of punishment. I hadn't expected the conversation to turn this way, and I felt bewildered. But I still wasn't as worried as my mother appeared to be.

'What does this old man look like?' she asked.

'Sheila,' my father said, 'you must be joking.'

I decided to take a risk, ignore him, and answer my mother. 'He's old,' I said. 'He doesn't have very much hair, and his head is shiny. He has wrinkly eyes, and he wears a black suit, like the one Daddy has. Except his has a flappy part that covers his ...' Here I paused, and lowered my voice, realising I was going to have to say – at the tea table, no less – a word I knew to be taboo. 'His bottom,' I whispered. Again, I couldn't help but feel rather grown-up.

I remember my father's face was quite red. I'm still not sure if he was angry with me for spinning a yarn – as he saw it – or angry with my mother for listening to it.

'Does he talk to you, this man?' she asked.

I shrugged. 'Not really, Mama. He just strokes my hair and says, "Goodnight, little one," and then he goes away.'

At the other end of the table, my father was making hissing, fizzing noises, like a punctured tyre held under water.

'Is there anything else about him?' my mother asked.

'Yes,' I replied. 'He wears white gloves on his hands.'

I helped to tidy the tea things away, and then I was sent to my room. I lingered on the stairs, hearing my parents talk in fierce whispers. At dinnertime, I was called back downstairs, and my father gave me a rather stiff dressing-down for telling fibs, and scaring my mother. She stood behind him, not looking at me. My punishment was going to bed early without pudding, and that night, the old man didn't come.

Years later, I would often walk past that house. I'd remember the scaffolding poles in the living room, the dens I built in the twisty rhododendrons in the garden. I'd remember my baby brother being born, and my mother putting her foot down about living in a building site. I'd remember us leaving soon after, Tommy still a babe in arms. But more than anything else, I'd remember the kind old man who wasn't real.

Except he was real, I was certain of it. I'd heard his voice, and felt the warm weight of his hand on my head. After I told my parents about him, he'd stopped visiting me every night – but he still turned up occasionally, when I most needed him. If there was a thunderstorm and I was afraid, or if I was hot and sick and miserable in bed, then he'd be there, with his comforting, white-gloved hands. One of the first things I ever looked up online – as soon as I got the new-fangled internet – was the history of that house. I discovered it originally belonged to an eminent, wealthy man: a Colquhoun or a Farquharson, one of those types. It was his *pied-à-terre*, a place in town away from his sprawling rural estate. The man was a bachelor, and most of the year the house was kept up by servants, only one of whom lived in. A butler, whose former room I guessed I must have slept in every night. The census listed one name only – Fraser – but whether this was his first or last name, I couldn't be sure. A butler, who for formal occasions must have dressed in a smart black tailcoat, and white gloves. I was seven when we left that house. Fraser was my first ghost.

Birch, Monday 10 January

The problem with the phased return was the monotony. Birch had been assigned desk work, almost exclusively, since she'd come back. This was partly, she knew, because she still couldn't drive, and also because she couldn't walk very fast – outside the confines of her office, she had to admit, she was a bit of a liability. However, she also strongly suspected that DCI McLeod was enjoying the opportunity to keep her on a short leash.

This afternoon, it was emails. Namely, the low-priority emails she'd saved in a folder marked 'Do later'. In these emails were links to online fire-safety trainings she needed to complete, minutes from meetings she ought to have read, attached documents she needed to file. In the old days, before she'd been shot, she'd occasionally wake up in the middle of the night in a cold sweat, thinking about the 'Do later' folder, and all the tasks she was putting off for some dreaded future day. Now that day had come, she cursed her past self. This week was her last chance to clear the decks before she went full-time, and she didn't think she was going to make it.

McLeod must have known about the 'Do later' folder. She imagined it must delight him to think of her as she was now: slumped behind her desk, clicking through a seemingly endless series of Equality & Diversity videos, on which she'd later be quizzed.

In the early stages of her sick leave, she'd allowed boredom to get the better of her: she'd begun to meddle in a case of

Amy's, telling herself it was fine, the case was small, McLeod would never find out.

'Yeah,' she said aloud, to the empty room, 'look how that went.'

Of course she'd got too involved. Of course the case had grown arms and legs. Of course she'd ended up in a violent altercation with a perp, because she'd gone where she wasn't meant to be, alone. Of course it had messed with her recovery – the physio team told her, mid-scolding, that she'd set things back by months. Of course she'd ended up reunited with the godforsaken crutches she'd hated so much. Of course she had. Of course.

'Just my luck,' she sulked. The finer points of the video she was watching – an achingly obvious tutorial on using appropriate language with members of the LGBTQIA+ community – were passing her by. She couldn't believe it was necessary to spell out in such basic terms the importance of not using homophobic slurs. Then again, she thought of some of her colleagues, and realised the training video had indeed been made for a reason.

On her desk, the phone rang, making her jump. It didn't ring all that often at the moment – word had got around that McLeod had basically benched her. Her heart fluttered, hoping the call might be something more interesting than the training video. Then she felt absurd. *Excited for a phone call*, she thought, lifting the receiver. *Jesus*.

'This is Birch.'

'It's me, Marm.' John at reception – perhaps the most familiar voice in the entire building – didn't need to announce himself. 'How's your afternoon?'

Birch smirked. 'Chock-a-block,' she said. 'I'd be rushed off my feet, if I could only walk properly.'

John laughed. 'Well, you're about to get even busier,' he said, and she could hear he was smiling. 'I've got a visitor for you.'

'Oh yes?' Birch kept her tone light, but she felt a flicker of panic. Was she expecting someone? Was it possible she actually had an appointment, and she'd forgotten it?

'There's a Winifred Fortune here, asking to see you.'

As the name registered, Birch felt something akin to falling backwards into water. Memories of times and places she hadn't thought of in years rushed up to meet her.

'Winnie's here?'

John chuckled. 'She said she wasn't sure you'd remember her.'

Birch shook her head in disbelief, though she knew John couldn't see her.

'Tell her I'll be down in five minutes,' she replied. 'If she's okay to wait.'

Winnie Fortune's smart, dark blue coat was the same one she'd been wearing when Birch had last seen her. They'd exchanged a quick, taut hug goodbye outside Birch's mother's funeral tea, an autumn day growing dark around them, haar wet and solid in the streets.

'Phone me,' Winnie had said, 'if ever you need anything.'

Birch recalled those words as she walked across the lobby, the rubber foot of her cane scuffing on the carpet, and realised she'd never phoned, or even so much as sent a Christmas card, in the years since her mother had died.

Winnie stood up from the chair she'd been perched on the edge of. 'Helen,' she said, and then, 'If I can call you Helen? Should I call you Detective?'

Birch grinned. 'Helen's fine,' she said. 'It's wonderful to see you, Winnie. I'm sorry I never got in touch, after …'

Winnie waved a hand, brushing away the rest of Birch's sentence. 'Ach, don't you worry your head about that. To be honest, I'm just glad you remember me.'

Birch's mouth fell open. 'Of *course* I remember you! I think about you often, when I think of Mum. She was so lucky to have had you as a friend. Truly, I ought to have kept in touch better. I'm sorry.'

Winnie made a teeth-sucking sound. 'Wheesht, hen! I said, it's fine. I've been keeping an eye on you from afar, anyway.' She glanced down at the cane, then, and Birch thought she might mention the shooting, but she didn't. 'Keeping track of your successes,' she said. After a pause, she added, 'Your mother would be so proud.'

Birch raised her free hand to touch her own cheek, feeling the heat rise in her face. She wanted to hug this woman, but it was too late now. She'd forgotten how kind Winnie was.

'Thank you,' she said, 'that means a lot.'

Winnie drew herself up a little taller in her smart coat. 'You always were such a clever girl,' she said. 'That's why I thought I'd come and talk to you.'

Birch blinked. She glanced backward towards John, but he was on the phone, his eyes downcast.

'You mean,' she said, 'this isn't just a social call?'

Winnie shook her head. 'I'm afraid not, hen. I mean, I'd absolutely love to catch up, and hear about everything you're doing, of course. But there's also something I'd like to pick your brains about. Something I'd like to report, I suppose.'

'You want to report a crime? Is everything okay?'

Something flickered in the older woman's eyes. For a moment, Birch thought Winnie might be about to cry.

'Not *really* okay,' she said. 'No. It isn't.'

Meeting Room C was the best space Birch could find at short notice. It wasn't an interview room, at least, but it wasn't desperately welcoming. It had been built in an awkward elbow of corridor and was, in truth, a glorified cupboard. The only window was narrow and high, and looked out on to the fleet yard. A riot van was parked about a foot from the glass, blotting out almost all the natural light.

'Sorry,' Birch said, ushering Winnie into a chair. 'This isn't exactly cosy.'

'It'll do nicely,' Winnie replied. She lifted her old-fashioned Gold Cross handbag and placed it on the small table in front of her. 'I don't expect special treatment.'

'I can offer you a coffee, at least – or tea, if you'd prefer?'

'No, no. I'd rather just get right to it, hen, if you don't mind.'

Birch nodded, skirted the table, and sat down opposite Winnie. She leaned the walking stick against the wall, placed her phone down in front of her, and thumbed open the Notes app.

'Are you going to record me?' Winnie asked. She eyed the phone nervously.

'Not at this stage,' Birch replied. 'I'll just take some notes, if that's okay. Memory like a sieve.'

At this, Winnie seemed to relax a little, though she didn't immediately begin to speak.

'So,' Birch said, 'what can I help you with?'

The older woman looked down at the table.

'Well, first of all,' she said, 'I hope you don't mind me just turning up. I'm sure it isn't the done thing. I just didn't know how else to contact you, really. I'm not very up on technology.'

Birch nodded along. She was used to this from taking witness statements; there was almost always a period of vague, settling-down chat to be had before anything useful was said.

'Don't worry,' she replied. She gestured in the direction of the cane. 'I'm rather confined to the office at the moment, so this is as good a way as any to get to talk to me.'

'That's good. I want to do things properly.'

'Of course.'

Birch leaned forward across the table, hoping to urge Winnie on.

'You maybe remember,' the older woman said, 'that I used to foster, on and off? I used to call it taking in strays.'

Birch had, in fact, forgotten this about Winnie, but now she was reminded, she recalled that yes, this woman's house had always been full of children.

'I remember,' she said. 'Mum used to talk to me about it sometimes. She worried that you took on too much.'

Winnie's eyes crinkled as she smiled.

'I know,' she said. 'Your mother always did fret about things. She didn't like it when I got older teenagers, especially – she thought they were too wild for me to handle. But I handled them.' She threw Birch a knowing look. 'You learn some tricks, the longer you do it for. And I've been doing it a long time.'

'I bet you're great at it,' Birch replied. 'I remember you babysitting Charlie sometimes. He used to love going to your house.'

Winnie's eyes seemed to lose focus, then, just for a second. 'Yes,' she said. 'I must ask you about Charlie, when we're done with all this. I read about him, in the papers …' She snapped back in, fixing her eyes on Birch's face. 'But I should get on, shouldn't I? I ought to tell you why I'm here.'

Birch smiled. 'Take your time,' she said.

Winnie pulled in a long breath, and then began.

'I'd been taking a break from fostering,' she said. 'In fact, I think I'd all but decided to retire from it completely. I'm sixty-seven now, you know – getting too old to be running around after weans. But then I got a call, about a girl named Linh. This was a couple of years ago. Linh had just turned fifteen. She'd been arrested by the police in Aberdeen after getting into an altercation with a man in the street. It turned out she'd been forced into prostitution, and this man was a punter who didn't want to pay. She'd all but scratched the bastard's eyes out, from the sound of things.'

Birch's eyes widened, but she didn't speak. Winnie was settling into her story.

'Linh was categorised as an unaccompanied minor,' she went on. 'She was too scared to say much to the police, but they managed to figure out she'd been trafficked into Europe from Vietnam. They found out that she'd spent some time at a shelter in the Netherlands – they call them protected reception centres over there. They're a bit more humane than our detention centres, and they're meant to shield the kids from being re-trafficked. But whatever shark of a man took Linh out of Vietnam found out where she was, and picked her up again. She ended up here, in Scotland, being put to work.'

Birch shook her head. 'It's disturbingly common, I'm afraid,' she said. 'I've heard similar stories a lot of times.'

'I don't doubt it,' Winnie replied. 'But I do wonder at the state of this world, the way we treat each other.' Her eyes went soft again, the way they had when Birch had mentioned her brother. But as before, she seemed to shake herself, and carried on speaking. 'Anyway – I got the call to see if I could foster Linh. They wanted to move her to a new place, away from Aberdeen. Away from the man who'd been forcing her to work, away from the punters she'd known. I'd never fostered an unaccompanied minor before – I'd only ever taken in Scottish kids. But I felt for the poor wee scrap. She spoke barely any English when I met her. She was a little lost soul. It was a lot of responsibility, but I didn't have any other placements at that time, and felt like I couldn't not help.'

'You're a good woman, Winnie.'

Winnie cocked her head. 'I try to do my bit,' she said. 'And Linh's been no trouble at all. We got her into school, and she likes going. She does her chores around the house. She picked up some English and made friends, but she isn't a party girl like they sometimes are at that age. She has no interest in boys whatsoever. She's never happier than when she's sat up in her room with her books. She told me she wanted to be a vet, because she loves animals, so for her sixteenth birthday we went down to the Edinburgh Cat and Dog Home and rescued ourselves a little ginger cat. Good lord, she loves that animal! She called him Lang. She told me it means sweet potato.'

Birch smiled, but Winnie must have sensed what she was thinking.

'Sorry, Helen,' she said. 'You must be wondering why on earth I'm telling you all of this.'

'I'm enjoying it immensely,' Birch replied. 'Linh is a lucky girl, to have been placed in your care. But I do have a horrible feeling that you're about to tell me something's wrong.'

'Yes.' Winnie's face darkened. 'I've come to talk to you because I believe Linh is missing.'

Birch frowned. She'd had the creeping suspicion that this was coming, but the way Winnie said it made her pause.

'You *believe*?' she repeated. 'You don't know?'

Winnie pushed her shoulders back. 'Oh, I feel almost certain,' she said. 'I have this terrible feeling, Helen, right down in my bones, that she's been taken. The person – or people – who trafficked her, I think they've found her again. But with kids like Linh, it's complicated. You need more to go on than just the bad feeling of some old wifey like me.'

Birch tapped a note into her phone. She needed to stay objective for now, but she knew only too well the kind of bone-deep bad feeling Winnie was referring to. She'd had the same feeling herself, many times, and not just in a professional context. She'd had it when Charlie reappeared, having been missing and presumed dead for so long. He hadn't needed to tell her a single thing about what he'd been up to for the past fourteen years: she'd already known that none of it could possibly be good.

'Tell me,' she said, 'why it's complicated.'

'Well.' Winnie shifted in her seat. 'I'm probably teaching my granny to suck eggs, here – you of all people will understand these things. Linh is seventeen now, you see. She's still a child, but she has full legal capacity. She's entitled to do a lot of things, these days, and though I think she's quite vulnerable, I'm not going to try and stop her. Since she turned sixteen, I've been letting her go to sleepovers with friends, for example. She even went on a little camping holiday last summer with a couple of other girls from school, though only for a few days, and only to Northumberland. I made her call me twice every day to check in. But she is independent – she does go off on her own.'

'And you haven't yet ruled out that she hasn't just gone to a friend's, or something?'

'No. But I have this *feeling*.'

Birch looked down at her phone, the few vague notes she'd made. 'How long has it been since you last heard from Linh?'

'Only a day,' Winnie replied. Her face reddened a little. 'I know that isn't long – I know it's very early to start panick-ing. But Helen, she went into town yesterday and hasn't come home, and she hasn't phoned or texted me to let me know she's okay. When I call her, the phone just goes to voicemail. I'm really very worried.'

Birch was nodding along. 'I can understand that,' she said. 'You mentioned that when Linh went on holiday, she called twice a day. Is it unusual for her *not* to call and check in? Would you say it's out of character for her?'

'Oh yes. It's not like her at all. She wouldn't want me to be worried.'

'I assume you've called round her friends? The people you think she'd most likely be with?'

'I have. In some cases I've spoken to their parents, as well. No one seems to know where she is.'

Birch's mind had begun to race. If Linh was indeed missing, then a variety of wheels would need to be set in motion. Birch would need to key in a missing persons co-ordinator to come on board. She'd need to get in touch with the Missing People charity, and secure their involvement. This could be complicated.

Calm down, Helen, she told herself. *It's only been a day. We don't know what this is yet.*

'Winnie,' she said, 'I'm sorry to ask this, I know it's a rather distressing question. But … do you have any reason to think that Linh might have wanted to run away?'

Winnie looked down at her hands. Birch noticed her neat nails, the stack of rings on her wedding finger: a diamond engagement ring, a plain gold wedding band, an eternity ring with diamonds and sapphires. She remembered that Winnie's husband had died young; that her mother had always said he was a good-for-nothing. The presence of those rings, still on Winnie's hand so many years later, suggested to Birch that her mother might have been exaggerating – she had rather liked to do that.

'Like I said,' Winnie replied, 'it's complicated.'

Birch leaned forward. 'You can tell me,' she said. 'I'm here to help.'

As though she knew Birch had been looking at them, Winnie began to twist the rings on her left hand, turning them round and round on her finger.

'I don't know how much you know about unaccompanied minors,' she said, 'but yes, they do sometimes run away.'

Birch tilted her head. She realised she probably ought to know more about unaccompanied minors than she did.

'Why's that?'

Winnie took another deep breath. 'Because,' she said, 'when they turn eighteen, they stop being unaccompanied minors, and they become adults. When that happens, the care system can't shelter them any longer, and they have to move into the asylum system. Many of the weans know about how unjust that system is: some have seen their parents failed by it. Kids like Linh, who've been in centres or children's homes, will have heard stories from peers. They know you can end up in a detention centre long-term, or you can end up being deported. Even in the best cases, where you're allowed to stay in the country, you can end up being moved away from all your friends, away from the life you've built. Imagine what that must be like for a teenager. Their friends are their whole world. There's no doubt that Linh was worried about all of that, and she knew it was coming up for her – and soon.'

'So ... you're telling me it's actually very possible that she might have run away?'

On the other side of the table, some sort of change came over Winnie. Birch felt it, like a wind blowing through the room.

'I was so worried,' Winnie said, her voice suddenly thick and choked. 'I was so worried that this would happen. That she'd be classed as a runaway, and nothing would be done about it.'

Birch's eyes widened. Instinctively, she held up both hands, trying to draw Winnie's gaze toward them.

'Hey now,' she said, 'hang on just a second. Let's not get ahead of ourselves. I haven't classed this as *anything*, not yet. I just want to run through the various potential scenarios.'

'He found her once before,' Winnie said. 'The trafficker. What if he's found her again, Helen?'

Birch narrowed her eyes. 'You think he'd continue to pursue her?'

Something moved across Winnie's face, then. Birch could see, for just a moment, that she regretted the decision to come and seek out her old friend's daughter, a person who, in spite of being a senior police officer, didn't seem to know anything about anything.

'Oh, yes,' Winnie said. 'This man wouldn't want Linh to stay in the system, either – not the care system, and certainly not the asylum system. He'd want to keep her, and earn money off her – that's what they believe they get, these traffickers, when they give so-called safe passage. The families think they're paying for their weans to get a better life somewhere. But the traffickers see them as chattels. Possessions. As far as he's concerned, the care system has stolen Linh from him. *I've* stolen her from him.'

Birch could see that Winnie had convinced herself of the worst-case scenario. The most terrible thing she could think of was surely what had happened.

'You've been worried,' Birch said, 'that Linh might disappear one day?'

Winnie's reply was fast. 'Yes,' she said. 'Ever since I took charge of her, really. They gave me training, showed me her case file. Just a teenager, and yet she had more history than some of us gather in a lifetime. They told me she was high-risk, and made sure I knew exactly what those risks were.' Winnie's eyes dampened. 'And I've grown so fond of her,' she added. 'We've grown fond of each other.'

Birch was nodding, trying to make her face do sympathetic things. She'd seen this a lot of times before: people called in to report crimes they were absolutely certain were taking place, before there was any real evidence. When you've spent years worrying that one specific, terrible thing may happen, it doesn't take much to make you feel as though your worst fears are coming true.

'You said earlier that Linh had no interest in boys,' Birch said.

'I did,' Winnie replied. Her face was a question.

'I have to ask that,' Birch explained. 'Anything to do with a missing teenage girl, and I have to ask about boyfriends.' She heard what she'd said, and held up a hand to correct herself. '*Potentially* missing, I should say. Obviously, I hope that you'll go home and find Linh sitting in your kitchen.'

Winnie was shaking her head, but not speaking.

'So, no boys at all, you're saying,' Birch said. 'No one who was interested in her, even?'

'Not that I know of.'

'But she had female friends.'

'Yes, a few. They'd hang around in a wee group, three of them.'

'These are the girls she went camping with, last year?'

'Yes.' Winnie reached over and snapped open the Gold Cross handbag. She rummaged for a moment, before taking out a packet of tissues, and plucking one out of the plastic wrapper.

'Okay,' Birch said. 'For things to progress, it would be handy to have their details.'

Winnie dabbed at her eyes. 'They're in my phone,' she said, and gestured back towards the handbag.

'Great. I'll get them before you go. The other thing it would be useful to have is a physical description of Linh. Can you tell me what she looks like?'

The tears Winnie had been holding back seemed to spill over, now: she pressed the tissue to her eyes, and then covered her face with her hands.

'Oh, Helen,' she said, her voice muffled and wan, 'she's awfie wee. She's just a wee girl.'

Bee, 1983

My second ghost was Martin's, although Martin wasn't dead. What happened with Martin made me realise there are many strange things in this world that we'll never understand. It also made me realise I was different. *Bad* different.

Martin was in sixth year when I was in first. He seemed to me like a proper grown-up: he was eighteen, and already had a car, a boxy black Mark 1 Ford Escort that he drove at wild speed along the street outside school. I can still hear the sound its tyres made as he skidded to a halt on the greasy cobbles, still feel the gritty slap as he aquaplaned standing water all over the school bus queue. Martin had repeated third year, people said: that was why he was the oldest person in school. I realise now that might have explained his latent anger, too, to a degree. Martin frightened me when not many things did. For that reason, I was drawn to him.

High school was a culture shock. I realised pretty quickly I'd been sheltered: walking with my mother and Tommy every morning to the primary school we both attended, only a few blocks away from home. I had felt no shame about taking Tommy's hand to cross the playground, little as he was – six years my junior. But at high school, I learned quickly that younger siblings were a terrible curse; they were *embarrassing*, the worst thing one could be. Also embarrassing: Clarks shoes, NHS glasses, parents, doing homework, being clever, reading books, and showing more than a passing interest in just about anything. I ticked every embarrassment box, and more besides.

It happened on a Thursday – I remember because PE was on Thursday afternoons. It was summer, so we were cross-country running: me, and twenty-or-so other first-year girls. I hated PE at the best of times – ashamed of my soft, white thighs and grannyish underwear in the changing room – and cross-country running was the absolute worst. We ran along the big, curved drag of Melville Drive in itchy shorts, while men slowed down their cars to jeer or blow their horns. Asthmatic – though I didn't know it then – I trailed behind the rest of the pack, so suffered mostly alone.

That afternoon, Martin was truanting, as I'd heard he sometimes did. I spotted him fingering the padlock on the green-painted pavilion at the end of Jawbone Walk. The other girls had already rounded the building – as the straggler, only I saw Martin insert a glinting thread of metal into the lock and jimmy it with practised hands. The padlock sprang from its hasp. I heard the soles of my feet slap-slap to a halt on the tarmac, a man somewhere behind me whistling lewdly from his car. Martin put his weight against the door and slunk inside. I shouldn't have stayed. And I swear, I'd have carried on running had I not seen the shadow: a grey column of cloud in the warm summer air, taller than a person but flimsy, shifting. It followed Martin into the pavilion, and he closed the door.

It was slightly ajar when I reached it, so I pressed my face to the gap. I could smell the building's old wood, the way decades of damp had sunk through it like brandy through a cake. It smelled like the old house, where we lived when Tommy was born – the house where I met Fraser, the old man in white gloves. But it also smelled like boys, the sweaty musk of them, and I thought of my male classmates spattering over this threshold in gangs, muddy off the park, to change.

I shuddered. The pavilion was gloomy inside, sunlight blocked from its windows by big trees. I couldn't see Martin, but I wanted to. I wanted to see what the shadow was made of, and find out how he got it to follow him.

I didn't open the door fully, but instead made a gap and wiggled through it. His hand against my mouth was almost instant: he'd been waiting there, his back against the wall. I felt him kick out diagonally, and the door scraped shut. His other arm went around my chest, pinning my arms to my sides. I whimpered, and he shook me, only once, but firmly.

'What the *fuck* are you doing here, you stupid little whore?'

I felt my eyes bulge. I'd heard these words before, of course, but never directed *at* me. As he said them, I felt little flecks of his spit land on my neck. His breath smelled like a cigarette just put out.

'You need to get gone, and I mean *yesterday*.'

His whole body was pulsing with anger, and I wanted to ask him why – all I'd done was catch him hanging about in a glorified shed. But his hand was still on my mouth, and besides, I was looking around for the shadow I'd seen. I could feel that it was in the room with us – a feeling like static behind my eyelids, like the heavy half hour before a thunderstorm. I should probably have felt afraid, but I didn't. I mainly felt a strange delight at feeling an older boy's body pressed so close to mine. Martin had gone still and tense, as though listening. I assumed he was thinking, figuring out what he was going to do.

Two things happened then. One: someone knocked softly at the door, and I felt Martin jump. And two, I looked up at the ceiling, but the ceiling wasn't there. Instead, there was the shadow, thicker now in the building's dim light and seeming to churn: a grey, dinner-table-sized roil above our heads.

'Fucking *shit*,' Martin hissed, and he let me go. I was frozen, mouth slack, watching the shadow he towed along behind him as he staggered to the door.

'You know I don't like to be kept waiting.'

The voice outside was low, the voice of someone not wanting to be overheard. But it was stern, and deep, and belonged to a man. A grown-up. For the first time since I'd panted to a halt on Melville Drive, I felt a stab of fear. I was somewhere I shouldn't be, during school hours, with a *boy*. With a much older boy. I was only twelve, but I had a sense of what this meant for me. Of what people would think. Of how my father would react.

But it was too late. The grown-up man shoved Martin out of the way, and stepped through the door.

'Look,' Martin said, his voice cracking, 'it's not—'

The man turned, and I saw him register my presence in the fuzzy light. I watched him look me up and down. He was tall, broad, dressed in a smart – if rather old-fashioned – brown suit. I was bad at guessing the age of adults, but suspected he was older than my father. He had a horseshoe-shaped beard and large hands that I shrank away from.

'Well, well, well,' the man said, still keeping his voice soft. He was smiling a nasty smile, and I could tell he was speaking to Martin, not me. 'Having a little assignation, are we?'

Behind the man, I saw Martin push his chest out. 'Maybe,' he replied, and I wondered if he was also guessing at what *assignation* might mean. He paused, looking at me, the shadow swirling and drifting like smoke around him. 'Beatrice was just leaving,' he added.

I blinked. I wouldn't have imagined that Martin knew my name.

The man laughed, and took a step towards me. I leapt backwards.

'Beatrice, is it? Well, what's a fine lady named *Beatrice* doing in a place like this?'

I was truly afraid now, but amid the fear, I felt a spike of annoyance. I hated having fun poked at me, and I also hated my full name.

'My name is Bee,' I said, trying to sound strident, but failing. 'And I'll go now, if you let me past.'

I balled my fists, and forced myself to close the gap between me and the man. The expression on his face changed in an instant.

'Oh, no you don't,' he said, and jabbed a fat finger at my face. I imagined how much it would hurt if he slapped me across the cheek, the way my father sometimes did.

By the door, Martin dithered. I could tell he wanted to wrench the door open and run, and I prayed that he wouldn't. I didn't know what kind exactly, but I knew I was in danger with this man.

'You can stay,' the man said to me, 'and watch. How about that?'

I cocked my head to one side, trying to understand what he meant. His face was a strange smirk I didn't like.

'Mate ...' Martin said, and took a step forward. 'She's not my— she's not ...'

'What?'

I wished the man would stop looking at me, but he didn't, even now Martin was speaking.

'She's only twelve,' Martin said. 'She's only a kid.'

The man appeared to consider this, though the strange expression on his face didn't change.

'I'll pay you extra,' he said, after a moment.

To my surprise, Martin looked as though he might be about to cry. I didn't want to look away from the man, but in my peripheral vision I could see the shadow was bigger now, swarming around Martin like something alive. Martin swallowed hard then; I knew, because I heard it.

'Double,' he said, in a small voice. He reached out and touched the doorhandle, a movement I saw register on the man's face, though he was still staring straight at me. 'Double, or I'm out of here.'

The man grinned, then, and the grin was shark-like, bloody. Martin let both hands fall to his sides, then he shrugged at me, and mouthed, *Sorry*.

'Deal,' the man said. Finally, he looked away, and I was free of his gaze.

When it was over, we walked back through the park together – or not quite together. Martin kept a few steps ahead of me, ready to quicken his pace and leave me behind if necessary. I knew he didn't want to be seen in my presence, but that knowledge didn't register as any sort of feeling in me. I was dazed, tongue-tied, unable to prevent my brain from flashing back to the pavilion, and what I'd seen. Martin kneeling on the ground in front of the man. The man knotting his fingers into Martin's hair. Martin retching and spitting on to the concrete floor as the man laughed.

'I don't know what the fuck you think you were doing,' Martin hissed. He didn't turn his head even slightly as he spoke.

I had no answer for him. I didn't know myself.

We walked a few more yards. I could still feel the cold sting of the pavilion's floor on the backs of my thighs: at some point, I'd sunk to the ground, afraid my trembling legs would no longer hold me up. I'd heard my classmates make their second pass of the cross-country course, pelting along the back of the building only inches from where I sat. The sound of the panting, chattering gaggle outside made things worse, some-how. They hadn't noticed I was gone. Or they'd noticed, and didn't care.

'Who was that man?'

I watched Martin's shoulders move up and down, a shrug.

'Some guy. I don't know.'

I frowned. I felt as though the ground beneath my feet was rocking – as though I were trying to walk along the deck of a ship on a high sea.

'But you— he knew you. You'd seen him before.'

'Fucksake,' Martin said, in a strangely matter-of-fact way. 'He's just a guy. One of my— one of the guys I ... do that for.'

The shadow was still there, draped around Martin's shoul-ders like a cape. I thought of the man's hands, of the wedge of folded notes he'd produced from a pocket, held in a shiny metal clip. The delicate way he'd peeled off two of them, test-ing the corners with his fingernails.

'For money,' I said.

'Why the *fuck* else would I do that?'

I wanted to tell him I didn't know. I didn't even really know what *that* was.

We walked on. Other people passed us, but I didn't regis-ter them. My head was full of the man, the way he'd turned towards me before he left the pavilion, the way he'd looked at me.

'You'd better forget my face, kid,' he'd said. 'I mean it.'

I'd known even before he said it that I'd carry the mem-ory of his face around with me for the rest of my life. He'd gestured at Martin, then – Martin, whose trouser legs were chalky with concrete dust, whose eyes were fixed on the floor.

'*He* has,' the man added. 'He knows better than to even look at me.'

In that moment, the shadow that hung around Martin had seemed to fill the whole room.

'I'm sorry, okay?' Martin said. We were nearing the school. I realised I had no idea what time it was. I didn't know if I'd been missed, if I was in trouble yet, how bad the trouble would be. He didn't sound sorry, but I knew he was. 'You shouldn't have seen that. Christ. You're only a fucking kid.' He popped his shoulders forwards, shaking himself. 'But you shouldn't have *been there.*'

We rounded a corner. I could see the school gates now.

'You know,' I said, 'you have this shadow that follows you around.'

Martin didn't respond.

'You have this shadow,' I said again. 'Not your shadow-shadow. More like … something like a ghost.'

For the first time since we'd set off across the park, he turned his head, just slightly, and I saw the white flicker of his right eye.

'What?'

I stopped walking. 'That's why I was there,' I said. 'That's why I followed you. Because of the shadow.'

Martin wheeled around. I was amazed. We were only metres from the school gates, anyone could have seen us talking.

'What is *wrong* with you?' The words were a snarl, and I was suddenly aware of how much taller than me he was, how much stronger. He windmilled an arm, and I thought he was going to hit me, but instead he pointed over my shoulder, back the way we had come. 'Do you have any idea what could have happened to you in there? How much trouble we might both have got in?'

I must have been frowning. The shadow was circling us both now, and I realised I could *hear* it. It sounded like television static.

'That guy,' Martin spluttered. 'He's a guy who likes to …' He trailed off, and I felt some of the fight go out of him. 'He likes kids,' he said, 'and you either know what I mean or you don't – I don't know. But you were in some fucking danger in there, and now you're messing with me about *ghosts*?'

I couldn't help it. I reached out a hand and touched the shadow. I expected it to move, to flinch away from me, but it didn't. I couldn't feel anything at all.

Martin was looking at me in disgust. 'You're crazy,' he said, straightening up. 'Fucking stay away from me, you hear? Don't ever talk to me.'

I opened my mouth to speak. *Can't you see the shadow?* I wanted to ask.

But he held up a hand. '*Ever*,' he repeated. 'Starting now.'

I closed my mouth again. He turned on his heel and walked away. The shadow followed, tugged like dry leaves on the wind.

I honoured his request, and never spoke to him again. Instead, I waited sixty seconds before crossing into the school grounds. I received a detention from Mrs White, the PE teacher, who assumed I'd simply dawdled through the cross-country course on account of laziness. I told my mother the detention was for running too slowly in PE, and she passed the information on to my father. He was reading the newspaper at the time, and simply rolled his eyes. I looked at my six-year-old brother across the dinner table, and thought of the smirking man in the brown suit, of Martin saying, 'He likes kids.' I excused myself and threw up my boiled chicken and potatoes and peas. I went to bed and lay awake, thinking of the pavilion, of Martin's shadow roaming through the space and growing, growing, until the whole building was filled with its static charge.

On Halloween that year, Martin drove his black Mark 1 Ford Escort westwards, through Currie and Balerno, and out of the city. He drove past the Harperrig Reservoir, up over the windswept moor at Tarbrax. He found a long straight on the A70, a place where he could pick up speed. It was night-time, lonely at 3am, and an egg-shaped waning gibbous moon hung in the sky. Martin fixed his eyes on that moon as he drove into the tree at eighty miles per hour, letting the bumper and the engine and the bonnet and the windscreen and the red speedometer needle and his body detonate into a million hot, brilliant shards.

When I dream about the crash, as I still do sometimes, I see the shadow hang awhile above the steaming wreck, as though waiting, like a dog, for Martin to return. But then it drifts upward, through the jagged branches of the ash tree and back the way it came, across the grassy barren of the landscape, a flash of dark reflected on the reservoir. And then it's gone.

Birch, Monday 10 January

Birch hobbled up the carpeted corridor along one side of the bullpen, headed for McLeod's office. Under the arm not braced on the walking stick was a stack of folders she was determined not to drop. She was thinking about Winnie, kicking herself for never having phoned her after the funeral. She was thinking about her mother, as she often did when she believed she ought to feel guilty about something. She knew that had her mother still been alive, Winnie would have been able to go round for a cup of tea and share her worries about Linh with someone who would listen, someone who'd say all the right things. Birch found herself resenting, the way she did almost every day, the fact that her mother had died. The fact that she'd had a difficult life, and then got ill. The fact that her treatment didn't work, and didn't work, and didn't work. The fact that Birch had had to send Winnie Fortune home, crying, sick with worry, and with no best friend to nip round to and confide in.

A new thought struck her, and she stopped, leaning on the stick, and cast around the bullpen. She was looking for her friend, Sergeant Amy Kato, whose desk was only a few metres away. Amy was sitting with her back to Birch, squinting at something on her screen.

Birch gave a low whistle. 'Hey, Kato,' she called, trying to keep her voice soft but also ensure she was heard over the general buzz of voices and photocopiers and ringing phones. It worked, because Amy's head flicked round. Birch couldn't wave, what with the files and the walking stick, so she gave an exaggerated nod of the head to indicate that it was she who had called.

Amy grinned, and practically leapt out of her chair. 'Helen,' she said, crossing the open space between them. 'You're outside the confines of your office! Has there been some sort of mistake?'

Birch laughed. 'The prisoner has been given extra time out of cell,' she said, 'for good behaviour.'

Amy grinned, and jerked her head towards the files. 'Off to archive those?'

'Yup. A little walk around the block. It's good for the war wound.'

'Need some help?'

Birch tried not to bristle. She'd grown very tired of those three words over the past few months. 'Thanks,' she said, 'but I'm good. Have to swing by McLeod's office on the way back, anyway.'

Amy raised an eyebrow. 'You in trouble?'

Birch snorted. 'What, you mean more so than usual? I don't think so. Just wanted his thoughts on something is all. But listen, let me ask you … how's the workload?'

Amy let out a short, mirthless laugh. 'Oh,' she said, 'it's a dream. Totally on top of everything, me. Not in any way waking up in a cold sweat at night thinking about paperwork.'

Birch smiled. 'I imagined you'd be snowed under,' she said. 'But how about the team? Anyone short of a job at the moment?'

Amy cocked her head. 'You need something?'

'I might, or I might not. A woman I know came in this morning to see me – Winnie, a friend of my mother's. She fosters kids – older teenagers, mostly – and one of them seems to have gone missing. She's worried.'

Amy had been smiling, but now the smile dimmed. 'Missing for how long?' she asked.

'We're still only at day one,' Birch replied. 'So I'm hoping it won't turn into anything. But this kid has … unusual circumstances. Like, even more unusual than most kids in the care system. So I'm just thinking ahead, in case it turns into a proper missing persons case.'

Amy was nodding. 'Let's say it does,' she said. 'What would you need from me?'

Birch looked past her friend, across the bullpen, without letting her gaze land on anything in particular. 'Family liaison,' she said, 'for Winnie. She's already pretty cut up about it, and it's only been a day.'

'You have anyone in mind?'

'Hey,' Birch said, 'you're the sergeant, remember? You know your team. Who's a good FLO and might have time to take this on?'

'Rema,' Amy said, almost before Birch had finished speaking. 'Rema's my best officer. I'm trying to make good use of her before she outperforms us all and ends up chief constable.'

Birch refocused her gaze to look at Amy again. 'Of course,' she said. 'Rema's great. She'd be ideal, if she's got space for it.'

Amy shrugged. 'None of us have space,' she said. 'Same old, same old. But if this turns bad, then I'm sure Rema would be all too happy to help.'

Birch winced. 'I really hope it doesn't,' she said. 'Turn bad, I mean.'

Amy flashed her a megawatt smile. 'It won't,' she said, 'I'm sure. Teenagers go walkabout all the time. She'll turn up.'

Birch had begun to nod before she realised what Amy had said. 'I never said it was a she.'

Amy grinned again. 'You forget I know you pretty well, Helen,' she said. 'If it wasn't a girl, you wouldn't be this worried.'

Birch blinked. 'Wow. How did you know that, when I hadn't even realised it myself?'

Amy waved a hand, as though presenting Birch with something. 'Oh,' she said, 'didn't I mention? I'm a police officer.'

It was 3.53pm when Birch reached McLeod's office, but she could tell he was already antsy to leave for the day. She saw a flicker of irritation cross his face as she walked in. His coat was slung over the desk, as though he'd been about to put it on.

'Helen,' he said.

'Guv.' She nodded towards the coat. 'This will just be a quick one, promise.'

He waved vaguely in the direction of a chair. 'I'm in no rush,' he said, without trying to make it sound true.

Birch was grateful for the seat: she'd been in since noon and would clock off herself in seven minutes, but her arm hurt from bracing against the walking stick, on top of all the other pain she was carrying around.

'Back to full-time next week,' McLeod said, brightly.

'Looking forward to it already,' she replied, aiming for sarcasm but sounding more weary than anything. In spite of herself, she added, 'It'll be good to get back to doing proper policework.'

McLeod raised an eyebrow at her from across the desk. 'I hope you're not assuming,' he said, 'that you can jump right back into a full command role, just because you're going full-time.'

Birch felt her shoulders sag.

'You'll be on that stick a while longer,' McLeod added, 'apart from anything else.'

She nodded – he wasn't wrong, after all – but she resented the fact that he seemed to be relishing the opportunity to keep her on the bench.

'I just mean,' she said, 'I'm looking forward to working on my own cases again, rather than catching up on paperwork.'

McLeod dropped his eyes. 'There are plenty of officers in this building,' he said, 'who'd give their eye teeth for a few weeks to sit and do nothing but paperwork.'

It was a snotty thing to say – *Listen, plenty of people would kill to have been shot and then beaten up so they could get on with their to-do list, so think yourself lucky* – but there was a smile in his voice, so Birch decided to laugh.

'True,' she said. 'I'm the most organised I've ever been. In a few weeks, I might be begging to go back to these halcyon days.'

McLeod was smiling properly now. 'I'm sure there'll be plenty more paperwork in your future, DI Birch,' he said.

Her own smile faded. She could tell he didn't want her there – not just in his office at 4pm on a Monday, but perhaps also, as she had begun to suspect, on his team. Since the shooting, she'd been dead wood he was having to carry – hadn't she? She wanted to ask him if he felt that way – as Dr Jane might have asked her, in one of their sessions – but DCI McLeod didn't really talk about how he felt.

'So,' he was saying, 'how can I help?'

Birch tried to straighten up a little in the chair. 'I was wondering if I could pick your brain,' she said.

'Oh yes? About what?'

'About unaccompanied minors,' Birch replied. 'Specifically, how often they become missing persons, and the outcomes of such cases.'

McLeod put his elbows on the desk, and steepled his hands. 'You're asking about young people who conveniently go walk-about on or around their eighteenth birthdays?'

'I might be. Is that very common?'

McLeod shrugged. 'It does seem to be a problem,' he said. 'They know they're about to become adults in the eyes of the law. They know that as an adult, one has to move out of the care system and make a formal application for asylum. They don't fancy doing that, so they disappear.'

'Where to?'

McLeod snorted. 'I suggest you use your imagination, Birch. Modern slavery, prostitution. The little swines would rather go through that than fill out the forms to seek asylum.'

Birch's eyed widened. 'With all due respect, sir,' she said, 'I think there's a little more to it than just filling out a form. I assume a lot of them are afraid of being detained.'

McLeod shrugged again. 'That's part and parcel of going through the system,' he said. 'After all, we can't make it too easy for these kinds of people to settle here.'

Birch literally bit down on her own tongue, but it was too late. The words were already forming. 'Just to be clear,' she said, 'we're still talking about children who've been trafficked into the UK and are living here without any support from family?'

McLeod threw an obvious glance at the clock on the office wall. 'You say potato,' he replied. 'Why are you asking me about this, anyway?'

Birch wanted to ask him what he meant when he said *these kinds of people*. But she was tired, and he wanted rid of her, and besides, she knew the answer.

'I had a woman come in and see me today,' she said. 'A Winifred Fortune. She was one of my mother's oldest friends, which is why she asked for me. Winnie's a foster carer, and a young woman in her care seems to be missing. An unaccompanied minor, originally from Vietnam.'

McLeod arranged his features into a knowing look. 'And she's seventeen, soon to be eighteen?'

'Yes, guv.'

'Missing how long?'

'Just one day, so far, so I haven't taken any action. She may yet turn up.'

McLeod let out another derisive snort. 'I doubt it,' he said. 'She'll get herself a cash-in-hand job in a nail bar, if she's Vietnamese. Or she'll go on the game. She'll fall through the cracks, as they say, deliberately. Put herself somewhere she can't be easily found.'

'You seem pretty certain.'

'Like I say,' he replied, 'it's a problem.' He was looking at his coat now.

'But … we'd investigate it as a missing persons case, right? If she doesn't turn up, I mean.'

McLeod sighed a long sigh. Birch wanted to tell him he was being dramatic, but knew better than to irritate him further.

'Yes, Birch. If your Mrs Fortune comes back, we'll be duty bound to investigate. It'll be a waste of everyone's time and resources, and we likely won't find the girl. But we'll do as we're told.'

'Great,' Birch said, though she didn't feel great at all. 'Should I start some paperwork on this?'

McLeod's eyes sharpened. 'Absolutely not,' he snapped. 'I can tell you're fond of this woman, so I'd say you've got a conflict of interest. Plus, you're …' He gestured at the walking stick she'd leaned against her chair. 'Well, as we discussed, you're still not fighting fit.'

Birch took a deep breath, preparing to respond, but McLeod cut in.

'I'll assign it to Crosbie,' he said. 'I assume you told this Mrs Fortune to keep in touch?'

Birch could feel that her face was suddenly hot. She hadn't anticipated that he'd take Linh's case away from her.

'I did,' she said.

'Good. You'd better call her and give her Crosbie's direct line. He can be the point of contact from now on.'

Birch thought about arguing. She would have argued, once upon a time, before – well, everything. McLeod had accused her on more than one occasion of having a brass neck. Recent events seemed to have stolen it from her. She found herself dipping her head and looking away. In that moment, she hated herself.

'Yes, guv,' she said.

'Good,' McLeod said again. He stood up, and made a show of brushing down his suit jacket with both hands. 'Now,' he added, 'unless there's anything else …?'

Birch felt around for the walking stick, and then clambered to her feet.

'Nothing else,' she said. 'Thank you, sir.'

She felt his eyes on her back even after she'd left the office, closed the door, and set off down the corridor. She made herself wait until she'd got into the empty lift before she allowed herself to swear.

'He's a racist,' Anjan said. 'Pure and simple.'

Birch gave him a *Lower your voice, please* look, and glanced around the restaurant. She needn't have bothered; they were eating in Viva Mexico, maybe the liveliest restaurant in the entire Old Town. Two plates of sizzling fajitas had just been delivered to the table next to them. Birch's own food was delicious, but she couldn't help feeling a pang of jealousy.

'He is,' Anjan went on. 'And you know it. That's why the things he said made you feel so uncomfortable.'

Birch looked down at her plate of half-finished veggie enchiladas. Anjan was right, of course. As usual.

'You do have a bit of a vendetta against him, though,' she said.

Anjan threw up his hands. 'Well,' he said, 'let's examine the facts of the case, shall we?'

Birch wanted to laugh. Anjan never stopped being a lawyer.

'First,' he began, 'James McLeod has never appreciated you. He's always made you feel like you're a bit of a liability, like you're making his life difficult, for the simple reason that you don't always subscribe to his way of thinking. Isn't that so?'

Birch paused, then nodded. She wondered if Anjan could tell from her face that she wished she'd never opened this particular can of worms. She wished she hadn't told him about Winnie, or Linh, or the conversation with McLeod and the case being given to Crosbie. She was even beginning to wish that she hadn't suggested coming out for dinner.

'Very well,' Anjan went on. 'So we've established that he's a bad manager, because only a bad manager makes their own inadequacies a problem for their staff.'

Birch decided to concentrate on her plate. She gathered a loaded forkful of enchilada and took a bite. She hoped that, if she gave him enough airspace, Anjan would eventually run out of steam.

'Second,' he was saying, 'it was James McLeod's fault that you were shot while working on Operation Kendall. The whole thing was badly handled, and he knows it.'

Birch glanced at Anjan's plate. 'Your food's going to go cold,' she said, but he didn't seem to hear her.

'Third,' he went on, counting on his fingers now, 'is Operation Stake. You being attacked by a dangerous criminal – on Police Scotland premises, no less – was a direct result of negligence on the part of James McLeod. He had a duty of care towards you that night, and instead of supporting you to do your job safely, he actively sabotaged you, and left you unable to call for back-up. Frankly, he's lucky you didn't die that night – and also that you're not a litigious sort of person.'

Birch rolled her eyes, and ate some more enchilada. Anjan had been a little too keen for her to sue Police Scotland for damages after Operation Stake, even though he knew she was mortified by the very idea.

'Four,' Anjan went on, 'McLeod has taken delight in the fact that you've been injured for months, and struggling with work. He has purposefully side-lined you, with no thought for the effect that might have on your mental health, and hasn't got involved in any meaningful way with your phased return.'

Birch didn't respond. She was chewing.

'Isn't that so?' he asked.

She put down her fork. 'Honey,' she said, 'I know you mean well. I know you're protective of me. But you're making me feel like I'm on the witness stand right now.'

For just a fraction of a second, Anjan looked frustrated. But then she saw what she'd said land, and he seemed to realise she was right.

'Sorry,' he said. 'Force of habit.'

'It's okay.'

Anjan looked down at his plate for a moment, then looked back at Birch. 'But just one more to add,' he said. 'Five: James McLeod is also a racist.'

Birch had been trying to smile, but it wasn't really working. 'I'll admit,' she said, 'the comment about nail bars did make me squirm.'

Anjan nodded, and finally picked up his fork to eat. 'Annoyingly,' he said, 'he might actually be right about that. Not the racial stereotype, obviously, just the fact that nail bars do sometimes employ unaccompanied minors. For me, it was his use of "these kinds of people". I've been referred to as "one of those people" my entire life. White people feel totally comfortable categorising brown people as other. They don't even attempt to hide it.'

Birch tilted her head, trying to make a sympathetic face. It made her squirm, sometimes, when Anjan talked about white people without making an exception for her. That proved his point, a lot of the time; she was learning to stop thinking of herself as special, as good, as above these kinds of criticisms. But it was a hard learning, and she felt embarrassed to have only just begun it now, in her forties.

'It's not on the same level,' she said, 'but I do also wish he'd learn to say sex work, not prostitution. Goodness knows we've all sat through enough training. He ought to know by now.'

Anjan was chewing. Birch waited.

'He knows,' he said, eventually. 'I believe he knows what he ought to say, and what he ought not to say. He just doesn't care enough to be mindful of that. There might even be a part of him that *enjoys* saying it.'

'You think he wants a reaction?'

Anjan shrugged. 'He was probably surprised he didn't get one from you.'

Birch put down her fork a little too forcefully, and it clattered on her plate. 'Oh God,' she said, 'you're ashamed of me, aren't you? You think I ought to have challenged him.'

'I am absolutely not ashamed of you.' Anjan reached across the table, and took her hand. Birch wanted to glance around to see if anyone was looking at them, but she stopped herself. 'I am a little surprised myself, though, I'll admit,' he said.

Birch gave his hand a small squeeze, then pulled away. She liked the gesture, but always felt a little like a daft teenager, holding hands across the table in a restaurant.

'Me too,' she admitted. 'I just sort of … let him get away with it. All of it. Saying those things, giving the case to Crosbie. Crosbie, of all people.'

Anjan cocked his head. 'You worry too much about Crosbie,' he said. 'He's not half the officer you are. You shouldn't let him get to you.'

Birch frowned. 'He doesn't get to me,' she said, then checked herself. 'Okay, maybe sometimes he gets to me. But mostly I think it's the other way round. Something about *me* gets to *him*. He just seems to hate me. He seems to have decided we're enemies – or at least rivals – so he's set up this dynamic between us that I can't seem to shake us out of. It's like a trap I fall into. I find myself feeling competitive, and yet, Crosbie isn't my competition. He's meant to be my colleague.'

Anjan was nodding. 'He hates that you know his secret,' he said. 'You know he's had to go to McLeod for help with his drinking – more than once, in fact. You know he's been sent to AA. More than likely, he's on a final written warning. Besides McLeod, you're the only person who knows that – and you know it because he was stupid enough to be drunk around you.'

'Only on the phone,' Birch said, wondering as she spoke why she felt the need to leap to Crosbie's defence. 'And only once.'

'Doesn't matter.' Anjan shrugged. 'You know. So it's not just McLeod he has to prove himself to. It's you as well.'

Birch closed her eyes for a moment. She realised her face was beginning to ache from frowning. 'If that's the case,' she replied, 'I don't get the enmity. Surely he knows he'd do a lot better with me if he worked at being a stand-up guy, you know? A good policeman. Why doesn't he just get on with it?'

Anjan's face twisted into a grim smile. 'Male anger,' he said. 'As you and I both know, it's both a mystery and a scourge.'

Birch poked at the food on her plate, wishing she could stop thinking so much. 'I do know,' she said. 'And since when was I a woman who'd allow herself to be pushed around by angry men? I mean, I've been letting McLeod get away with banishing me to my office for weeks. I've been letting Crosbie crow about the fact that I'm walking wounded. I've been allowing it all to happen. But I'm just so tired.' She glanced at the walking stick, which was leaning against the edge of the table. 'I feel like all the fight has gone out of me.'

'Of course you're tired,' Anjan said. 'You've been struggling with pain. Being in pain is incredibly tiring.'

Birch looked down at the space between the edge of her plate and the edge of the table. She could see where she'd dropped crumbs and they'd settled into the tablecloth's weave.

'It's not just that,' she said, in a small voice. 'I mean I'm tired of everything. Not just the pain, not just not being able to work. I feel like I'm tired of *life*.'

Anjan was quiet. He stayed quiet for so long that eventually Birch looked up, as though to check he was definitely still there. He was watching her, his brow furrowed.

'Helen,' he said, 'what are you saying, exactly?'

She looked down at her plate again. She could feel a lump forming in her throat. *Don't you dare cry, Helen.*

'I'm saying …' She trailed off, rallied, and then tried again. 'I think I might be saying … maybe you're right. About McLeod. About everything, really.'

She risked another look at him, but he was still frowning. He hadn't understood. She took a deep breath.

'I'm saying,' she said, 'that I don't know if I can do it anymore. I'm saying I don't think I'm up to the job.'

Bee, 1987

I hadn't ever really made friends, and I didn't particularly care: my favourite place in the school was the library, and I was happy to spend time there alone. It was a chilly, imposing place, not at all like the cosy libraries I'd seen in films; the librarian, Mrs Muchtie, had set it up to function like a panopticon. The desk at which she sat was slightly raised; to pay a fine or get your chosen book stamped out, you had to ascend two carpeted steps and teeter there on the edge of Mrs Muchtie's makeshift dais. The rest of the room was laid out like a clock, with the raised desk at its centre and the shelf stacks angled away from it, making strange diagonal corridors that Mrs Muchtie could watch at all times from her swivel chair. Among the things she wouldn't tolerate were loitering, whispering, giggling, and the consumption of food or drink of any kind. These were, as far as I could tell, among my classmates' favourite things, so the library was always blissfully quiet. I'd wolf my packed lunch in the corridor outside before settling in to read something 'wholly unsavoury', as my mother would have said. My favourite was Agatha Christie's *A Pocket Full of Rye*, the one with the maid dead and strung up with clothesline, a peg on the end of her nose.

In fourth year – the year I turned sixteen – I got heavily into Shakespeare's tragedies. *Macbeth*, which we'd studied the year before, was my favourite. As well as carrying copies of each individual play, the library also had a massive *Collected Works of William Shakespeare*, a book so large I struggled to heft it over to my favourite lunchtime seat each day. It was that book I chose to read, though it was reserve only and couldn't be taken home. I loved its onion-skin pages, and the places where students before me had underlined sections in silvery pencil, ploughing a channel in the paper that ghosted on to the pages below.

One day, the book felt different; as soon as I picked it up, I could tell someone else had held it recently, perhaps only minutes ago. The knowing prickled in my fingertips like static. Cradling its weight in my arms, I opened the book and flicked through to my favourite scene in *Macbeth*: Lady Macbeth's 'Come, you spirits' soliloquy. Tucked between the pages was a Post-It note, which read, *Bee I need to talk to you – meet me behind Chemistry at lunch xx Melody*. Feeling Mrs Muchtie's eyes on me, I continued turning pages, trying to look nonchalant, though my heart had begun rattling in my chest. Melody Rowe was a popular girl – low down on the in-crowd league table, but a member of the hockey team nevertheless. I'd spoken to her perhaps three times in four years. I couldn't think of a single reason that Melody Rowe might need to see me. Surely the note was some sort of trap.

Balancing the book against the shelf, I slipped the Post-It note out and crushed it in my fist, before dropping the crumpled yellow ball into my duffle coat pocket. With some effort, I slid the book back into its space on the shelf.

'Not staying today?' Mrs Muchtie watched over the tops of her glasses as I crossed the room to the door. I could detect no emotion in her voice, couldn't tell if she was pleased I was leaving, or disappointed.

'I just remembered I have …' I paused, trying to think of a reason she'd buy – I was sixteen, of course, and not realising that Mrs Muchtie probably didn't care whether I lived or died, let alone what I did with my lunch hour. 'Detention,' I sputtered, eventually, and then fled, clattering off down the corridor as though I might be pursued.

I got halfway through the building before my pace slowed. I needed to think: Melody seemed harmless in comparison to some of her friends, but wouldn't it make sense, then, to make her the messenger? The hockey girls might want to lure me somewhere, for ... something. I didn't know what the something could be, but I knew it couldn't be good.

I ducked into the ground-floor girls' toilets, the safe ones – there was a staffroom right across the corridor, close enough that any illicit smoking could be easily sniffed out by a passing teacher. The bad girls – the ones with the cigarettes and Doc Marten boots and safety pins through their earlobes, the ones even the hockey team feared – used the bad girls' bathroom on the second floor. This one was fine. I could hide out here for a minute and figure out what to do.

Locking myself in the nearest stall, I pulled the balled Post-It out of my pocket. I closed the toilet lid, sat down and smoothed Melody's note against my thigh. *Bee I need to talk to you – meet me behind Chemistry at lunch xx Melody*. Again, I felt a prickle in my fingertips, a warm feeling, like lightly brushing the fur on an animal's back. I closed my eyes, and realised that, touching the note, I could *see* Melody Rowe standing behind the Chemistry block, almost as clearly as if I were walking towards her. She was alone, glancing around as though afraid to be seen, hugging her own waist with one arm. The other arm was bent towards her face, her free hand busy twirling the same strand of permed, streaked hair over and over again. I could see that Melody was more afraid of me than I was of her: knowledge that hit me like a cold slap to the face. I leapt up from the toilet and opened the lid, screwing the Post-It into a pellet once more. I threw it into the bowl and pulled the chain, watching until the note had washed away. Then I shouldered my school bag, turned left out of the toilet block, and headed for Chemistry.

It was a grey day, overcast and blustery, a typically Edinburgh sort of day. Melody was shivering in a thin school shirt, her hair wrapped round her finger just the way I'd seen. Her skirt was rolled at the top to make it shorter; Melody wasn't as thin as some of her hockey-girl peers, and I could see the little fabric bulge it made around her waist. Below the skirt she wore white knee-high socks, the kind I coveted, but wasn't allowed to buy. My mother sewed my school skirts herself: monstrous, baggy creations with straight seams and a hem that fell to mid-calf – the worst possible length.

'There'd be no point,' she'd say, whenever I asked about the socks. 'No one would ever see them.'

I let out a little cough, announcing my presence, and Melody turned to face me.

'Hi, Bee.' She threw me a nervous smile, and I saw the glint of braces on her top teeth. 'I wasn't sure if you'd come.'

'I got your note,' I said, and heard the hard edge of wariness in my own voice.

Melody glanced behind her, then back at me. 'Did you … bring it with you? The note.'

I shook my head. 'I flushed it,' I said.

She smiled properly then, a smile of relief, though it didn't last long. I could feel a strange fizziness radiating out of her. It was fear.

'You're smart,' she said, and I was taken aback. This was maybe the nicest thing anyone at school had ever said to me. 'I knew you'd know what to do.'

I took a step closer to her. 'What's up, Melody? What's going on?'

Her face crumpled. She looked down at the short stretch of tarmac between us. After a moment of silence, she took a long breath in, and I could tell she was trying not to cry.

'People say that you – know things,' she said. She didn't look up at me.

'Know things?'

'Yeah. That you're a bit, um – psychic. Or something.'

I blinked. When I didn't respond, Melody let out a short, wet laugh.

'I know it sounds mental, okay?' she said, 'But at this point, I'm desperate.'

I was still processing. 'People say I'm psychic?'

She shrugged. She was still looking at the floor, but I could see her eyelashes were damp. 'Well … you're a witch, aren't you? Like in *The Witches of Eastwick*. That's what I've heard.'

I was staring at her now, goggle-eyed, unsure how to react. I wasn't stupid; I knew people whispered about me. I knew I was considered *weird*. I'd assumed it was my embarrassing home-made clothes, and the hand-me-downs from my mother, and my lack of knowledge about anything even the slightest bit cool. I hadn't seen *The Witches of Eastwick*, for example. It was an eighteen certificate, which meant Melody must have either snuck into the cinema or watched a pirated video copy at somebody's sleepover. I couldn't have snuck anywhere, even if I'd wanted to, and I'd never been invited to a sleepover in my life.

But Melody was still talking.

'You do,' she said. 'You know things. You always do so well in tests and stuff, because you know the answers.'

I snorted. 'No,' I said, 'that's because I *study*.'

She didn't seem to hear me. 'Then there was that time,' she went on, 'when you said you didn't want to sit next to Malik in French because he had tonsilitis. And he didn't even get tonsilitis until, like, three days after that.'

I was shaking my head as though denying her story, but yes, she was right – I *had* known that Malik had tonsilitis. Though I hadn't yet been diagnosed asthmatic, I knew that getting sick was no picnic, so I didn't want his germs and wasn't afraid to say so. But I hadn't realised my behaviour that day had been noteworthy.

'And,' Melody added, 'last year you told Jeanine Peoples that Joel was dating Lara, when he wasn't. He was dating Cassie. But it turned out he was *cheating* on Cassie with Lara, and it was a total secret until way later. But you knew.'

I was starting to feel light-headed. This whole interaction was too bizarre for me to fully take in.

'Do you even *talk* to Jeanine Peoples?' I asked. It was hardly the most pertinent part of what Melody had said, but I couldn't believe that a lowly swot kid like Jeanine would ever have had the ear of hockey girls like Melody, Lara and Cassie.

Melody sighed. 'Sometimes,' she said, clearly irritated by the question. 'She wants to be popular, and every so often she tries to get in with us by telling us her little snitch facts. That time it really backfired on her, though. Cassie was *furious*.'

'With Jeanine? Shouldn't she have been furious with Lara?'

Melody looked up at me, at last, but only so she could roll her eyes. 'I *told* you,' she said, 'Cassie didn't find out that the Lara thing was true until way later; she thought Jeanine was just being a bitch. But it *was* true, and you knew about it.'

'Okay?' I said. I couldn't summon up any memory of offering this information to Jeanine Peoples, and that bothered me.

But it was information that I had, indeed, known. I just hadn't really thought much about *how* I knew it.

Melody was looking at the ground again. 'Okay,' she replied. 'So you know stuff. And I need your help.'

I realised then, in a way I never had before – in spite of what had happened with Martin and the shadow-ghost cast over him by his unbearable pain, which I could see, though no one else could – that yes, I did know things. I knew things other people didn't know. I knew things it was impossible for anyone to know. Because I knew in that moment what Melody was going to ask me – and worse, I knew the answer.

She was biting her lip. 'Look,' she said. 'You can't tell anyone. You really, really can't tell anyone.'

I took another step towards her. 'Who am I going to tell?' I realised that sounded too harsh, because Melody's eyes were properly wet now. 'I won't tell anyone,' I said. 'I'll take it to the grave, I swear.'

A tear finally escaped from her eyelashes, and ran down her face. It was grey.

'Quick,' I said, aiming for a light tone, the sort of tone friends use. 'You'd better just say it, or you're going to ruin your make-up.'

I watched her try to smile, but it didn't really work. She hiccupped a breath in, and then one out.

'I need you to tell me,' she said, 'if I'm pregnant or not.'

I tried not to react. I tried to make my face do absolutely nothing.

'Why don't you just go to the pharmacy,' I said, 'and get a test?'

Melody rolled her eyes heavenward. 'Oh,' she said, 'like that would be so easy. My friends would know, or they'd find out. Or worse, one of my *parents'* friends would find out. Someone would find out. This way, only you have to know.' She paused, and I saw her throat contract as she swallowed. 'If it's true,' she added, in a sort of strangled voice. 'Maybe it's not true.'

I closed my eyes for a moment. Melody was one of the youngest in our year, still only fifteen. Her mother was on the PTA. Her family went to church. I understood. I didn't need to be told how bad this could get for her.

I opened my eyes, and began to nod.

Her eyes widened. 'Yes? You're saying yes? It's true?'

I kept nodding, like I didn't know how to stop. I felt like one of those stupid fuzzy nodding dog toys. 'Yes,' I whispered. 'I'm so sorry.'

Her face twisted, and she let out a sob, then clamped both hands over her face. 'You're sure?' she said, between her fingers.

I felt a stinging cold in my chest, like I'd swallowed an ice cube whole. Was I sure? Lying about this – or guessing at it – would, I knew, be incredibly cruel. But yes, I was sure. Melody was pregnant. I could see her life as she knew it ending, right there, around us.

'I'm sure,' I croaked.

Hands still raised, she pressed her fingertips into her eye sockets. 'Oh god,' she said. 'Oh god. Oh god.'

I was close enough, just, to reach out and touch her. I couldn't quite make myself do it.

'How did you ...?' I tailed off. That was a stupid line of questioning. I sounded like a stupid virgin. In that fleeting second, I decided that being a stupid virgin was actually no bad thing. But I changed tack. 'Who ...' I asked. 'Who did you ...?'

She uncovered her eyes and looked at me. Her hands were daubed with mascara, and her face was ruined. When she spoke, it was so quiet I had to take a second to process, to check I'd heard her properly.

'Joel,' she whispered.

If it hadn't all been so terrible, I'd have laughed. I could see why she didn't want her friends finding out.

'*Fucking* Joel,' I spat.

She laughed then, a desperate sort of laugh, so unexpected that it made me jump. 'Yeah,' she said, 'I have been. Me as well.'

Her eyes weren't laughing.

'That guy's a total prick,' I said, surprising myself. It was true, he was, and I'd long thought so, but until this moment I would never have dreamed of voicing such a strident opinion within anyone's earshot.

Melody had covered her face again.

'Listen,' I said. Now I did reach out towards her, placing one hand on her shoulder. She didn't acknowledge the gesture, but she also didn't flinch away. I gave her the slightest shake, because it seemed like the right thing to do. 'This isn't your fault, okay? This is *his* fault. He should have ...' I thought of all the words I could use for the thing I wanted to describe, all the euphemisms I'd heard my peers employ, and I couldn't bear to allow any of them to come out of my mouth. 'He should have used protection,' I said. Even that made me cringe.

Melody was shaking her head. 'No,' she said, her voice muffled by her hands, 'it was me. It was all me. I'm a horrible person.'

'You're *not*.' Without thinking, I'd raised my voice. An echo bounced off the Chemistry block wall: *not, not, not*.

Melody dropped her hands and wiped them against her thighs, leaving snotty trails on her skirt. 'I am,' she said. 'And now I'm dead, too.'

I started shaking my head, so she grabbed the arm I'd braced between us. My hand was still on her shoulder.

'Listen, Beatrice, I mean it. I am so dead. My dad's going to kill me. My *mum's* going to kill me.' I watched her eyes widen and her pupils dilate as the final realisation hit her. 'And then the worst part is, I'm going to end up with a fucking *baby*.'

I shuddered, unable to help myself. I genuinely couldn't think of anything worse.

Melody swatted my hand away, then reached out and gripped both my arms, just above the elbows. We were so close now that I could smell her Charlie body spray, and see the little individual flecks of mascara smeared on her cheeks. I had the stray thought that had I wanted to, I could have kissed her. I let myself wonder, just for a second, if I did want to, and decided I didn't. But I could have.

'What am I going to do, Bee?' She shook me then, much harder than I'd shaken her. I felt glad I was wearing my duffle coat so that her fingernails couldn't press into my skin. 'What can I do? Tell me what to do.'

I thought for a moment. My head felt fuzzy, full of TV static, but beneath the static was a picture I could almost make out.

'You have an aunty, right?'

She stopped shaking me. 'What?'

Gently, I tugged both arms away from her, and she let go.

'You have an aunty. Your aunty who lives in London.'

She blinked three times, slowly, and cocked her head at me. It made the grey tears shift to run diagonally across her face. 'How did you know that?'

I raised one hand and tapped my own temple with my forefinger. 'I know things, remember?' I said, then felt stupid. It sounded lame.

But she was nodding, wanting me to go on.

'You should tell your aunty in London,' I said. '*Don't* tell your parents. Just your aunty. She'll know what to do.'

Melody was nodding more vigorously now. Teardrops cascaded off her chin. 'Okay,' she said, pulling in a snotty breath. 'Okay. I'll ring her tonight.'

I realised I was also nodding. 'She'll know what to do,' I said again, hoping it was true. I didn't know how I knew this stuff, and it was freaking me out.

Melody looked like she might say something, but then we both jumped. The bell for the end of lunch was ringing.

'*Shit*,' Melody hissed. 'Oh god … what day is it?'

I frowned. 'Wednesday.'

'Shit,' she said again. She had begun pawing at her face, trying to wipe away the daubed mascara. It wasn't working. 'I need to get to French. But I can't. I need to fix my make-up.'

I held out a hand towards her, though I didn't touch her again. 'You don't,' I said. 'You really don't.'

She narrowed her eyes at me then. 'Shut up,' she spat. 'I look a state.'

I was still holding my hand out towards her, as though she were a drowning person I wanted to save. 'No,' I said, 'I mean … you don't have to go to French. And you should leave your face, because it'll help.'

She huffed out a breath at me. 'What are you *talking* about?'

I diverted my held-out hand, waved it vaguely in the direction of the school reception. 'We're going to the sick bay,' I said, with more conviction than I felt. 'We'll tell the nurse you've got terrible period cramps. She'll believe you because, look, you're crying. Like, they're really, *really* bad cramps. She'll send a note that you need to skip French, and you can take forty-five minutes to clean up and get yourself together.'

She was looking at me as though I'd just done some sort of complicated magic trick. 'I can do that? They'll let me do that?'

I threw her a grin. 'I mean, sorry to say it, but you look like death. They'll believe you.' I turned to face the way I'd pointed, and took a step. 'Come on,' I said. 'It'll be okay. I'll come with you.'

Melody paused for a moment, then repeated the action of rubbing her hands down the sides of her thighs, the way she'd done earlier. 'But,' she said, 'you'll get into trouble. You're meant to be in class, too.'

I shrugged, perhaps a little too theatrically. I'd never, ever been late to class, and the idea *was* making me a little queasy – but she didn't need to know that.

'Doesn't matter,' I said, and beamed at her. The smile was genuine: in that moment, I felt cooler and more rebellious than I ever had before. Lateness be damned: I might just have successfully made friends with Melody Rowe.

I jerked my head in the direction of the main building, and began to walk. Melody hesitated, just for a second or two, but then, out of the corner of my eye, I saw her toss her hair back over her shoulder, and follow me.

Birch, Tuesday 11 January

Birch had come to the realisation that there were just two types of people: people who had tidy desks (Amy Kato, of course, was one), and people who had messy desks. She was a messy desk person. It was as much a part of her as her stubborn fringe that wouldn't sit flat, or the fact that when she'd had a few glasses of wine, she laughed just like her mother. Right now, she was leaning back in her office chair and taking inventory of said mess. Two used coffee mugs, one a freebie from the International Crime Co-Ordination Centre. Its slogan read: 'THE TRUTH IS any one of us could be involved in an international crime investigation. BE READY' – wording that always made Birch chuckle. Beside the 'real' mugs were three empty cardboard cups she hadn't yet carried over to the recycling bin. Four sugar packets, intact, and two wooden stirrers. A block of neon Post-Its, the top one scribbled on. The old cow-shaped milk jug from her mother's kitchen, which she hadn't been able to throw away. Instead, one day after the funeral, she'd brought it to work with her and turned it into a pen pot. A copy of yesterday's *Edinburgh Evening News*. A copy of the *Scotsman* from sometime the previous week. An unruly heap of paperwork – which seemed never to shrink – and three buff-coloured box files, which Birch was slowly filling. Biros. Paper clips. An ugly photo frame Charlie had made her in high school woodwork class, many years ago – he'd painted it bright red and daubed her nickname, *Nella,* along the top in blotchy yellow script. In the frame was a photo of the two of them as children, playing in the surf on Portobello Beach. Next to it was a small plant pot, half-filled with crusty soil and brown leaves. It was the remains of a plant her colleagues had bought for her birthday, her first year at Fettes Avenue. It had died within six months, though she'd watered it. Over-watered it, Amy reckoned. Birch hadn't known there was such a thing.

The drip started up where it always did: a little seam of water had formed at one edge of the ceiling tile right in the centre of the room. The first few drops of water fell sound-lessly, absorbed by the regulation grey-brown office carpet-ing, and Birch didn't notice them as she fretted over her desk inventory. But after a while, enough water had soaked into the spot under the ceiling tile that a puddle began to form, and then the drips fell with a regular *tick-splat, tick-splat* sound. Now she looked up, frowned at the drip, and cast around for something to shove under it while she figured out what to do. One of the coffee mugs would work – it was only a small leak, after all. But when she glanced back up, the drip had become a trickle, like a tap had been turned on right above that ceiling tile, and the tile itself was beginning to sag with accumulated water. *I ought to check*, Birch thought, *to see if there's been an all-staff email about works in the building*. But before she could reach for her laptop, the ceiling tile gave way – followed by the one beside it, then another – and what had been a drip only a minute ago was now a small waterfall. Little rainbows thrown by the harsh office lighting danced in the air around the pillar of water. The carpet was already becoming soaked; Birch could hear the squelch it made under the stopper of her stick as she hobbled out from behind the desk and over to the door.

Outside in the bullpen, her colleagues were working away as usual. Birch watched Amy cross the room, heading back to her desk from the photocopier. Out there, the water was already ankle-deep, but Amy picked through it in her smart high heels as though the flood were simply not happening. The PC monitors glowed and hummed, though the water level was now above their sockets. What had been a feeling of vague unease turned to terror, and it held Birch's chest in an icy grip. She tried the door handle, and it didn't move. She rattled it, and it wouldn't give. The door was mostly glass, so she rapped on it loudly, shouting *Hey!* as her colleagues walked by. No one blinked. The flood was rising rapidly, now almost at her knees: she felt its weighty pull as a throbbing pain in her bad leg. It had to be going somewhere, all this water; she could feel a current in it, as if she'd stepped into a river. Out in the bullpen, Amy threw back her head and laughed at something, the strange ebb-tide now lapping at her waist. A movement in Birch's peripheral vision made her turn her head in time to see her cluttered desk lose contact with the floor and begin to float. The coffee cups barrelled over, and Charlie's teenage woodwork project toppled off the lip of the desk. The red frame bobbed on the surface of the water for a moment before going under, and Birch let out a strangled sort of cry.

The officers she'd been able to see sitting in chairs at their computers were now completely submerged. Amy, petite as she was, was still standing by the photocopier – Birch could see it glowing faintly under the torrent like some alien deep-water fish – while the water inched over her shoulders. Birch yelled her friend's name, yelled for help, eventually just yelled, a series of wails that became increasingly animal as she made them. Her walking stick floated by, and she grabbed it, hitting the office door with all the strength she could muster. Nothing happened: she couldn't even make a scratch on the glass. One by one, she watched as her colleagues disappeared without a struggle; for a moment, Amy's long black hair floated on the surface like seaweed, until it too was gone. The water was strangely warm, though its waves were now high enough to break across Birch's face like a series of blows. She closed her eyes. The current was strong, and she was tired. What was left, if all of this was washed away? Who was she without this office, these people, this job …

Birch jolted awake, as she'd half known she would. The dream was so familiar now, and it played out in almost exactly the same way every night. Except this time, it wasn't night; Birch was slumped in her office chair, her neck bent at a strange angle. The desk from her dream was now in front of her. She'd fallen asleep at work.

She lurched upright, cheeks burning with shame. Outside, it was almost dark; 4pm had come and gone. She should have left for home by now. Birch rubbed her eyes, her heart rate ticking up. How long had she been asleep? Anyone could have walked past the office, glanced through the door and seen her. Had McLeod seen her? She covered her face with her hands.

'Oh God, Helen,' she whispered aloud.

Her bad leg hurt, and her shoulders ached from sliding down into a strange position in the chair. She'd fallen asleep. How could she have fallen asleep?

'You're going back to full-time next week,' she hissed. She could feel her face flushing with embarrassment. How many people had seen her dozing in her chair? Even if McLeod wasn't one of them, he might be told. She didn't want to imagine what he might say, or the smug look he'd wear while he said it.

'For goodness' sakes,' she said, a little louder now. 'You have to get a *grip*.'

She checked the time again, and realised she could take another dose of painkillers if she wanted to: enough time had elapsed. Her hand hovered beside the drawer where she kept the pills. *Did* she want to? Sure, things hurt, but weren't the drugs part of the problem, these days? Weren't they part of the reason she'd just been literally asleep on the job? Birch had read the list of side effects so often she could have recited them word for word. They didn't say it in so many words, but the meds definitely blunted her edges, made her softer. Slower, less effective. All the things McLeod kept hinting at. She could try to explain to him that she slept badly at night, waiting for the pills to kick in and quiet the pain, but then felt herself fighting their side effects through the day, too. She shook her head. He'd only say, *See, Helen? You're just not firing on all cylinders right now. Best to keep you on desk work for the foreseeable future, don't you think?* And the woman she was now – the strange, pliant woman she seemed to have become – would most likely nod, say, *Yes, guv*, and wander back to her office as if still in the dream.

She gave her head a shake, took a deep breath in and held it. She counted to four in her head, then let the breath out slowly. Dr Jane had taught her this technique for times when she felt like her thoughts were doing things she hadn't asked them to.

'Okay,' she said aloud. 'Name the feelings, Helen.' She felt idiotic, talking to herself this way, but she'd learned it helped to pretend that Dr Jane was also in the room somewhere, standing just outside her field of vision.

'I feel like my meds are making me bad at my job,' she said, then paused. 'But no,' she went on, hearing her voice as though it were Dr Jane's own, 'that's not the feeling, is it? What's the feeling? I feel *worried* that I'm bad at my job.' She paused again, assessing the statement, and then the truth occurred to her. For a moment it took her breath away, how different it felt to actually identify a feeling as opposed to guessing. She let out a low whistle. Therapy really was a magical thing.

'I feel shame,' she said. 'That's it. I feel shame.'

Birch slid into silence for several minutes. She imagined explaining all this to Dr Jane, come their next session. *I was asleep on the job. Perhaps I've been asleep on the job all this time, all these weeks. And I feel shame.* No response, of course. This was the part she struggled with: the part that came next. If Dr Jane *were* here in the room with her, what would she say? Birch didn't know. In the bullpen outside, some of her colleagues were packing up for the day. She could hear people shuffling to the break room to wash up their coffee cups, shoulder on their coats. Someone called out 'Cheerie-bye!' across the office. Birch straightened up. She could have been home by now.

'What was I even *doing*?' she muttered. She poked at her laptop's trackpad until the screen came to life, then she tapped out her login details. Predictably, up sprang the email inbox, her old nemesis.

'Oh yes,' she said. 'Of course.'

In front of her was the email she'd drafted to Winnie Fortune.

Dear Winnie,

I gave you a call this afternoon to see if you'd heard anything from Linh, and left a message on your voicemail.

She stopped reading for a moment, reaching for her phone. Had Winnie called while Birch was dozing, and she'd missed it? No: the phone showed no missed calls. She let out a short, fast breath, then carried on.

I'm getting in touch here, too, just to make sure you're kept up to date. Obviously, I very much hope that Linh has come home, or that you've heard from her, and what follows can now be disregarded. Please do get in touch and let me know if that's the case.

In the meantime, I should tell you that I've spoken with my commanding officer, DCI McLeod, about Linh's disappearance, and he's given me some useful context to work with. He has also suggested that Linh's case be taken forward by my colleague DI Alan Crosbie. I'm still recuperating after my period of long-term sick leave, and DCI McLeod feels I am not in a position to head up a case like this at the present time.

Birch paused, feeling her nose wrinkle. Reluctantly, she shifted the cursor into the email text and then deleted 'DCI McLeod feels'. She re-read the sentence, understood it was better and more professional as a result of the edit, but let out a snort anyway, and then read on.

DI Crosbie's contact details are at the bottom of this email. If Linh has not returned home or been in touch with you in the twenty-four hours since you and I last spoke, then please do get in touch so we can begin a formal investigation. Please note that I have also made enquiries about the allocation of a family liaison officer who will be able to support you in this event. DI Crosbie's team will be able to provide more information on this in due course.

Here, Birch paused again. The paragraph she was about to read was too personal, she knew – it was too wrapped up in her relationship with Winnie, and Winnie's relationship to her mother. But also contained within it was her disappointment at McLeod for giving her case away before it had even begun, and with the annoying awareness that what he'd done probably was for the best.

'Name the feeling?' she said, hearing the bitterness in her voice. 'Pissed off, that's the feeling. I'm a control freak who hasn't been able to control anything for bloody months, and I'm sick of it.'

She could imagine Dr Jane's face, then: the slight raise of the eyebrow, the nod. The face that somehow managed to say, *I totally understand.* But still Birch couldn't imagine the other side of the conversation.

'I guess that's why people keep going to therapy,' she said, accustomed now to the sound of her own voice in the empty room. 'If you already knew what your therapist was going to tell you, what would be the point?'

The final paragraph of the email read:

I'd really appreciate it if you could keep me in the loop, of course – you have my private mobile number and should feel free to get in touch whenever you like. If there is to be an investigation into Linh's whereabouts, then I can only apologise for the fact I won't be leading it. I understand that you came to see me, specifically, and I'm sorry I'm not in a fit state to do the job you need me to. But I will be ready to help you in whatever way I can, so please do just shout. You know where I am.

'I should delete that,' Birch said, to Dr Jane and to no one. 'I should just tell her about Alan, and then sign off.'

She nodded decisively, as though settling the matter, then, without making the edit, closed her eyes and hit 'send'. When she opened them again, the email had gone.

'Who cares if it sounds personal?' she muttered, checking the Sent Items box to see that it really had gone. 'It *is* personal.'

The phone rang and she snatched it up, hoping it was Winnie, calling back.

'This is Birch,' she said, but her shoulders sagged when she heard the reply: it was only the familiar voice of John, calling from reception.

'There's a lady down here asking to see someone,' he said, and once again Birch's ears pricked up. Yes, coming to speak in person might be more Winnie's style. But John went on, 'A Mrs Crozier.' Birch frowned as he paused, seemingly receiving a correction – she couldn't immediately place the name. 'Sorry,' John added, '*Ms* Crozier.'

'She's asking for me?'

There was another pause.

'DI Crosbie suggested,' John replied, 'that you might be the best person to speak to.'

Birch rolled her eyes. Presumably this was a random wild goose chase that Crosbie couldn't be arsed with. Not content with taking the case she'd wanted, he was now sending her all the stuff he *didn't* want. She stifled a yawn, still groggy from her accidental nap. She could tell John she ought to have left by now – *Sorry, Ms Crozier will have to make an appointment.* But she'd just been literally asleep on the job – for how long, she wasn't sure. Going home now wouldn't make amends, but this – whatever this was – might.

'Send her up, John,' she said.

Beatrice Crozier seemed extremely normal: under her long winter coat were dark blue jeans and navy Converse hi-tops. She looked like a friendly librarian, or a kindly teacher. She wore no make-up, and looked for all the world like the average Scottish woman: indeed, perhaps it was her averageness that gave Birch the feeling that they'd met before. Beatrice's face felt like a line from a song she couldn't quite recall. Looking at her made something in Birch's brain itch.

'I'm sorry,' she said, 'but before we start, can I ask … Beatrice?'

'Please,' the woman said, 'call me Bee.'

'Bee,' Birch repeated. 'Okay. Is it possible that we've met somewhere before?'

Bee smiled. 'I wondered if you'd remember me.'

'Oh,' Birch said, 'thank goodness. I thought I was going mad. But I'm so sorry – I *do* remember you, but I cannot for the life of me remember where from.'

'That's not surprising,' Bee replied. 'I had a couple of disastrous dates about nine years ago with a guy who was a bit of a lowlife. When I ended things, he didn't take it well. You came to my house a couple of times when he was banging on the door.'

Birch closed her eyes for a moment. 'Banjo Robin,' she said. 'Of course. That man is like a bad penny, as my mother would have said.'

Bee laughed. 'You're right,' she said. 'But I learned something from the experience. Sometimes, it's better to just be alone.'

Birch felt a pang of sadness at that, but didn't get a chance to speak.

'You've come a long way since then, though,' Bee said. 'You're a detective inspector now.'

'For my sins,' Birch replied. She felt a strange feeling creep up the back of her neck. What did this woman know about her? Why was she here?

'Anyway,' Birch said, straightening her shoulders a little. 'You're not here to make small talk. You're here for ...' She tailed off. 'Well, why don't you tell me what you're here for.'

'I have some information for you,' Bee replied, 'though I'm afraid I can't quite tell you what it pertains to. It could be a case you're working on, or ... well, it could also relate to a crime you're not yet aware of. But if my past experience is anything to go by, if you're not already investigating this, then you will be soon.'

Birch felt her eyelids fluttering. She was beginning to understand why Crosbie had bounced this woman over to her. 'I'm terribly sorry,' she said, 'but I'm afraid that didn't make much sense. You're here with some information, you said. Do you believe you've witnessed a crime?'

The other woman's eyes shifted. 'In a manner of speaking,' she replied.

Birch tried not to sigh. She wondered what Crosbie had decided this woman was. Was Beatrice Crozier a concerned citizen who thought that maybe she'd seen something a bit untoward and wanted to report it, just in case? Or a person who truly did know something the police ought also to know, but who didn't want to get themselves into any sort of trouble by sharing it? She'd just begun to come down in favour of the former when Bee spoke again.

'You see, DI Birch,' she said, 'I'm – well, I suppose I'm what a lot of people might call a psychic.'

Birch blinked. Whatever she might have expected from this woman, *that* was not it. 'A psychic,' she repeated, trying to stop her mouth from flapping open. 'Like a fortune-teller, you mean?'

Bee's brow immediately furrowed. 'Oh no,' she said. She looked stung, as though Birch had reached out and slapped her. 'No, not that.'

Birch found she was also frowning. 'I'm sorry,' she said. 'I thought it was all much of a muchness. A psychic is a fortune-teller is a medium, and so on. Am I wrong?'

Bee sighed: a sigh of irritation, but also, it seemed, sadness. 'See,' she said, 'this is why I don't talk to people about … this stuff. The things I know. But yes, DI Birch, I'm afraid you *are* wrong: they're different things. A fortune-teller claims to know your future. A medium communicates with the dead.'

Birch raised an eyebrow. 'Okay. So what does a psychic do?'

Bee closed her eyes for a moment, as though recalling something. 'A psychic is someone with additional faculties of perception that cannot be explained by natural laws.' She paused. 'At least,' she added, 'that's what the dictionary says about psychics.'

Birch dipped her head to one side. 'And what do you say?'

Bee shrugged. 'I just know things,' she said. 'Sometimes – often, in fact – I wish I didn't. But I do.'

Birch sat back in her chair. She glanced at the desk drawer where she knew her pills were stowed. This woman – this seemingly real, flesh-and-blood woman – felt like a strange apparition, a fever dream. Birch made a fist under the desk, pressing her fingernails into the palm of her hand. She could feel the sensation; she was awake. This weird meeting was real.

'And you've come to tell me that you … know something that pertains to a crime?'

Bee sat forward slightly. 'A missing person,' she said. 'Yes. I believe so.'

In spite of herself, Birch felt her pulse quicken, just slightly. 'What sort of missing person?' she asked.

'A missing girl,' Bee replied. 'Not a child, but – a young girl. Teenage, maybe. I've seen her. I think she's being held captive somewhere.'

Birch wanted to reach for her phone, to record this inter-action somehow – not least, simply, because of how bizarre it was becoming. But her nails were still pressing into her hand.

'You've seen her?'

Bee dropped her gaze. 'Not literally,' she said. 'But I've … well, I suppose you might say I've seen a vision of her.'

Birch closed her eyes for a moment. A feeling was grow-ing inside her, starting behind her breastbone and spreading outwards. A hot feeling: she realised it was anger. Crosbie was hazing her, wasn't he? He'd taken the missing teenage girl case off her, and now he'd sent her … well, this. It had to be some sort of wind-up.

'Listen,' she said, trying to keep her voice level, 'I'm not sure why you're here, but I have to tell you that you're skirting dangerously close to being guilty of wasting police time.'

Bee opened her mouth to speak, then closed it. The two women sat in silence for several moments, Birch's words – a threat, she realised only after she'd said them – hanging in the air between them. It felt like a long time before Bee spoke again.

'I know how I sound,' she said, her voice smaller than before. 'I promise you, I do. To be honest, I'm surprised you've let me say as much as I have. I assumed I'd be summarily dismissed as soon as I opened my mouth. But I had to tell someone. I saw something like this once before, and I didn't speak up, and I've hated myself ever since. So here I am. I'm doing it this time. I'm telling you: I've seen a young girl in distress, being held captive by a man, and you ought to investigate. There. That's it.'

Birch sighed. She wanted to like this woman. Beatrice Crozier seemed so – well, normal. Plausible, even. A reluctant psychic. *But no*, she reminded herself. *She isn't normal. Normal people don't say this kind of thing. Normal people don't try and lure you in.*

'I'm sorry,' Birch heard herself saying, 'but if I go to my commanding officer and tell him we need to investigate a missing persons case – or indeed anything – on the basis of – what? Evidence from a psychic vision? – it would be more than my job's worth. I'd be laughed out of this place.'

Bee looked down at the edge of Birch's desk. 'I thought perhaps I could make you understand,' she said.

Birch got to her feet. 'I do understand,' she said. 'Perhaps not why you're here, but I understand what you're like – you, and people like you. I've tangled with so-called psychics before. And I'm afraid my prior experience has not left me with a great deal of patience for this sort of "seen in a vision" stuff.'

Bee looked up at Birch, her face pale.

'If you have any real evidence,' Birch went on, 'that someone has committed a crime, or is intending to commit a crime, then I'd be more than happy to hear it. But I'm afraid that psychic evidence, or spectral evidence, or any other evidence that might be considered supernatural in nature, cannot be taken seriously.'

Bee regarded her for a moment, as though deciding how to respond. Birch realised that, now she'd finished speaking, it was strange to still be on her feet. She contemplated sinking back into her seat, but the gesture felt too much like backing down. Her hip hurt. She wanted this woman to go away.

'You have a brother, don't you?' Bee seemed to have decided to change tack.

Birch felt her eyebrows lift, but forced herself to remain calm. 'I do,' she replied. 'But if you think that telling me that will persuade me of your psychic ability, I'm afraid I am unmoved.'

Bee wasn't looking her in the eye; rather, Birch realised, the other woman was looking past her – almost *through* her – as she went on.

'Charles,' Bee said. 'You call him Charlie. He's in prison.'

Birch forced herself not to roll her eyes. 'Yes,' she said, her voice turning icy. 'That's a matter of public record, and very easy to find out.'

'He killed someone,' Bee went on, as though Birch hadn't spoken. 'A woman. An older woman – someone he liked. He didn't want to do it, but his hand was forced. He couldn't stop it.' Her eyelids flickered as she spoke. 'There was so much blood.'

The hot feeling in Birch's ribcage had pulled into a taut wire she wasn't sure she could prevent from snapping.

'He made a plea deal,' Bee was saying, her gaze still unfocused. 'Information on the gang he was in, all those years you thought he was missing – enough evidence of their activities to put the big boss man behind bars. The man who made him kill her. And in exchange, they lowered the charge. Murder to manslaughter. Twelve years.' Bee's gaze seemed to zero back in, and she met Birch's eye. 'He's a good man, really, isn't he? Charlie. He's just a man who made mistakes.'

Birch realised how little she wanted to hear her brother's name in this woman's innocent-looking mouth. The hot wire in her chest broke, sending anger whiplashing through her.

'Enough!' She brought her palm down on the desk between them, startling Bee into silence. 'I'm not interested in your theatrics, Ms Crozier. I want you out of my office.'

Bee pushed back her chair, slowly, and then stood. If she was afraid of Birch, she didn't show it: her face looked mainly sad, and rather drained.

'I'm sorry,' she said. 'I didn't mean to. I just know things.'

Birch narrowed her eyes. 'You know the details of my brother's case,' she said, 'because they were widely reported in the papers. You've been away and googled me, that's all. It's called hot reading, I believe. I'm not stupid, Beatrice. Like I say, I've met people like you before.'

To Birch's surprise, Beatrice Crozier lifted her chin, and held her gaze. 'With all due respect, DI Birch,' she replied, 'I don't believe you have.'

Birch could feel the anger – an old anger, one she'd thought long buried – threatening to engulf her. She needed rid of this woman.

'Please leave now,' she said, her voice quiet but firm. 'I believe you've said all you need to say.'

She thought that Bee might argue, but the other woman only paused for a moment. Then she let her eyes flick away from Birch's own, and she turned her shoulders slightly in the direction of the office door, ending their stand-off.

'I suppose I have,' she said, 'for now. I'm sorry if I've upset you, Detective Inspector.'

Birch bit her tongue – literally sinking her teeth into the tip of it, so she wouldn't speak again – and watched as Bee scooped her handbag from the floor, and shuffled out of the room. Only when the other woman's footsteps had faded did she allow herself to sink back into her chair, and resume the deep breathing Dr Jane had taught her.

Name the feeling? Rage. Annoyance. Confusion. The feeling of salt in an old wound.

'Fucking Crosbie,' Birch spat.

It was after 5pm now. Somewhere on the floor above, she could hear a hoover running. She knew many of her colleagues would stay far later than five – though she couldn't see from where she was sitting, Birch would bet any money that Amy Kato was still at her desk in the bullpen – but plenty of others were leaving.

Birch glanced at her walking stick, propped against the desk, and then looked over at the door. *Get up*, she thought. *Come on, it's time to go*. But the command felt muted, and her body wouldn't obey it. Her brain was busy with questions: what the hell *was* that? What had Beatrice hoped to achieve with that little stunt? How much had Crosbie known about what she might say when he decided to send her over to Birch's office? Was it some sort of practical joke? Then the questions changed, and Birch found herself pressing a hand to her own forehead, perhaps in a vain attempt to stop them. Had she been too harsh? What if Bee really did know something? What if the missing girl she was talking about was Linh? And yes, Linh! Why hadn't Winnie called her back? Was it because Linh was home? She hoped, rather than believed, that was the case. With a missing person, every hour was crucial – doubly so in the case of a kid like Linh. Why hadn't Winnie updated her? Had she seen the email yet? What was going on?

She reached for the desk phone, lifted the receiver, and dialled Crosbie's extension. It only rang twice before he picked up.

'Crosbie.'

'Alan, hi. It's Helen. I'm glad you're still here.'

'Birch,' Crosbie replied, his tone stiff. 'What can I do for you?'

Birch sighed. Crosbie had been distant with her ever since Operation Stake, and an ill-advised phone call he'd made to her while under the influence. She hadn't wanted to snitch to McLeod, but when she did eventually raise it, it turned out their boss already knew. Crosbie was getting help through a partner organisation, and Birch was genuinely proud of him. *What you're doing is so hard,* she wanted to tell him. *It took my dad forty years before he could do it. But you're doing it.* Crosbie would, of course, hate to hear this. Anjan was right: he hated that she even *knew* he was in AA.

She was about to answer his question when he cut in, a sneer in his voice. 'How did you get on with Mystic Meg?'

Birch closed her eyes. 'Yeah ... What *was* that, exactly? Some sort of joke?'

She could practically hear Crosbie shrug.

'No idea,' he said. 'John phoned it up to me. "There's a psychic down in reception," he says.'

'And you said?'

Crosbie snorted. 'I said, "Absolutely not, pal." I'm doing actual policework, here. No time for that sort of nonsense.'

Birch's eyes were still closed. 'Whereas *I*,' she said, 'have nothing better to do than be messed about by random members of the public, right?'

The smirk in Crosbie's voice eased off a little. 'Well,' he said, 'I mean ... it's not like you have any active cases right now, is it?'

Birch opened her eyes again. She wanted to spit. 'That was constable work, Alan,' she said, 'and you know it. I'm sure you found it very amusing, but please don't send me any more bullshit like that.'

He tutted. 'Oh, come on, Birch,' he replied. 'Learn to take a joke.'

She opened her mouth to rebuke him, but felt relieved when he carried on talking. She hadn't been entirely sure what she'd been going to say, but it wouldn't have been anything good.

'Is this why you're calling me?' Crosbie asked. 'To tell me off about Psychic Sandra, or whatever her name was? I hope you asked her for this week's lottery numbers.'

Birch paused, making sure that when she answered him, her voice would be level. 'Actually,' she said, 'I'm just wondering if you managed to get hold of Winifred Fortune. I know McLeod passed that on to you, and I've been trying to call her myself, but—'

'Oh, yes,' Crosbie cut in. 'I spoke to her this morning.'

Birch blinked. She waited for him to say something else, but he didn't.

'So, Linh,' she sputtered. 'Is she still unaccounted for?'

'It appears so.'

Birch's heart had already begun sinking, but now it plummeted. All thoughts of Beatrice Crozier fell from her mind.

'Shit,' she said. 'So we have a missing person on our hands.'

Crosbie was quiet for a moment. 'Not necessarily,' he replied. 'I'm trying not to jump to any conclusions.'

Birch frowned. 'It's been forty-eight hours, though, right? And Linh is under eighteen.'

'Yes,' he said, and Birch could tell he was trying to be patient. 'I'm aware of all of that. I just think we should give it a little longer before we set all the wheels in motion.'

'*Why?*' She hadn't meant to say it out loud, but the word seemed to fall from her mouth unbidden.

Crosbie didn't answer immediately, and she wondered if he was counting to ten in his head.

'Because,' he said, 'of – oh Christ, what's it called? The thing – the principal whereby the simplest explanation is also the most likely.'

So this is why Winnie hasn't called me back, Birch thought. *She thinks I didn't want the case and just handed it off to this bozo.* Winnie would, Birch imagined, take a dim view of Crosbie's philosophising.

'You're talking about Occam's razor?' she said.

On the other end of the line, she heard him click his fingers.

'That's the one,' he said. 'I'm thinking … Occam's razor suggests that the most likely explanation is *not* that she's a missing person. Not in the true sense.'

She's seventeen, Birch wanted to say, *and out there on her own*, but she held herself back.

'I don't think I'm following,' she said.

'Well, there are two possible explanations that are far more likely. One, she's a seventeen-year-old girl who's slept over at a friend's house and her phone's run out of battery, or she's gone off somewhere with some lad or other, and she'll eventually come trailing home carrying her stilettos in her hand.'

Birch's eyes widened. Crosbie's imagined version of Linh didn't chime at all with the quiet girl Winnie had described.

'Two,' Crosbie was saying, 'she *has* gone missing, but on purpose. She's disappeared herself. If that's the case, we're unlikely to ever find her, and she'll only go and disappear again if we do.'

Birch began nodding a slow, grim nod. 'You've been talking to McLeod.'

'Of course,' Crosbie replied. 'And I think he made a lot of sense. We don't want to devote man hours to this unless it's ... well, you know. Real.'

She found herself stifling a desperate sort of laugh. 'I think,' she said, 'that a seventeen-year-old non-native English speaker with a history of trauma needs to be looked for, personally. Isn't everything else just window dressing?'

Crosbie went quiet. It was ominous. Birch was pretty certain she hadn't talked him round.

'What are you thinking, Alan?'

Still, he didn't speak for a moment.

'I'm thinking,' he said, at last, 'that that's exactly why McLeod gave this case to me.'

'I'm sorry?'

Crosbie sighed. 'You care too much, Birch. You get too involved. Let's face it, we're not talking about some vulnerable child here, are we? Be real. This girl has been trafficked halfway across the world. She's been in the sex trade. Somewhere in Aberdeen there's a punter she malkied half to death, for Christ's sake. She can hold her own, wherever she is.'

Now it was Birch's turn to be quiet. She listened to the blood sloshing around in her own ears, and thought about how, if it weren't for her godforsaken leg, and the godforsaken walking stick, and the past godforsaken few months, she'd march over to Crosbie's office and malkie *him*.

Eventually, Crosbie cleared his throat, and she realised she had to say something.

'I really hope,' she managed, 'that you're right, Alan. Because it's a hell of a gamble if you're not, and this girl turns up dead somewhere.'

She heard him straighten up in his chair.

'Yes, well,' he said. 'That's my risk to take, isn't it? Given that it's my case.'

Birch closed her eyes. The palms of her hands itched. In that moment, she felt like she could have set fire to the entire profession and every cynical, jaded Crosbie-alike it had produced. But she also felt like she could cry, and she mustn't cry.

'Besides,' Crosbie was saying, 'it's only a few hours. If there's nothing more at noon tomorrow, then we'll start putting things in place. And don't,' he added, hearing her take a breath, getting ready to speak, 'give me chapter and verse about the first forty-eight hours and how crucial they are. I do know how to do my job, no matter what you think of me.'

Birch sagged in her chair. She wished she'd never called him. She wished she'd argued with McLeod about keeping the case. She wondered how disappointed Winnie was that she hadn't. She couldn't be more disappointed than Birch was in herself.

'You've no idea,' she said, quietly, 'what I think of you, Alan.' She could feel that urge to cry – or perhaps to yell something unwise and unprofessional – building in the back of her throat. It was time to get off the phone, before she said or did something that could get her in trouble. Crosbie didn't seem to have anything more to say, anyway. 'Thanks for giving me an update,' she added. 'Fingers crossed for Occam's razor.' That bitter edge again – she couldn't hide it. *Time to go, Helen.*

'Goodnight, Alan,' she said, then slammed the phone down before he could respond.

Afterwards, she took another few deep breaths, holding them for the count of four, then letting them go. To her surprise, this tamped down the urge to cry, and she filed that information away for future use. But a few deep breaths could do nothing about the rest of it, and no amount of naming the feelings could unknot the tangle of anger and frustration she felt, thinking of Linh, a girl who would always be missing and could never go home, whether she was indeed out on the street somewhere or in Winnie Fortune's cosy Colinton living room. Closing her eyes against her own ridiculousness, Birch lifted the phone's receiver and waited for the dial tone, making sure Crosbie wasn't somehow still listening, before placing it down again. Then she let herself do the only thing that felt like it would help: she brought her fists down hard on the desk, one, two, three, four times, hard enough that her hands throbbed with the impact.

'*Bast*ard,' she spat. 'Absolute total and utter *bastard.*'

Bee, 1988

I hadn't, of course, made friends with Melody Rowe. Melody Rowe didn't talk to me again after I had dropped her off that afternoon, still sniffling, at the school reception desk, and then waited until the nurse had come out of the little room with the low, narrow bed and guided Melody inside. But I knew – because I knew – that during the Christmas break that year, she'd gone to visit her aunt in London, and something had been done about the baby, because no baby was ever forthcoming. A rumour spread around the school that Melody had begged Joel to have sex with her, and he'd only done it because he pitied her so much – that was what he told Lara and Cassie, and when they confronted Melody, she went along with it. I supposed she didn't want to lose her place in the school's social pecking order. By the time we all came back to school after New Year, everyone talked about her as though she was a desperate slut who couldn't get her own boyfriend, and when we passed in the corridors she scowled at me, and I knew – because I knew – that she thought I'd started the rumour. I hadn't; it was Joel himself, bragging to his rugby pals. I knew, because I knew. But I never told.

Was I more aware of the whispers about me because Melody had talked to me about them? Or was I more aware of them because they got worse? I couldn't tell. But after I helped Melody, I seemed to go from being a lone weirdo nobody really bothered with to being a target for mindless high-school violence. Someone scratched the word 'devil'

and a pentagram into my locker door, and then someone
– maybe the same someone – told the teachers *I'd* done it.
For only the second time ever, I was sent, dumbfounded,
to detention. One day, a tiny, shaven-headed second-year
kid ran up to me in the English corridor and launched a
small projectile at my face, then pelted back to the safety of
his shoal of friends. His missile was a ball of paper, which
bounced off my temple, causing gales of childlike laughter.
When I picked it up and unfolded it, it was a page from
the Bible, hastily torn. I almost laughed. Underlined in
pencil was Exodus 22:18: 'Thou shalt not suffer a witch to
live.' No way some little second year came up with that. It
was a put-up job, a dare. I wondered, often, how much of
that stuff was Melody, seeking revenge for the rumour she
thought I'd spread.

I tried not to let it affect me, and did as I had always done:
mooching around alone, holing up in the library, lingering
after the last bell had rung so the others could disperse before
I began the walk home. I didn't talk to my parents about it,
because I knew there was little point. My mother would want
to complain to the school, an act that could only bring more
and greater humiliation. And my father would see it as a failing in me: *Why can't you just be a normal girl, Beatrice? Why
must you always rub people up the wrong way?*

I didn't really get it. I wasn't like the girls with safety pins
through their ears. I wasn't like Melody and her cultish hockey
friends, all sleeping with the same stupid boy and making
fools of themselves. I hadn't shaved myself a mohawk and
dyed it blue like Dawn-Marie Tait. I didn't take diet pills or
throw up in the bad girls' toilets. Okay, I was weird, but so was
everyone, weren't they, in their own ways? I knew they were,
even if they didn't.

That week – that particularly bad February week – we were all just back from half-term, and everyone was giddy. Spring was coming, and the air in the corridors felt thick with pheromones. I still looked out for Melody's streaked perm, would always turn my head if someone walked by wearing Charlie body spray. I didn't really know why, then, but I did sometimes recall that moment behind the Chemistry block when she'd grabbed me by the arms and I'd considered whether or not I wanted to kiss her. More than anything, she intrigued me. I wanted to talk to her. I wanted to ask her what had happened in London, what her aunt had done. I wanted to ask if she ever thought about the baby that never happened. Had she given it a name?

I was in one of my ruminative daydreams that morning, the morning of the stones. It was a wet, late-February Wednesday, and I'd walked to school only half awake. Nearing the school gates, I passed the spot where Martin had said, *You're crazy, don't ever talk to me*, and I slowed down for a moment to think about him, as I often did. It had been over four years now since he'd died alone under that tree on the lonely verge of the A70 and become an urban legend – *there was a guy at this school once who went mad and killed himself* – though only my year group, who'd been first years at the time, actually remembered Martin. I imagined I was the only one who *really* remembered him, because I could still hear the exact sound of his voice – the voice of a boy trying too hard to sound like a man. *She's only twelve. She's only a kid.* I could still smell his tarry, cigarette smell, and if I tried, I could remember how his arm had felt, pinned around my chest that day in the pavilion, before the bad thing happened.

'Witch!'

The first stone hit me between the shoulder blades, hard enough to make me hiccup out a strange, coughing breath.

Another stone glanced off my school satchel as I wheeled around. It was that same gaggle of second-year boys – the ones who'd thrown the ripped-out Bible verse at me a few weeks before. They were still a good twenty feet away, and I thought, as I turned to face them, how small they all were, how like actual children they still looked, though they must have been thirteen years old. I'd reached my full adult height by then, and could easily have knocked any one of them to the ground, but that was why they ran in a pack. There were maybe twelve of them advancing on me, pebbles and two-pence coins in their hands.

'Stone the witch!' one of them yelled, and launched another missile. This one missed me, and glanced off the parked car I was standing beside. I saw it chip the paintwork. It was Mrs White's car.

'Look!' I yelled, pointing, assuming they'd knock it off if they realised they'd done something they could really get in trouble for. But if they cared, they didn't show it, and another stone flew at me, hitting me in the thigh.

'What the fuck?' I said, and they all laughed. I felt a mixture of fear and complete disbelief. It was 8.35am, broad daylight, and we were literally feet from the school gates. People could see them doing this. Didn't they *care*?

'Freak!' one of them shouted, and let loose the final stone. I raised my hands to block its trajectory, but was too late. The rock – a biggish one, about the size of an egg, only sharp – hit me square on the left cheekbone, and opened a bright red wound underneath my eye. I must have cried out, because it hurt like nothing I'd ever experienced before. My father had slapped me a time or two, and I'd fallen down and hurt myself plenty as a kid, but this was different. My teeth crashed together with the stone's blow, and my eye socket detonated into a hot ring of pain. A glitchy rainbow blossomed on my vision, like the aura before a migraine. Through it, I could see the kids' faces were a silent chorus of *Oh shit, what have we done.*

I put my fingertips up to my face, and touched the place where the stone had hit. They came away red.

'You little *scumbags!*' I screeched. I stooped to pick up one of their stones from the ground and then lobbed it blindly back in their direction, but by then they were already scattering. I watched, mouth open in shock, as they ran for the gates and disappeared, one by one, into the schoolyard's morning crowd. Plenty of faces had flicked round to watch their little sideshow, and I could see that people were pointing and whispering, their heads cocked close to one another. No one did anything to stop the second years as they clattered away from the scene of their crime. No one came back out through the gates to help me, or see if I was okay. I stood on the pavement, blood running down my face, and stared at them all. I felt like I was looking into some terrible enclosure, full of mindless, milling zoo animals. I couldn't walk through those gates and past them; I just couldn't make myself. I was a good student – whatever else I was, I prided myself on being a good student – and had never even been tempted to truant. But that morning, I couldn't not. I couldn't go and sit among them while they turned the story of what had just happened into passed notes and Chinese whispers. Their hypocrisy was baffling. I knew – because I knew – things about some of them that I could have weaponised, if I'd wanted to. I knew things that could have been turned into taunts, into rumours that would have made their school days unbearable. I'd never done it, because I had no right knowing those things and having no idea how I knew them. I'd never done it, because some part of me still thought I might be allowed to slink back into obscurity, go to my classes, sit my exams, and get the hell out of there without incident. But now, it was too late. *Incident* had happened.

The first bell of the day was ringing, and I was standing bleeding in the middle of the street, my whole head beginning to throb. I watched as they all began streaming into the building, chattering together, heading off to their respective registration classes. Some of them turned back to look at me, waiting to see if I'd cross the threshold of those gates and fall in line. But I couldn't do it. I waited until the building had swallowed up the last of them, then I turned on my heel and, trying to keep my bloodied head high, walked away into the morning.

I got as far as the block of public toilets on the corner of Bruntsfield Links. I hadn't planned to go in there – I don't know where I'd planned to go – but people were staring at me. Adults, strangers. I didn't like it when adults looked at me for too long – not since that day in the pavilion with Martin and the man in the brown suit. I let myself into the cold, tiled Ladies' with its dim block lighting and stainless-steel trough sinks, and slung the handle of my satchel over a hand dryer, not wanting to place it on the stinking floor. The mirrors were the anti-shatter kind you get in circus funhouses, so I couldn't see my reflection all that clearly, but I could see that the second years had made a real mess. My left eye was rapidly swelling and turning purple, as though I'd been punched. The stone had made a two-inch cut along my cheekbone, which stung when I touched it. Blood had pooled in the cut and then run down my face and neck in one thin stream, like a brown-red tear. It was drying now, becoming a crust I could chip off with my fingernails. I looked like I'd been in a prize fight, but hated that I hadn't. I hated that I'd done absolutely nothing to stop the second years. I should have grabbed at least one of them as they clattered past me – I could have got hold of the back of his collar and planted him face-down on the pavement. I'd have got in trouble, of course, but it would have been worth it. Now I was going to be in trouble anyway, for truanting, and my assailants had got away with it. Something ugly ignited in me then, as I pawed at my bloodied face with a wadded handful of toilet roll. It smouldered in me like a hot coal: if I ever got the chance to hurt those little boys, any of them, I would. I'd played nice for four years, trying to live a quiet life, but I wouldn't anymore. I'd hurt them back – starting now.

'Liam Torrance,' I said, beginning to count on my fingers. 'Sam Burke, Daniel Burnett and Cameron Tait.' Cameron was Dawn-Marie's little brother. The others had names I'd heard simply because they were known for being little tearaways. 'I don't know the others, but I could point them out to you. They were all second years.'

The school nurse had patched up my face properly, cleaning my wound with a stinging Dettol-soaked cloth, and then sticking it closed with little butterfly plasters.

'If it doesn't start to knit,' she'd said, her face so close to mine that I could smell the ghost of her morning toothpaste, 'then you'll need to go to A&E, and have proper stitches.'

I blinked at her. 'Will I have a scar?' I asked.

She winced. 'Very possibly, Beatrice,' she said. 'I'm sorry.'

I shrugged then, feeling more like a teenager than I ever had before. 'Good,' I replied.

I'd marched back on to the school grounds halfway through first period, and gone straight to reception. The story I'd decided on was that I hadn't truanted, I was just late – school reception was where you went when you were late, to get a little yellow slip to take to class. The receptionist – whose name was Mrs Mackie – had let out a yelp when she'd seen me standing on the other side of the desk. The yellow slip was not discussed; I was packed off to the sickbay with no questions asked, while Mrs Mackie phoned for the rector.

Now, Mr Johnstone was nodding as I listed the names of my tormentors. Outside the sickbay sat a bright orange plastic chair, where students who were waiting for the nurse were put to bleed or whimper while she saw to somebody else. More than once, I'd walked past the sickbay door and the orange chair to see a kid parked there with a plastic sick bucket on their lap, left to get on with it. Mr Johnstone had dragged that vomit chair into the room, and was perched on it, studying my swollen face.

'Liam Torrance,' I added, when he didn't speak, 'is the ringleader, though. He's thrown stuff at me before.' I decided the rector didn't need to know that the *stuff* of *before* was only a screwed-up piece of paper.

'This happened earlier this morning, you say?'

The school nurse was still in the room with us, and I noticed she was nodding, as though not sure which of us Mr Johnstone was speaking to.

'Yes,' I said, 'before registration.'

'And did anyone see this incident?'

I smiled what was probably quite a nasty little smile. If he was hoping I'd lied about any of this, he was going to be disappointed.

'*Everyone* saw it,' I replied. 'Everyone who was waiting outside school. It happened right by the gates.'

Mr Johnstone and the school nurse exchanged a look.

'Where, exactly, Beatrice?' he asked.

'On the pavement,' I said, wondering if he'd been listening to me at all. 'Right by Mrs White's car. I told you, they scratched the paint.'

'Ah yes,' he said, 'I remember.' He stood up, then, so decisively that it made me jump. 'I think you could come along to my office, Beatrice. These are serious allegations.'

I tried very hard not to let out a derisive snort. Of course, he'd rather believe I was lying than believe I'd been pelted with stones. But my left eye was now almost swollen shut, the state of my face pretty hard to ignore. The nurse had made me an ice pack in a strange blue cloth bag to press against it.

'Take it with you,' she said, as I trailed out of the sickbay door after Mr Johnstone. 'Just bring it back when you can.'

Mr Johnstone's office wasn't far from reception, but by this time, second period was chucking out, and a whole raft of my classmates passed by in the opposite direction as I followed the rector down the corridor. They gawped at my swollen face, the collar of my white blouse now red-brown with blood. I stared back at them, though instinct told me to drop my gaze, do what I'd always done, and try to disappear. I caught the familiar Charlie scent, and Melody walked by, her face a mask of shock. Had she done this? Had she put those kids up to it?

I hate you, I mouthed, though it wasn't true.

She looked down at her feet and hurried away.

We'd reached Mr Johnstone's office door, and he ushered me into the anteroom, where his secretary sat behind a desk, apparently busy, though for the life of me I couldn't think what work she could possibly have to do. I looked around at the wood-panelled room with its photos of *Dux* medallists shaking hands with past rectors, rugby teams arranged in rows around their ribboned trophies. I'd never been in here before, and it felt like a weird little temple to the cult of the school. Above the secretary's desk was a portrait of the Queen.

'Miss Henderson,' Mr Johnstone said, and the secretary looked up. 'Please can you consult a timetable, and discover the whereabouts of the following boys?' He looked at me.

'Liam Torrance,' I said, using the same contemptuous tone of voice as I had before. 'Sam Burke, Daniel Burnett, and Cameron Tait. All S2.'

Mr Johnstone gave a short nod, and then looked back at Miss Henderson, who was scribbling a note.

'Phone up their current class teachers, please, and have them sent here immediately.'

Miss Henderson nodded, and I smiled. Good. I was going to be in a room with them. They were going to see what they'd done to my face.

Mr Johnstone was holding open the door to his office. I stepped through, demurely, and sat down on an offered chair to wait for my assailants. I thought about Lady Macbeth and didn't speak, while Mr Johnstone paced a short stretch of floor beside the window and avoided looking at me. *Look like th' innocent flower, but be the serpent under't.*

Cameron Tait was the first to arrive. I had almost felt bad for naming him, because although he'd been carrying stones like all the others, he hadn't actually thrown one. But then, I reflected, as he sidled into the room, he also hadn't stopped it. He hadn't stayed behind while the others ran away, to see if I was okay. Even if he wasn't a bully, he was a coward. And yes, I could see it on his face: he was afraid. Afraid to have been called into this room, afraid of what that meant. Afraid of me.

'Sit down, Cameron,' Mr Johnstone said, and went back to pacing.

Cameron picked up the chair furthest away from me, and moved it another two feet towards the far wall. Then he sat down.

'I'm sorry,' he said, in a sort of stage whisper, 'about your face.'

I heard him perfectly – I was sure Mr Johnstone had, too – but I fixed him with a look and said, 'Sorry, what was that?'

Cameron sniffed, put his hands in his lap, and looked down at them. 'Doesn't matter,' he said.

I was right. He *was* a coward.

Liam, Sam and Daniel all arrived together. I guessed that they'd either all been sent from the same class, or each had guessed the others were coming, and they'd waited for one another outside the door, because in truth, they were cowards, too. Nevertheless, Liam swaggered in with a wide grin on his chubby kid face, like he'd been called up by the rector to receive the award for Student of the Year. Sam and Daniel, his sheep-brained little goons, followed in his wake. I saw both of them flinch as they saw my face, but Liam didn't even look at me. I could tell from the way he flopped into a chair without being asked that this wasn't his first time in Mr Johnstone's office. All the seats, save Mr Johnstone's own, were taken now, so Sam and Daniel each struck a typical teen boy pose, leaning against the back wall of the room.

'Mr Torrance.' Mr Johnstone stopped pacing, and moved to stand behind his desk, facing the five of us.

Liam's grin widened.

'Is that sweatshirt regulation school uniform?'

Everyone glanced at Liam. Instead of his school jumper, he was wearing a black sweatshirt emblazoned with the famous Nike swoosh, and the word NIKE in half-foot letters. Liam didn't reply, and his expression didn't change, but I saw his eyelashes flutter slightly.

'I thought not,' Mr Johnstone said. 'If I see you out of uniform again, then that's a detention, do you understand?'

'Yes, sir,' the kid sneered. 'Sorry, sir.'

'Good. Now then, boys. I'd like you all to have a look at Beatrice, here.' He gestured towards me.

I hadn't expected this, but forced myself to hold my head up, and be looked at.

'Look at her face,' Mr Johnstone said.

Liam eyed me with one eyebrow raised and a smirk, as though he were looking at something deeply comical. Daniel and Sam both watched me uneasily, their eyes flicking back to Mr Johnstone every couple of seconds to see if they were allowed to look away yet. Cameron looked past me from across the room, not wanting to make eye contact, and I could see the fear in his face. I was glad at least one of them was intimidated.

'Beatrice's injuries,' Mr Johnstone said, 'were sustained during an incident outside school this morning.' Had I known the name for it then, I'd have rolled my eyes at his use of the passive voice. 'Do any of you know anything about that incident?'

Sam and Daniel shook their heads, immediately and vigorously. They knew, alright; it was Sam Burke who'd shouted *Stone the witch!*, and whose thrown rock had chipped the paint off Mrs White's car.

'No, sir,' Liam said, widening his eyes in a cartoonish display of fake sympathy. 'But wow, *Beatrice*, that looks pretty bad. Are you *okay*?'

I ignored him. I didn't need to respond to his taunts. When he'd sat down next to me, I'd felt the same pricking feeling in my hands that I had a few months ago, reading the note left in the library by Melody Rowe. These days, I recognised the feeling for what it was: there was something about him to be known, though I hadn't figured out what it was yet. I was too busy watching Cameron. Cameron was looking down at his hands again, a thin line of sweat visible on his forehead.

'What about you, Cameron?' I said. 'Did *you* see anything this morning?'

Mr Johnstone held out a hand towards me. 'I'll ask the questions, thank you, Beatrice.'

But Cameron still couldn't meet my gaze.

'Boys,' Mr Johnstone said, 'I'm a busy man, and I don't have time to beat around the bush, here.'

I saw a slight smile scuttle across Daniel's face upon hearing the word 'bush'. Pathetic.

'If it'll speed things up, I can always call your parents in, and talk to them about it.'

Beside me, Liam gave an elaborate shrug. But Mr Johnstone wasn't looking at him; he was looking at Cameron. Sam and Daniel were, too. He shuffled in his chair, and let out an awkward cough.

'What do you think, Cameron?' I asked. 'Should we get all our parents in?'

Mr Johnstone glared at me. I was talking a big game, but desperately hoping it wouldn't come to that; I was already struggling to figure out how I was going to explain the black eye to my father.

'No,' Cameron replied, his voice a quiet croak. He paused for a moment, before adding, 'We were just messing around.'

For the first time since he'd walked in the door, Liam's shit-eating grin disappeared. I saw him tighten one hand around the arm of his chair.

'I'm sorry,' Mr Johnstone said, stepping out from behind his desk and placing his body between Liam and Cameron. 'What did you say, then? I didn't quite hear you.'

Cameron cleared his throat. 'I said,' he replied, his voice still weedy, but stronger, 'that we were just messing around. We didn't mean for anyone to get hurt.'

Sam and Daniel exchanged a worried glance.

'I see,' said Mr Johnstone. 'So you boys *were* throwing stones outside the school gates this morning.'

'Not us,' Liam said, a little too quickly. 'I mean, not me, anyway.' He turned his face away from me, but I could tell he was scowling at Cameron. 'I don't know what *Cameron* might have been doing, though.'

Mr Johnstone turned, then, unexpectedly, and I saw Liam jump in his chair as the rector loomed over him.

'Really, Mr Torrance? Is that so?'

Liam pasted the shit-eating grin back on to his face, though I could see it took some effort. 'Yes, sir,' he said. He risked a look at me. I noticed he had a small gold stud in his left earlobe. 'I'm not sure why Beatrice told you *we* were there. I suppose it must have been' – he paused for emphasis – 'mistaken identity.' From the way he sat back smugly in his chair, I could tell this was a line he'd rehearsed, presumably off the back of his previous visits to the rector's office.

Mr Johnstone threw Liam a smile that didn't reach all the way to his eyes. 'Well,' he said, a little too brightly, 'if that's the case, then you gentlemen won't mind at all if I have a word with Cameron in private.' He shifted his gaze to Daniel and Sam, who immediately looked at their shoes. 'Will you?'

I could see Liam was trying to make eye contact with Cameron, but Cameron was picking the skin off one of his thumbs. He looked like he might cry.

'That's fine with me,' I said, rising from my chair. They all turned their eyes on me – all except for Cameron. I jerked my head towards the door. 'Come on. Let's let Mr Johnstone and Cameron have a chat.'

Liam couldn't hide it now: his face was a mask of sheer hatred for me. He knew as well as I did that Cameron would last about five seconds before he squealed on the rest of them.

Daniel knew it too. 'Shouldn't one of us stay …?' he said, letting his voice peter out to nothing at the end of the question. It was the first time he'd spoken since he entered the room, and Mr Johnstone didn't seem to hear him.

'Thank you, Beatrice,' the rector said. 'You can go back to class, for now. Miss Henderson will prepare you a note to take to your teacher as an explanation for your lateness for period three.'

I nodded.

'Boys,' he went on, 'I'd like you to wait outside in the reception area, so I can call you back once I've spoken to Cameron.'

Cameron looked up at Liam through his eyelashes, and then flicked his gaze immediately away.

'But sir—' Liam was attempting to protest, but Mr Johnstone held up a hand, the same way he had when I'd asked Cameron if he'd seen anything.

'Don't worry, Mr Torrance. Miss Henderson will provide notes for each of you, too. There are seats in the reception area; please go and wait quietly there. And bear in mind that members of the public may be going in and out of that area, so I expect you to behave in an appropriate manner.'

He was addressing all three of them, but looking only at Liam.

'Yes, sir,' Sam and Daniel chorused, their voices dull.

I waited until the three of them had trooped out of the room, then followed. As I stepped back into the anteroom, I heard Mr Johnstone lift the telephone receiver.

'Mrs Mackie,' he said, 'there are three young men from second year coming to sit in the reception area for a short while—'

The door closed behind me, and I heard nothing more.

Miss Henderson was standing next to her desk. I took notice of her properly now, in a way I hadn't before. Though she wore a grannyish tartan skirt, and her hair was pulled into a high, neat bun, I saw she was wearing Doc Marten boots on her feet. I smiled, and she smiled back.

'Here you go, honey,' she said, and handed me a slip of paper. I skim-read it, and saw it was a boilerplate note, with a gap where she'd written my name in blue pen.

Beatrice was not in class today as he or she was called to Mr Johnstone's office. Please call Miss Henderson on extension +100 if you have any queries. Thank you.

When I looked up, I saw that Miss Henderson's smile was tinged with a look of concern.

'Get some arnica cream on that eye when you get home,' she said, 'if you can find some.'

I smiled properly now, showing my teeth. It made my face hurt, but felt worth it. 'Thanks,' I said.

Upon leaving Miss Henderson's strange little room, I could see Liam, Daniel and Sam dawdling ahead of me along the corridor. They were clearly in no hurry to go and sit in reception. Even from a distance, I could see that Liam was gesticulating angrily at the other two. Quietly, I moved into earshot behind him.

'Fucking little grass,' he spat. 'Once we get this over with, we'll fuck him up, okay? He lives down Gorgie somewhere. I know the way he walks home. You two meet me at—'

I waited until I was right behind them, then piped up. 'Planning your next assault, are you, lads?'

Only Daniel visibly jumped, but I knew I'd startled all three of them.

Liam rounded on me. 'Fuck off, snitch,' he spat. 'Next time I'll hit you in your stupid cunt mouth.'

I let out a short, unbidden laugh. It was bizarre to hear such a small person say such adult things. 'Big words,' I said, 'for a kid whose voice hasn't dropped yet.'

I watched the insult land. For a moment, Liam had no comeback.

'Yeah?' he spluttered. 'Well … when do your *balls* drop, you fucking tra—'

He was within reach, so I shot out one hand and pushed him, hard, on the shoulder. He wasn't expecting it, and toppled to the ground. Daniel and Sam danced backwards, letting him fall on to the waxed linoleum floor of the corridor. All three gawped at me, but I didn't see them. I was looking down at my hand, which seemed to crackle with static where I'd made contact with Liam's body. When I'd touched him, I'd seen what it was I could know about him, about his future. I'd seen the thing I'd sensed, sitting next to him in Mr Johnstone's office. It was by far the worst thing I'd ever known about anyone.

'Shit,' I whispered.

Liam was clambering to his feet. 'You're damn right,' he said, taking my shocked expression for remorse at having pushed him. '*Now* who's been assaulted?' He reached out and pushed me back, but he was only small. I teetered, but didn't fall. '*Now* who can go snitching to Poncy Johnstone, eh?'

He pushed me again, but I'd anticipated it, and didn't really budge. Each time he made contact with me, I saw more clearly the terrible thing that was coming.

'Don't,' I said, holding up both hands. 'Don't touch me.'

He grinned, but the grin was laced with a look of suspicion. 'What's up, freak?' he said. Daniel and Sam had resumed their positions behind him. 'You scared of me again now?'

I looked at him, and could see the kid he really was: a sad little boy whose dad worked offshore and was barely ever at home. A little heartbroken child who'd cried himself to sleep so many nights, missing his daddy. And now I knew what I knew.

'Don't,' I said again. My voice was quiet now. 'Don't do this, Liam.'

His grin only widened. 'You snitched on me,' he said. 'And that little prick Cameron is going to get us all bollocked. But guess what? I'm gonna make your life *hell* in this school – we are, aren't we boys?'

Behind him, Sam and Daniel nodded, as though pro-grammed. I wondered where the hell he got off talking like a gangster from a movie, this sad, angry little thirteen-year-old who, for all he disdained school uniform and wore an earring, was only five feet tall in a fair wind.

'And,' he added, puffing out his chest, 'when your little brother comes up to high school, we're gonna make life hell for *him*, too. We're gonna fuck him up.'

Something happened inside me, then – I couldn't stop it. The ugly, smouldering coal that had ignited somewhere in my chest as I wiped the blood from my face that morning shattered, fill-ing my whole body with sparks. My vision guttered in and out – I knew for the first time what people meant when they used the expression *I saw red*. I knew what I was going to say, and I knew I shouldn't say it, but honestly, I couldn't stop it.

'Your dad's going to die,' I said.

The grin froze on Liam's face. 'What the fuck?' he said. Over his shoulder, Daniel laughed nervously.

'Long before my brother gets to this school,' I said, 'your dad's going to die. There's going to be an explosion.' I could see it happening, in my mind's eye: not just an explosion, but a series of explosions. The terrible wail of alarms. Men shouting to each other, unable to be heard. The sound of rotor blades. Fire in the waves. The sea itself on fire. I wasn't really looking at Liam anymore, but through him. How was that possible? How could the sea be on fire?

Liam pushed me again, then, and this time I staggered backwards, shaken out of the vision.

'What the *fuck*?' he said again, and to my surprise I saw tears in his eyes. 'Why the *fuck* would you say that?'

The red mist had subsided. I knew he wouldn't hurt Tommy. He wouldn't even meet Tommy; by the time Tommy got to high school, Liam would be gone. Where? I didn't know. But I knew it was nowhere good.

'I'm sorry,' I said, my voice softer now. 'I'm so sorry. I shouldn't have told you that.'

This seemed to unsettle him even more. 'Stop it,' he said. 'Stop fucking talking about my dad.'

Sam and Daniel were gawping at him. He seemed to have shrunk. I'd done it: I'd hit upon his most terrible, secret fear. It was going to come true. I knew it was.

'I'm sorry,' I said again, though the word felt empty and useless. 'It's going to be—' I couldn't find the words. 'There's going to be nothing anyone can do,' I whispered.

Liam was backing away from me, now. Daniel and Sam stepped aside, and he slipped between them. 'You bitch,' Liam spat at me. 'You total psycho *bitch*.'

He turned on his heel and ran. Sam, Daniel and I stood there together, watching him pass through reception and keep going – on down the corridor, growing smaller and smaller as he went, until he reached the corner where the building turned, and disappeared.

Five months later, on 6 July 1988, the Piper Alpha oil platform exploded and sank into the North Sea. Liam never came back to school after the summer break, but Mr Johnstone led a special assembly in memory of Liam's father and the other 164 men who lost their lives in the disaster. I stayed off school that day, though it was the first day of fifth year – too physically sick at myself to be present. But Daniel and Sam had already done what I'd anticipated they would: by the time I returned, everyone knew what I'd said to Liam that day in the corridor, all those months before. I'd been a weirdo back then, but now I was a pariah. Not a single student in the whole of that school ever spoke to me again.

Birch, Wednesday 12 January

Birch had slept badly. She'd slunk into work the next morning feeling sheepish, waiting for McLeod to call her in for a telling-off, or for one of her colleagues to make a wisecrack about her sleeping on the job. She tried to focus on the 'Do later' folder, its contents now limited to the most mundane of administrative tasks. But her mind was wandering, and she couldn't stop looking at the clock. Crosbie was waiting until noon. Wherever Linh was, she'd spent another night alone, and un-looked-for. There was still no reply from Winnie – no phone call, no email back. Birch didn't exactly blame her: Winnie was already certain of the worst-case scenario. She was convinced that Linh's trafficker had returned to take her away again. In light of that conviction, she must have found Birch's initial inaction maddening, and Crosbie's further stalling downright hurtful. And what if Winnie was right? Birch shivered. Linh could be on another continent by now. It didn't bear thinking about.

Instead of thinking about it, she opened Google and typed in the name 'Beatrice Crozier', not really sure what she was looking for. A website, perhaps, advertising Bee's supernatural services, offering personalised psychic readings for a fee. Testimonials from suggestible people desperate for help with their seemingly insurmountable problems. A Facebook page, at the very least. But to her annoyance, she found very little. A few social media accounts, none of which seemed to belong to the correct Beatrice Crozier. Some ancestry.com results for a woman in Randolph County, Georgia, who'd died in 1898. Illustrations from the Beatrix Potter books scattered among the scant image results. Birch sighed, closed Google, opened up the PNC, and typed in Bee's name.

And yes: here were a handful of results listing Beatrice Crozier, born 5 April 1971, as a witness. Twice to domestic disputes, once to breach of the peace. One of the calls Bee had made herself. At two of them, PC Helen Birch was listed as an attending officer. All of them involved Banjo Robin being carted away to the drunk tank. Birch sighed. She already knew all of this. The clock's minute hand was inching towards 11am, and she still didn't know anything new about Beatrice. She felt irritated, though she didn't even really know why she was looking.

When Amy rapped on the glass door of the office, Birch jumped. Her friend grinned at her, and let herself in.

'Penny for your thoughts,' she said.

Birch felt herself blushing. Bee's PNC results were still open on her screen.

'Sorry, Kato,' she said, 'no can do. Not a single thought I can give you.' She tapped the side of her head. 'There's nothing in here.'

Amy raised an eyebrow. 'With all due respect, marm,' she replied, 'that's bullshit. I know your thinking face, and that' – she pointed directly at Birch – 'is most definitely it. What's up?'

Birch sighed. She'd already decided not to tell Amy about her strange visit from the so-called psychic. Amy was a smart woman, but she was open-minded about some pretty 'woo-woo' ideas. Birch was still worried that her response to Bee may have been a little harsh. She knew why, and where the anger she'd felt had come from. None of it was anything she wanted to get into with Amy. Amy was too good a police officer; she'd have follow-up questions.

'Honestly,' Birch said, 'there really are no deep thoughts going on here. Just some worries, I suppose.'

Amy tilted her head. 'About this case that might not turn out to be a case?'

Sure, Birch thought. It was true: running underneath the curiosity about Bee, there was a deeper vein of worry about Linh, and Winnie, and Crosbie.

'Yeah.'

'I heard McLeod made it Crosbie's problem.'

Birch nodded. 'You heard right.'

Amy snorted. 'Say no more,' she said. 'You'd think he could have let you have this one. You're back to full-time hours next week, for goodness' sakes.'

'There, you see.' Birch smiled, though she knew it was a poor effort. 'No penny required. Those are my thoughts exactly.'

Amy placed one hand on her friend's desk, and leaned over to see what was on Birch's laptop screen.

'Hey,' Birch said, angling the screen away. 'What are you doing?'

Amy laughed. 'Checking you're not watching TikToks on Police Scotland's dime.'

Birch made a face. 'I don't know what a TikTok *is*,' she said, 'let alone how to watch one.'

Amy was still chuckling at her. 'I know, marm,' she said. 'I was actually just checking on a hunch. And I was right.'

'Oh yeah? What was your hunch?'

Amy flipped her shiny sheet of hair off one shoulder. All she'd seen, Birch realised, was the familiar search results page from the PNC.

'That you're not doing anything even remotely important,' Amy replied, 'and so you should come for a ride-along with me.'

Birch's heart leapt. She could think of nothing better than getting out of this miserable office, not least so she could stop killing time counting down the seconds before Crosbie finally cracked and opened a missing persons investigation. But she mustn't seem too keen.

'Why?' she asked. 'You feel like you need some help?'

Amy shook her head. 'Not especially,' she replied. 'I'm just going to take a statement from someone. I thought you could use the fresh air.'

Birch closed her eyes. 'Oh god,' she said. 'You've heard, then …'

Amy looked at her. 'Heard about what?'

Birch glanced around, though they were in a closed room and no one could possibly have overheard them. 'About me falling asleep,' she said.

'What? Where?'

'Here!' Birch gestured at the desk in front of her. 'Here, in this very room, yesterday. I woke up out of a pretty deep doze – deep enough that I was dreaming. I'm absolutely mortified about it.'

Amy glanced behind her, back through the glass door and towards the bullpen. 'Really?' she said. 'Well, you shouldn't be. As far as I know, nobody noticed. Certainly no one's mentioned it to me. Besides, I've seen plenty of our mutual colleagues taking forty winks at their desks over the years. We're all human, Helen.'

Birch couldn't help frowning.

'I mean it,' Amy said. 'I really don't think that's a big deal, so try to stop worrying, will you? Come on this ride-along with me; you'll like it.'

Birch glanced at her walking stick. 'I'm still pretty slow these days,' she said. 'You're sure I won't be a liability?'

Amy laughed again. 'We're only going to a nail salon in Leith,' she said. 'There'll be no chasing bad guys down dark alleyways.'

The mention of a nail salon called up the memory of McLeod's theory about Linh: *She'll get herself a cash-in-hand job in a nail bar. After all, we can't make it too easy for these kinds of people to settle here.* She tried not to wince.

'Hey, it's *Leith*,' she said. 'Never say never.'

Amy pressed a hand to her chest. 'On behalf of the people of Leith,' she said, mock-horrified, 'I'm offended.'

Birch threw a final glance at Beatrice Crozier's name on her laptop screen, then closed it and reached for her walking stick. 'Listen,' she said, 'I used to work at Gayfield Square. In the People's Republic of Leith, anything can happen.'

Amy was beaming now. 'So you'll come along?'

Birch was on her feet, hooking her coat from the back of her chair. 'Of course,' she said. 'You might need back-up. At least, that's how I'm planning to justify it to McLeod.'

It was a dreich day. Amy squeezed her car into a space on Manderston Street, and for a moment, the two of them sat there in silence, watching rain spatter on to the windscreen.

'Still glad you came along?' Amy asked.

Birch couldn't explain how thrilled she was to be doing something that definitely counted as work but didn't involve being confined to the four walls of her office, so she simply nodded.

'Let's do this thing,' she said.

They made their way out on to Leith Walk. Birch could sense Amy curbing her usual pace to wait for her, and for the millionth time cursed the bad hip and Operation Kendall and the walking stick and Operation Stake. But the weather wasn't so bad once you were out in it; it was squally sea-weather, a fickle wind which funnelled the rain into occasional gusts.

'Quite invigorating out here, isn't it?' Birch said.

Amy had bunched her hair into a thick twist in her hand, trying to prevent it from flying in all directions. 'Sure,' she said, screwing up her face.

Leith Walk was, in spite of her wisecracks earlier, one of Birch's favourite places in Edinburgh. They were at the bottom end, near the Newkirkgate shopping centre and the Central Bar, a pub Birch had spent a goodly amount of time in as a young uniformed officer at Gayfield Square. But this wasn't the street she remembered it being: gentrification had hit hard, and a lot of the landmarks she would once have used to navigate were gone. As she and Amy made their way up through the Walk, she quietly mourned the Punjabi Women's Kitchen and the Leith Sale Rooms. The locals pub that would live forever in her memory as Bar Sienne had passed through a variety of iterations and currently claimed to be a trendy cocktail bar called The Mother Superior. At the corner of Smith Place, they passed the Arthur Williams bench, and Birch recalled the handful of times she'd talked with the gentle homeless man – arguably Leith's most famous resident – who for two decades had slept in the doorway of the Majestic Wine Warehouse.

'You're a bit quiet,' Amy observed.

Birch shrugged. 'Just remembering things,' she said. 'This was my old stomping ground for such a long time.'

Amy came to a halt. 'Here we are,' she said, and they both looked up at the building in front of them. 'I guess you don't remember this.'

Birch shook her head. The salon was squeezed into a narrow shopfront, the space inside more a corridor than a room. Its shop sign had been hand-painted in a traditional style, the words 'Lucky Seven Parlour' emblazoned in black and red against a yellow background, alongside an illustration of a manicured hand holding the four sevens from a deck of playing cards. In the window was a pink neon sign announcing 'Nails Tattoos Piercings' to the world outside. Birch could hear the familiar Hammond organ line of a Pink Floyd song drifting from the other side of the door.

'No,' she said. 'This was definitely *not* here when I last worked this beat.'

'Come on,' Amy said, glancing at Birch's cane. 'Let's get inside and get you sat down.'

'Jesus, Kato, I'm not your grandma,' Birch replied. But Amy was already over the nail salon's threshold, holding up her warrant card. Birch hobbled in behind her.

'And this is my colleague,' Amy was saying, 'Detective Inspector Birch.'

Birch decided against flashing her own badge. The job title alone seemed enough for the slight bewildered-looking young woman in front of them. This was constable work, really. Birch suspected Amy of having an ulterior motive.

'I'll get Carol,' the young woman said. Birch noticed she had the words 'Love' and 'Hate' tattooed on her knuckles. Her nails were, of course, immaculate. 'Carol's the owner.'

'Thanks,' Amy said. 'Is it alright if we sit?'

The woman was already several feet away. 'Of course!' she called, over her shoulder.

Birch tried not to sink too readily into the nearest chair – one of two that backed on to the window – though she was glad of it. While she and Amy waited, she marvelled at the salon's clever use of space. The slightly bowed window they were sitting in was clearly a sort of miniature reception area: it had a little MDF podium with a laptop on it where customers could be booked in. Along the length of the space were three café-style tables with a chair on either side, each table equipped with objects Birch could only assume were standard paraphernalia for a nail technician. At the far end of the room was a chipboard hoarding, painted in the same style as the sign outside. The lettering read 'Tattoo & Piercing'; Birch knew the partition was a licensing requirement, but felt disappointed that she couldn't see the set-up on the other side.

'It's quiet,' Amy said, and she was right: only one of the tables was occupied. The nail tech and her customer chatted together in low voices, apparently oblivious to the presence of the two policewomen.

'January,' Birch replied. 'Everyone's too skint for nails.'

Amy fanned her own hands out in front of her, palms down. 'Not me,' she said. Her nails were a tasteful wine red, and looked perfect as far as Birch could see. 'I could do with a fresh set, actually. Fancy it, once we're done with questioning?'

Birch laughed. 'I *knew* it,' she said. 'I knew there was a reason you hadn't just sent a couple of constables down here.'

Amy folded her hands back into her lap. 'Like I was going to pass up the chance to come to a nail place,' she said, 'and call it work.'

Birch was shaking her head in faux disbelief. 'Yeah,' she said, '*work* – remember that? You can't just stay after and have your nails done in the middle of the day.'

Amy threw her a mischievous look. 'Not just me,' she said. 'We. You're getting yours done, too. It'll be lunchtime after this. When did you last take a proper lunch break?'

'No, listen—'

'Exactly,' Amy said, holding up her hand. 'The answer is you've never taken a proper lunch break. So I think you can, on this one occasion, take an hour.'

Birch fell silent. She was still on phased return until the end of the week – a fact Amy seemed to have temporarily forgotten – so would actually clock off at 1pm anyway. And what Amy did with her lunch break was up to Amy.

'But,' she said, 'I've never had a manicure in my life, Kato. It's not my thing.'

Amy tutted. 'Nonsense,' she said, 'it's everyone's thing. Seriously, it's my treat. You need a bit of me-time.'

Birch laughed nervously. 'Is it me-time if I'm being forced into it? I don't even know what *happens* in these places.'

Now Amy let out a full-blown snort laugh. The nail tech at the nearby table glanced up, mildly alarmed. 'It's a *nail bar*,' Amy said. 'What do you think happens?' Birch must have been frowning, because she added, 'Don't sweat it, Helen, you're not going to be tested on it afterwards.' She nudged her friend in the ribs. 'Live a little, why don't you? Do something you've never done before.'

Birch opened her mouth to reply, but a woman who must have been Carol was bustling down the length of the salon towards them. Birch guessed that Carol was around her age – early forties – but she looked intimidatingly glamorous. Her hair was dyed pillar-box red and piled into an elaborate beehive on the top of her head. She wore a fuzzy red angora sweater that Birch would never have chosen herself, but coveted anyway, and a black leather pencil skirt with fishnet tights underneath. She reached out to shake first Amy's hand, then Birch's. Her nails were long, bright red, and coffin-shaped.

'Carol,' she said, 'hi. You're Amy? We spoke on the phone?'

'Amy Kato, yes,' Amy said. 'This is my colleague, DI Birch.'

'Helen's fine,' Birch cut in.

Amy was eyeing the nail tech and her client. 'Is there anywhere we can go to speak privately?' she asked.

Carol jerked her head backwards. 'Come through to the back office,' she said. 'Just be warned, it's a bit of a squeeze.'

They followed Carol back the way she had come through the narrow little salon. Birch glanced at the tables as she passed them. Each had a rack of polish bottles mounted on the wall behind it, one labelled 'Pastel', the middle one 'Bright', and the third 'Glitter & Iridescent'. Passing the tattoo and piercing partition, Birch peered inside the little space. It held a black, wipe-clean tattooing couch with a stool next to it for the artist, along with a ring light and two shelves with boxes of latex gloves, sterilised needles, kitchen roll and other supplies. The tattoo machine's cables snaked across the floor, and wound around the base of a wheeled trolley full of inks in all different colours. Birch had always wondered about getting a tattoo. The overpowering disinfectant smell that wafted out of the little space made her think that if she ever got round to it, this would be a safe place to come to.

'Here we are,' Carol said, holding open a door at the far end of the shop marked 'Staff Only'. Another door, next to it, was marked 'Powder Room'.

Amy sidestepped into the little office, which contained only a narrow desk and two chairs. Carol followed Birch in, and Amy gestured that the other two women should sit down. Before Birch could protest, she held up both hands.

'Helen,' she said, 'I insist. Have a seat. I'll stand and grow good, as my dad would say.'

Carol had already settled herself into what must have been her usual workspace. 'Sorry,' she said, 'I did say it was a bit of a squeeze.'

'Don't worry,' Amy replied. She was standing behind Birch's chair now, between her and the door, but Birch could hear her fishing in her handbag, presumably for something to record the interview on. Sure enough, Amy added, 'I'd like to either record our conversation, or take notes. Recording would be easier, but I'll only do that if you're okay with it.'

Carol was already nodding. Birch wanted to ask her how she kept her lipstick so perfect.

'That's fine with me,' Carol said.

'Great,' Amy replied. 'Okay. So if you could begin by stating your name for the record.'

Carol nodded again. 'My full name is Carol-Anne Carruthers,' she said, 'but I just go by Carol.'

'Lovely, thanks.' Amy cleared her throat, and raised her voice a little. 'And it's Wednesday the twelfth of January, eleven thirty-five am.'

'Also present,' Birch said, 'Detective Inspector Helen Birch. Just sitting in.'

Carol shuffled a little in her chair, settling in for the interview, the way people did. She smoothed the pencil skirt over her knees. Birch wondered if Carol was surprised that two quite senior officers had turned up to question her, but if she was intimidated, she didn't show it. She seemed at ease, in fact; Birch could tell she was someone who was accustomed to talking to people all day.

'Can you start,' Amy was saying, 'by just briefly going back over what you said on the phone when you called 101? Just say a bit about why you got in touch with us.'

'Sure,' Carol replied. 'So, basically, I've been getting a bit of trouble from … well, I don't know who he is, really. This bloke who keeps phoning up the shop, asking for one of my former employees.'

Birch could feel Amy nodding.

'Can you tell us what you mean by trouble?' Amy asked.

'Well,' Carol said, 'it started just after Christmas. We re-opened between Christmas and New Year, so it would have been about the twenty-seventh or twenty-eighth of December. We'd had a decent day, and everyone had gone home, but I'd stayed behind to catch up on emails and things that had built up over the festive period. So it was outside our working hours, when the phone doesn't usually ring, but it rang. And it was this guy.'

'Did he give his name?' Amy asked.

'No,' Carol replied, 'I'm afraid not. But he asked if he could speak to Kim, which caught my attention because … well, *I* was kind of keen to speak to Kim myself at that point in time.'

Birch leaned forward slightly in her seat.

'Oh yes?' Amy said. 'Who's Kim?'

Carol gestured vaguely back through the door, in the direction of the salon. 'Kim works here,' she said, 'or she did. The last week before Christmas is really busy for us, and Kim was booked out for the whole of Christmas Eve. But she just never showed up for work, which resulted in some very disappointed clients. She didn't call, didn't text, didn't email – just didn't turn up. And I haven't seen or heard from her since. Not a dicky bird … until this random bloke phones up asking to speak to her.'

Amy was quiet for a moment. 'What did you tell him, that first time he called?'

Carol's face flushed, ever so slightly. 'I might have been a bit short with him, to be honest,' she said. 'I told him Kim didn't work here anymore, and as far as I was concerned, she needn't bother ever coming back. I thought it might be her dad or something – he had an accent a bit like hers. So I figured maybe the message would get back to her that I was pissed off.'

'And that was that,' Amy said. 'You thought.'

Carol nodded. 'Yeah. I felt a bit bad immediately afterwards, you know, for snapping at him. I realised I wouldn't have done that with a woman, because I would have assumed that a woman was one of Kim's clients. But because it was a man, I maybe made a connection in my head that I shouldn't have. And then I wondered afterwards if I'd made him angry.'

'Because he called back.'

'Yeah,' Carol said again. 'Not the next day, but the day after. And he asked again to speak to Kim.'

Birch had kept quiet long enough. It felt weird that she wasn't participating. 'You're sure it was the same man?' she asked.

Carol nodded. 'He had the same accent,' she said, 'and he called at about the same time of day. Evening time, after it had got dark. I was here on my own.'

'You think that was deliberate?' Amy asked.

'Maybe,' Carol replied. 'I still wasn't spooked at that point, but as it went on, I did get a bit rattled.'

'Because he kept calling,' Birch said.

'Yes. We were closed on Hogmanay, but I came in to do some bits and pieces back here in the office. He phoned that evening, and then he phoned again on the Monday, when we opened up after New Year. He's phoned at least once a day since then, and sometimes more than once. I think he's also been calling my mobile – at least, I've been getting a lot of calls from a private number.'

'And you think it's this same man,' Amy said.

'I think it could be. I don't pick up private numbers.' For a moment, Carol looked down at the floor. 'I got some hassle from an ex a few years ago, and now I only pick up numbers I know.'

Birch wanted to shake her head. She assumed 'some hassle from an ex' was probably a euphemism for stalking behaviours. She wished more women would report these things – women like Carol who'd likely been told that no one would care about their stupid problems, probably by the same ex-boyfriend who was causing them.

'That's very sensible,' Amy was saying. 'But as you're not sure about the calls to your mobile, let's focus on the calls to the shop phone for now. When he calls, does this man always say the same thing? What's his tone like? You mentioned to 101 that his manner is quite threatening.'

'A bit, yeah,' Carol said. 'That first time he called, he was pretty polite – just like, "Hi, is Kim there, can I speak to Kim?", that sort of thing. Then the second time it was the same, but when I said that Kim didn't work here anymore, he wanted to know where she was. His tone wasn't threatening then, either, but it was sort of demanding. I thought it was a bit odd for some random dude to ask for a young woman's whereabouts without saying, you know, "I'm her dad, I'm her boyfriend," or whatever. Just to demand that information, it made me think maybe he was bad news for Kim. And although I was a bit peeved with her, I still wasn't going to respond well to that, you know? So I said something that I now realise was a bit stupid.'

Birch leaned forward fully now, resting her elbows on her knees. 'And what was that?' she asked.

Carol screwed her eyes closed before she spoke again. 'I said, "I'm not telling you that" – or, "I'm not telling you where she is." Something like that.' She opened her eyes again. 'I think he assumed that meant that I knew where she was, and just wasn't going to tell him – when what I *should* have said was, I don't know where she is, because that's the truth. I don't.'

'You don't know Kim's home address?' Amy asked.

'Oh, sure,' Carol replied. 'We have an address on file for her. But Mandy – the girl you met on reception, just now – she's been by the place a couple of times on her way into work, and tried the buzzer. No answer. So I don't even know if Kim still lives in that flat or not.'

'Even so,' Birch said, quickly, 'it was obviously right not to give this man any of Kim's details. You've done all the right things, Carol; there's no need to beat yourself up.'

Carol sighed. 'Thank you,' she said, 'that's good to hear. But still, I think that was bad wording on my part, because saying "I won't tell you"' – Carol raised her manicured hands and made the bunny-ears gesture, twice in quick succession – 'instead of "I don't know", that seems to be what's made him keep calling. And with every call, he gets angrier with me.'

'So, it escalated,' Amy said, 'after that second phone call?'

Carol winced. 'Yep,' she said. 'Now when he calls, he's pretty abusive. And threatening. It went from "Where's Kim, please," to "Tell me where Kim is, you stupid bitch." And then more recently, it's become, "Tell me where Kim is or I'll come there and make you tell me." When he started saying things like that, that's when I called 101.'

Birch wished she could see Amy's face, get a sense of what her colleague was thinking.

'That was exactly the right thing to do,' Amy said, and Birch nodded vigorously in agreement.

'Have any of the other employees here had to deal with this man?' she asked.

Carol shook her head. 'It's weird,' she replied, 'there have been times where the phone has rung and someone else has picked it up, and the line has just gone dead. A few times like that, just recently. That happens occasionally, of course – when we answer, we always say, "Lucky Seven, Carol speaking," or, "Lucky Seven, Mandy speaking," or whoever. And I think sometimes people think, shit, that wasn't who I meant to call, and they just put the phone down. But there's been a few of those hang-up calls just recently, and I've wondered if it's him – if he'll only say his little piece if he knows it's me.'

'That's interesting,' Amy said, and Birch could tell from her voice that she was making some sort of mental note.

'You mentioned that this man has an accent,' Birch said. 'You said it sounds a bit like Kim's. What kind of accent is it?'

Carol looked down, pulling the sleeves of her fluffy sweater over her hands.

'I – sorry,' she spluttered. 'I – honestly, I don't know how to describe it without sounding … kinda racist.'

Birch cocked her head. 'That's okay,' she said. 'How about I word the question a different way. Where is Kim from?'

Carol lifted her chin again, and met Birch's eye. 'Oh,' she said, obviously relieved. 'Yes, that's a good way to approach it. Kim's from Vietnam, originally.'

'It could be a coincidence,' Amy said, as they made their way back down Leith Walk towards the car.

Birch's jaw was set. She was hobbling as fast as the cane and her bad leg would allow, and trying to ignore the resulting pain.

'Yeah,' she said, 'it could be.'

Birch had spent the remainder of Carol's interview forcing herself not to hijack Amy. As far as Amy was concerned, they were there to take a witness statement in relation to a case of nasty phone harassment – that was all. Birch had fallen silent, listening carefully. She suddenly had a lot of questions, but none of them were appropriate for that particular moment – and besides, Carol probably wouldn't have been able to answer most of them.

'My money's on a coincidence,' Amy was saying. She'd wrapped her hair around her fist again, the wind even stronger now that they were walking into it. 'I'm working from the hypothesis that this man on the phone is a suitor of Kim's, and he's doing to her exactly what Carol described *her* ex doing. Hassling, I think, was the word she used.'

Birch crinkled her nose. She was trying not to get distracted, but … 'Did you just use the word *suitor*? What is this, *Pride and Prejudice*?'

Amy laughed, and the laugh was caught up and carried over her shoulder by the wind. 'Well, *I* don't know,' she said. 'Is there a name for a man you might once have been interested in but now aren't, and can't get rid of?'

'Scumbag?' Birch suggested.

'Yeah,' Amy replied, 'that fits. Guys can be pig-headedly persistent, even when they *know* they're not helping their cause. They just have to have the last bloody word.'

Birch couldn't help smiling. 'Tinder going well lately, is it?'

Amy raised an eyebrow. 'Thank goodness for the block button,' she said. 'But seriously. Our phone man sounds a lot to me like a spurned lover who can't stand that he's been ghosted. He doesn't care how many women he freaks out if he thinks he can get the information he wants.'

They walked into a smatter of rain, and Birch squinted. 'That's totally plausible,' she said, 'sure. But what if it's not that?'

They were nearing Manderston Street now. Amy was digging in her handbag 'Well,' she said, 'if you rule out sex as a motive, you turn to look at money. Could our phone man be a loan shark?'

Birch tilted her head, considering it. 'I suppose so,' she said. 'Though I might have expected him to turn up in person by now, if he thought there was any chance Carol was standing between him and a repayment.'

Amy brandished the keys. 'That's a good point.'

As they rounded the corner, the wind died down a little, blocked by the high tenements opposite. Instinctively, Birch reached up to her forehead and began trying to smooth down her fringe.

'So,' she said, 'next up is *my* hypothesis.'

Amy didn't look at her. Birch fancied she saw a *here we go* look cross her colleague's face, though she might have been doing what Dr Jane called *projecting*.

'Go on,' Amy said.

They were nearing the car. Birch waited until Amy had unlocked it, and they'd both got inside.

'I want to go back to the office and see what I can find out about Kim,' she said. 'Because listen, I know it's not much to go on, but two young Vietnamese women going missing within a couple of weeks of each other? That feels significant, to me.'

'Of course,' Amy replied. 'But Kim isn't missing, necessarily. She seems to have quit her job and been out the two times her co-worker came by, but that doesn't mean she's missing.'

'No,' Birch admitted, 'it doesn't. But there's also the fact that someone's looking for her. Our man on the phone has lost track of her, and so has Carol.'

She fell silent, then, thinking about when Charlie had become a missing person, all those years ago. Except he hadn't, not really – her brother had become a hidden person. A person who didn't want to be found.

'So, come on,' Amy said. 'I know you've done more than that, in your hunch-addled brain. You're like a chess grandmaster, always fifteen moves ahead of the rest of us. Let's say she *is* missing. Where does that rabbit hole go?'

Birch grimaced. 'Only bad places,' she replied. 'But what I'm wondering is this. Does this guy on the phone maybe have something to do with Kim arriving in Scotland in the first place? Winnie told me that once a trafficker is contracted, they see the trafficked person as their property. They think that in exchange for moving that person somewhere, they get to own their whole life thereafter. If their person goes missing – even if she's just taken off somewhere nice of her own volition – they're going to get pretty mad about it, right? And be very persistent, I'd imagine.'

Amy was quiet for a moment. 'I know you know this, marm,' she said, 'but I feel like I have to point out that not every Vietnamese person in Scotland has been trafficked here.'

Immediately, Birch felt her face flush. She recognised the same feeling she'd had in the restaurant with Anjan creeping over her again: the desire to be given a free pass. *Of course I don't think that,* she thought, *I'm not the sort of person who—* but she stopped herself.

'You're right,' she said. 'I'm sorry.'

Amy's expression softened. 'Hey,' she said. 'I'm not saying it's a bad theory. It's certainly one possibility, based on what little we know right now. I just want to ask, with all due respect, if you'd have jumped to that conclusion on the basis of Carol's evidence had we interviewed her, say, last week. If you weren't already thinking about another young Vietnamese woman – one you know *has* been trafficked –

would you have been so ready to fit Kim into that same narrative, too?'

Birch sat in silence for a moment. The wind had changed: rain was scattering sideways over the car windscreen now, making little diagonal flecks on the glass.

Amy had her hands on the steering wheel, but didn't move to start the ignition.

'You know,' Birch said, eventually, 'you're a bloody brilliant officer, Kato.'

Amy spluttered, ready to deny it, but Birch held up her right hand, and let it hover in the air between them.

'Now,' she said, 'don't be modest. That was an extremely diplomatic and elegant way of telling me, quite rightly, to get back in my box. I bet DCI McLeod wishes he had even half your smarts when it comes to wrangling me and my runaway mouth.'

'I hope that didn't sound like a telling-off,' Amy said.

'Not at all. It sounded like what it was: a very classy way of saying, "Calm down and stop being such an eejit," *woman.*'

Amy sighed. 'You're not an eejit,' she said. 'You just get … overexcited, sometimes.'

Birch pressed the hand she'd raised against her forehead. 'Trust me,' she said, 'I'm an eejit. I sound like one of these true crime nutters, hopping on to the back of some wild piece of speculation like that. Thanks for not letting me ride off into the sunset on it.'

Amy grinned, and turned the key in the ignition. 'I'm sure there's still time for that,' she said. 'But maybe it's a good idea to get you back to the office – see if you can't dig up some actual evidence to work from, eh?'

For a fleeting second, Birch considered the fact that actually, it was now almost one o'clock. Had she wanted to, she could have gone home. But for the first time in a long time, she had something to be curious about. Something she was keen to go and get her teeth into – even if it did, as Amy had suggested, turn out to be nothing more than a woman who'd quit her job and was ignoring her particularly persistent ex-boyfriend. Had Dr Jane asked her to name the feeling, Birch would have told her that for the first time in months, she felt *useful*.

'Sounds good,' she said, as Amy pulled out of the parking space and began to rev along Manderston Street. 'Let's do it.'

At the first red traffic light they came to, Amy braced her hands on the steering wheel, palms flat, and examined her nails. 'I still think,' she said, 'we could have stayed and got our manicures.'

Birch nudged her friend as the light turned green. 'Eyes on the road, Kato,' she said. 'And don't you worry – I feel confident there are plenty of manicures in your future.'

As she peeled out on to Leith Walk, Amy threw her friend an eyeroll.

'Trust me,' Birch added, with more emotion than she'd intended. 'I'm psychic.'

Bee, 1991

I made it to the end of fifth year, and got out. I had decent grades. I wrote an essay about *King Lear* that won the school's essay prize that year. My mother put the little certificate up on the wall in the downstairs bathroom, then took it down again in an act of silent protest when I told her I'd decided not to stay and do Sixth Year Studies. I wasn't going to go to university, so what was the point? My mother dropped hints and offered to phone up the school and see what could be done if I changed my mind, but I wasn't going to. I knew – because I knew – that after a couple of weeks of cajoling, she'd loosened any and all hope she'd pinned on me, and transferred all that hope to Tommy instead. *He'd* be the one to do all the things she'd wanted to, but never done. If anyone was going to make her happy, it would have to be him. Poor kid.

To my surprise, my father approved of the decision.

'Quite right,' he said one night at the dinner table, after I'd brushed off yet another of my mother's pointed comments. 'Bloody waste of time, a university degree. I never went to university, and have I ever regretted it? I have not. Why spend all those years toiling when all you get at the end is a piece of paper that says you're clever?'

My mother tried to protest, but he cut her off.

'Beatrice *knows* she's clever,' he said. 'She doesn't need some fancy professor in an ivory tower to tell her that.'

That one small remark was like a warm shawl I pulled around myself for weeks afterwards. It was the most loving thing my father ever said of me.

I got a job as a garment sorter in the Jenners Depository. Every day, I walked through the Meadows from our house in Marchmont, made my way over George VI Bridge and down the Mound to Princes Street, where I caught a bus. The bus carried me through the West End, past Haymarket station and Donaldson's School with its fancy turrets and immaculate lawn. I rode all the way to the Murrayfield Stadium, where I alighted. I liked a walk at either end of the journey – a journey that made me feel a little more grown-up, and a little less afraid of the world – every day.

My job was to sort through defective clothes that customers had returned, and to handle written complaints. These would appear in my workstation overnight, spirited down to me from the mail room as though by fairies. The clothes came to me on a van once per week, and it was my job to examine each item, ascertain its fault, and decide its eventual fate: could it be fixed up, retagged and returned to the shop floor? If so, my little workstation was equipped to do minor repairs: the re-fitting of a press stud, the closing of a seam. If not, I baled the items and passed them on for disposal. What "disposal" meant, I didn't know, and didn't much concern myself with – but recycling wasn't much of a thing at that time. I assumed they were incinerated: soft cashmere cardigans and smart tweed coats sent up in a smog-choked pyre and then raked down into ash, ready for the next bale. I never failed to check the pockets, and earned myself a little extra cash every now and then in forgotten change.

Complaints were more labour intensive; every complaint posted to us required a hand-typed response. More often than not, customers sent their items back to me along with their missives. I received shoes with snapped-off high heels or flapping soles, and regularly, scraps of fabric cut from a garment and folded or stapled or paper-clipped in alongside the letter. *I took the item home, whereupon I discovered a moth hole in the left sleeve. The hole is hereby enclosed* – and I'd fish in the envelope to find a two-inch square of what was once a jumper, neatly swatched with pinking shears, the tiniest pin-prick of a defect in the centre, barely visible to the naked eye. My replies were achingly polite, and usually came with a refund. Our customers were always right, even when they were vandals who'd wrecked a perfectly decent sweatshirt over the tiniest flaw. Some of them lost buttons and complained that they shouldn't need to sew them back on. Occasionally, women would write to complain that the garment they'd bought didn't suit them – it wasn't their colour – and shouldn't the shop assistant they'd dealt with have told them that, prior to purchase?

That job taught me a great deal about my gift – though I couldn't bring myself to call it that. It didn't feel like a gift, though I wasn't melodramatic enough to think of it as a curse. It simply was what it was, and in the absence of any better term, I began to think of it as the Knowing.

I learned that some people were easier to know – to *know* know – than others. Some people seemed to wear their hurts and fears on the outside, and to me they looked like open wounds, bleeding on everyone around them. There was an old man I saw every day when I got on the bus: he liked to latch on to whoever sat next to him and launch into a barrage of chatter. I tried not to sit too near, because sadness hung in the air around him like smoke on a still day. To the strangers he engaged, he'd talk about the weather, football, Edinburgh traffic, the headlines of the moment. But I knew – because I knew – that he was poor and lonely and rode the buses every day in winter on account of them being warm. His head was filled with the noise of explosions, and he could call up the sickening taste of trench gas on his tongue, unbidden. He'd lied about his age to enlist young, and was the only member of his entire platoon not killed in the mud at the Third Battle of Ypres. He never said this aloud to anyone, but I knew.

It was easier to be around people who didn't make themselves known. The foreman in my corner of the warehouse was a big, bear-like man named Jock, who strode around in dark blue overalls and old-fashioned boots with nails in the soles. He knew my name but called me 'Daphne and Blossom', and routinely hailed me with the words, 'Will ye no pit the kettle oan, hen, ah'm gaspin'.' I'd call him over to my station if I got an especially daft complaint – those letters with the squares of cut-out jumpers were his favourites – and he'd hold the flimsy paper in his paw-like grip and read and laugh, sometimes until he had to wipe away tears.

'Ach, this wan's a *scunner*,' he'd say, handing me back the crumpled missive. 'Go an write back, an tell him fae me: away an bile yer heid!'

Either Jock was unknowable, or there was nothing to be known. I couldn't discern anything about him, either in his past or still to come. Learning that some people were impervious to my particular form of sight felt like a blessing – a break from the weight of all the things I knew. I still lived with my parents then, and knew of my mother's affair from the first night it began. She'd been at the bingo, we thought, and she'd come home late – well after Tommy had gone to bed. I'd stayed up reading a novel – I remember it was

The Trick is to Keep Breathing by Janice Galloway – while my father clicked through the BBC Ceefax pages, looking for bulletins about Kuwait. My mother breezed into the living room wearing lipstick, her cheeks flushed, and before she'd even opened her mouth to speak, I knew.

'Och,' she said, pointing at the clock on the mantelpiece, 'it's late! I never even realised.'

My father didn't look up at her, but pointed the remote in the direction of the TV. 'They're bombing the bastard Iraqis,' he said, 'look. About bloody time, too.'

My mother padded over the rug to the armchair, where I was sitting, cat-like, with my legs pretzelled up underneath me.

'Hello, darling,' she said, and bent down to kiss me on the cheek. I stared at her – it had been years since she'd last kissed me. 'How was work today?'

I dog-eared the page I was on, and tossed my book to the floor. 'Fine,' I said. I wondered if I could really smell after-shave on her, or if my imagination was adding that detail because I knew. I realised why she'd made a show of coming over, of kissing me and asking me the question. She wanted me to ask her something back, so she could ream off the story she'd been rehearsing as she made her way home. I glanced at my father, who was still stabbing at the remote. Okay, I'd play along.

'How was your evening?' I asked.

'*Well*,' my mother began, delighted, 'you wouldn't *believe* the carry-on Sandra and I had, trying to get back across town from the bingo. *Hon*estly, the *buses* in this city ...'

While she talked, I studied her. I wanted to see where she'd really been – wanted to know who this man was she'd been out with. They hadn't slept together. She'd met him a few days before, when they'd both sat down on the same park bench in Princes Street Gardens and she'd asked him for the time. He was married, too. I could see him, if I concentrated hard. He was a deeply ordinary-looking man, and balding quite severely, which my father was not. Earlier that night, she'd met him on the North Bridge and got in his car, and they'd driven to a restaurant in Musselburgh, where they knew no one.

'*Then*,' she was saying, 'they had us alight at the Waverley Steps, even though we'd been told the bus would be fixed and move off in five minutes or so. Sandra and I stood in the cold there for I don't know how long. Honestly, I could have *walked* in the time it took them ...'

I wanted to laugh at her, and tell her to stop, and sit down, and be normal. I wanted to tell her there was no need for this little charade. She hadn't *done* anything: she'd gone out for dinner in Musselburgh with some accountant who drove a brown car. She'd eaten some lukewarm spaghetti and told him how her life felt dull, as if the accountant could offer anything other than a rehashed version of this same beige, middle-class existence. I wanted to tell her my father wasn't listening, anyway, so she might as well tell the truth. I wanted to yell at her, too, because I knew that nothing was going to come of it; yes, they'd sleep together eventually, in some crappy hotel room by the airport, and then he'd get cold feet and go back to his wife and stop picking up the phone when she called. She'd spend the rest of her life assuming she hadn't been good enough, when the truth was he was just another man like my father – a man with a nice, quiet life he didn't want upturned. A man who valued his own comfort over absolutely anything else.

'They're all like that,' I said, interrupting her. 'Isn't that what they say, about men?'

I saw a jolt of fear tighten her lipsticked mouth.

'And buses,' I added. 'Men and buses. They all come along at once, don't they? And none of them can be relied upon.'

I didn't blame her. My father's preferred way of living was to have everything quietly and smoothly provided for him without him ever having to see the logistics. He mostly treated us as though we weren't there – me, my mother, and even Tommy, though the older Tommy grew, the more my father spoke of him as 'my son and heir', a statement I always rolled my eyes at. Everything my parents owned was on tick, being paid off in tiny instalments by my father's middle-management salary. To have an heir, didn't you need to leave behind something – anything – of value?

I managed to live with them for another four years. The balding accountant put a stop to my mother's affair, and she became very thin. Dieting became the new love of her life: the kitchen cupboards filled up with chocolate-flavoured SlimFast shakes and packets of Ryvita. She bought Cindy Crawford's *Shape Your Body* on VHS and danced bizarrely around the living room to it with all the curtains closed. She was trying to disappear – I knew – because she couldn't stand that she'd made a fool of herself with another man, only to be turned down.

Living there was bearable, because it meant I could save my wages for important things. First, I learned to drive, something my mother had never done and therefore frowned upon. But I was good at it, partly because a forklift had been introduced to the warehouse earlier that year, and I'd been trained to operate it, though I didn't often need to. The vehicle had very little in common with a car, but it taught me how to do things with my feet and hands at the same time: accelerate while lifting the control beam, signal left while bringing the forklift to a halt. Same difference. I passed my test on my first try, a thing my father told me only bad, over-confident drivers do.

My station at work was blessed with the arrival of a computer, so I learned how to operate that, too. Now my paper clothing slips were replaced with electronic forms I could fill out and print. I loved to stand by the dot-matrix printer and listen to its weird song as it stuttered out the day's reports. The floor around it was littered with the little perforated strips people tore off the sides of the paper absent-mindedly as they waited. Jock retired early, claiming technology had come to take his job. They recruited a new foreman – a man named Eric, about whom I immediately knew things I wished I didn't – but Jock could never really be replaced.

I might have stayed longer in the family home, but the Knowing became too much. In the spring of 1994, Tommy turned sixteen. I was twenty-three, and had managed to save up almost £10,000, though my parents didn't know it. It helped that I didn't have friends; my co-workers were either men, or women considerably older than me. They had children, and mortgages, and secrets I didn't want to have to carry. I'd never had a boyfriend, for the simple reason that I wasn't sure I really wanted one. The thought of bringing a man home to meet my parents flooded my chest with a cold, sloshing fear. Besides, I could only stand to date someone if they were unknowable. It wouldn't be fair for me to know more about a man – or woman, I occasionally reminded myself – than they knew about me, especially when I didn't have any choice.

Tommy, of course, didn't have the Knowing. After Melody Rowe and the baby that never happened, I'd thought about asking Tommy if *he* ever knew things about people without knowing how he knew – or I fancied that perhaps I could test him for the Knowing by asking a series of careful questions. However, the older Tommy grew, the more obvious it became: he had no gift, or curse, the way I did. One night after work he crashed into my room as I was reading, and flopped down on his stomach at the end of my single bed.

'Bee,' he said, 'what the hell is wrong with girls?'

I looked up from the pages of *Trainspotting*. 'Don't you have the ability to knock on a door?' I asked. I'd actually hit a particularly grim scene in the book and felt grateful he'd barged in when he had, but nevertheless, there was a way to be a person.

'Sorry,' he said, not sounding it. 'But seriously. Girls. What is their problem?'

I chucked the book down on the bed beside him. 'You're going to need to be more specific,' I said.

He raised both hands and covered his face, though whether he was exasperated with me, or with womankind in general, I couldn't tell. Then, suddenly, I knew something. I knew there was a girl at school Tommy wanted to have sex with. I knew he had a box of condoms hidden in a toffee tin in his bedside drawer. I knew he'd memorised the condoms' expiry date, as though it were a deadline.

'Ew,' I said, aloud.

He looked at me, around his hands. 'What?'

Inwardly, I shook myself. I'd promised myself, after Liam Torrance, that I'd never let anyone else find out I had the Knowing. Not even Tommy. Especially not Tommy.

'Nothing,' I said. 'Just … you and girls. Why would I want to get involved in that?'

He wormed around on the bed until he could face me, clasping his hands together in a desperate praying gesture. 'Look,' he said, 'I know, okay. But please? I need help to understand what's going on.'

'With girls.'

He was beginning to blush. 'With *a* girl,' he said. 'This girl I really like.'

'From school?'

I already knew. I knew her name was Eilidh, that she was a sporty type, with long, shiny brown hair in a ponytail, and long dark eyelashes that meant she never needed to wear make-up. She wasn't a hockey team girl, though: she had cool parents who took her indoor climbing at the fancy new centre on Pier Place.

'No,' Charlie was saying, 'from the Girl Department at Jenners. Of course from school.'

I reached out and gave him a gentle shove. 'Sorr-ee,' I said. 'You want my help, or just to take the piss?'

His face turned sincere. 'I want your help, I do.'

'Okay,' I said, bracing myself, 'tell me. But no gory details, please. I don't want to hear about how long her tongue is, or anything.'

I couldn't stay there after that. I couldn't stay, and know things against my will about my little brother's sexual exploits. I still wasn't entirely sure what the rules of the Knowing were – if there were rules at all – but physical proximity was definitely a factor. I'd known something was going on with Melody Rowe from touching her note, but I hadn't known she was pregnant until I got to the Chemistry block and stood within an arm's length of her. When Liam Torrance had shoved me that day in the corridor, with each contact he'd made, I'd seen a different, flickering snap-shot of his future. My mother's first illicit evening with the accountant only opened up in front of me when she crossed the living room and bent to kiss me. I figured if I no longer slept every night only feet away from Tommy, I could stop knowing about him and Eilidh and the condoms in the bedside drawer.

After a few weeks, I came to know that she wasn't going to date him. *Not because you're not a sweet guy,* she'd say, when he finally plucked up the courage to ask her out. *But because you're a guy. I'm afraid I'm just not into guys – you know, like that.* Sure enough, a few days later, he came home from school dejected, and sat through dinner silently, his eyes downcast. My mother had cooked a chicken casserole she wouldn't, herself, eat. It was Tommy's favourite, but I watched him push the food round and round his plate. I didn't think I could stand the pointless dance of asking him what was wrong and having him clam up and refuse to say. I'd dealt with a particularly aggravating complaint at work and didn't have the energy. Instead I offered to wash up, and my mother sent him into the kitchen to help me dry and put away.

'It's Eilidh, isn't it?' I said. No point prevaricating.

He nodded.

'That sucks,' I said, riffling my hand through the dishwater to froth the Fairy Liquid. 'But hey, you can't blame her for being gay.'

He fumbled a plate, and it smashed on the floor at his feet.

In the next room, my mother made a noise of exasperation. 'Was that one of my good serving plates?' she called.

'No, Mum,' I yelled back. 'It was just one of the Hedgerow set.'

I heard the scuff of her slippers on the living room rug. Tommy was still boggling at me when she arrived in the doorway.

'Oh, Tom,' she said, seeing the shards at his feet.

He juddered slightly, then, like a shut-down machine coming back to life. 'Shit,' he said, looking down at the shattered plate. 'Sorry, Mum.'

'*Language*,' she said, but she was already turning back in the direction of the TV and her armchair. 'Be a bit more careful, please. And mind your fingers, picking that up.'

We both stood there for a moment, watching her go, then Tommy held out a hand in my direction. I made a little dressage-step away from the sink, swung open the cupboard under it, and handed him the dustpan and brush.

'How did you know that?' he said. 'About Eilidh? You didn't go and *talk* to her, did you?'

I snorted at him. 'Don't be ridiculous,' I said, 'I don't even know what she looks like.' This was a lie. I could have picked her out of a line-up – because of the Knowing, but also from Tommy's rapturous descriptions of how *pretty* but *cool* and *unaffected* and *chilled out* she was.

'I've just been thinking about her,' I went on. 'And come on – a girl who goes indoor climbing and doesn't wear make-up? Very likely gay.'

He slung me a look. 'Don't be homophobic,' he said, and bent to start picking up the wrecked Hedgerow plate. He looked angry, and I realised he thought I was saying he was stupid for not realising by himself.

'I'm not,' I said, 'really. And listen – you're not heartbroken, are you? You're sort of down, but … not the way you would be if she'd told you, "Nah, I fancy the captain of the rugby team."'

Tommy clattered the broken china together in the dustpan as he straightened up. He didn't respond straight away. I waited while he carried the shards to the pedal bin, and toppled them in.

'Yeah,' he said, coming back to me. 'You're right. Why *is* that? Why is it better if she fancies the captain of the hockey team instead? Why is it better if she fancies a girl?'

I shrugged. 'Don't ask me,' I said. 'I know nothing.'

For the first time that evening, he laughed. 'Hey,' he said, 'you knew Eilidh was a lesbian.'

I looked at him. The next day, I'd start making enquiries about a place to rent.

'I don't know anything else,' I lied.

Birch, Wednesday 12 January

After the visit to the Lucky Seven Parlour, Birch couldn't face the idea of returning to her desk. Amy had delivered them both back to Fettes Avenue, where they'd hoped to find Crosbie briefing his team on the opening of an official missing persons case for Linh Fortune.

'He said noon,' Birch told Amy, as they climbed the steps – Birch leaning on her friend's elbow – from the car park to the main building. 'He promised me, yesterday evening, on the phone.'

And yet the bullpen, when they walked into it, seemed to be in business-as-usual mode.

Birch nudged Rema's elbow as the younger woman passed her. 'Anything?' she asked.

'Marm?'

Birch nodded in the vague direction of Crosbie's office. 'Anything yet on Linh Fortune?'

Rema shook her head. 'Not yet,' she replied, and Birch thought she caught the edge of something caustic in the other officer's voice when she added, 'He's out to lunch just now.'

Birch turned to look at Amy, releasing Rema back to her duties. 'He's taking the piss,' she muttered. 'He's doing this on purpose.'

To her surprise, Amy looked down at the floor between them. 'I mean …' Amy faltered, but then seemed to decide to carry on speaking. 'I'm sure he's not doing it as a personal slight towards *you*, marm.'

Birch huffed. 'I wouldn't be so sure,' she replied.

Amy followed Rema's retreating back with her eyes. 'Well,' she said, clearly trying to lift the mood, 'it *is* lunchtime. If there's nothing doing just yet, want to chum me down to the canteen?'

Birch leaned on her stick, considering. The ride-along to the nail bar had set a gear whirring in her brain that felt familiar but rusty, as though it had lain dormant for too long. Something fizzed in her arms and hands; perhaps it was adrenaline. She needed to do something to burn it off, and sitting in the staff mess watching Amy pick cucumber out of her sandwich wasn't going to cut it.

'You go, Kato,' she said. 'I'm going to take some time to think.'

Birch had ignored her colleague's raised eyebrow and obvious unspoken questions. She'd waited for as long as she could stand – not all that long – after Amy had left the bullpen. Then she'd fished out her phone, opened the Uber app, and summoned herself a car. No one in this place seemed to care what she did, as long as she did it quietly. Well, she could do some quiet policework, couldn't she?

'If Crosbie isn't going to bother doing his job,' she hissed, hobbling into the lift, 'then I'll just have to do it for him.'

She lucked out with the driver of her Uber; he possessed, as some of them do, the preternatural ability to sense whether or not their passenger wishes to chat. A bookish-looking man named Lukasz, he clarified her destination and then, in under thirty seconds, turned up his radio and began to hum quietly along.

Birch looked out at the passing shopfronts as they toiled through lunchtime traffic along Ferry Road. She was headed back to Leith: her new destination was only about a mile from the Lucky Seven Parlour, where they'd just been. Why hadn't she asked Amy to drive her somewhere else before they headed back? Why didn't she want her colleague to accompany her? She imagined these questions might also intrigue Dr Jane. It was something to do with frustration at her loss of independence, Birch decided. It had been months since she'd been able to drive her own car, or even so much as rise from a chair in a decisive fashion. Meeting with an informant – as Birch was on her way to do – was often done in pairs. She could easily have asked Amy to accompany her – *It makes sense, Kato, as we're in the area* – and Amy would almost certainly have agreed. But Birch was tired of being so dependent on other people.

As the Uber turned into Sailmaker Road, slowing as it approached her destination, Birch realised it may also have something, somehow, to do with Beatrice Crozier. Meeting the so-called psychic yesterday had upset her in a way she hadn't yet got a handle on. It was unlike her to keep things from Amy, and a weird interaction like the one she'd had with Bee was just the sort of workplace morsel she'd usually offer up to her friend over coffee in the bullpen. She was worried that Amy would scold her: for being overly harsh with Bee, for failing to take her visit seriously, for neglecting to probe further into the reason Bee had come to the station in the first place.

'I didn't do due diligence,' Birch murmured. Amy would – however gently – have said so.

'Sorry, hen?' Lukasz had brought the Uber to a stop, and was peering at her in the rear-view mirror.

Birch gave her head a shake. 'Nothing,' she said, a little too quickly. 'Don't mind me. Just thinking aloud.'

Lukasz grinned as she pushed open the car door. 'You were saying, "Five stars for this guy," right?'

Birch laughed. 'Oh yes,' she said, 'of course.'

Alyona's flat was high up in the block, its immediate out-look the huge, twisted sculptures of the Salamander Street scrap-metal yard. Beyond that, industrial warehouses – the no-man's land of Leith Docks – and then, in the distance, the sea. Birch stood on the open walkway outside Alyona's front door, feeling the icy bite of the sea wind as she looked out in the direction of Fife. As she raised her hand to knock, she felt the familiar buzz of her phone in her hip pocket. The display read *Police Scotland Fettes Avenue*.

She sighed, and swiped to answer. 'This is Birch.'

'Afternoon, marm.' It was John again. 'You're not at your desk?'

She winced. She'd hoped no one would realise she'd gone. 'No, John, I'm out and about just now. What can I do you for?'

He paused. In the short silence, Birch could hear his reluctance to answer. 'Ms Crozier is here again, asking to see you.'

She felt something heavy in the pit of her stomach. Bee had come *back*? Birch heard Amy's voice in her head: *She knows you didn't do due diligence, too.*

'Oh, for goodness' sakes,' Birch said aloud, without really meaning to. Behind Alyona's door, she could hear shuffling sounds. Her informant was coming out to see who was on the doorstep.

'Listen,' Birch said, aware she sounded snappish, 'I'm sorry, John, but I'm down in Leith, meeting with an informant. I don't know how long I'll be. If Ms Crozier wants to see me, she'll have to come back another time.'

There was another brief pause: time enough for Birch to feel guilty for her crabbit tone.

'Understood,' John replied. 'I'll pass that on.'

She huffed out a breath. From the other side of the door came the sound of locks being undone. She hoped she hadn't disturbed her informant partway through a session with a punter.

'Thanks. And tell Ms Crozier she may want to phone first, next time?'

Birch hung up the call just as Alyona opened the door. Though flustered by John's news of Beatrice Crozier, Birch felt relieved to see that she clearly hadn't arrived during business hours. Alyona's hair was pulled back into a loose ponytail, and there was no make-up on her puffy face. She looked Birch up and down, and sniffed.

'Police again,' she said, her tone derisive, but a sly smile on her lips. 'Every day of my life, police.'

Birch pasted on her most winning smile. 'Hello, Alyona,' she said. 'I hope I'm not interrupting anything?'

The other woman leaned out of the door and peered around, as though checking to see if Birch had been followed.

'I was napping,' she said. 'Big booking tonight. A real high roller. I want to be fresh.'

'You look great,' Birch replied. 'And I won't take up too much of your time. I just wondered if there was any chance of a cup of tea?'

Alyona rolled her eyes, but stepped back into the hallway and beckoned with one long, blueberry-milk-coloured nail for Birch to follow her.

The flat was a chic place of business; Birch recognised its design. It would impress high-paying clients with its clean lines and sparse, tasteful décor, but it could also be packed up swiftly and abandoned at the first sign of trouble. Alyona had been a Police Scotland informant for only a handful of months, coming on board after Operation Stake. Thus far she'd had little to report, but her proximity to a handful of Edinburgh's higher-end scumbags made her a useful investment for the future. And her price was low: an unspoken agreement that Police Scotland would turn a blind eye to the work she did.

Birch leaned against the spotless worktop as Alyona clattered cupboard doors, making tea.

'Your face is looking great,' she said, offering up another warm smile. 'They're doing a brilliant job.'

Alyona lifted two fingertips to her cheek, touching the web of faint scars. When she and Birch had first met, Alyona had still been using heavy make-up to cover the acid burns an angry pimp had left on her face. The difference Birch could see in her now suggested her first round of corrective surgery had been a great success.

'The doctor is so good,' Alyona replied, and Birch saw she was blushing. 'I tell her she has magic hands.'

'I'm so glad it's working out for you,' Birch said, and meant it. Alyona handed her a steaming mug of strong, dark tea.

'Me too,' she said. 'It means more clients now, and that's good.'

Birch was unsure how to respond to this, so didn't. She took the tea and cupped it in her hands.

'You want to go through?' Alyona asked, gesturing in the direction of her spotless living room. Birch would have liked to sit down – leaning against the counter was making her bad hip ache – but she sensed a reticence in the other woman, so shook her head.

'This is fine,' she said, 'I really won't take up too much of your time.'

Alyona gave a *suit yourself* shrug. 'So,' she said.

'So,' Birch echoed. 'I've come to ask you for some help.'

'Of course. With a client of mine?'

Birch shook her head. 'Not this time. I'm working on—' Birch paused, reminding herself whose case she was about to refer to. 'Well, I'm working alone at this moment, but ... there's a case we're looking at. A missing person. A young woman.'

A look of concern crossed Alyona's face. 'Someone I know?'

'No,' Birch replied. 'Probably not. She's young, only seventeen. Vietnamese. Her name is Linh. L-I-N-H.'

Alyona was frowning, trying to place the name. 'I don't think I know her,' she said. 'She's a working girl?'

Birch couldn't help but grimace. 'In a manner of speaking,' she said. 'She's not a sex worker. She was trafficked here from Vietnam, via Europe.'

Alyona sucked her teeth, a noise of disgust, but didn't speak.

'She worked in the sex trade in Aberdeen for a while,' Birch went on, 'but then she got out. Came to live in Edinburgh. She's been in a great foster home, she's been attending school, doing well. Now, all of a sudden, she's gone missing.'

Alyona took a sip of her tea. 'Got a picture?' she asked.

Birch fumbled with her phone. Winnie had brought a Polaroid with her, that first visit to the station, and laid it on the table in front of Birch. The photo was of a sweet-looking girl with long, shiny black hair, smiling shyly at the camera. She wore a pistachio-green hoodie and a silver pendant in the shape of a cat. She looked a lot younger than seventeen. Birch had taken a photo of the Polaroid with her phone, sensing that Winnie wouldn't have been happy to part with it. Now she turned her phone screen in Alyona's direction.

Alyona leaned in to study the image. 'Poor kid,' she said. '*Varóbushik.* Just a baby.'

'I know.' Birch flipped the phone back around, glancing at Linh's smiling face again before thumbing the screen blank.

'You think she's been put back to work? Her pimp took her, maybe?'

Birch winced. 'I hope not,' she said, 'but it's possible. Or it's possible she'll end up back on the street before too long. I've come to ask if you could keep an ear to the ground for me?'

Alyona squinted at her. She didn't know this idiom.

'Ask around,' Birch explained. 'See if anyone's seen her. Any of the girls you know.'

The other woman nodded. 'You know who her pimp was? Who the man is, who might have taken her?'

Birch shook her head. 'No leads yet,' she said. 'We don't even know if she *has* been taken. But if you hear anything about a man shopping around a young Vietnamese girl, then please let me know immediately, will you?'

'I will. I've got your number.'

Birch took a long drink from her cup of tea, aware it was untouched. It was still pretty hot; her throat burned as she swallowed it. 'Call me any time,' she said, placing the mug down on the worktop. 'If you hear anything at all, even if you're not sure it's relevant. I should pick up, but if I don't, leave me a voicemail. Is that okay?'

Alyona laced her fingers around her own tea mug. 'Sure,' she said. 'Anything I hear, anything I see, I'll let you know.'

'Thanks.' Birch levered herself into a fully upright position, trying not to cringe as her bad hip complained. She reached for her stick, leaning against a nearby kitchen unit. 'That's it,' she added. 'I told you I wouldn't take long.'

Alyona smiled. 'I like you, DI Birch,' she said. 'Time is money – you understand this.'

Birch grinned, and began her slow walk back towards the front door. Alyona followed, and stood on the threshold as Birch stepped back out onto the walkway.

'These men,' Alyona said, her face suddenly pulled into a grimace, 'who traffic little girls? These *parazit*? I don't know the English, but ...' Alyona worked her jaw, and then she spat on to the frosty floor of the walkway. 'That's what I think of them.'

Birch nodded. 'We'll find her, okay? I promise.'

Alyona gave a single, short nod. 'If I can help,' she said, 'I will.'

Back on Sailmaker Road, Birch opened her phone to hail a return Uber, and was once again confronted with the photo of Linh in her green hoodie and cat necklace. *Varóbushik*, Alyona had said. *Just a baby.* Birch shivered, and flicked the photo away. Somewhere, a clock struck the hour: 2pm. Linh could be moving further from their grasp with every minute.

Nearby, someone honked a car horn, and Birch jumped.

'Hey, Helen!'

She looked up, and saw Amy Kato parked only feet away, her driver's window wound down, one arm stuck out of it, waving. Birch felt her face flush. How had Amy known where she was? Why had she come here?

'Don't book a taxi!' Amy yelled.

'I haven't!' Birch called back.

She saw her friend roll her eyes.

'Well, get over here, then! I've come to give you a lift.'

Birch pocketed her phone, leaned on her stick, and swung her good leg out on to the road. She crossed it as quickly as she could, then rounded her friend's car and opened the passenger door.

'Going maverick, are you?' Amy asked, as Birch climbed into the car. 'Why didn't you just ask me to bring you to see Alyona?'

Birch's cheeks were burning. She'd hoped she could slip away, visit her informant and get back to Fettes Avenue without anyone realising.

'I didn't think of it until after we got back to the office,' she said, hoping this wasn't too obvious a lie. 'Plus … you know, I'm not supposed to be working on this case.'

'Hey,' Amy replied, 'you'll hear no judgement from me. I doubt Crosbie would have had the nous to come and speak to Alyona. Did she give you anything?'

Birch shook her head. 'She's going to keep an eye out, though.'

'You trust her?'

Birch nodded. 'Completely. She's a good asset, and she knows a lot of people. If Linh ends up working the street anywhere in this town, Alyona will tell us.'

'Good.' Amy started the engine. 'That's also progress.'

Birch fastened her seatbelt as they pulled slowly away from the kerb. 'Also?'

Amy nodded. 'Yeah. I came to get you because Crosbie's finally picked up the ball. He's leading a briefing at half two, and I thought you might want to be there.'

Birch snorted. 'I doubt *he'll* want me to be there. But okay, that's good, I guess. Half past two is only two and a half hours late.'

Amy turned the car out on to Salamander Street. 'I mean, it's seventy-two hours late, if Linh went missing on Sunday afternoon, right?'

'Right. That was the last time Winnie saw her.'

Amy was quiet for a moment. 'What's the deal with you two, anyway?' she said then. 'You and Crosbie, I mean.

You used to get along fine, and then suddenly ... well, you know.'

'Suddenly he's a pain in my ass?' Birch laughed. 'Listen, it's complicated. I can't really talk about it. But ... Crosbie's got some stuff going on. So do I, I suppose.'

Amy shrugged. 'Who among us doesn't?'

Birch could feel her face returning to its normal colour. 'Good point,' she said, 'well made.'

They drove a little further in silence, passing at a frustrated crawl through the roadworks on Bernard Street.

'Kato,' Birch said, after a while, 'how did you know where I was?'

Amy grinned. 'You told John at reception. He told me.'

Birch shook her head. 'I only told John I was in Leith, didn't I?'

'Meeting an informant. And I thought, which informant in Leith would Helen Birch be visiting if she was worried about a missing teenage girl who used to be in the sex trade? It's not rocket science.'

Birch laughed. 'Fair enough.'

'Plus,' Amy said, 'I lucked out. I'd just pulled up there when you walked out of Alyona's block.'

'Nice timing.'

Amy made a toothy clicking sound. 'Maybe I'm psychic, too,' she said.

Birch felt a flicker of panic. Had John told Amy about Beatrice Crozier? 'What?'

The jumpy tone in her voice made Amy turn her head to glance at her. 'You're psychic. You said that earlier.'

Birch closed her eyes. *Jesus, Helen, get a grip.*

'So I did,' she said.

Amy hung a left on to Dock Street: a shortcut, Birch assumed, to avoid the lights.

'So, I looked up Kim,' Amy said, 'the girl from Lucky Seven.'

'Oh yes?'

'Yeah. Since I was forced to have lunch *on my own*.' Amy gave a theatrical hair flip. 'At my *desk*, no less.'

'Hey, I didn't force you to do that.'

Amy tutted. 'Well, anyway. I looked her up on the PNC.'

'And? Anything interesting?'

'Nothing at all at first,' Amy replied. 'But then I remembered that Vietnamese folks use different naming conventions for official documents and other formal things, even if they do things the Anglophone way informally. I had "Kim" in the first name bar and "Le" for the surname. I switched them around, and bingo.'

'What did you find?'

'A few driving records,' Amy said, 'but the dates of birth were all wrong, if Carol's correct in saying she's in her early twenties. However, there was a custody record, for one Le Thi Kim. Born in 2000, so that matches. This record is from 2009: a Mrs Le Hoa Diep took custody of nine-year-old Kim. The relationship given is "aunt".'

'You think it's her?'

Amy nodded. 'It could well be.'

'Well, if it is, we know Kim didn't come here as an unaccompanied minor, the same way Linh did. Did it say she was born in Scotland?'

Amy shook her head. 'No, no place. Just date of birth. The middle name is useful intel, though. That'll help us track down Kim's last known address.'

They passed the Leith Theatre, hitting a series of lucky green lights along Ferry Road. Birch sat quietly, watching the clock on Amy's dashboard.

'You okay, marm?' Amy asked. 'It feels like you've gone somewhere.'

Birch raised a hand and rubbed it across her forehead.

'God, Kato,' she said, 'I'm such a jerk. I'm sorry.'

Her colleague looked alarmed. 'Whatever for?'

Birch gestured out of the windscreen, towards nothing in particular. 'Well, for being … Anjan would probably say, for being a racist.' She waited for her friend to say something, but Amy only cocked her head. She was frowning. 'Maybe that's a bit strong,' Birch added, hopefully.

'I couldn't tell you,' Amy said, 'because I'm not sure what you mean.'

Birch sighed. 'Well,' she said, 'I've done two things I'm ashamed of. Firstly, I've hijacked your phone harassment case by making it all about Linh's case instead – which, actually, isn't a case yet, and even after this afternoon's briefing, it's going to be Crosbie's, not mine. Secondly – and much worse – the instant that Carol told us her missing employee was Vietnamese, I started thinking that she and Linh *had* to be connected in some way. Simply because they're from the same place. That makes as much sense as assuming two cases are connected because the victims in both have blond hair. So, I apologise. For both things. I ought to know better.'

Amy's head was still tilted over, though her eyes remained on the road. Birch felt a prickle along the back of her neck.

'You know,' Amy said, 'I think it's good that you've reflected on that. On the second part, I mean. But we already talked about that stuff after we left Lucky Seven, so you know my thoughts. The first part, though? The hijacking of my case? I can't say I'm mad about that. In fact, I feel quite relieved.'

Birch raised an eyebrow. 'That's not what I was expecting you to say.'

Amy smiled as she made the left on to East Fettes Avenue. 'I know,' she said. 'But ... earlier, when we were talking to Carol? I started to hear all the cogs in your policework brain start to turn. I could *see* that all of a sudden, something clicked, and you were racing off in your mind to think about all the possible scenarios, to try and join all the dots. And do you know what I thought in that moment?'

Birch shook her head.

'I thought,' Amy said, '"Thank goodness, she's back." That exact phrase.'

The hot prickle at the back of Birch's neck began to creep up towards her face. '"Thank goodness she's back"?' she repeated. 'It wasn't more like, "Oh bloody hell, she's off on one again"?'

Amy immediately shook her head. 'Not at all,' she said. 'I've been a bit worried about you, you know. Ever since Operation Stake. That night, when you ...' Amy trailed off.

'... Rode in all guns blazing, like a total idiot?' Birch suggested.

'No,' Amy said. She brought the car to a halt, waiting to turn right on to Inverleith Place. 'Wait, I'm trying to find the right words. That night, when Operation Stake ... came to a head, I suppose is the correct term. I think that's the last time you were really *on it*, you know? You were doing that brilliant Helen Birch thing that you do – follow the hunch first, ask questions later. And you were spot-on, though everyone else doubted you.'

Birch held up her index finger, to show she needed to add something. 'Except my dad,' she said.

Amy gave one long nod, and made the turn. 'Except your dad,' she said, 'of course. Thank goodness for him, otherwise you'd have been all alone that night, and who knows what might have happened to you.'

Birch reached out and touched the handle of her walking stick. It represented her ongoing recovery from that night, when she'd found herself alone, off radio, and cornered by a perp. Had her father not been keeping tabs on her … She shivered. It didn't bear thinking about.

'But what I'm getting at,' Amy was saying, 'is the fact that, that night, you were on top of your game, policing wise. You'd figured it all out, and the rest of us were useless. But since then … well, to be honest, it's felt a bit like you've locked your police brain away in some sort of Pandora's box, and you don't dare open it again.'

Birch felt something touch her right temple. She was surprised to find it was her own hand, touching her head as though checking it was indeed still attached to her body. 'No offence to her,' she said, 'but I've been in therapy for six months, and Dr Jane has yet to say anything to me that's hit the nail on the head quite like that.'

Amy flipped her hair. She wasn't preening, but Birch could tell she was pleased that her read of the situation was correct. 'I've known you a long time, Helen,' she said. 'Longer than Dr Jane has. But my main point is that earlier, talking to Carol, I saw a bit of that Birch spark coming back, and I was pleased.'

Birch tried to scoff, but Amy's face was serious as she made the final turn and steered the car into the boxy shadow of the Fettes Avenue campus.

'I mean it, marm,' she said. 'We've missed you round here.'

The prickling sensation that had been spreading over Birch's face had now become a full-on blush. 'Well,' she spluttered, 'that's very kind. To be honest, I actually felt a bit of something coming back to life myself, earlier. I was thinking I'd tell Dr Jane that for the first time in ages, I actually felt—'

Amy pulled into the car park. 'Yourself?'

Birch nodded as the car came to a halt. 'I was going to say *useful*,' she replied. 'But yes – that, too.'

Amy delivered Birch as far as the doors of the briefing room Crosbie had booked.

'You going in?' she asked.

'I probably shouldn't. Like I say, I'm probably not wanted.'

Amy snorted. 'Do you *want* to go in?'

Birch tried not to let her face give her away. *Of course I do*, she thought. *This should have been my case, not his.*

'Sure,' she said.

Amy gave her a nudge. 'Then do it,' she said. 'If I may be permitted to psychoanalyse you a little more, marm, it feels like you've been trying to fight the fact that this particular case is personal to you. First off, it's a fight you're losing, if you don't mind my saying. And secondly, taking things personally isn't always a bad thing. You know who taught me that?'

Birch didn't. 'Who?' she asked.

'You,' Amy replied. 'You did, with Operation Citrine, when in spite of everything, you helped put Charlie away. That case was intensely personal for you, but you went ahead and did your job nevertheless.'

Birch allowed her mind to drift back to the precious five minutes she'd spent with Charlie in the holding cell after they brought him in. He'd been missing fourteen years – living invisible in a criminal underworld – and McLeod had given her only five minutes to talk to him before he was formally charged. The final five minutes where he was still just her little brother.

'It's never been your style,' Amy was saying, 'to let a personal connection get in the way of good policework. I don't see why you should start now.'

Birch thought of Winnie Fortune, and her decision to seek out Birch in person. Winnie had wanted her running the case.

'True,' she replied. 'You're right. And besides, there's no harm in me sitting in. I'd just be spending my afternoon pushing paper around my bloody desk, otherwise.'

Amy smiled. 'Exactly,' she said. 'Annoying Crosbie is a much better use of your time.'

Birch grinned. 'How about you?' she asked. 'Are you following up on our mysterious phone man?'

Amy nodded. 'Yeah,' she said. 'My feeling is, now that we have a few more details on Kim, the most obvious next step is to track her down, and see if she can tell us who the harassing guy is. It might be possible to wrap this up in about half an hour, in the event that she says, "Oh yeah, that's my pain-in-the-ass ex-boyfriend, sorry about him."'

'That's if Carol and the salon folk decide not to press charges.'

Amy made a 'Hmm' sound. 'We'll see,' she said. 'I'll look up Kim on the electoral register, see if she really has moved away from the address she gave to Carol. Fingers crossed I can track her down, have a chat, and put a stop to this thing.'

Birch threw her a fake smile. 'Wouldn't that be nice, eh?'

Amy tutted at her friend. 'Listen,' she said, 'it does happen, you know. Sometimes things *are* just straightforward.'

Thanks to her bad leg, it was tricky for Birch to enter a room unnoticed, but this meant she felt the small, unkind thrill that came with seeing Crosbie's face fall as she shuffled into the briefing room. Amy had driven back from Leith as fast as she could, but nevertheless, Birch was ever so slightly late. As she ducked into a free chair near the back, Crosbie cleared his throat in a pointed sort of way, and for a moment she thought he might be about to stop the briefing and tell her to get out. But of course he carried on, positioning his gaze on a spot somewhere just above her head, and never looking directly at her.

'So,' he said, 'as I'm sure you're all realising, there are a lot of mitigating factors at play in this particular disappearance.'

Birch looked around at the small team Crosbie had put together. Apart from Rema, she didn't think anyone in the room could be counted among the force's best and brightest. Crosbie had not prioritised this case; he clearly felt his better officers had more important things to be working on.

'We have very little to go on,' he was saying, 'beyond Linh's personal history. According to Mrs Fortune, there's no boyfriend in the picture. No hangers-on, either – no male attention of any kind. But of course, that's only as far as we *know*. You don't need me to tell you that nine times out of ten, when a teenage girl goes missing, there's a boyfriend or ex-boyfriend or unsuitable older man wrapped up in it somewhere. So let's keep that particular avenue open. I don't just want to take Mrs Fortune's word for it – let's be talking to Linh's school friends. Let's be having a look at her social media activity. If there's even the slightest suggestion that there's a boy on the scene, we need to speak to that boy as a matter of priority.'

There was a general nodding of heads around the room.

'I also think we need to explore,' Crosbie went on, 'the possibility that Linh has decided to disappear her*self*, in order to avoid being processed through the asylum system. Now, I'm not saying this is definitely what's happened, but I *am* saying …'

He trailed off. For a fleeting second, he met Birch's eye.

'Occam's razor,' he said, flicking his gaze away. 'I trust you're all familiar with the concept.'

It was all Birch could do to keep from snort-laughing. A couple of seats away, she saw a young constable open Google on his phone and type in *ockham's razor*.

'If Linh *has* decided she needs to disappear,' Crosbie was saying, 'then she will – if she's smart – have done some ground work first. Maybe she's been on the lookout for a cash-in-hand job, for example. Maybe she's been talking to our local working girls. She has been on the game before, so she knows she could make money that way.'

Birch closed her eyes, as though doing so might block out the things Crosbie was saying. He was talking about Linh as though she were a grown woman – as though she were a criminal, almost. Birch felt like raising her hand to point out that Linh had been fifteen – perhaps younger – when she'd been forced into the sex trade. But there was no point interrupting. The information was in Crosbie's notes. He knew.

'That means it's time to check in with our friendly local toms,' Crosbie went on, 'see if there's any talk of a new girl on the block.'

Birch wondered if Crosbie was being extra abrasive because she was there. He must have known she was itching to challenge him over his language. Again, she considered butting in and doing it, but she stopped herself. She hadn't challenged McLeod the other night, either. She wasn't entirely sure what was stopping her, but it made her feel sick and weak. She made a mental note to talk to Dr Jane about it.

The young PC who'd been searching Google raised his hand, and Birch felt a stab of hope. Had he read her mind? Was *he* going to challenge Crosbie, so she didn't have to?

'Yes,' Crosbie said, gesturing towards him. 'PC Howard.'

The constable cleared his throat. 'So,' he said, 'I was wondering. If she's a runaway, how likely is it that she's left the City of Edinburgh? Is there anywhere further afield we think she might head to? And does she have the resources to get there?'

'All good questions,' Crosbie replied. 'We know she's spent some time in Aberdeen, though Mrs Fortune seems adamant that Linh wouldn't return there. I'm told she doesn't have a bank account, but does receive a weekly allowance which is overseen by Mrs Fortune. That's given to her in cash, so it's possible she's been saving up a little fuck-off fund.'

For a moment, Birch allowed herself to entertain the possibility that what Crosbie was describing might be true. Linh was seventeen, after all – seventeen-year-olds weren't stupid. They could definitely be manipulative. Perhaps it was possible that Linh had led Winnie to believe she was a sweet, studious kid who loved school and her friends and her cat, when in fact she was hoarding her pocket money and planning to disappear into the black economy at the earliest possible opportunity. But no: Birch couldn't make the idea stick. Winnie Fortune had been taking care of teenagers for decades. There wasn't a kid on the planet who could pull the wool over her eyes. Crosbie was presenting the scenario he hoped was true; if Linh really had disappeared to avoid the asylum system, then she'd fit neatly into his narrative, and make his life a lot easier. He and his team could exhaust the avenues he'd listed thus far and, finding nothing, shrug it off, write up their reports, and move on to the next case. They'd have looked for her. They'd have done their jobs. But, they'd lament, you can't find a person who's determined to stay lost. *Whit a wee shame, onyway lads, whose round is it?*

Birch realised she was shaking her head. She could see it happening, right there, in front of her.

'Something wrong, DI Birch?'

A few heads flicked round. Crosbie was looking at her, waiting for her to answer. She was still shaking her head.

Yeah, she wanted to say, *you're an arsehole.* Instead, she found herself rising from her seat, biting her bottom lip to prevent the words from sliding out of her mouth.

'Sorry,' she said, feeling around for her stick. 'I just realised, I—' She paused. She had been going to say, *I just realised I need to be somewhere else,* but where else could she possibly need to be? In her office, completing out-of-date risk assessments?

'I just stepped in for a moment,' she said. 'But I don't think I'm needed here.'

Crosbie threw her a nasty smile, and Birch wanted to yell at him, right there, in front of the entire team, that it wasn't her fault she'd found out about his drinking – it was his. She wanted to point out that she'd carried his secret faithfully. As far as she was aware, only she and McLeod knew, and no one else had the faintest inkling. She hadn't even told Amy, earlier, when her friend had asked outright to know what was going on. Birch didn't always agree with Crosbie – indeed, if she was honest, she rarely did – but she respected him too much to turn the knowledge she held about his personal life into gossip.

Birch realised that she'd been standing there, leaning on her stick, for just a little too long.

'I have no doubt,' Crosbie said, his voice smooth as oil, 'that you have more important things to be doing.'

You shit, she thought. *You know full well that I don't.* But she simply nodded, and turned her back on Crosbie and his assembled team. The room was a weird, held breath: the whole group waiting for her to leave before they resumed the business of the briefing. As she reached the door and pushed it open, Birch felt a wave of tiredness so strong that it almost knocked her over. She realised she'd walked out because she'd had enough. She'd simply had enough.

Bee, 2000

I'd wanted to move closer to work, but couldn't afford the New Town. I feared the debatable lands of Dalry and Gorgie – I was leery, as a young woman alone, of the football fans who regularly streamed up and down the thoroughfare between Haymarket and Tynecastle Stadium. Corstorphine felt like a different world, a separate place that wasn't quite part of the city. And besides, I was no longer sure about my little corner of the warehouse, where I worked largely ignored and certainly never promoted. In the end, I didn't move far from the family home, settling on an attic bedsit on the corner of Spottiswoode Street and Warrender Park Road. Not far, but far enough. I no longer knew the contents of Tommy's bedside drawer.

The bedsit was at the very top of a tenement, its ceiling so steeply pitched that I could only stand up straight in the dead centre of the room. The landlady who showed me around had curlers in her hair and a liver-and-white spaniel who ran riot through the building as we talked. There was a single bed tucked under the eaves, and along the back wall ran a couple of metres of countertop with a sink, a microwave, and an electric two-ring burner that I knew would smell of singe whenever I plugged it in. The shared bathroom was outside on the landing, its shower cubicle leaning slant and patched with duct tape. A voice in my head said *Take it*, so I took it without any further thought. It was cheap, and quiet. My thoughts could settle here. I even wondered – naively, I realise now – if the Knowing would subside and leave me be now I'd come to be alone.

I didn't hate it, but it tired me out, navigating a world where people saw me as a stranger, while I parsed the intimate details of their lives from a look, a touch, a brush in the street. I often wondered how it would feel to 'fess up to my gift – or curse – and tell the people I encountered all the things I knew. I imagined myself booking a Saturday off and walking the length of Princes Street, passing between the throngs of shoppers, listening for the signals they gave off. I imagined stopping each person about whom something was revealed to me. *Hi, you don't know me, but I know that your best friend Stephanie's baby wasn't fathered by her husband, but by yours. Hi, I'm Beatrice, please go back to the doctor as soon as you can. Hi, you should leave, and take the kids, because it's only going to get worse. Hi, your house is on fire. Hi, someone you love is dying. Hi, I'm Beatrice. I know it hurts. I know you want it so badly. I know you miss her. I know you're hopeful in spite of it all. Hi. I know. Because I know.*

I imagined it might feel cathartic. I imagined I might get arrested, carted off to some facility. I imagined I might get beaten up, or followed home, or clung to, begged for more information, begged to be told it wasn't true, *Take it back, please*. I imagined it often and knew I'd never act on it.

The millennium approached, and I itched for change. Nights, after work in my bedsit on Spottiswoode Street, I made pasta or noodle dinners on the two-ring burner and watched my tiny black-and-white TV. It was 1999, a boom time for celebrity psychics; they were wheeled out for every panel and talk show and even, sometimes, for the news. What were their predictions for the new millennium? What would happen when all the world's clocks ticked over to the year

2000? Was the Millennium Bug real? Were the evangelicals correct? Would planes fall from the sky? Would Jesus come back? Would the Four Horsemen of the Apocalypse ride through the streets? Someone, somewhere had decided that viewers couldn't get enough of this stuff.

The only part of it I enjoyed was spotting the real psychics. They were few and far between; most of the 'gifted' were, I could tell, charlatans chasing after their fifteen minutes.

'Within the first ten years of the new millennium,' one woman said, 'we'll have the cure for cancer. I believe that all cancer will be eliminated by the year 2025.'

I rolled my eyes. She was a white woman wearing a turban and a bindi on her forehead. Her cheekbones glittered under the studio lights with mauve iridescent powder, like the wings of a beetle. I was embarrassed for her, and angry with her. She was wrong, but people would believe her; people who were sick, or who loved people who were sick, would take hope from her words, and that hope would be dashed. Then they'd hate her, and they'd most likely come to hate all psychics. This was the reason I couldn't ever tell anyone about the Knowing. Because of people like her.

But very occasionally, there'd be a late-night talk show with one quiet woman or man who'd predict something I immediately knew to be true.

'There's going to be a war,' one man said. His hair was grey, and he wore a beige shirt and a striped red tie that bled on camera. He looked more like a car salesman than a TV psychic. 'Within the next five years,' he went on, 'we're going to be at war. And it's going to be the most terrible mistake.'

My stomach flipped. If I closed my eyes, I could see my father sitting in front of the TV that evening my mother came home and I knew she was having an affair. I could see the footage he'd been watching that night, and in the weeks that followed: fuzzy night-time shots of desert cities far away, endless tracer rounds from anti-aircraft fire streaking between tower blocks, eerie in night-vision green. Except it wasn't that same footage, but new footage. The man in the bleeding tie was correct: the same thing was going to happen all over again, and once again we'd learn nothing, achieve nothing.

I handed in my notice at the warehouse, and my colleagues clubbed together to buy a sheet cake with the words 'Best of Luck, Beatrice!' piped on the top in bright pink icing. We all went out for a drink in the Haymarket pub; it was nearly Christmas, and the bar was decked out with tinsel and fairy lights. The stereo played Will Smith's 'Will2K' and 'Caught Out There' by Kelis. Everyone was talking about the Millennium Bug and the havoc it might wreak in just a couple of weeks' time. Eric the foreman said he'd been stockpiling watercooler bottles in his garage in case the mains water went off; if it did, he said, there could be looting, riots, martial law. I imagined myself stranded high in the tenement eaves on Spottiswoode Street as tanks rolled over the cobbles below, and I kept quiet. I didn't believe in the Millennium Bug, but I felt a nagging sense of unease I couldn't fully ignore. Something *was* coming, the Knowing told me – something big. I didn't know what, yet, but the worry of it grew in me like a persistent weed.

That worry kept me from going out on New Year's Eve, though I'd been invited. Tommy was at uni by then, finishing up an engineering degree and making our mother proud – at last – in the process. Always a social butterfly, I think he felt sorry for his lonely, attic-dwelling spinster of a sister, and he sometimes invited me out to the bars where he and his dreadfully young-seeming friends would argue about politics with a fervour that exhausted me. They seemed to believe that by talking enough, they might actually change the world. I joined them occasionally, but not often, and decided very quickly that an evening of drinking and discussing George W. Bush was not the way I wanted to spend my last night of the old millennium.

Also not high on my list of ideal New Year's Eve celebrations was going round to my parents' for dinner, but that was what I ended up doing, following a long and increasingly obvious campaign of emotional blackmail on my mother's part. My parents had never been great celebrators of Hogmanay, but this year, my mother pointed out, as though no one else had noticed, was special. The occasion needed to be marked. As the day approached, I had no better offers and very little food in the house. The sense of something impending – something big, and most likely bad – now felt a millstone I was carrying around. If the apocalypse was arriving with the chimes of midnight, then I guessed it made sense to be with the people I loved most in the world. The fact that those people were my parents – that after almost thirty years on the planet, they were the best I had – did not fill me with joy. I needed to do something about my life. If we survived, I pledged, I'd fix it. I'd change things. I'd do something radical. The Knowing felt like a small voice in my head, mocking me. *No you won't,* it said, *and what's more, you know it.*

Even though only days ago she'd made Christmas dinner with all the trimmings, my mother pulled out all the stops that Hogmanay. She'd moved into what she called the 'maintenance phase' of her most recent diet, which meant she'd stopped eating only grapefruit or drinking only powdered shakes, and was attempting to eat like an actual human animal once again. Every time she did this, she'd immediately regain all the weight she'd lost in the starvation phase, and usually more. That evening, registering her face at the front door and handing over the obligatory bottle of white wine, I thought she looked the best she had in years. Her hair was shiny, and when she smiled, there was pink in her cheeks.

'Don't look at me,' she said, as I hugged her. 'I'm becoming so monstrously fat again.'

'Mum. You're, what? A size fourteen?'

She snorted at me. 'A Marks and Spencer's fourteen,' she said, 'maybe, if I'm lucky. But anywhere else I'm a sixteen, and you know what that means.'

It meant she thought she was a failure. I felt a pang of something for this woman I'd lived with for over two decades, but whom I'd never seen happy. I think it was sadness, but it was tinged with a slippery anger I couldn't quite get a handle on.

She fussed around me as I took off my winter coat and gave it to her to hang up. I slipped off my boots and scuffed along the familiar, carpeted path to the dining room. My father must have been upstairs; I could hear the floorboards overhead shifting as he moved around.

'We're almost there,' my mother said, slipping past me into the kitchen. I watched her as she stood in the doorway, tying on the apron she'd removed to answer the door. 'I've made salmon en croûte. Your father wanted beef, but I find it a little heavy for an evening meal.' She brandished the white wine I'd handed her. 'This will be perfect,' she said, and disappeared from view.

I stood clasping the back of a dining chair with both hands, looking around at what had always been the family meeting room, the place where we gathered to eat and talk and argue and sulk and celebrate. I'd laboured over homework at this dining table; I'd watched my mother sew the cushion cover or plate bag or skirt zip I'd been supposed to make myself for home ec class; I'd flicked food at Tommy and been sent to my room. I'd laid my head on this dining table's polished surface – breathing in the smell of Mr Sheen – and cried. I felt like I could do it again, right then, at 7.30pm on Hogmanay, in the final hours of the old millennium.

'Do me a favour,' my mother called through from the kitchen, 'would you, Beatrice? Go to the bottom of the stairs and shout for your father. We'll eat in five minutes.'

I padded back into the hallway in my stockinged feet. I paused halfway to look at the large framed photo of my parents' wedding day. My mother was almost unrecognisable, her beaming smile pulling focus in spite of the strange netted fascinator she'd chosen to wear in place of a veil. My father had filled out since, and his hair had greyed, but he was otherwise identical to the sombre-looking man in the picture who was leaning, just ever so slightly, towards his mother, who stood on his right-hand side. She was a neat woman in a twill skirt suit and a small, serious hat, her mouth ever so slightly open, as though she'd just whispered something to him, her only son. She'd died before I was born, suddenly, of bowel cancer she'd suspected was there but never told anyone about because the symptoms caused her too much shame. Looking at that photo then, more closely than I ever had before, I knew she'd disapproved of my mother. Not because of the Knowing – it was simply written all over my grandmother's face.

It took a moment to dawn on me. I walked the rest of the length of the hall – maybe six more steps, in total – and with each one the knowledge crystalised in my mind a little more. As I arrived at the bottom of my parents' carpeted staircase, I saw it in full: the thing I'd been worried about for the last few weeks, the thing I'd known was coming but couldn't yet make out. It wasn't the Millennium Bug, and it wasn't the end of the world – at least, not for anyone other than me, perhaps, and my mother, and Tommy. My knees gave way, and I hugged the newel post to hold myself up.

Bowel cancer. My father had it, too. Had it, or would soon have it, and it would be the thing that killed him. I stood looking up to where the stairs made their turn, the wallpaper's pattern swimming in front of my vision. I listened to my father – the strong, stubborn, belligerent father I'd never really loved – moving around in my parents' room. He was going to die, and I knew it. Could my knowledge stop it, or slow it down? I didn't know. I let go of the newel post and dropped to my knees on the bottom step of the stairs. My eyes were dry, but a bubble of panic seemed to be filling my chest. I was going to have to tell him, the person whose judgement I feared the most, about the Knowing.

'Beatrice,' my mother trilled, 'have you shouted your father?'

I pressed my palms into the stair carpet, leaning forward so hard that when I lifted my hands, the heels of them were pocked with tiny acrylic whorl marks.

'Dad,' I croaked, but my voice was barely a whisper. I coughed, and pushed myself back up on to my feet. Once again, I leaned on the newel post, not sure I could stand with the weight of the thing I now knew.

'Daddy,' I called, in a voice that cracked the word down its centre, 'can you come down? We need you.'

'Beatrice, you're worrying me. Do you think perhaps you need to see a doctor?'

I sighed. Across the table, my mother's fork hovered over her slab of salmon en croûte. 'No, Dad. I'm saying *you* do.'

I'd told them as soon as they'd sat down at the table. I was amazed I'd managed to hold it in long enough for my mother to serve out the various vegetables, one spoonful at a time. As I'd talked, my father's expression had slowly changed from one of annoyance to one of concern.

'Listen,' he said. 'Your mother and I, we realise you're having a difficult time lately.'

I blinked. This was news to me. 'I am?'

'Well.' They exchanged a glance that told me I'd been the topic of conversation in the house for some time. 'You've left your job, you don't yet have another, and—'

'I have savings, Dad. And I'm applying for things. Something will come up in the New Year.' I knew it would, because I knew. It was thanks to the Knowing that I'd felt confident in my decision to quit the warehouse job. 'I'm not in any sort of trouble.'

'Okay,' he replied. 'But … you live an unusual sort of life, Beatrice, you have to admit. We can't help but feel that … Well, we worry that you're maybe not very happy.'

I felt bewildered. I'd just dropped the bombshell that my father had cancer – cancer I believed would turn out to be terminal – and thrown in for good measure the fact that I knew this because I was, to use the hated term, psychic. I wasn't sure what response I'd expected, but it wasn't a talking-to about the fact I hadn't ever come close to getting married, which was what my father was getting at. I wondered if perhaps that had been the pretext for this Hogmanay dinner all along. *We really ought to get Beatrice round so we can sit her down and ask her when she's going to find a nice man to settle down with.*

'Dad, did you hear what I said? I think you're sick. No – I *know* you're sick. Isn't that what we ought to be talking about?'

My mother was unusually quiet. It was beginning to unnerve me.

'I feel fine,' my father snapped. 'What we ought to be talking about is what's happening to you. What's making you say these things.'

'The fact that I know them,' I said. 'The fact that they're going to come true! I'm trying to help—'

'There's nothing helpful,' my father cut in, 'about coming here and ruining the Hogmanay dinner your mother has worked so hard to cook for you.' He gestured at my mother's face. 'Look, you've upset her. And you've upset me.'

I didn't think my mother looked upset. If anything, she looked thoughtful.

I placed my hands palm down on the table on either side of my plate. 'Look,' I said, trying another tack, 'I know what I'm saying is very hard to hear. I know it makes me sound insane. But I promise you, I'm not insane. I know things. I know you have cancer, Dad.'

He snorted. 'How do you know?'

'Because I know.'

'That isn't an answer.'

My mother finally let go of the fork she'd been holding aloft since I'd begun speaking. It clattered on to the edge of her dinner plate, then fell on to the floor. I felt my father jump. I did, too. We both turned and looked at her.

'It's true,' she said, 'that Beatrice has always … known things.'

'Sheila.' My father's voice was a blade.

'But she has. Remember the ghost, at Mount Pleasant?'

My eyes widened. Mount Pleasant was the house where Fraser had appeared at night to tuck me in. I was amazed to find my mother remembered him.

'There *was* no ghost at Mount Pleasant,' my father said, a little too quickly. 'We went over this at the time.'

My mother was frowning. 'Well,' she said, 'what about that day when Tommy was a baby?'

My father closed his eyes. He knew what she was referring to, but I didn't.

'What day?' I asked.

My mother looked at me. 'You don't remember? It was at Mount Pleasant, before we moved, when Tommy was still very little. I was in the back kitchen, doing the ironing, and you were playing in the garden while I watched you. Tommy was down for his nap – I'd left him sleeping completely soundly in his cot.'

'Sheila,' my father said again. My mother ignored him.

'All of a sudden,' she said, 'you came to a total stop, stock-still. You looked like you'd been hit by lightning. And then you came running inside, shouting, "Mama, Tommy's hurt, Tommy's hurt."'

I could feel my eyes widening. I had absolutely no memory of the day she was describing.

'I told you,' my mother was saying, 'that everything was fine, and Tommy was asleep in his cot. But you insisted he was hurt. Eventually I agreed to go upstairs with you and look in the cot.'

My father was shaking his head. He was angry now, I could see that.

'His face was grey,' my mother said. 'He'd stopped breathing. They say babies can do that – they hold their breath, and then it makes them faint. I think that was what had happened; there was no other way to explain it.'

I realised I was holding my own breath, listening. 'What did you do?' I asked.

'Well,' my mother said, 'it gave me such a scare, seeing him that colour. I scooped him up and just … well, shoogled him around, really, and said his name over and over. It must have done something, because he came round.'

'Thank god,' I whispered.

My mother shook her head. 'Well, no,' she said, 'it was thanks to *you*. I'd never have known – how *would* I have known? But you knew.'

My father held out his hand towards her. 'Sheila,' he said, a third time.

'She *did* know,' my mother insisted. 'She did.' She turned to look at me again. 'I walked you and Tommy over to the Royal,' she went on, 'after it happened. I wanted to get him checked out. The doctor said it was very lucky I found him when I did. Had he been left like that for too long, he'd have had brain damage.' Her eyes were damp now. 'You saved your baby brother's life,' she said.

My father brought his hand down, hard, on the table, making the cutlery rattle. My mother let out a small, strangled sound.

'*Enough* of this nonsense,' he said. He glared at my mother. 'Stop encouraging her! You've always encouraged her.'

I rolled my eyes, feeling like a bratty teen but doing it anyway. 'Oh yes,' I said. 'God forbid I ever be encouraged in doing anything.'

My father rose from the table, unlocking a memory from when I was small. He used to do that when I was misbehaving: stand, and draw himself up to his full height in order to tower over me. It had been an intimidation tactic – but now when I looked at him, I saw a man shrinking into himself, growing smaller. I realised for the first time that my father no longer frightened me.

Now he was standing next to my chair.

'Do not cheek me, Beatrice,' he said, his voice low. 'I warn you.'

I stood up, so we were eye to eye.

'Ted,' my mother murmured, 'please.'

I wasn't scared. I put my face close to his. 'All my life,' I said, 'you've ignored me. You've stopped listening whenever I've started speaking. You've sat behind your newspaper and ignored your way through my entire life so far. But you are *not* going to ignore this.' I realised my voice was rising, but I couldn't stop it. 'I don't care if you believe in the Knowing I have. I don't care if you think I'm mentally ill. I don't care what you think of me at all, Dad – I've given up trying to win your approval, because it's clearly never going to happen.' I was shouting now. 'But you are *not* going to ignore me when I tell you you're sick. You have cancer, and if you ignore it, then you *are* going to die.'

He hit me then, square in the face. A hard, open-palmed slap. I reeled. My father had never liked me, often belittled me, sometimes raged at me, and generally just tuned me out – but he hadn't raised a hand to me in twenty years.

My mother screamed. Though everything was happening very fast, I still managed to register her response as annoying. It had always bothered me when men started fighting in films and the women around them would respond by screaming. I didn't think it was a thing people did in real life.

The slap had buckled me sideways, and I found myself leaning over with one elbow on the dining table. My father wasn't sticking around to find out what happened next; he was already walking across the room towards the door. Storming out had been another of his specialities when I was a kid. He didn't like to give anyone the right to reply.

I didn't think; I was too angry. My face stung where he'd hit me. There was an empty side plate next to my bent elbow. I grabbed it, straightened up, and before I had a chance to stop myself, hurled it at my father's retreating back. It shattered against the doorframe, only inches from his ear. My mother wailed.

He spun around. 'You little bitch,' he said, and I almost laughed. His tone of voice was so matter-of-fact.

'Let me tell you,' I said, 'all the things I know.' I felt like my heart was boiling in my ribcage, but my voice was so calm that it frightened me. It frightened him, too – I could see it in his face. He didn't believe that I knew things, but he also didn't want to hear them.

'I know,' I said, 'that you only married Mum because you got her pregnant. I know that when the two of you were young, she loved you *so much*, she'd have done anything for you. And you were ambivalent, weren't you? Happy to go along with it, because you were getting your leg over, but otherwise ...'

I glanced at my mother, expecting her to look upset, but to my surprise, I saw she was nodding. I was saying things she'd figured out for herself, long ago.

'But then you fucked up, didn't you, Dad? You got her pregnant. And then you had to get serious.'

Still standing in the doorway, my father scoffed. 'This isn't impressive,' he said. He waved an arm vaguely in my mother's direction. 'This isn't stuff you mysteriously *know*, Beatrice. This is stuff *she's* told you.'

The way he said *she*, with such derision, made me want to throw something else at him. I wanted to throw the candlesticks, the silverware, my mother's precious serving plates, the whole damn dining table at my stupid, pig-headed father.

'Would she have told me,' I said, 'about the conversation you had with your mother, the night before the wedding?'

His face froze. In my peripheral vision, I saw my mother cock her head to one side. This was news to her.

'You begged her, didn't you, you cowardly shit? You begged her to let you run away, go overseas, go anywhere. You were going to leave my mother at the altar, weren't you? And me, too – tiny and unborn as I was. You were going to leave us both.'

'Nonsense,' he said.

I glared at him. 'Is it, though?' I asked. 'Is it nonsense? Or did Grandma Eileen tell you that you'd got yourself into this mess, and – as much as she also hated it – you had to stick around and deal with it? Even Grandma Eileen – a miserable, bitter old woman who only cared about herself and you – even *she* thought it would have been wrong for you to run out on us. Isn't that right?'

He was looking at my mother now, shaking his head.

'Sheila, she's making this up,' he said. His voice shuddered slightly on the final syllable. 'She's lying. She's always been a liar.'

My mother was looking at me. Her face – usually such an open wound of a face – was inscrutable. She seemed to be studying me, weighing something up.

'You always say that,' she replied, after a pause, her gaze still fixed on me. 'All her life you've said that – Beatrice is a liar, Beatrice makes up tales, Beatrice has a vivid imagination. You've said it so many times that I came to believe it. But do you know …'

She trailed off, and finally turned her head to look at him. His face was red. I could tell he was impatient, waiting for her to finish speaking so he could bluster some more.

'I'm just now realising,' she went on, 'that in almost thirty years, I've never, ever seen evidence that our child is a liar. Not even once.'

I held my breath. I tried not to think about all the times I *had* lied to her, the way that kids do: little lies, like the day of Martin and the pavilion, when I'd explained away my detention to her. But in that moment, I realised that the main lie I'd told – not just to her, but to everyone in my life – was a lie of omission. I'd never told them all the things I knew, and this was why. This moment. The devastation it was causing.

'Sheila,' my father said.

My mother blinked, a slow, deliberate blink, like a reptile. 'I believe her,' she said, quietly. 'I believe that you probably did have that conversation with your mother.'

My father threw up his hands, a *that's ridiculous* gesture.

'I believe,' my mother went on, 'that you wanted to leave us. You've never wanted us, have you, Edward?'

My father looked at me. 'Do you see what you've done?' he demanded. I shrugged.

'It took me a while to realise it,' my mother was saying. 'Took me maybe six years or so. Beatrice is right: I loved you so dearly when we met. I *would* have done anything for you. I'd have died for you. And when we got married, I was so happy, because I thought it meant something.' She rose from the table, knocking her chair over backwards in the process. It thudded on the carpet, making me jump. 'But after we had Beatrice, I started to realise that you hated it. All of it. Me, her, fatherhood. That bloody falling-down house at Mount Pleasant. All that crashing around and swearing you did. You were just livid with yourself, weren't you? Livid at the trap you'd set, and then fallen into.'

I could see patterns starting to swim in front of my eyes, unaware I'd been holding my breath. I realised that my whole family had spent the last twenty-nine years setting up emotional dominoes, each of us carefully placing them so that eventually, at precisely the right moment, they'd all topple in a beautiful, terrible, unstoppable cascade.

'Then I got pregnant again,' my mother said. 'And when it was a boy, I was so relieved. I thought, "Thank God, this will fix it." I gave you a son. I did my job. But even that didn't make you happy, did it?'

At this, my father began shaking his head, slowly at first, and then more vigorously.

'No,' I said, speaking for him. 'That's not quite true, is it, Dad? You do love Tommy.'

To my surprise, I saw his eyes were suddenly damp. He paused. 'I love all of you,' he said, and his voice was a croak. 'In my way.'

My mother snorted. 'In your *way*?'

I swallowed hard. I hadn't quite understood the extent of the pent-up anger my mother had been carrying around, unaddressed. I had been naive.

'Well,' she said. The single word hung in the air like the chime of a dreadful bell. She looked at me, and there was a question in her eyes. I knew what it was – because I knew – without her having to ask.

'Mum,' I said, 'you don't need my permission.'

She blinked. I could see, in that split second, that I'd convinced her. She believed me, about the Knowing. I saw any remaining doubt fall away from her face.

'As we're telling home truths,' she said, turning back to my father, 'here's one for you. I tried to leave you, once. In the end, I couldn't do it, but it wasn't because I didn't want to. And I was mad as hell that it didn't work out, let me tell you.'

My father's face was pale.

'When?' he asked.

I spoke before she could. 'In 1991,' I replied. 'It started the first night of Operation Desert Storm. I remember, because I was at home with you, listening to you shout at the TV. Mum went out to dinner with another man. She thought he was going to save her from you.'

I was looking at my father, but out of the corner of my eye, I saw my mother's mouth fall open.

'Sheila?' my father said.

She simply nodded.

'You told her about this?' he asked.

I shook my head. 'No, Dad,' I replied. 'Like I've been trying to tell you: I know things. I just know things.'

It was as if I hadn't spoken.

'Who was he?'

My mother's face was stony. She was quiet again, and again I could sense her weighing something up. 'It doesn't matter,' she said, after what felt like a long silence. 'Ted, I want a divorce.'

Birch, Wednesday 12 January

Birch stumbled out of the building, still too angry with Crosbie to really think straight. The physio team had encouraged her to walk short distances – like the distance between Dr Jane's consulting room and work, or the distance between Manderston Street and the Lucky Seven Parlour – but getting to and from home each day would have been too far for even her pre-gunshot, unencumbered self to commute on foot. For perhaps the first time in her life, she wished she could walk that distance now. It was five miles, give or take, and might, in the past, have taken her two hours. Such a long walk home would have given her plenty of time to stew over Crosbie, over Winnie and Linh, over McLeod, over the relentless dream of the whole damn edifice that was Police Scotland being flooded out and washed away. Instead, she contemplated summoning another Uber – she'd become reliant on them lately – but decided against it. She was spending too much on transport, and besides, she didn't think she could stand to risk having to make polite small talk with a total stranger while they crawled through the endless Seafield traffic. She thought briefly of Anjan – level-headed Anjan, who was still assuring her on a daily basis that if ever she needed anything, he'd be there – but dismissed the idea before it was even fully formed. Anjan's caseload was heavier than ever, and although he'd never let on, she knew a distress call from her at 3pm on a Wednesday would seriously mess with his day.

'Besides,' she said, quietly, standing on the concrete Fettes Avenue steps and frowning down at her phone, 'I'm not in distress. Not really.'

She thumbed open her texts, and found the thread from her father.

Hi, Dad, she wrote. *Any chance of a lift home from work this afternoon?*

She looked at the message for a few seconds, still weighing up her various options, before hitting send. When she looked up, Beatrice Crozier was standing a few feet away, watching her. Birch jumped.

'Jesus,' she said. 'How did you get there?'

Bee looked a little wounded.

'Sorry,' she said, 'I didn't mean to sneak up on you.'

Birch looked the other woman up and down. Again, she noted how ordinary Bee looked. She bore none of the trappings that Birch might have associated with a psychic. There were no signs of patterned scarves or occult jewellery. *But then,* Birch thought, *these people are clever. That's how you were taken in before.*

Bee took a step towards her. 'Your colleague,' she said. 'The man at the desk. He said you were out this afternoon.'

Birch felt a prickle on the back of her neck. 'I was,' she said. 'I came back, briefly. But now I'm going again. Going home.' She nodded down at the stick she was leaning on, wondering why she was explaining herself. 'Phased return,' she added.

Bee smiled, but it was a wan smile. 'You're recovering well,' she said.

Birch snorted. 'So I'm told.'

The other woman looked down at the floor. 'I'm not stalking you, DI Birch,' she said. Birch raised an eyebrow, and Bee went on. 'I promise. Your colleague told me to go, but I said

I'd talk to someone else. I was just waiting ... not waiting for *you*. But then I saw you, and—'

'Well,' Birch said, 'I'm afraid I've clocked off now. No longer on duty.'

'Okay.' Bee glanced through the glass doors behind Birch, back towards the reception area. 'In which case, I guess I'll go back in.'

Birch sighed as the other woman made to walk past her. She put a hand out to touch Bee's elbow, stopping her. 'You're not going to get anywhere, you know,' she said. Bee stopped, level with her now. Once again she seemed to be looking not at Birch, but through her, the way she had the day before. 'Not with this psychic schtick. None of my colleagues will listen to it, either.'

Bee's gaze still didn't clarify. Birch could see the faint freckles on the older woman's cheekbones.

'They haven't had the experience you had, though,' Bee replied. 'They haven't been targeted by a fraudster.'

Birch felt something lurch in her chest. Her brain began a frantic scramble, thinking back all those years. Who had she told about that whole business – anyone? Her mother, and her mother was dead. No one else. She'd been too ashamed of herself. Had her mother told someone?

Bee was still talking. 'A woman came to you a few months after Charlie went missing,' she said. 'She timed it well, didn't she? There weren't any leads, and the police were losing interest. You were desperate – understandably. You wanted to be able to tell your mother something. Anything. Anything would have been easier than getting her to accept that her son had simply disappeared into thin air.'

Birch pulled in a long breath. She felt light-headed suddenly. 'How did you ...?'

'Know?' Bee asked. 'I couldn't tell you. But I know she was horribly plausible. I know she told you she'd seen Charlie. Not seen him, but *seen* him – envisioned him. She told you details about him you didn't think anyone else would know. And then she asked for money before she'd tell you any more.'

Nausea churned in Birch's gut. She'd worked hard all these years to bury the memory of her own stupidity.

'I only did it once,' she said, quietly. 'Only one payment – my mother was ready to try absolutely anything to find him. She was devastated when we realised. We both felt so cheated.'

Bee was nodding. 'I didn't know that yesterday,' she said, 'when I first came to see you. I only came to know it then, a moment ago, when you touched me. I'm so sorry that happened to you. Please understand, if I'd known, I'd have taken my concerns to someone else.'

Birch took a step backwards, leaning hard on her stick. This interaction was making her queasy, and her mind raced. Surely she was still, somehow, being had? There was no possible way that Bee was for real. She opened her mouth to speak, but found she couldn't say anything.

'It's okay,' Bee said, 'I'll go back inside. You need to get home. Sorry, again, about yesterday.'

As the other woman walked back towards the building, Birch swayed in the cold air, feeling the aggressive push and pull of her own thoughts. Half of her wanted to call Beatrice back, ask her more, offer to start over. *Tell me what you know, and I'll listen this time. I'll trust you.* The other half of her burned with the ancient shame of her past mistake. *Fool me once, shame on you. Fool me twice …*

'I *won't* get fooled again,' she hissed, aloud. Shaking her head, she became aware of her phone vibrating. Her father's reply: *On way :) da x*

If Jamieson was busy, he didn't let on. Birch knew it took around ten minutes to get out of his house in Boswall Parkway, get into the car, and drive to Fettes Avenue – ten minutes, as long as the traffic was good. Her father got to her in under six, and she wondered just how far above the speed limit he'd been.

'Afternoon, Michael Schumacher,' she said, as she dropped into the passenger seat of his scruffy little van.

'Och, dinnae jest, hen,' he replied, his tone serious in spite of the playful gleam in his eye. 'It's awfie sad whit happened tae that man.'

She raised an eyebrow. 'Nice deflection,' she said. She leaned across to kiss him on the cheek. It was something she'd started doing, because she found, to her surprise, that she liked it. It still felt wrong, somehow, to hug her father – he'd been a stranger to her for such a long time – but she wanted him to know she appreciated him.

'I hope I'm not taking you away from anything,' she added.

He laughed, and pulled away from the kerb. 'Ah widnae say so,' he replied. 'Nae work on the day, so ah wis just ditterin' in the hoose, ken. Got up, watched *Loose Women*, read the paper. Tae be honest wi ye, ah wis a wee bit bored.'

Birch snorted. '*Loose Women*, eh?'

He waved a finger at her. 'Dinnae take the piss, okay? They speak some sense oan that show.'

'I've no doubt.'

Jamieson was quiet for a moment. 'They speak some shite an' aw,' he added, and Birch laughed.

'Keeps you up to date with the pressing issues of the day, though.'

'Aye,' he said. 'Today there wis some wifey oan sayin' she thinks her husband's ghost still lives in the hoose wi her. Pure shite, bit it's a laugh. How's the day been fer yersel, hen?'

Birch felt the smile fade from her face. She sighed. 'Two words for you,' she said. 'Alan Crosbie.'

Her father made a noise of derision. '*That* roaster,' he spat.

Ordinarily, Birch hugely enjoyed the fact that her father talked about her male colleagues as though he'd been personally insulted by each of them. He'd met McLeod, and formed an unshakably negative opinion that Birch had no real desire to try and change, but all he knew of Crosbie was what he'd been told. Jamieson's resulting hatred for the man was, Birch knew, a sign that she moaned about him too much. But right now she didn't care; frankly, he fucking deserved it.

'Whit's he done?' Jamieson asked.

Birch opened her mouth to speak, then paused. The ire she'd felt as she staggered out of the briefing had been replace with confusion around her interaction with Bee, and suddenly she wasn't sure that she had the strength to tell either story to her father.

'Crosbie's usual thing,' she replied, after a moment. 'He's basically being a belligerent bastard, and it doesn't make a whole lot of sense. He's been given a case that should have been mine, and it's like … he's taken it on, because it's something he can hold over me. "Ha ha, I got given this, I'm the golden boy and you're the poor relation," that kind of thing. But in terms of the case itself, he just really can't be arsed with it. He doesn't *want* it, not really. So he's phoning it in.' Birch felt a little light come on somewhere in the dark recesses of her brain – a thing that sometimes happened in therapy. 'I guess I'm annoyed about it because I'd have done a good job,' she added, 'while he's going to do a bang-average one – in fact, bang-average would be the best case scenario.'

Jamieson snorted. Birch literally bit her own tongue as he sped up to nip through an amber light.

'He's a wee puke,' he announced. 'Cannae stand the fella, mysel. His heid's up his arse.'

Birch turned to look at her father. He kept his eyes on the road, but his gaze flickered.

'Whit?' he said.

She blinked. 'What do you mean, "whit"?' She enjoyed imitating him – though whenever she did, she reminded herself of Charlie. 'Dad, have you *met* Crosbie?'

Her father brought the van to a stop at the Commercial Street junction. ''Course,' he replied. 'He's in ma meeting, huv ah no said?'

Birch bounced the heel of one hand off her own forehead. 'Wow,' she said. 'Of course he is. Of all the AA meetings in all the world, Alan Crosbie has to walk into that one.' A thought struck her. 'Does he know you're my dad?'

Jamieson nodded. 'Aye,' he said, 'that's how ah ken it's the same gadge. He comes up tae me a few weeks back in the break, wee cup o tea in his haund, an he asks me straight up if ah'm related tae a Helen Birch.'

Birch's eyes widened. 'And what did you say?'

'Ah says, "Fuck no, that wifey's a fuckin' danger!"' He laughed, and Birch joined in, though she felt queasy again. 'Whit dae ye think ah said, ye daft besom? Ah says, "Aye, that's ma wee girl."'

'And what did he say?'

Jamieson shrugged. 'No a lot. Jist like, "Aye well, we work thegither," or some such. An then aff he wanders wi his wee cup o tea.'

Birch turned back to face the road. They were moving slowly through the Shore now, passing the Granary pub and the Clock Café.

'Things suddenly make so much sense,' she said.

Jamieson was watching the traffic, but she saw him dip his head to one side, a question. 'Whit does?'

'Well,' she replied, 'Alan's been so weird with me lately. Since Operation Stake. I thought it was because I'd found out about his drinking, and maybe that he thinks I snitched on him to McLeod. Not that it mattered, because McLeod knew anyway, but I've been thinking that maybe Alan takes a dim view of me being a grass. Even though I'm not one.'

Jamieson let out a short gulp of laughter.

'Like ah say – his heid's up his arse.'

'I won't argue with that,' Birch said, 'but now I'm thinking, maybe it's not that at all. Or it *is* that, but it's also the fact that you're in the same AA meeting as him. He seems to have this idea that I'm judging him for something, that I'm looking down on him. Maybe he thinks you're telling me things he's said in AA.'

It took a fair bit to shock Jamieson Birch, she knew, but at this, he looked shocked. 'Helen,' he said, slowing down the van so he could look at her. 'Ah wid *never*. He could say whitever he liked in that room – onything. Ah wid never repeat it. It's the rules.'

Birch held out a hand, as though she might place it on his arm, though she didn't reach out all the way. She recalled touching Bee, the way the other woman had seemed to look through her. She dropped her hand again.

'I know, Dad,' she said. 'I know how important that confidentiality is.'

Jamieson nodded. 'An he ought tae ken the same,' he added. 'He ought tae ken that naebody in that room wid ever clype.'

Birch was nodding, too. 'True,' she said. 'Besides, if he's worried about it, why doesn't he find another meeting?'

Jamieson shrugged. 'There's no many,' he said. 'An it's a nice group tae be in. Ah widnae want tae leave, before ye ask.'

Birch touched her chest in an unbidden, defensive gesture. 'I wasn't going to!' she said. 'I'd never ask you to leave your group. I know how important AA is to you. And I'm so, so glad you've kept going.'

Jamieson seemed to draw himself up, just slightly. 'Aye, well. Ah widnae stop, either. It's fer you an Charlie that ah dae it, ken? Ah've got ye both back in ma life, an ah'm no losing ye again.'

Birch felt both a swell of emotion and a spike of annoyance at this. She wanted to say, *You didn't lose us in the first place, you chose to walk out.* But with the help of Dr Jane, she was learning to keep that annoyance under control.

There was a pause, which felt heavy in the still air of the van.

'Well,' she said, 'we really appreciate it, Dad.'

Jamieson refused her offer of a cup of tea, which nettled Birch, but she didn't feel like she could press him on the subject after she'd pulled him away from his day off. She'd wanted to ask him about unaccompanied minors. Jamieson worked in the building trade, often on jobs that were quiet, cash in hand, with the expectation that nobody asked any questions and, as a result, nobody was told any lies. She assumed that there must be young men who'd fled the asylum system working in the same sort of way he did – and she knew he crossed paths with a lot with people he referred to as 'foreigners', an expression she couldn't seem to stop him using.

'But it's true, hen,' he'd say, genuinely confused by her consternation. 'They *are* foreign. Ah'm no sayin' they're bad lads, bit they're foreign.'

She'd wanted to ask him about these *foreigners* – where were they actually from, did he know? Did they get paid the same money as he did? How were they treated? He'd most likely have been evasive, of course. She knew Jamieson was proud of her, but he still couldn't shake the bone-deep distrust for police that he'd developed as a man who had often lived and worked in the grey areas at the very edge of what was legal.

'Ah wis a pissheid fer years,' he'd told her. 'Ah've slept in a cell mair times than ma ain bed. An let me tell ye, Helen, ye ought tae be careful. There's some hard, mean bastarts work as polis.'

She couldn't argue, because he wasn't wrong. She often wondered what cruelties he'd suffered at the hands of bored late-night desk sergeants.

Robbed of her opportunity to question him, she stood on the pavement at the end of the Portobello prom and watched as he turned the van around and then drove out of sight. It was almost four o' clock, and the January dark was gathering around her. The tide was out, the sea a black, seething slab in the middle distance. As she looked across the Forth, she saw a stretch of pinprick streetlights come on, all at once, in faraway Fife.

The house felt cold and unwelcoming as she hobbled in over the threshold. She stood in the dark hallway debating, as she had many times that winter, whether or not to put the heating on early. She'd set the timer to come on at 8pm, so her bedroom would be warm when she went upstairs to bed each night, but to knock off again at 10.30pm, by which time she ought to be under the duvet with a hot water bottle. This was part of the reason she hated the recurring nightmares she'd described to Dr Jane; when she woke up in the middle of the night of late, it was always bloody freezing.

She was still dithering at the bottom of the stairs when she heard the familiar creak of the front gate, and the scuff of footsteps up the path. She realised that someone was about to knock on the door, and when she answered it, they'd see she'd been standing in the dark, still bundled in her winter coat. Who could possibly be coming to see her at 4pm on a Wednesday? She flicked on the hall light at exactly the same moment the knock came, then reached out and opened the door.

'Kato!' she said, genuinely shocked to see her friend standing there.

'Evening, marm.' Amy was grinning, but as she looked Birch up and down, her smile faded. 'Oh shit,' she said. 'Are you on your way out somewhere? I don't want to interrupt.'

Birch shook her head. 'Not at all,' she said. 'I actually only just got in.'

'Oh.' Amy frowned. She looked like she was re-evaluating whatever situation had led her to Birch's front door. 'Well – okay, listen, this was a daft idea. I should probably just—'

Birch laughed. 'Kato,' she said, holding up a hand. 'Why don't you tell me why you're here, and we'll go from there?'

She saw Amy's shoulders relax. 'Right, yes. Sorry.'

Birch smiled. 'You want to come in?'

'Well …' Amy hesitated. 'I was actually calling to see if you wanted to come out.'

Birch cocked an eyebrow. 'For a drink? You're clocking off early!'

Amy shook her head. 'Sadly, no. On another ride-along. I looked up Kim's address, and it turns out she lives not far from here. As she's a neighbour of yours, I thought I'd see if you wanted to come with.'

Birch glanced at the hall clock. 'Okay I take it back,' she said, 'about clocking off. It's after four. Don't you want to leave this till tomorrow?'

Amy shrugged. 'I feel like I might as well do it now, while it's in my teeth, you know? Plus, Carol's colleague from the parlour went round to try and see Kim during working hours, and no one was in. But the electoral register tells me she lives in a multiple occupancy flat. If we go later in the day, it's more likely that someone will be in – if not Kim, then maybe one of her flatmates.'

'True,' Birch said. She paused for a second – perhaps not even a second – considering the offer. Then she reached out and scooped up her handbag from the bottom step of the stairs, where she'd placed it only moments before.

'Okay then,' she said, 'let's go. Saves me putting the heating on for another couple of hours, anyway.'

It took Amy less than five minutes to drive them from the back of Birch's house to Ramsay Place: a short, nondescript street full of parked cars and classic Edinburgh sandstone tenements.

'Wow,' Birch said, as Amy executed a flawless reverse park, 'you weren't kidding when you said it wasn't far.'

'Right?' Amy said. 'Kim's one of your neighbours.'

Birch squinted up past the orange streetlights at the towering tenement building. 'What floor is this flat on?'

'Second,' Amy replied. 'You going to be okay on the stairs?'

Birch was unbuckling her seatbelt. 'I'll be fine,' she said. 'I might just be a bit slow.'

Amy had managed to park only a few feet away from the building. The door was a pale sage green, the paint flaking and curling in the salt air. The promenade was only two hundred metres or so away, and Birch knew that had the tide not been out, she'd have been able to hear the sea.

'Just out of interest,' Amy said, as they crossed the pavement together, 'who was that I saw you speaking to, earlier?'

Birch had been looking at her own feet, but jerked her head up to look at Amy. 'Who?' she asked, perhaps a little too sharply. 'When?'

Amy raised an eyebrow. 'Before,' she replied, 'as you were leaving work. I looked out of the stairwell window and saw you chatting with someone. A woman with long brown hair.'

Birch dithered. *Tell her – why don't you just tell her?* But if she told Amy about Bee, she'd have to tell her about the other time – the previous time. The fake psychic she'd given money to. She'd have to talk about her own shame.

'Oh,' Birch replied, trying to lighten her tone. 'Just some woman saying she had some information to impart about something. I told her I was off-duty, on my way home. She said she'd go in and find someone else.'

Amy's raised eyebrow was still raised, but they'd reached the door. The doorway was gloomy, and instead of saying anything else, Amy peered at the bell board, then reached up and pressed a buzzer. For at least two minutes, there was silence.

'No one home,' Birch said, but Amy had raised her hand to press the buzzer again. In the moment before she could, there was a crackle: someone in the flat had picked up the receiver.

'Hello?' The voice was tinny and small in the speaker.

'Hi,' Amy trilled, and Birch recognised the practiced register of her voice: *Yes, it's the police, but don't panic, nothing bad has happened.* 'My name's Amy Kato, I work for Police Scotland. I'm looking for a Kim Le.'

There was a pause, but the sound of static told them the person on the other end was still there.

'You'd better come up,' the small voice said. Then they heard the clunk of the entry button, and the buzz as the door unlocked itself to let them in.

'Bingo,' Amy whispered, pushing open the door and stepping inside to hold it for Birch. Birch didn't respond. The way the person in the flat had said 'You'd better come up' felt ominous. She was pretty sure that person wasn't Kim.

The tenement was unusual, in that the flats' front doors were not inside the stairwell, but outside, on the back of the building. When they reached the second floor, Amy and Birch stepped out on to a long concrete walkway with railings, pot plants and washing lines. If she looked over her shoulder, Birch could make out the flat roof of the local social club, and, in a gap between the neighbouring buildings, she could see a tilted half-moon coming up over the dark mirror of the sea. The flats' front windows looked out over the walkway, and though most were dressed with net curtains, Birch averted her gaze in order to avoid nosying in at the lit-up, early evening scenes inside.

Amy stopped outside a red front door. Its paint was also peeling. Above the door knocker was a faded hand-made sign which read 'Le, Smith, Lewandowska' in black marker pen. Underneath, and in smaller writing, were the words 'All other mail, please return to sender'. Birch felt a pang of nostalgia for her years spent living in shared flats, then checked herself; there wasn't much to be nostalgic about.

Amy didn't need to knock – the person on the other side of the door had been waiting for them, listening, the way Birch had listened only minutes ago to Amy's footsteps advancing up her garden path. The door opened, throwing a rhombus of light out on to the walkway. On the threshold stood a petite woman with dyed lilac-coloured hair and a septum piercing.

Birch guessed she was about thirty. A fat black cat rubbed around her ankles.

'Hi, you're police?'

Birch caught the hint of an accent: Polish, she guessed, with a name like Lewandowska.

Amy nodded, holding up her warrant card. 'Yes,' she said. 'I'm Detective Sergeant Amy Kato, and this is Detective Inspector Helen Birch.'

Again, Birch decided against showing her own badge. Alarm was already registering on the young woman's face.

'There's nothing to worry about,' Amy added, 'we're just following up some enquiries. I mentioned that we're looking for Kim Le. Is she at home?'

The black cat miaowed once, twice, as though answering, and Amy laughed. The woman looked embarrassed.

'Don't mind him,' she said. 'He thinks it should be his food time. I'm sorry, I don't know where Kim is right now.'

Birch frowned. 'By that, you mean … she isn't home, or you haven't seen her for a while?'

'I haven't seen her for a while,' the woman parroted. She bent down and scooped up the cat, who miaowed again. 'I'll be honest, I'm not sure if she even lives here anymore.'

Amy glanced over her shoulder at Birch. Birch gave a nod.

'Do you mind if we come in, Ms …?'

The woman took a step backwards into the lit hallway. 'Lewandowska,' she said. 'Magda.'

'Magda,' Amy repeated. 'I promise we won't take up much of your time.'

The woman stood still for a moment, then took another couple of steps back. 'Sure,' she said.

Amy stepped inside, then held the door for Birch before closing it behind her. Birch felt immediately enveloped by warmth, and the mingled smell of incense burning, and something delicious cooking.

Magda was walking away. 'Come through to the kitchen,' she said. 'I need to stir my soup. And feed this cat.'

Birch followed Amy and Magda along the narrow hallway. The woodchip wallpaper was painted a pale yellow, and on the walls were odd, mismatched pictures in brightly coloured frames. The doors off the hallway were all closed except for the penultimate one. As she passed, Birch glanced in at the flat's living room: a poky space with a classic Edinburgh press, a stopped-up fireplace with fairy lights coiled behind its grate, and one sagging sofa bedecked with patterned throws. The flat was messy, and shabby, and cosy. It felt relaxing to be there.

Magda waved them into the kitchen, a room whose only window was above head height and looked out on to the enclosed stairwell. The room had red walls and brightly coloured tiles, and a tall fridge that fluttered with notes and flyers and photographs and postcards and many, many novelty fridge magnets. In one corner was a small table and, behind it, an old church pew that looked like it might have come out of a skip.

'Please,' Magda said, 'sit down.'

Amy shuffled into the gap between the pew and the table, and sat. Birch followed suit. The hard, narrow seat reminded her immediately of childhood, and trailing into church behind her righteous mother, Charlie's little hand held in her own. Magda turned her back on them. On the hob was a huge soup pan, sitting over a low flame. Magda dipped a wooden spoon into it, and stirred.

'So,' Amy said, 'we've come here hoping to speak to Kim. But you haven't seen her in ... how long, would you say?'

Magda shrugged; Birch saw her shoulders go up and down. Apparently satisfied with the soup, she laid the spoon down beside the hob, and turned to face them.

'Not since before Christmas,' she replied. 'Maybe the twentieth of December, or sometime around then. She went out one day, I thought to go to work. Then she just ... hasn't come back.'

'So that's nearly a month,' Amy said.

'Yes. I have started to get worried, just these past few days. Next week we need to pay the rent.'

'You've only just started to get worried? Is it normal for Kim to be away for long periods of time?'

Magda shook her head. 'No,' she said, 'but you know, it was Christmas. Kim isn't from here, she's from Vietnam. I assumed she just went home for the holidays. Vietnam is far away. She'd probably go for a long time.'

Amy cocked her head and made a face that said, *Good point.* 'Have you been away yourself, over the festive period?' she asked. 'Is it possible Kim could have been here more recently, and you missed each other?'

Again, Magda shook her head. 'I didn't go home to Poland this year,' she said. 'I had to work.' She smiled, then, unexpectedly, and added, 'Christmas retail, you know?'

'Ah yes,' Amy said, 'I do know. That's really helpful, though – that means we know Kim definitely hasn't been at home in all that time.'

Magda's smile faded. 'Wait,' she said, 'do you think something bad has happened to her? She's missing? Like, in a bad way missing?'

Amy held up her hands. 'No, no,' she said. 'No one's saying that, not yet. We're not sure where Kim is at the moment, but we don't yet have any evidence to suggest that anything bad has happened to her. You might be right, in fact – maybe she did just go home for the holidays.'

Birch cleared her throat. She felt weird just sitting there, not talking. 'In this time that Kim has been … away,' she said, 'have you had any contact with her? Have you texted or called her, or heard from her by email – anything like that?'

Magda looked down at the cat, who was winding himself awkwardly around her ankles. 'I texted her a couple of times,' Magda said, 'just, like, two days ago. Just to remind her about the rent. But I haven't had any answer. I thought maybe, if she's in Vietnam, she doesn't have service. Or her phone doesn't work there.'

Birch could see they were worrying this woman. A seed of worry had already begun to grow in her mind, but their arrival at the flat had caused it to bolt. Magda was clinging to the idea that Kim was in Vietnam. It was a tempting theory.

'You have another flatmate, right?' Amy asked. 'There are three names on the front door.'

Magda nodded. 'Yeah,' she said, 'there's also Emma. She's not here right now, though. She's a nurse, so she works long hours.'

'That's okay,' Amy said. 'I assume Emma hasn't mentioned hearing from Kim at all?'

'No. I just asked her yesterday, actually. We were talking about the rent money, how we'd pay it if Kim doesn't come back. Emma hasn't seen her, either, or talked to her.'

'Okay,' Amy said. 'Now, this is an important question. Has anyone else been here in the past few weeks, looking for Kim?'

Magda's eyebrows lifted. 'Like, police?'

'Like anyone,' Amy replied.

'I don't think so.'

Birch leaned forward. 'Has Emma mentioned anything to you about anyone coming round looking for Kim? Or has anyone phoned either of you, looking for her?'

Magda frowned at Birch as though she thought she might be mad. 'No one,' she said. 'No one's been here, and I don't think anyone would have my number. No one I don't know, anyway. I promise you, I haven't heard anything about Kim.'

Birch tried to relax her posture. It was difficult, on the narrow pew. She'd rattled Magda, and she hadn't meant to.

Amy glanced at her, before changing tack. 'What can you tell us about Kim?' she asked.

At Magda's feet, the cat miaowed again. Magda looked down at him. 'Bart, shh,' she hissed. 'Food time is five o' clock! Ten minutes!'

Amy laughed.

'Sorry,' Magda said. 'What can I tell you about Kim? I don't know. She's quite young, only maybe twenty, I think. She's lived here in Scotland for longer than me, though, since she was a kid. She's a – I don't know the word. She does people's nails.'

'A manicurist,' Amy offered.

Magda pointed one index finger into the air. 'Manicurist,' she said. 'Yes. She works at a place in Leith. The Good Luck Parlour? The Lucky Parlour?'

'Lucky Seven Parlour,' Birch said. 'We were just there, earlier today.'

'Ah,' Magda said, 'Lucky Seven. Yes, she works there. And sometimes she does nails for people in their houses as well, like … bridal nails, for weddings, that kind of thing. But just sometimes. Not very often.'

Birch and Amy exchanged a look. A missing young woman who sometimes worked alone in clients' homes? That was an avenue to follow up.

Magda was stalling. 'I don't know what else to tell you, really,' she said.

'How long has Kim lived here?' Amy asked. 'How did you come to be flatmates?'

'Oh,' Magda said. 'Yes, I can tell you about that. Emma and I already lived here, and we had a spare room … then the landlady put the rent up. We asked if we could have another flatmate and she said yes, so we put an ad up in a few places. Kim messaged me on Facebook, I think. A few people asked us about it, but she seemed like the best person, so we said yes and she moved in. She was so excited; it was her first time living away from her family.'

'She told you that?' Amy asked.

'Yeah. She lived with her aunty and uncle before this, she said. They lived in Glasgow. She told us she'd got very tired of living there – her uncle was quite controlling, I think. She said her family were trying to set her up with some Vietnamese guy, but she didn't like him. He was old, I think – too old for her.'

Amy took out her phone, and thumbed in a note. Birch wasn't surprised: this felt important.

'Do you think,' she asked, as Amy typed, 'that Kim had fallen out with her family? Or was it not that serious?'

Magda dipped her head to one side. 'I think they didn't always agree,' she replied, 'but she still talked to them. She used to phone them up a lot – I heard her speaking on her phone in Vietnamese. I didn't understand, of course, but she always sounded pretty happy. She would laugh and make jokes. I think things were okay with them, she just didn't want to live there anymore.'

'You mentioned this older man,' Birch said. 'Did he ever come here? Did you ever see him, or meet him?'

Magda shook her head. 'That was all back in Glasgow,' she said. 'I don't think Kim ever saw him again after she moved here. She sort of moved here to get away from having to date him, I think. She really wasn't interested.'

Amy typed something else.

'Okay,' Birch said. 'What about other men? Did Kim ever have a boyfriend here in Edinburgh, that you knew about?'

'I don't know about *boyfriend*. I do know she went on dates sometimes, like from Tinder, you know? Emma sometimes has dates, too. They always tell me where they're going, what bar, what time.' She smiled. 'They say I'm like the mother of the flat.'

Birch matched her smile. 'That's a very sensible thing for them to do,' she said. 'And you're doing an important job, being that person.'

Magda laughed. 'I don't know what I'd do if one of them never came home,' she said. Then her face fell. 'Wait. Is that maybe what's happened to Kim? You think some man ... maybe the Glasgow man ... he's done something to her?'

'We don't know, Magda,' Birch said, 'but we promise you, we're going to find out. Wherever Kim is, we're going to find her.'

Bee, 2010

I didn't know how to feel about the fact that the Knowing had ended my parents' marriage. I rattled through a series of extreme emotions during the first few months of the new millennium. I felt horrified, of course, that I'd ruptured our family unit, but also glad that I'd provided the catalyst my mother needed to get free. My father wasn't a monster – he was guilty of selfishness and perhaps of neglect, nothing more than that. But being married to him had robbed my mother of thirty years of other opportunities, and I was happy that she might now get to make up for lost time, for a life only half lived. I also felt strangely vindicated; I'd been right, after all. Telling other people about the Knowing was a mistake. It caused upset on a seismic scale. And it made my life much worse, having my parents – my mother, especially – know about it. In the years that followed, she became morbidly reliant on my input and advice.

'I'm thinking,' she'd say, having called me on the fancy smartphone I quickly regretted having bought for her, 'that this man might not be quite what his dating profile says he is. Can I read it to you, and you can tell me if … you know. If you get a feeling about him?'

I always got a feeling about them. It was depressing, how readily my mother bounced from the frying pan of her failed marriage and into the fire of online dating in her sixties. I'd hoped she might travel, go to university, take up pottery, do something for herself. But my mother didn't know how to be alone. She'd moved out of her parents' house and straight into the marital home with my begrudging father. The job she got soon after she left him – working in the Marks and Spencer Food Hall on Princes Street, the first real job she'd ever had – didn't suit her. I realised with some disappointment that she didn't want to reinvent herself. She was just hoping she could upgrade to a slightly more attentive man.

I didn't like the sound of any of the profiles she read out to me over the phone. These men had grown-up children of their own – children I'd have to meet and be polite to, if things progressed. I was suspicious of the men for being divorced, and hoped the Knowing would tell me if their wives had left for reasons that might put my mother in harm's way. I tried to tell myself she was having a nice time, getting her hair done for dates and being told she looked lovely by men who drove Volvo estates and bagged Munros and had names like Roger and Nigel. For his part, my father didn't speak to me for six long years. I sent him cards on his birthday and Father's Day and at Christmas, and occasionally I'd try to phone him on the number Tommy assured me still worked. He never picked up. I assumed we were forever estranged – I'd done it, I'd made it happen, I deserved it – and tried to go on with my life.

The job I'd known would materialise was a manager's job in a charity shop in Tollcross. The pay was meagre, but otherwise, I loved it. I inherited a roster of enthusiastic volunteers from the previous manager – volunteers who kept the shop floor running like a Swiss watch while I got on with the heavy lifting. The back shop was my favourite place; I was never happier than when the sort room was filled to the roof with bags and I could spend an entire afternoon discovering what was inside. I loved the story that every bag told, loved the way that each donation revealed something about the person who'd gifted it to us. Sometimes I'd put my hand into a bag and the Knowing would show me a whole series of snapshots from that donor's life as I touched each garment and shoe. Other times I got no information at all, but could nevertheless imagine the tales each item told. I got to see all life in those bags, from the tragic binbag full of unworn baby clothes, their tags still attached, to the satin wedding dresses carefully folded between crumbling sheets of tissue. I moved through my thirties in the back room of that shop, learning who I was: a woman who loved nothing more than to be alone, and quiet, watching as the world changed, knowing more, perhaps, about the people around her than she did about her own self.

It was Bonfire Night, 2006, when I received the phone call from Tommy. It had taken six years for my father to actually get sick – or rather, to begin to show symptoms serious enough that he'd finally swallowed his pride and sought help – and throughout that time I'd hoped beyond all hope that for once, the Knowing had been wrong. It was a rainy Tollcross teatime, a Sunday, the 23 and 27 buses sloshing through the standing water outside my closed-up shop. Every so often I'd hear the crackle of a firework nearby. I'd come in to work up the rotas and potter around, happier in that sort room than in my own home. My mobile rang, and I knew without looking that it was Tommy, and why he was calling, and what he was going to say.

'Bee, it's me.' He sounded tired.

'Hey, sweetness.'

'You home?'

I held up my pricing gun, close to the phone, and rattled it. 'Sort room,' I said. 'In my happy place.'

'Mate, it's a Sunday night.'

I laughed. 'Best time to be here,' I replied. 'I get the place completely to myself. I'm queen of all I survey.'

It was hard, keeping my voice light, pretending he wasn't about to say what I knew he was about to say. But I'd never told Tommy about the Knowing. I knew my father hadn't, either – he wouldn't want to give the idea any credence. And I'd sworn my mother to absolute secrecy, going so far as to check in with her every so often, just to make sure she hadn't let slip.

'Listen,' he said, and I braced myself for it. 'Maybe I should call you back when you're at home.'

I shook my head, though he couldn't see me. 'It's fine,' I said, 'I'm happy to talk.'

He paused. 'Okay, but … I've got some bad news.'

'About Dad?'

'About Dad.'

I closed my eyes. 'Tell me,' I said.

My father's ability to repress and compartmentalise truly astounded me. I went round the following weekend with Tommy – my first visit to that house since Hogmanay 1999. My father greeted me as he always had, opening the door, saying my name, and planting a dry kiss on my cheek. It was as though the falling-out, my mother leaving, their divorce, and all the intervening six – almost seven – years had never happened. He was greyer, and thinner, but otherwise he was himself in every possible way.

The house, meanwhile, was radically changed; my mother had taken most of the furniture from the ground floor. Gone were the Ercol sideboards with their crystal vases and knick-knacks. Gone was the dining table that had felt, for so many long years, like the dead centre of that house. Gone were the hideous serving plates my mother treated like treasure. What remained was my father's armchair, the sofa, and the coffee table. A new, vast, flat-screen TV balanced on a stand that was too small for it. The curtains looked faded now I saw them again, and the carpet had a path thinned into it between the armchair and the door. Everything seemed dusty, and just a little unloved.

'They've said I need surgery,' he told me, as Tommy clattered around in the kitchen, making cups of tea. 'I've already told your brother. They're going to remove part of the bowel, and then see where we're at. But I'll probably get chemo as well. See if we can't prevent the bastard thing from coming back.'

I nodded along, until he stopped talking. He glanced back towards the kitchen door, to check for Tommy. Then he looked me in the eye for the first time since I'd walked into the house.

'I want you to know,' he said, 'that I believe this is a coincidence, and nothing more. I won't hear you tell me that you knew about this, or that you tried to warn me. Do you understand? We won't discuss that.'

I blinked. I was impressed. I'd never heard my father articulate a boundary so clearly. I'd never heard him communicate so well.

'Of course,' I said.

Tommy appeared in the doorway, three mugs clutched precariously in his fist. In his other hand, he carried a plate of biscuits.

'What's important is the treatment, making sure you get what you need,' I said. 'We're both here to help with that, however we can.' I looked at my brother as he handed me my steaming mug of tea. 'Right, kid?'

Tommy nodded. 'Right,' he said.

My father was still looking at me. 'I won't die of this thing,' he said.

Of course, I thought, *of course he has to prove me wrong.*

He sat up straight in his scruffy armchair. 'I absolutely refuse to die of it.'

My father had his last day of chemo the day Rosie Cole disappeared. I didn't know it then, but that night, I'd go home to bed and dream of her, locked up in the cellar in Mountcastle, under the trapdoor and the black-and-white linoleum floor. I wheeled him into the ward past the bell, and saw him look up at it. I wondered what he was thinking – whether he'd want to ring the infernal thing, or not. Yes, he was finishing chemo, but only because he was about to finish his life. His place in the hospice was booked. Tommy and I had been to see the room the previous week. They'd given him a corner suite on the ground floor, with two vast windows that looked out over rolling lawns. Perspex bird feeders had been attached to the glass outside, and as we looked around, little sparrows and finches kept alighting to peck at the birdseed. There was a hospital-style bed with electronic controls, an accessible toilet and shower, and a big TV. He'd have everything he needed.

'He reads newspapers,' I said to the nurse who showed us round. 'It's his favourite thing.'

She made a note. 'Let me know which ones,' she said, 'and we'll have them delivered.'

I'd held Tommy's hand as he cried, looking at the room, and I fought in silence against a terrible déjà vu. I'd never been here, but I'd seen this room before. I'd watched my father die, in my mind, that New Year's Eve as I sagged against the newel post at the bottom of my parents' stairs. I'd heard him take his final, rattling breath. He did it here.

He sent me away, that final chemo session, the way he some-times did. I think it made him uncomfortable, sitting beside me for that length of time, trying to find the right things to say. We'd never had anything in common, my father and I, other than my mother and Tommy, and now only one of those things remained. My mother hadn't shown much emotion as I'd told her the news: the cancer had spread, the chemo wasn't working, we were looking into hospice care, the end was nigh. I knew – because I knew – that she felt guilty for leaving him, but also that she felt intense relief. It was happening, but it wasn't happening to her. I begrudged her nothing. After all, it was me who'd set her free.

I'd got used to wandering the corridors of the hospital, a cup of lukewarm coffee in one hand. I'd learned where the quietest seating areas were, where I'd be bothered and where I wouldn't be, where I could avoid encountering people I'd know things about that I really didn't want to know. That day, I headed for the hospital chapel, which seemed to be the only place they'd soundproofed against the rattle of trolleys and the endless beep of machines. The lighting in there was slightly less stark than the rest of the rooms I'd been in, and quiet organ music floated through the space from unseen speakers. Sometimes there were other people there, but the unwritten rules of that room kept anyone from speaking. In the chapel, I could sit for hours and feel content. I felt like, had I wanted to, I could have laid down on the carpet tiles and slept for a hundred years.

That day, when I pushed open the heavy chapel door – always soundless on its hinges, like someone came round to oil them every night – I was greeted by the sound of coughing. At the front of the room, between the pews closest to the altar, someone had parked a wheelchair. An old man was sitting in it, bent over and retching. Two IV bags hung from a stand beside him. Even from the doorway, I could see he was in bad shape.

I sidled into the room and hovered, waiting for the retching to stop. There was no one else in the room – no family member keeping an eye on him, no nurse. It wasn't the done thing to approach people who'd come to sit in the chapel, but I decided it was more important to check on him than it was to respect the code of silence. I shuffled down the aisle, wincing as he heaved and wheezed.

'Excuse me,' I said, as I drew level with the wheelchair. 'I'm sorry to bother you, but … are you okay? Do you need me to call someone?'

He bought a quivering hand up to his mouth. I could see the knobs of his wrist bones, the skin on his arms blue-white and thin as paper. I tried not to look at the cannulas, the way they lifted the veins up close to the surface of his arms. The wisps of hair left on his head looked just like my father's: a few strays clinging on where the chemo had spared them. This man had cancer, too.

He brought the coughing under control, and hauled in a breath. Then he turned to look at me.

'You'd better forget my face, kid. I mean it.'

I staggered backwards. He hadn't spoken, of course; the voice was in my head, a dredged-up memory from twenty-seven years ago. I'd disobeyed him. I'd never forgotten that face with its violent grin, hanging above me in the dim light of the pavilion. Now it was looking back at me once again – thinner, paler, the eyes cloudy and dull – that self-same, terrible face.

'I'm fine,' he whispered, even as I backed away. 'Just dying.'

I knocked my leg against a pew, and let out a little yelp of pain.

'It's alright,' he said. He seemed to be accustomed to people recoiling at the sight of him. 'It's nothing contagious.'

I leaned back against the pew, attempting to steady myself. I felt as though I'd been thrown from a plane with no parachute

– I was falling face-first into my own past. The events of that day in the pavilion came rushing up to meet me: Martin pressing his hand over my mouth. The man refusing to shift his gaze from my face, even as I cowered and squirmed. Martin kneeling on the dusty floor in front of him, the shadow roaming in circles around them like a caged thing. The smell of sweat and fear. *Forget my face, kid. I mean it.*

'What are you doing here?' I breathed.

He shrugged. It made him cough. 'Trying to atone for my sins,' he croaked.

I straightened up. I wanted to slap myself in the face, make myself come to, stop my vision from swimming. 'And what sins would those be?'

He looked down at his lap. He didn't seem fazed by the fact that a strange woman had marched up and begun questioning him. He shifted his feet in the wheelchair's stirrups, and I saw the chunky plastic monitor on his ankle.

'You don't want to know,' he said. 'I've done a lot of bad things in my life.'

I was quiet for a moment. I realised I did want to know, but the voice of the Knowing wouldn't speak to me. This man's shame was like a high wall between us; I couldn't see him, not clearly.

'And you've been punished, it looks like,' I said. I pointed to the ankle bracelet.

He smiled. 'Oh yes,' he said. 'Once upon a time, they'd have locked me up and thrown away the key. But these days, they let you out to die. They know where I am at all times, of course, but this way they can call themselves humane.'

I straightened up, and closed the gap I'd made between us. 'Do you mind if I sit?' I asked, indicating the empty pew beside his wheelchair.

'Not at all,' he replied, and there was genuine surprise in his voice. 'You're not repulsed?'

I was, but more by the memory of him than by the husk he was now.

'My father's dying, too,' I said. 'Cancer. It's his last chemo session today.'

'Ah. Then you know what a rotting old man looks like.'

I shrugged. 'His treatment isn't working anymore,' I said. 'It's getting to be his time.'

He took a couple of wheezing breaths, and I thought he might cough again, but he didn't. 'You seem resigned,' he said.

'I am. I knew it was coming. I knew well before he did. I'm a … I'm psychic, you see. I know things.'

He wheezed again, and the wheeze turned into a rattle, and the rattle intensified into a laugh. He laughed for a few seconds before the laugh turned into a cough and, once again, he began retching. His eyes were wet. I'd amused him.

'You don't believe me,' I said. My voice was cold.

He shook his head. 'Surely,' he said, between two long, sucked-in breaths, 'that's not unusual?'

'I don't know. I don't usually tell people.'

'Really? Don't you types like to advertise your … what would you call them? Your gifts? I thought you were all about extracting money from credulous fools.'

'Not me,' I said.

He coughed some more. From somewhere in the folds of his hospital gown, he produced a tissue. I watched him spit into it, then fold the little gob of phlegm into a tight square.

'Go on then,' he said, his voice tart. 'Tell me my life story. See if you can cold-read a dying old man.'

I laughed, and the laugh was hard and flinty. 'You're not going to like it,' I said.

'I'm not going to believe in it,' he replied.

I smiled. 'There was a day,' I began, 'twenty-seven years ago, that changed everything. Perhaps you don't remember it, but I can see it like it was yesterday. It was a sunny after-noon, and you went down to the pavilion on the Meadows Park. You went there to meet the boy you liked, the one you paid to suck you off and keep quiet about it. Remember that? You'd come from work that day, and you were wearing your brown suit.'

He looked at me then, properly, his eyes boggling. 'Who are you?' he croaked. 'Who the fuck are you?'

'That boy's name was Martin,' I said. 'Did you ever know that? His name was Martin, and he was eighteen. A few months after that day, he stopped showing up to the pavilion. Do you remember?'

He stared at me.

'I said,' I repeated, my voice like ice, 'do you *remember*?'

He nodded. I could hear the breath rattling in his chest.

'The reason he stopped turning up,' I went on, 'was this. Martin killed himself. He killed himself over the shame and the trauma of what you did to him.'

I watched his eyelashes flutter.

'Who sent you here?' he whispered.

I barked out a laugh. 'What do you care? I thought you didn't believe in this stuff.'

He coughed again, a prolonged bout of spluttering. 'Listen,' he said, 'I'm dying, okay? I've been in prison for the past twelve years, and now I'm dying. Whatever you think you're here for, I promise you, I've suffered. They've made me suffer.'

I narrowed my eyes. 'What did they get you on? What charge?'

He looked down at his lap again, shaking his head. I reached out and clamped a hand around his arm. He jumped. His flesh felt like the onion-skin pages of the ratty old *Complete Works of Shakespeare* that might, as far as I knew, still be sitting on its shelf in Mrs Muchtie's library.

'Tell me,' I said.

'Possession of child pornography,' he whispered.

I sat back a little. I could feel the gap between his ulna and radius under my palm.

'That day was important,' I said, 'wasn't it? Because up until then, you thought you were safe. You thought you weren't doing anything wrong. Martin was eighteen, he was a consenting adult. You were just going to a rent boy; that was okay. That was what you told yourself, wasn't it?'

He hauled in a breath. It sounded like a wave dragging rocks down a beach.

'*Wasn't it?*'

He nodded the smallest and slightest of nods.

'But that day,' I said, 'there was a girl there. She was small, and she was scared. She was twelve – not even a teenager. She was a child. And you made her stay there, and watch what you did.'

He closed his eyes. I could see the line of his eye sockets jutting out where his eyebrows ought to have been.

'That was the catalyst, wasn't it? Her being there. You couldn't get quite so excited by Martin after that. You realised you needed someone younger. You couldn't deny it anymore.'

He opened his eyes, and I saw they were wet: not with the exertion of coughing, but with tears. 'Beatrice,' he said. 'You're Beatrice.'

I found I couldn't speak, so I nodded.

He lifted his free hand and made to put it on top of mine, still resting on his arm. I snatched my hand away.

'Don't,' I hissed.

'I've thought about you,' he said. 'I've thought about you often, since that day. I've never forgotten you.'

A wave of nausea came over me. 'Don't say that. Don't you dare fucking say that to me.'

He was shaking his head. 'I don't mean it in a sordid way,' he said. His voice was pleading now. 'I mean, I've thought about how wrong that was of me. I knew I'd scared you. I hated myself for wanting to scare you. I've often thought about what I'd say to you, if I could speak to you again.'

I straightened up. I wanted to hit this man, abject as he was.

'Well,' I said, stiffly, 'I'm here now.'

He let his head loll forward on to his chest. 'I'm sorry,' he said. 'I'm so sorry. I'm sorry for all of it. For all the terrible things I've done.'

I snorted. 'Pathetic,' I spat. 'That day in the pavilion, you pinned me there and wouldn't look away. Now you can't even look me in the eye.'

He raised his head. I watched his eyes pinball around as he focused, briefly, on the cross above the altar.

'Forgive me,' he said, quietly. Then he turned his head and looked at me. 'Forgive me,' he said again, louder this time. 'Please, Beatrice. I'm dying. I've only days left on this planet. Hours, perhaps.' He held up his hands, beseeching. The cannulas strained in their fixings, and I thought I might vomit. 'Forgive me. Forgive a stupid old man.'

I leaned backwards, away from his grasping fingers. I stood up, pushed my shoulders back, and took a deep breath in. The nausea eased, ever so slightly. I waited a moment, looking at the altar. The cross had a little figure of Jesus hanging from it, a halo carved around his head and painted gold, his face and hands impossibly white.

I leaned down over the wheelchair, and put my face close to his. I could smell the hospital on him: the thin scent of urine, the frightening tang of strong drugs.

'You can rot in hell,' I whispered.

I straightened up and moved along the aisle, listening to his cough intensify as I walked away. I stepped out of the chapel and into the glare and noise of the corridor outside. Hanging there, only feet away, was Martin's shadow: a pillar of shifting grey air that tumbled gently around on itself like a colony of moths.

I smiled. 'Have at it,' I whispered. 'He's ready to go.'

I held the chapel door ajar long enough for the shadow to slip inside. Then I closed it behind me, and let the sound-proofing do its work.

II.

Birch, Thursday 13 January

Kim's uncle had refused to sit down for the interview. He set himself up in the corner of the room, leaning against one wall with his arms folded, while his wife took the seat offered to her at the interview table. Birch thought Hoa Diep Le looked like a kind woman: she was petite, but sturdy, wearing delicate gold rings, and her nails looked like tiny works of art. Her husband, who shook hands with Birch and Amy but did not speak, was tall and angular. Birch wondered if perhaps his silence came down to a lack of confidence in speaking English.

'You should call me Hannah,' Hoa Diep said, 'and my husband is Jonathan.'

Amy frowned at the papers she'd placed on the interview table between them. 'Are you sure?' she asked. 'I don't mind …'

The older woman cocked her head. 'You're not Vietnamese,' she said. She managed to make it sound like both a statement and a question.

Amy shook her head. 'I'm half Japanese,' she replied, 'half Scottish.'

Hoa Diep – *Hannah*, Birch thought – nodded slowly. 'People who aren't Vietnamese,' she said, 'find it easier to use our Scottish names. And we like them. We chose them, after all.'

Birch smiled as the older woman let out a musical laugh. She seemed easy with them, the sort of person who was probably easy with everyone. Her husband, however, had yet to meet Birch's eye.

'Okay,' Amy said, 'Hannah.' She glanced up. 'And Jonathan. You're sure you wouldn't like to sit?'

Kim's uncle gave the slightest shake of his head. Birch felt the hairs on the back of her neck prickle.

'Right, then.' Amy shuffled the papers in front of her. 'Well, I want to thank you both for being so accommodating over the phone, and for coming in to see us today. It really was kind of you to offer to come to Edinburgh.'

Hannah nodded. 'We want to help,' she said, 'however we can. We want to cooperate.'

Birch flicked an eyebrow upward at the use of that particular word, but Amy was already speaking again. 'We really appreciate that. Now, I know we already spoke a little on the phone, but because I'm taking a formal statement, I may have to ask you to repeat some of that information again, or talk about it in more detail. Is that all right?'

Hannah nodded again. 'Of course,' she replied. Behind her, Jonathan did not respond.

Birch cleared her throat. 'I'm sorry, Mr Le,' she said, 'but we do need you to just confirm that you understand that you're here to give a statement, and that you consent to this conversation being recorded.' His silence was pissing her off already, and they hadn't even got started.

Jonathan blinked at her, slowly, and then opened his mouth to speak for the first time since he'd entered the room. 'I understand all of that perfectly, Detective Inspector Birch.'

Birch looked at Amy. No problem with his English, then.

'Very well,' Amy said. 'Then we can begin. As you know, we're here to talk about Kim, your niece. As I said on the phone, she hasn't been formally reported missing, but we've discovered that she hasn't been at her flat or attended work since before Christmas. Our initial attempts to ascertain her whereabouts have been unsuccessful, and therefore, I'd like to suggest to you that we set up a missing persons file for Kim, and begin a full investigation.'

Across the table, Hannah was frowning. 'I feel so guilty,' she said, 'for not realising. For not coming to you, or someone, and reporting it.'

Birch leaned forward slightly. 'Why didn't you? Realise, I mean.'

Hannah looked down at the table top. 'Kim ... she's an independent girl. She's spirited.' The older woman risked a shy glance at Amy. 'I like that. I raised her that way. But ... these past couple of years, we haven't got along so well. She hasn't been in touch with us so much. Not since she moved to Edinburgh. It happens sometimes that I try to call her and she doesn't answer. I leave messages and she doesn't reply. Sometimes she replies after three weeks. I just ... I hadn't realised yet that I needed to worry.'

Amy pressed her mouth into a sympathetic line. 'Tell us about Kim's move to Edinburgh,' she said. 'I understand she lived with you before that, in the family home?'

Hannah nodded. 'Yes, she's been with us since she was twelve. Her parents – my sister and her husband – they died in a car accident, back home.'

'I'm sorry,' Amy said.

Hannah lifted both hands off the table, and then placed them down again. 'Thank you,' she said, 'but it's okay. It was a long time ago. We were happy to take Kim. My sons were all getting older and flying the nest, and I'd never had a girl. It was nice for me, to have her around.'

'You got on well?' Birch asked. 'You'd say family life was ... good?'

Hannah nodded again. 'Absolutely,' she said. 'Kim was a good girl. She worked hard in school. She made us proud.'

From the corner, Jonathan let out a snort. Birch saw a flicker of embarrassment cross Hannah's face.

'You don't agree?' Amy asked, turning her face towards him.

Jonathan shrugged. 'Kim was a good student,' he said. 'She's a bright girl. She could have been a doctor. Instead she decided to do nails. Of all the things she could have done.'

Hannah looked down at her own nails. 'That's *my* profession,' she said, her voice quieter now. 'My husband wanted something better for Kim.'

Birch tried to meet Jonathan's eye. 'We understand, Mr Le,' she said, 'that there was a man in Kim's life. A man you were keen for her to spend time with?'

He let out a cold laugh. 'You understand correctly,' he said. 'I said to her, "Kim, you are eighteen now. If you're not going to build a decent future for yourself, then I am going to do it." I introduced her to Liem. He's the son of one of my oldest friends.' He pulled a face, and waved his hand as though swatting a fly. 'She dismissed him, after only moments.'

Hannah's eyes were still downcast. 'Liem is a brilliant entrepreneur,' she said. 'He does business all over the world.'

Birch saw Amy scribble a note.

'You were keen for her to give him a chance?' Birch asked.

Jonathan snorted again. 'She ought to have married him,' he snapped. His voice was suddenly louder. 'I told her, another chance like this will not come along! We are talking about your future!'

Hannah appeared to be fighting tears.

'We pushed her,' she said. Her voice seemed to be growing smaller as Jonathan's grew larger. 'Maybe we put too much pressure on her. But we just wanted for her to be happy. We wanted to make sure she was secure.'

'She's a lazy girl,' Jonathan spat. 'She was too lazy to build a proper career, and too lazy to be a wife.'

Hannah's eyes darted back towards her husband. '*Với làm im lặng*,' she whispered.

'So ...' Birch held up both hands, her palms facing Hannah. 'Kim opted to leave the family home and ... live alone for a while?'

Hannah took a deep breath in through her nose. 'Yes,' she said. 'She moved here, to Edinburgh, and started working as a manicurist.'

Birch nodded. *I can see why,* she thought. 'And how were things left? Between Kim and Liem, I mean.'

'Liem was patient,' Hannah replied, 'at first. We all thought that perhaps Kim just needed a few months, you know, to find herself. She was young.'

From the corner of the room, Jonathan made another noise of derision, but didn't speak.

'But now we think perhaps Kim has missed her chance with him.'

Jonathan sucked his teeth. 'Stupid girl,' he said.

Birch bit down on her bottom lip to keep herself from answering him. Amy scribbled another note.

'How about your relationship with Kim?' Birch asked. 'How have things been between you, since she moved? It sounds like you communicate less often than you used to.'

Hannah nodded. Again her face had creased, as though she might become upset. 'I think Kim is angry with us,' she said, 'for not supporting her choices in life. She could always be quite moody. Now she will only get in contact if she is feeling very good towards us, I think.'

Birch mimicked Amy, trying to project sympathy in Hannah's direction, though still deeply irritated by Jonathan. 'We'll need to speak with Liem,' she said, 'and see if he knows anything about Kim's whereabouts.'

Hannah turned her head and looked squarely at her husband for the first time since they'd started speaking. 'He's out of the country, I think,' she said.

'New York,' Jonathan added. The words sounded bitter in his mouth.

'No chance Kim may have gone with him?' Birch knew it was a long shot.

'Sadly,' Jonathan replied, 'no. He's on a business trip. Even if she hadn't squandered her chances with him, he wouldn't want her tagging along.'

Hannah's brows were knitted. Birch wondered how she'd managed to stay married to this man.

'Is there anywhere you could suggest,' Amy was saying, 'that we could look for Kim? Anywhere we could go and make enquiries? Might she be staying with friends? Any favourite haunts you could tell us about?'

Hannah put one hand up to her face, and then the other. After a moment, she covered her eyes, as though trying to block out the question. 'I'm so sorry,' she said, through her fingers. Her voice sounded damp. 'I couldn't tell you. I don't know. I feel like I don't know her anymore.'

'What did you think?' Birch was following in Amy's wake, the younger woman clicking away just a little too rapidly on her high heels.

'I didn't like the uncle at all.' Amy gave her head a shake, causing a ripple effect in her waterfall of hair. 'Like, not at *all*.'

Birch leaned heavily on her stick, swinging her bad leg through the long strides she was taking. 'Me neither. He seemed weirdly aggressive.'

'Right? It *was* weird, wasn't it? Like ... your niece is missing and you're berating her and calling her stupid? Really?'

Birch huffed air through her nose. 'Exactly. And I mean, way to immediately make yourself into a suspect.'

Amy began to slow down. They were approaching Birch's office door.

'That struck me, too,' she said. 'He got my back up and made me think, "Okay, we really need to be keeping an eye on this man." But then I'm also thinking ... why would he do that, if he had something to do with Kim's disappearance? Surely if he was guilty, he'd want to be nice as pie. So there's a part of me thinking the opposite, too.'

Birch was nodding. 'We need to follow up on this Liem, though,' she said. 'Because even if Uncle Jonathan isn't directly involved, he seems pretty keen for Kim to be in a relationship with this guy.'

'A guy who conveniently happens to be out of the country,' Amy added.

'Bingo. We should look into the possibility that he's taken Kim with him, I think. And if that turns out to be the case, I wouldn't be at all surprised to discover that the uncle helped make it happen.'

Amy reached the office door and pushed it open. 'I'll get a DC on to obtaining Kim's passport records,' she said. 'What did you think to the aunt?'

Birch hobbled over the threshold. Alan Crosbie was sitting at her desk – *at* it, in *her* chair. She felt a spike of annoyance. 'She seemed pretty legit to me,' she replied. 'Kind of what I expected. Worried. Feeling a bit guilty.'

'A bit embarrassed by her husband.'

'Yeah,' Birch replied, 'which I get.'

Crosbie waved a hand. 'Afternoon, ladies,' he said. 'You've summoned me here, so would you care to acknowledge my existence?'

Amy raised an eyebrow. 'Hi, Alan,' she said.

'Would you care to get out of my seat?' Birch couldn't help herself. 'I'm walking wounded over here.'

Crosbie pursed his lips, but didn't say anything. Instead he stood, and stepped out from behind the desk with the overzealous care of a dressage horse. As Birch lowered herself into her padded office chair – disturbingly warm, thanks to Crosbie – Amy sat down on one of the two more quotidian chairs on the far side of the desk. After a moment's petulant pause, Crosbie joined her on the other.

'So,' he said, 'you called, Kato? What do you two want to talk to me about?'

Amy gestured vaguely at the file she'd brought with her from the interview room: Kim's file. 'I think it's high time we declared Kim Le a missing person,' she said. 'More to the point, I think we need to start talking about a possible link between Kim and Linh Fortune. That's why I want to bring you in, Alan.'

Crosbie sat back in the chair, hitching one ankle up on to the opposite knee as though relaxing at a bar. 'Because they're both Vietnamese,' he said.

'Because they're both Vietnamese,' Amy repeated, 'and roughly the same age and same physical description, and – crucially, I feel – because they're both *missing*.'

Crosbie cleared his throat. Birch wondered if he was going to argue.

'Fair point,' he said, after a pause. 'I'll share my notes on the Fortune case with you, Kato, if you share yours on the Le case.'

Amy nodded. 'Of course.'

'What's your primary lead at the moment?' he asked, still sounding like he didn't really care to hear an answer. 'Who's your number-one suspect?'

'This older man from Glasgow,' Amy said. 'Liem, he's called. We've just learned that he's overseas, and that worries me. I'd like to gather some more information on him. The details the aunt and uncle gave me weren't particularly useful. They seem to be a fan of his, but literally just because he's a businessman and he has money. They didn't comment at all on his personality.'

Crosbie looked at Amy. 'Is that sort of attitude common,' he asked, 'in Vietnamese culture?'

Birch saw a look of mild disgust flash across Amy's face. *You wouldn't ask her that*, Birch thought, *if she was white.* 'I think you'll find,' Birch cut in, trying to keep her tone light, 'that that's the thinking of mothers and aunties the world over. My mother certainly wanted *me* to marry a rich and success-ful man.'

Crosbie coughed up a laugh.

'The aunt also told me,' Amy went on, 'that this man is in his forties. Which … isn't ancient, but probably *feels* ancient to a twenty-year-old.'

'And the expectation was that Kim would eventually marry this guy,' Birch said. 'I mean, no one with any sense wants to even think about marriage when they're twenty.'

'Right,' Amy replied. 'But it seems like the family were very keen on the idea. I think Hoa Diep has good intentions – I could see how she'd want to take responsibility for mak-ing sure Kim is well taken care of. I guess she really feels the weight of the legal guardianship she's taken on. But she doesn't seem to have realised the pressure she was applying.'

Birch was nodding. 'And if Liem was keen, he'd no doubt be adding to that pressure himself.'

'Yeah. I can see why the poor kid felt like she had to move cities.'

Crosbie seemed to have perked up a little. They were presenting him with a scenario he could buy. 'So you're suggesting,' he said, 'that this guy gets upset that he's been ghosted, as the young ones say, and comes to find Kim. Then what? He abducts her?'

'Worst case,' Amy says, 'yes. But I also think it's possible he came looking for her and she got spooked, and ran away somewhere. She already ran away from Glasgow, so we know she's not afraid to uproot herself.'

'So in that scenario,' Birch cut in, 'this Liem guy could be the crank caller who's been threatening Carol at Lucky Seven.'

Amy nodded. 'Either way,' she said, 'we need to track down this bloke and have a word.'

Crosbie had picked up a pen and was twirling it between his finger and thumb. 'So, how does this link to my case?' he asked. Birch disliked the added emphasis he placed on the word *my*. 'Let's say this is our perp, and he's started abducting women. What interest would this guy possibly have in Linh?'

Amy put her hands on the table, flat, palms up. 'That's where I'm drawing a blank,' she said. 'It just feels like a huge coincidence that two young Vietnamese women disappear from practically the same postcode area within three weeks of one another.'

Birch turned to Crosbie. 'What can you tell us?' she asked. 'What's *your* primary lead at the moment?'

Crosbie started clicking the pen's mechanism, over and over, which set Birch's teeth on edge.

'Until now,' he said, 'we've been operating on the assumption than Linh is a runaway.'

Birch raised an eyebrow. 'It's still only an assumption? No evidence yet?'

It was wicked of her, she knew, to nettle him, but he deserved it.

'We've spoken to some local working girls,' he said, still clicking the pen. 'And of course they're all claiming they've never seen anyone matching Linh's description in their lives. I've sent constables around the city's nail bars with Linh's photo. Nothing yet, but we'll keep trying.'

Amy sat back in her chair. 'So you've exhausted the obvious avenues,' she said. Birch thought the statement sounded rather pointed, and tried not to smile.

'Personally,' Crosbie replied, 'I've been focusing on the hunt for a man in Linh's life. We all know when teenage girls go missing, the first thing you look for is the involvement of a teenage boy – or some love interest, whoever he may be. Mrs Fortune is determined that Linh showed absolutely zero interest in boys, but we all know how manipulative teenagers can be. Or how secretive – perhaps that's what I mean.'

Birch made an *I'm not so sure* grimace. 'I dunno,' she said, 'Winnie's a smart woman. She's housed many a teenager. It would take a *lot* of stealth behaviour to keep a boy around without her at least beginning to suspect.'

Amy was quiet, thinking. 'Though it might be easier,' she said, after a moment, 'for an adult man to orchestrate that.'

Both Birch and Crosbie turned to look at her.

'I mean, think about it,' she said. 'If Linh had met an older man, an adult – a man we know has been on the lookout for a young, Vietnamese wife in recent times, let's say – he may well have been able to orchestrate meetings with her without

Winnie Fortune ever knowing. Teenage boys are daft and useless, but grown adult men can be, as we know, extremely calculating.'

'So you're saying,' Crosbie replied, 'that our older man from Glasgow might have not only gone looking for Kim, but also gone looking for a Kim replacement?'

Amy threw up her hands. 'I'm saying it's the only theory I have at the moment. I realise it's pretty flimsy. But people don't just disappear into thin air. You're right, Alan – with missing young girls, there usually is a man involved, somewhere.'

Birch found herself thinking of Charlie, the fourteen years she'd spent fruitlessly searching, only to find he'd been living one city over all along. *Sometimes people do disappear into thin air*, she wanted to say, but she bit down on her bottom lip and kept quiet.

'So the next obvious thing to do …' Crosbie was saying.

'Is to track down this mystery man, Liem,' Amy replied. 'Yes. It feels like he's the only lead we have, right now.'

Crosbie laughed unexpectedly, and Birch jumped.

'Well,' he said, 'unless you count the bloody mad woman who's been phoning me up lately.'

Birch tilted her head towards him. 'Which woman?'

Crosbie snorted. 'That charlatan claiming to be a psychic. You spoke to her the other day, Birch, remember?'

Birch winced as Crosbie turned to Amy, and continued speaking.

'You know how we get these weirdos every so often,' he said. 'We've all been trying to fob her off, but this one is particularly insistent. When she phoned me earlier today, I'm afraid I gave her short shrift.'

Amy was frowning.

'What did she say?' Birch asked. Her pulse was beginning to quicken.

Crosbie rolled his eyes. 'Probably the same thing she's been saying to you. All about this vision she's had: a young woman has been abducted and is being held somewhere. Of course she couldn't tell me where, or by whom. It was all very vague and woo-woo, like these people go in for.'

'So,' Amy chimed in, 'what did you say to her?'

He shrugged. 'I said, listen, bad call this time, lady – what you're telling me doesn't match the description of any case we're working on. Better luck next time.'

Amy threw Birch a look, and Birch knew what it meant: *That does, actually, match the description of a case we're working on.*

'And she went away?'

'Oh, god no. She's been pretty tenacious, hasn't she, Birch? But she did change tack, and said, "Well, maybe this girl is missing but you just don't realise it yet. Maybe it's not a case yet, but that doesn't mean I'm not for real." Blah blah blah. She tried to tell me she'd predicted something else, years ago – something about that missing kid, Rosie Cole.'

Amy's eyes widened. 'I remember that,' she said. 'I studied that case at Tulliallan.'

Birch could feel her face getting hot. Why was she feeling so uncomfortable right now? She knew the answer: because she'd kept her conversations with Bee a secret from Amy, and now Amy knew it, and would want to know why.

Crosbie looked at Birch, and seemed to take her silence as a question. 'It was a little kiddie,' he said, 'who got snatched by her pervert neighbour. He kept her in his cellar for a while – what was it, Kato? A couple of weeks? You have to remember it, Birch – it was only 2010! Mind, we found her in the end. Safe and well.'

Birch scoffed. The sound came out half strangled. 'Apart from the lifetime of trauma,' she said.

'Sure.' Crosbie waved the hand still holding the pen. 'Apart from that. Anyway, Mystic Meg tries telling me that she knew where Rosie Cole was hidden all along. Knew from the day she was abducted, apparently. Funny how hindsight is twenty-twenty, eh? They always knew all along, these people, but only ever after the fact.'

Amy was looking down at the table top.

'So, how did you leave it?' Birch asked.

Crosbie shrugged again. 'In the end, I had to put the phone down,' he said. 'The woman just would not shut up. She was really giving it some about how she felt terrible, having failed to come forward and tell us about Rosie Cole all those years ago. "I won't make the same mistake again," she says to me. "This time I'm doing the right thing, whatever it takes." Aye, sure, hen. It became obvious that she'd keep spinning shite at me for as long as I stayed on the line, so I cut her off.'

Birch looked at Amy.

She was shaking her head. 'You know, Alan,' she said, 'sometimes this sort of thing is a tactic a witness will use to provide information in a way that feels safe for them.'

Crosbie frowned. 'How do you mean?'

'Well,' Amy said, 'to use a very heavy-handed example – let's say someone has witnessed a violent crime. They want to do the right thing, and report what they've seen, but they're afraid of retaliation, or they can't get past the idea of being a grass, or they don't want their identity to be known, or perhaps a combination of all three. In a scenario like that, it's not unheard of for someone to call the police and claim that the information they have was obtained through supernatural means. They saw it in a vision, or whatever. It makes them feel safer, reporting it through that lens, you know?'

Birch turned to look at Crosbie, who had the good grace to look a little shamefaced. She felt shame, too – this thought hadn't really crossed her mind. She'd been so busy worrying about whether Bee was trying to trick her or not.

'You think I should have paid more attention to this woman?' Crosbie asked.

Amy threw him a kind smile. 'Yes,' she said, 'but there's no need for you to worry about it. As it happens, I took a call from Beatrice Crozier myself earlier this week. I understand she's been calling a lot, trying to talk to anyone who'll listen. I decided I'd be interested to hear what she has to say, even if it is just nonsense.'

Birch's eyes bulged. Amy had known about Bee? For how long? 'So …' she asked, 'what did you do?'

Amy was still smiling her kind smile. 'I've invited her in for a chat,' she replied. 'She'll be downstairs in about' – Amy paused, and looked at her watch – 'twenty minutes.'

Fortunately, McLeod was nowhere to be seen as Bee and Amy alighted from the lift and stepped out into the CID bull-pen, where Birch was waiting. A couple of heads turned to see who'd arrived, and as they flicked away again, Birch gave thanks for Beatrice's nondescript appearance.

'Just along here,' she said, shambling back towards her office as fast as her aching hip would allow. She reached the office door, and held out one arm to indicate that the other two women should enter first. 'Here we are,' she said. She remembered too late that Bee had already been here; neither woman required her help finding the room.

Amy stepped into the office, and Beatrice followed. Feeling strangely like a naughty school child, Birch cast a furtive glance around the bullpen before following them inside. She was surprised to see that Crosbie, who had still been in his chair beside the desk when Amy left to go downstairs and fetch Bee, was no longer in the room. Clearly, he had decided to opt out of this particular meeting. Bee took up the seat Crosbie had been occupying, and Amy sat down beside her. The two women waited while Birch got settled, and leaned her stick against the arm of her chair.

'I'm unsure where to start,' Bee said. She was looking at Amy. 'I don't know how much DI Birch or DI Crosbie might have told you.'

Amy leaned forward slightly. 'I suggest,' she said, 'that you assume they haven't told me anything. Whatever you have to say, I'd like to hear your version.'

Bee took a deep inhale, then, and seemed to hold her breath for a few seconds. Birch wondered if she also knew about Dr Jane's calming breath technique. But then the other woman exhaled, and began to speak.

'Ten years ago,' she said, 'you dealt with the case of a toddler named Rosie Cole. She went missing from her own back garden, and as far as anyone knew, it was as if she'd vanished into thin air.'

We know, Birch wanted to say, but she reminded herself that Amy only knew the case as an example in a textbook. Besides, Bee seemed to be settling in.

'Rosie was missing for almost two months,' she said. 'I remember Police Scotland doing fingertip searches, draining the pond in Figgate Park. I remember the newspaper reports that speculated Rosie was dead, or that her parents had killed her, or that she'd been snatched by child sex-traffickers. But then they found her. She was a few doors down the road, in a neighbour's cellar. She'd been there that whole time.'

Bee paused, and a silence began to fill the room.

'If you don't mind me asking,' Amy said, 'why is this important?'

Bee looked down at her hands. Birch noticed she'd laced her fingers together in her lap. The knuckles were white.

'Because,' she said, 'I knew where Rosie Cole was, that entire time. Or rather, I knew where she *wasn't*. I knew she wasn't dead. I knew she wasn't in the pond in Figgate Park. I knew her parents didn't deserve the journalists bothering them at all hours of the day and night. I knew she was in a cellar, under a bungalow, somewhere on the 49 bus route. I'd seen all that, and I never told anyone. I withheld information that could have been vital to that case.' She sniffed.

Birch slid open the topmost drawer of her desk and held out a box of tissues. Bee took one.

'Thanks,' she said. 'I've never forgiven myself for not saying anything.'

Birch wanted to look at Amy, see what her face was doing, but Amy was facing Bee fully, focused on the other woman's voice.

'Why didn't you say anything?' Amy asked. 'Police Scotland must have made appeals for members of the public to come forward with information.'

Birch nodded. 'We did, as I recall,' she said. 'With those kinds of cases, we always make clear that no detail is too trivial. Even if it might be nothing, it could be something.'

Bee was shaking her head. 'I don't think you under-stand,' she said. 'I knew that information because I saw it in a dream. Or … a vision. Whatever you want to call it. The

248 *Claire Askew*

first night Rosie Cole was missing, I dreamed I was in the kitchen of a white bungalow with leylandii in the garden. I saw a night bus go past, the N49. The kitchen had a black-and-white linoleum floor, with a loose flap you could pull up to find a trapdoor. The trapdoor led to a cellar with a dirt floor. In the dream, I climbed down into it, and I could feel that there was someone there with me. Someone – something – was crying. At first, I thought it was an animal. But it wasn't. It was Rosie.'

Bee was twisting the tissue between her fingers now, and Birch couldn't help herself. She let out a little cough, making Amy look over at her. Amy gave the slightest shake of her head. Birch wondered if they were both thinking the same thing: how much information about the Cole disappearance was in the public domain? The detail about the black-and-white floor could have been obtained from a newspaper photo. The rest was probably easy enough to find. Why dredge up all this drama about a decade-old case in the first place?

'I thought about coming forward,' Bee was saying, 'when Rosie's case got really high-profile. I did see those appeals for information from the public, and I thought about it. But who would believe me? Especially because …' Bee paused, and swallowed hard. 'At the time,' she said, 'my father was very ill with cancer. He was dying – he had his last day of chemo the day Rosie went missing, and in the two months she was gone, he died. I was at the hospice most days, visiting him. I was supporting my younger brother, who took it very hard. I had a lot on my plate. But also, I thought that might be held against me, you know? Oh, this crazy woman's turned up babbling about a dream – but her dad's dying, she's obviously just not coping. There was a part of me that thought I might be sectioned, or detained in some way. I was selfish. I made a decision to keep quiet.'

Birch remembered her mother's brief spell in hospice care, how emotionally draining those couple of weeks had been. Bee's mention of a younger brother touched a painful nerve somewhere inside her; by the time their mother died, Charlie was already missing. Their mother never got the chance to say goodbye to her only son, and towards the end, after they upped the morphine to keep her comfortable, she asked for him over and over again. Birch gave up on the truth, and told desperate, tearful lies. *He's on his way, Mum. He'll only be an hour.* Or, *He was just here, while you were asleep – he's just gone to get a cup of tea.* Birch begrudged this woman's story, tragic though it was – she'd *had* a little brother, there, with her, in the room. She hadn't had to invent him, time after heartbreaking time.

'And you regret it now,' Amy was saying. 'You regret your decision not to come and see us.'

'Yes,' Bee replied, shaking her head a little, as though to dislodge the memory of that time. 'After Rosie was found, I promised myself that if ever I knew anything that important again, I'd tell someone. I'd tell the police. Because ...'

Bee looked down at her hands, then at Birch, then at Amy. Amy leaned forward a little, indicating she ought to go on.

'Because,' Bee said, 'sometimes I know things. I know things about people I've never met before. Strangers. I can walk past someone in the street, and suddenly know some intimate detail about their life without ever having spoken to them. I don't really think of myself as a psychic. I just ... *know* things. Ordinarily, I have to be in physical proximity to someone for the Knowing to occur. And then the closer I get to a person, the clearer the Knowing becomes.'

Birch frowned. She fancied she could recall a slight prickle in her fingertips where she'd brushed Bee's arm outside the station the day before, and Bee had looked through her, and told her things no one else could possibly have known. 'But presumably you'd never been in close physical proximity to Rosie Cole?'

Bee shook her head. 'No,' she said, 'something about that was different, and I'm not sure what. I was physically close to her in my dream, but I'd never met her or been anywhere near the house where she was found. It's been a mystery to me ever since it happened. And now it's happened again.'

'Yes,' Amy said, 'DI Crosbie told me …' She stopped herself.

Good girl, Birch thought, *don't lead the witness*. 'Never mind DI Crosbie,' Birch cut in. She enjoyed the way the sentence felt in her mouth. 'You tell us, Bee. Tell us about this new … happening.'

Bee was nodding. 'I've been having dreams,' she said. 'Weird dreams. Dreams that feel different.'

'Different to what?' Amy asked.

Bee gave a nervous laugh. 'I know this sounds stupid,' she said, 'but … different to other dreams. They're more real, more vivid, or … something. It's hard to explain.'

Birch wanted to tell Bee that she knew exactly what she meant – she'd been having those kinds of dreams herself, lately. But she stopped herself. This could still all be a con job, couldn't it? Though, when she thought about it, Birch couldn't figure out for the life of her what Bee's end goal might possibly be.

'The first one,' Bee was saying, 'wasn't especially eventful, but it was frightening. I was in a small, pitch-black space, and I felt violently ill. I mean really, really nauseous.

Somewhere very close to me, someone was crying. A girl. I could tell she was extremely upset, hysterical even, but she was also trying to keep as quiet as she could. This went on for what seemed like a very long time. And then I woke up. This was just the other night, I should say. Sunday night. Or the early hours of Monday.'

Birch could feel Amy's attention sharpening. Linh Fortune had last been seen on Sunday afternoon.

'And when you woke up,' Birch said, 'what then? What did you think of that, in the cold light of day?'

Bee shrugged. 'I tried to tell myself it was just a dream,' she replied. 'A weird dream, but a dream like any other. But something nagged at me. That dream … it had *felt* the same as the dream I had about Rosie.'

Amy was looking intently at Bee, as though urging her to go on. 'And then you had another dream,' she said.

'Yes,' Bee replied. 'A couple of nights later, and it had that same feeling. But it was different: I wasn't in the dark space anymore, and I didn't feel nauseous. I was standing in the living room of a house, with my back to the window. In front of me was a young girl – a teenager, I'd say – asleep on a sofa. She had a blanket over her, but she was shivering, and I realised it was very, very cold. I could see my breath in that room, even though I was indoors. And I felt a strong urge to shake this girl awake, to warn her about something, though I didn't know what. Before I had chance, I woke up.'

Birch was quiet. Across the desk, she could feel Amy dithering, too. She wondered if Amy wanted to ask the same things she did: what did the girl look like? Did the house have any distinguishing features? Was there anyone else in the building with you? Those questions crowded her throat, and she had to swallow them down. Because this wasn't a witness statement, and it might never turn into one. It might never turn into anything. It might all be a huge waste of everyone's time.

Finally, Amy spoke. 'I feel like I have a lot of questions,' she said, 'but I sense...'

'That there's more,' Bee replied.

'Yes.'

'You're right,' Bee said, 'there is more. Because just last night, I had another dream. It started the same way. I was standing in the same place, in the living room of this house. Back to the window, and the sofa in front of me. This time there were two girls sleeping there, sort of top to toe, you know?'

Birch nodded. She and Charlie used to sleep that way as kids, staying over in their grandparents' spare room.

'And again I wanted to wake them up, and warn them about something, because I had this horrible feeling of foreboding, of something bad about to happen. This time, I was able to walk over and look down at them, and I was struck by how young they both looked. One of them was hugging a soft toy – a ginger cat, I think, though it was hard to tell, because it looked so well-loved. It broke my heart, that, and I didn't know why. I stood over them, watching them sleep, desperate to warn them about this terrible feeling I had – but I couldn't seem to reach out and touch them. It was like the dream wouldn't allow it, wouldn't let me interact. So I just stood there, wondering what to do. And then I heard a noise.'

A movement outside the office door caught Birch's eye. Faces were turning upward in the bullpen: there seemed to be a general pricking-up of ears going on out there.

Shit, she thought.

Amy hadn't noticed. 'What was it?' she asked.

'Someone moving around upstairs,' Bee replied. 'Footsteps shuffling. I didn't want to leave the girls, but I stood there listening, waiting to see if whoever was up there would come down into the living room and show themselves. I felt strangely responsible, like I ought to stand guard, you know? But no one ever appeared. And after a while, I simply woke up.'

Birch could hear footsteps now, someone bearing down on the office door at full steam. She winced, and nudged Amy. 'Incoming,' she said.

McLeod didn't knock. He barely even paused on the threshold. One minute, the door was closed, and the next, he was in the room, and the room felt suddenly very small.

Birch felt Amy sit up very straight. Bee hadn't turned to see who'd walked in, but her eyes went very wide. For a split second, Birch allowed herself to imagine what psychic insights Bee might be gathering as a result of being in close physical proximity to her boss. She tried not to smile.

'Afternoon, guv,' she said.

Crosbie appeared in the doorway behind McLeod. *Of course*, Birch thought.

'Would someone,' McLeod began, 'like to explain to me what exactly is going on in this room?'

Amy opened her mouth to speak, and Birch held up a hand to indicate that she shouldn't – that she, Birch, would handle it. But neither of them got the chance to say anything, because Bee had risen from her chair. She turned to face McLeod, and held out a hand to him.

'My name is Beatrice Crozier,' she said.

McLeod looked down at Bee's extended hand as though he didn't know what it was. For just a moment, he seemed unsure what to do.

'Beatrice,' Birch cut in, 'this is DCI McLeod. And DI Crosbie. I believe you two have already spoken.'

Crosbie wrinkled his nose. 'John told me she'd been escorted from the reception area by you and Sergeant Kato.'

Birch snorted at his brand-newness. John had told him no such thing: he'd already known Beatrice Crozier was here.

'And your immediate thought was what? To clype?'

She felt McLeod's gaze zero in on her.

'Birch,' he barked.

She closed her eyes, to prevent herself from rolling them at him. McLeod was allowed to say things like *We can't make it too easy for these kinds of people to settle here*, but heaven forbid she be allowed to call Crosbie what he was: a wee schoolyard clype.

'Detective Chief Inspector,' Bee was saying. She was trying to make him look at her, and he didn't want to, Birch could tell. 'I have what I believe is some important information to impart. Information I believe may assist with a case, or perhaps with the prevention of a future crime. Sergeant Kato and Detective Inspector Birch have been good enough to listen to what I have to say.'

He looked at Amy now. Birch wanted to step in front of her, screen her from his glare.

'Have they now?' he said.

'Yes,' Bee said. 'And I have more to say, if you'd care to listen.'

McLeod snorted. 'No,' he said, 'I don't think I do care to. I've been made aware of your behaviour over the past few days, Ms Crozier. I am aware that you've been phoning this police station on a regular basis, and turning up unannounced to harass my officers. I have absolutely no interest in anything you have to say, unless you intend to make a formal witness statement and impart information relating to events that have actually, physically happened.'

Bee opened her mouth.

'Have the things you've told my officers actually, physically happened, Ms Crozier? In your presence, or in the presence of another witness or witnesses?'

Birch saw Bee's shoulders drop: a rabbit going limp in the fox's jaws.

'I don't—'

He drew himself up taller. 'Well, have they?'

Birch glanced at Amy, but Amy was watching Bee.

'I'm afraid,' Bee was saying, 'that right now, I can't say for certain. However—'

McLeod held up a hand. 'However, nothing,' he said. 'Listen, DI Birch may be perfectly happy for you to set up your crystal ball in her office and trip out your nonsense, but in my book, all you're doing right now – all you *have been doing, all this past week* – is wasting police time.'

Bee shook her head. 'Detective Chief Inspector, I assure you—'

'Enough,' he snapped. 'Our time is being wasted with every word you speak. I suggest that, in order to escape a criminal charge, you pack up your wares and get out of this building as fast as you possibly can. Do I make myself clear?'

There was a short, charged pause, in which Birch had the chance to wonder if Bee might actually argue with him. *Don't* she thought, *please, I beg you. This is already bad enough as it is.* Thankfully, Bee seemed to have decided the same thing. She was still wearing her long winter coat, and didn't actually have any wares to pack up. The silence seemed to break, though nobody spoke; Bee simply turned to Birch and Amy and gave a nod. Birch felt unsettled by the look in her eye. It seemed like a look of fear. Bee had tried and failed to share the burden – real or imagined – that had settled on her. She'd come looking for help, and hadn't received it. They each watched as she skirted around McLeod and Crosbie, and walked, head down, out of the door.

Diary, Thursday 13/01

At the protected reception centre, they told me that if he ever came back for me, if he ever took me, if anyone ever took me, I should try to keep a diary. Write down the dates and times, the order things happened. Make a thing the case workers could read. Help people understand.

Here is what I know.

I was always in awe of Luke, maybe because I met him when I was younger. He was so tall. I hadn't met very many white men in my life, not to talk to. We lived in Ha Tinh province, in a place where not many tourists came. I was curious about Luke, and a little bit afraid. The first thing he told me was that his name was Luke, like in the Bible. He wore a gold cross on a chain around his neck. I didn't know who Luke-like-in-the-Bible was, but I tried to be polite. He'd come to visit with my parents, though I didn't know why. I helped my mother to make a dinner that this white man would eat: pork mince omelette, pumpkin soup, steamed vegetables, cornbread, rice, eggs. My sisters and I laughed behind our hands at Luke, who looked so large perched on his small stool at our table. He spoke Vietnamese okay, but slowly, and with an accent that made everything he said sound funny. My father looked at us sternly. Luke was important. We had to respect him.

I was the eldest, at thirteen. I knew my parents were figuring out what to do with me. I wasn't stupid; my father was a fisherman, and I knew things had been hard since the

Formosa spill. The water still wasn't clean after two years. I think my parents worried it might never be clean, and things would get harder and harder. They'd decided I was old enough to go somewhere else – somewhere better. My English was good, and I was a hard worker. They told me Luke had offered to take me to Europe. He'd find me a job there, they said. He'd promised I could still go to school. They'd pay him the money to take me there, and I'd work at my job to cover my food and a place to live. We all thought that maybe I could even earn enough money to save and send home. Luke started coming to dinner at our house more and more often. He sat – awkward in his tall body, like he was wearing clothes that were too big – and listened as we talked about this plan. I was scared, because I didn't really know him, and because I had never been anywhere so far away, and because I knew I would miss my sisters, and because no one could tell me when I might be able to come back. But Luke told us stories about Europe, about the opportunities there. He talked about castles and kings and queens, about snow and ice and being so cold that your breath makes fog in the air. He ate our food and brought us little gifts and complimented my mother on her cooking. Looking back, I feel like an idiot. I never once asked what he was doing there, in our kitchen, in our little town in the middle of nowhere. I never asked why me – why did he specifically want me to come to Europe with him, do this job, have this new life? Now I know it wasn't me, I wasn't special – I was just thirteen, and naive, with parents who needed help and believed his lies. He took their money, and then he took me. He told them I'd be safe, I'd be so safe. He made it sound like the place we were going didn't *have* danger. I believed him.

It was Sunday 9 January. I walked to the end of my road and caught the 26 bus into town. I got off on Princes Street, and walked to meet my friends, Josie and Beth, outside TK Maxx. It was 1pm, and Beth, who's always hungry, hadn't even finished hugging me hello when she asked what we'd do for lunch. We looked around TK Maxx first – it was busy, and we didn't find much, but I did buy a light blue card holder with a ginger cat on the front, because it looked just like Lang. Josie bought a huge brick of nougat with almonds and pistachios embedded inside, and Beth told her that even one bite would pull out all her teeth. Then we crossed the road and went down the Waverley Steps into Princes Mall. I don't like the food court there: it's noisy and crowded and none of the restaurants are very good. But Beth and Josie like it, because it's cheap and because no one looks at us funny when we laugh and mess about. Also you can get a huge cup of Fanta the size of your own head, which was what I did.

Princes Street was busy, because of the January sales. Too busy, we decided, so instead of going back out of Princes Mall the way we'd come, we walked down through Waverley Station instead, and out of the other side, on to Market Street. I keep thinking that if anyone is looking for me, they could look at the CCTV from the station concourse, and see me there, laughing with my friends, not knowing anything was going to happen.

We climbed up the stairs of Fleshmarket Close, all three of us complaining the whole way about how steep it was. Those steps never get any sun, and they were icy in places. I felt very sad for the homeless man asleep in a doorway halfway up the climb.

We came out on to Cockburn Street, and called into some shops. None of us had any money to spend, really – not after bus fare and TK Maxx and burgers for lunch – but we had fun anyway. I tried on a lot of woolly hats, because I am always cold here. Sometimes I'm even cold in the summertime. We joke that I'm always cold, Beth is always hungry, and Josie is always early because she's so afraid to be late. When we went camping together, Josie woke up at 6am every day and sat around bored while Beth and I slept.

It started to get dark around 3.30pm, and by then all three of us were cold, so we walked up to the Royal Mile and went into Starbucks. It was busy in there, and all the windows were steamed up. We found a tiny table, which was really meant for only one person, but we squished round it. We drank hot chocolates and sneakily ate some of Josie's nougat, which didn't pull our teeth out but felt like it might. Trying to talk with nougat in your mouth is very hard but also very funny, and we did that for what felt like ages, until I was crying from laughing so much.

I knew my bus was at 5.32pm. Beth and Josie were both getting a train, so we walked back to Waverley Station and I stood on the platform with them until their train came. After they'd gone, I felt the strange feeling I always have when my friends leave, and I'm alone. I get more alert, somehow, like a switch clicks on in my head. When I'm with Beth and Josie, I don't look at the other people around us – I barely notice they're there. But when I'm alone, I look at everyone. When I'm alone, I'm always checking for danger.

I decided I'd climbed enough stairs for one day, so I didn't walk back up the Waverley Steps. Instead I did something stupid, which was take the lift. It's a glass lift, and if you stand with your back to the doors, you can look out over the whole of the Old Town. I like it best when it's dark and you can see all the city lights – and by that time it was totally dark. I got into the lift, which was empty, and I turned my back on the exit doors.

I was right; the city did look beautiful. I could see lit-up windows in buildings at the back of Cockburn Street, where we'd just been. I could see the big banner on the City Arts Centre, a massive painting all floodlit, advertising an exhibition. I could see that on North Bridge the Christmas lights were still up, and seeing their colours made me happy. I kept looking until the last moment, until the lift made its *ping* sound and a robotic female voice said, 'This is: Princes Street.'

But it wasn't Princes Street, not really. It was a dark little corner on the roof of Princes Mall. I'd forgotten that was where the lift came out. I'd forgotten it was fifty yards from the street itself. I'd forgotten that after 5pm on a Sunday, there'd be nobody around up there. I'd forgotten, just for a minute, to be careful.

And *he* was there. When the doors opened and I turned around, he was there, as though waiting to get into the lift himself. I always thought if I ever saw him again, I'd feel the most horrible terror. But instead, it took me around ten seconds to even realise who he was. I saw his face, and thought, *I know that man, who is that?* Then he got hold of me, and I knew.

Birch, Saturday 15 January

The Dean Cemetery wasn't Birch's favourite place to be on a Saturday morning. She sat uneasily on one of the wrought-iron benches beside the path, trying to focus on the task at hand. She'd drunk the lukewarm coffee she'd brought along, and now fretted with the empty paper cup, unable to see a bin anywhere. The task at hand was marking her mother's birthday. It was etched right there on her gravestone: 15 January 1951.

Her mother had always liked that her birth date was a palindrome: 15/1/51. She'd always hated that her birthday was so close to Christmas, and closer still to Hogmanay.

'No one ever has any money,' she'd say like clockwork, every year. 'That means everyone with a birthday in January gets dreadful presents.'

Birch had tried not to let the pressure of that remark get to her, but it did. She always made sure her mother's birthday present was, if anything, fancier than her Christmas present. She routinely spent more money than she really intended to. As a younger woman, she'd wander for hours through John Lewis, deliberating between an enamel brooch and a pair of buttery leather gloves; between thermal slippers and a tufted pyjama and dressing gown set. In the end, she'd just buy all the items on her mental shortlist, and then her mother would tell her it was all far too much, Helen, and that she shouldn't have. The best present she'd ever found was a portable home steamer, which her mother liked so much that she threw away

her iron. It had cost Birch, then twenty-two, an entire fort-
night's grocery budget.

She tried to hang on to that memory, but it slithered away.
The bars of the wrought-iron bench were stubbornly cold, in
spite of her thick winter coat. A keen wind blew through the
cemetery, making her cheeks sting.

Birch was preoccupied. She felt troubled by McLeod's
outburst in her office two days before, and the way the
encounter had ended. After Bee had left, Birch had been
bracing to be yelled at; even Crosbie, whose fault it all was,
had begun to look nervous in the silence that followed Bee's
departure. But McLeod had maintained that silence for an
unusually long time. They'd all listened to the thud of the
lift's doors opening, and the slow whirr – usually just part
of the daily background noise of the building – as it carried
Bee down through the floors, away from them. McLeod had
kept his eyes on Birch the entire time, regarding her with
an expression she couldn't accurately describe. After what
felt like an eternity, he'd given a nod, as if satisfied – though
that look on his face suggested he was anything but. Then,
to Birch's bewilderment, he'd simply turned on his heel and
walked away. Crosbie had stood in the office doorway for
a few more seconds, his mouth opening and closing like a
fish, before he, too, disappeared back in the direction he'd
come. Birch had felt in the quiet that followed that both she
and Amy were waiting, expecting McLeod to turn around,
come back, and say, *Just kidding, here's your bollocking.* When
it eventually became clear that there really were going to be
no further repercussions, the two women had turned to look
at each other.

'Pardon my French,' Amy had said, 'but … what the fuck?'

Someone was advancing along the cemetery path towards her. Birch sighed. She liked the cemetery at this time of year, because very few other people ever came here. Now, it seemed she might be required to exchange pleasantries with a fellow mourner, and she really wasn't in the mood.

She busied herself with the contents of her handbag, which was sitting on the bench beside her. As the other person's footsteps crunched closer along the frosty gravel path, Birch pretended to rummage for a tissue. Surely, no one would interrupt her reverie, if—

The footsteps came to an abrupt halt.

'Good morning, Helen.'

Birch jumped, and looked up. It was Winnie Fortune, wearing her smart, dark blue coat and matching navy blue gloves. Her Gold Cross handbag hung in the crook of one elbow, and in the same hand, she carried a bunch of super-market flowers.

'Winnie,' Birch said. 'You're here.'

Winnie gave a single nod. 'As you see,' she said.

Birch felt a sudden lump in her throat. 'You've come to see my mum,' she said.

Winnie allowed herself a small smile. 'Of course. I'd never let Joan's birthday go by without a wee visit.'

Birch grabbed at the strap of her handbag. 'Do you want me to—?'

Winnie held out a hand. 'You stay where you are, hen,' she said. 'You've as much right to be here as I do. Mind if I join you, though?'

Birch shook her head. 'Not at all,' she said. 'Please, sit.'

Winnie came to rest at the opposite end of the bench, close enough to touch, but maintaining a marked distance.

She placed the flowers between them on the seat, their plastic wrapper crunching.

'She'd have been an old lady by now,' Winnie said, after a pause. 'Like me.'

Birch was unsure how to respond to this. She didn't feel as though she could agree. 'I wish I'd made more of her birthdays,' she said, instead. 'You know, when she was alive. If I'd known that she'd die so young, I'd have thrown her a massive bash every year, with balloons and a disco.'

'She'd have hated that,' Winnie replied, not unkindly. Birch laughed, and then they both fell silent, staring across the path at the gravestone.

'I'm surprised we haven't met like this before,' Winnie said. 'Here, I mean. On this day.'

Birch nodded. 'It doesn't often fall on a day I can be here,' she said. 'If I'm working, then … you know. And they lock this place early in winter.'

'True.'

They settled back into silence. Birch thought of all the things she wanted to say to Winnie, but she couldn't figure out where to start. The weight of those unspoken things felt like nothing at all when she thought of all the things she wished she could say to her mother. She wondered what Winnie was thinking, but knew it would be inappropriate to ask.

'Your Detective Inspector Crosbie,' Winnie said, startling Birch, 'is a real piece of work.'

Birch hiccupped out a laugh. She hadn't expected that. 'I know,' she said. 'I'm so sorry, Winnie.'

Winnie turned towards her then, looking at her properly for the first time since she'd sat down. 'What happened, Helen?'

Birch found she couldn't hold the older woman's gaze. 'DCI McLeod took Linh's case away from me,' she said.

'I wasn't expecting it. I really thought he'd let me keep this one, given my connection to you. So when he said he was assigning it to Crosbie, it took me by surprise. I didn't fight for it. I should have, but I didn't. I'm so sorry.'

Winnie shifted on the bench, and Birch could tell she was still looking at her. 'I'm sorry, too,' she said. 'I should have phoned you. But ... I've been so frustrated, this past week. It feels like nothing is happening, like no one is *doing* anything.'

Birch nodded.

'I know,' she replied, 'and I understand why you'd feel angry with us all – with me, too. But I promise I've been doing what I can behind the scenes. I want you to know that I've been advocating for Linh. It's because of me that you have Rema, for example.'

'Yes, I suspected you might have had something to do with that. Rema is wonderful, by the way.'

Birch smiled. 'Isn't she just? She's one of the best officers Police Scotland has.'

When Birch allowed herself to look up, she saw Winnie was nodding, slowly.

'She's helped me a lot,' the older woman said. 'Helped me to ... well, just to keep body and soul together, I suppose.'

Birch looked over at her mother's headstone once again. 'We're going to find her,' she said, her voice relaying more conviction than she'd realised she felt. 'We *are* going to find Linh.'

Winnie didn't reply, but she did reach into her sleeve to retrieve a handkerchief.

'It may not be my case,' Birch went on, 'but I want you to know that I've been doing what I can. DI Crosbie hasn't been taking her disappearance seriously enough, in my opinion. I'm sure, from your dealings with him, that you'd agree.'

Winnie dabbed at her eyes. 'Yes,' she said, 'I do.'

'I want you to know that I've been trying to keep him right. Trying to hold him to account.'

Hearing herself, Birch thought of Dr Jane. She realised she sounded pleading – she wanted Winnie to thank her, to tell her she was doing a good job. She realised, with a degree of embarrassment, that in that moment, she'd settle for *anyone* telling her she was doing a good job. She imagined Dr Jane asking her to analyse that, and found she didn't want to.

Winnie took a moment to compose herself. 'I'll tell you what's frustrating, Helen,' she said. 'It's the complete lack of information. DI Crosbie doesn't tell me anything, and Rema, I think, isn't allowed to. I know Crosbie and his officers must be doing *something*, but hearing nothing at all about it makes me wonder. Does anyone care about Linh at all? Does anyone care that this wee girl is missing?'

Birch turned her shoulders so she was facing Winnie squarely. 'I care,' she said. 'I care very much. And my colleague, Sergeant Amy Kato, also cares. Amy's involved in this case now, which can only be a good thing. I promise you, the wheels are turning; what needs to be done is being done. But I know it's painfully slow, and it's difficult to be in the dark.' She wanted to add, *I've had someone I love go missing. Trust me, I know what it's like.* But again, she thought of Dr Jane, who'd no doubt find an extremely diplomatic way to say, *Stop making it about you, Helen.*

Winnie was looking at her intently, her eyes wet. 'Can you tell me anything,' she asked. 'Anything at all?'

Birch could feel the emotion behind the older woman's words, and the temptation to tell her not just something, but everything, felt extremely strong. It wouldn't be especially risky;

Winnie wouldn't repeat anything. If she wanted to, Birch could repeat to her those comments of McLeod's that had made her so uncomfortable. She could tell Winnie how Anjan had later confirmed they were racist. She could tell her that Crosbie's first assumption had been that Linh had decided to go into sex work in order to avoid the asylum process – she could tell her he'd even sent constables out to interrogate the local working girls. She could even tell her about the strange materialisation at Fettes Avenue of Bee, with her cryptic dreams. It felt incredibly tempting to spill every detail of the case – of the two cases, Birch reminded herself, because Kim Le was also missing – to this civilian who couldn't possibly understand what any of that really meant. But no. Birch gave her head a small shake. However she was feeling about Crosbie, about McLeod, about herself, she was still a policewoman. There were still rules.

'I'm so sorry, Winnie,' she said. 'I want you to know that as soon as we know anything new, as soon as there's anything we *can* tell you, we will.'

Something changed in Winnie's eyes, then; Birch saw her retreat behind something. She sniffed in a short, hard breath. 'Yes,' she said. 'Of course. You have to say that.'

They fell into an uneasy silence once more, both looking at the gravestone in front of them. Birch had chosen the font and the wording herself; she liked the looping white 'J' at the front of her mother's name, the elegant slant of it. She traced the lettering with her eyes, trying to tell herself she'd been right not to say anything else to Winnie. Then a thought occurred to her, and she turned back to face the older woman once again.

'Can I ask you something? About Linh.'

Winnie looked up. 'Of course,' she said. 'Anything you need to.'

Birch tried to think of a way to phrase the question that would sound casual, that wouldn't cause alarm.

'Does Linh … does she have a stuffed animal? One she's particularly attached to, I mean?'

Winnie sat up a little straighter. 'Wait,' she said, 'are you asking because – have you had a sighting of Linh? Has someone seen her?'

Birch winced. *Maybe*, she thought. *Sort of.* 'I'm afraid I just need you to answer the question,' she replied, hating herself for how police-like she sounded.

'Well,' Winnie said, 'I suppose the answer is yes … in a manner of speaking.'

Birch cocked her head. 'What does that mean?'

She saw Winnie take a deep breath, as though calming herself. The question had got her hopes up, Birch knew. She felt cruel for doing it, when it was based on almost nothing.

'It's not a soft toy she has,' Winnie replied. 'It's a backpack. She takes it everywhere with her. She had it with her when she—' Winnie paused. 'She had it with her the last time I saw her,' she said.

Birch could feel her pulse rising. 'Can you describe this backpack?' she asked.

Winnie nodded. 'I already told DI Crosbie this,' she said, 'but yes. It's a fluffy backpack in the shape of a ginger cat. Less fluffy these days, really, because she's used it so much. I'm sorry to say it's rather ratty now. But she won't be parted from it. Even though she's seventeen, and it's a bit babyish, to be honest. It's the only possession she still has from her home in Vietnam, so you can't begrudge her being attached to it.'

Birch realised she was standing up. She wanted to peel out from the bench and start running.

'Helen?' Winnie said, looking up at her. The older woman's face was a mix of concern and hope. 'What's wrong? Have I said something important?'

Birch glanced down the path in the direction of the cemetery gate, and the road beyond. For the five hundred millionth time, she cursed her busted hip and the fact that she couldn't currently drive. She'd need to call a taxi, or an Uber ...

'Sorry,' she replied. She felt like she'd been slapped, hard, in the face, and it has disorientated her. 'I can't really ... I don't know. But ... Crosbie hadn't told me about the backpack, you see. Otherwise ...'

Winnie was frowning. 'You're not making any sense, hen,' she said.

Birch reached down and grabbed her handbag. 'I know,' she said, 'and I'm so sorry. I hope I haven't ... worried you, or anything. But I have to go now. Hopefully we'll have something for you soon. Some news.'

Winnie still looked utterly confused, but Birch had begun to feel that if she didn't speak to Amy immediately, she may explode. She didn't trust herself not to blurt out the whole thing to Winnie, instead.

'Thank you for coming to see Mum,' she said, and before Winnie could respond, Birch turned her back. As fast as her bad hip would allow her, she walked away.

She hadn't wanted to call Crosbie, but she knew she needed to. However she felt about it, Linh's case was assigned to him. For this lead – she was trying to persuade herself that it was, in fact, a lead – to be pursued, he'd need to be involved.

'This had better be good, Birch,' he said, letting himself into her office without knocking. He was carrying his coat over his arm, and in the same hand clutched a Hibs scarf.

He brandished it at her. 'I was on my way to Easter Road, you know.'

Amy teetered in behind him, balancing three large coffees in a cardboard tray. 'Hello, Alan,' she said.

He glanced at her. 'Kato,' he said. He looked back at Birch. 'Any chance we can make this quick? More to the point, any reason why it couldn't just be a phone call?'

Birch accepted the coffee Amy was holding out to her. She was already sitting in her own seat, behind the desk she'd begun to think of more as a prop from her flood dream than as a useful object in the real world. She indicated that he should take the other seat, the one Bee had sat in less than forty-eight hours before. Glancing at Amy, she saw her nod. They were ready to begin.

'I didn't want to call you, Alan,' Birch said, 'because I feared you'd put the phone down on me. You're not going to like what I have to say, but I need to make sure that you hear it.'

Crosbie closed his eyes. 'Oh Jesus,' he said. 'This is about the bloody psychic, isn't it?'

Birch glanced at Amy. Neither of them knew, yet, what she was about to say. She took a deep breath. 'Beatrice Crozier knows something,' she said. 'How she knows it is irrelevant right now, but she knows something. It's my belief that she *has* seen Linh Fortune. I think she's a legitimate witness in this case.'

Crosbie fixed her with a dead stare. 'You've lost it, Birch,' he said. 'You have just completely flat-out lost it.'

Amy tilted her head to one side. 'Marm,' she said, 'what's making you say this?'

Birch looked past Crosbie in the direction of her friend. 'Kato,' she said, 'you were there on Thursday, when

Ms Crozier ... gave her testimony. Tell me what you remember about her description of the girl she said she'd seen.'

Something changed in Crosbie's body language; Birch could tell, even though she wasn't looking directly at him. He hadn't, of course, bothered to ask either her or Amy about what might have come out of their conversation with Bee. He had, as usual, already made up his mind. Now he was receiving new information.

'She said,' Amy replied, 'that she saw a girl, and later two girls, asleep on a sofa. She said it was cold in the room, cold enough for her to see her own breath. She described the first girl as having a blanket pulled over her, but still shivering.'

'Yes,' Birch said. 'And what else?'

Amy was quiet for a few seconds, remembering.

'Oh yes,' she said. 'She'd seen that one of them was holding a stuffed toy. A ginger cat, she thought.'

Birch looked back across the desk at Crosbie. 'Thanks, Amy,' she said.

Crosbie met her gaze. The confusion on his face seemed genuine. 'I'm sorry,' he said, 'but I seem to be missing something.'

Birch didn't move her eyes, but she addressed Amy again. 'Kato, you're closer to this case than I am. Do you happen to know what personal effects Linh Fortune had on her when she was last seen?'

Out of the corner of her eye, she saw Amy shake her head.

'No,' Birch said. Crosbie wasn't looking at Amy, and she wanted to be sure he knew the answer. 'I thought not. I don't think many people have that information, do they, Alan? You do, Winnie Fortune does, and Rema, presumably. Maybe a few officers who've looked at Linh's file. Does that sound about right?'

Crosbie didn't respond. He still looked confused.

'I suppose what I'm asking,' Birch went on, 'is for you to confirm that it's not a matter of public record, what Linh was wearing when she disappeared, or what items she had with her?'

Crosbie began to shake his head, but slowly, as though answering her might constitute stepping into some sort of trap.

'So you haven't yet made a public appeal of any kind, asking for witnesses to contact us if they've seen someone matching Linh's appearance? Her appearance hasn't been described publicly?'

Crosbie shrugged. 'Not yet,' he said, 'no. Birch, what *is* this?'

Birch held up a hand. She was enjoying this process more than she ought to be, she knew. 'One more question,' she said. 'When you sent constables out to speak to local sex workers about Linh, did they disclose Linh's appearance based on what she was last seen wearing?'

Crosbie shook his head more definitely this time. 'No,' he said, 'I don't believe so. They went out with a photograph Mrs Fortune gave us permission to use. It was about a year old, she said, but a decent likeness.'

'Right,' Birch said, 'thank you. This confirms to me, then, that Beatrice Crozier could have had no easy way of knowing that one of the things Linh had on her person when she disappeared was a backpack. A fluffy backpack in the shape of a ginger cat. A backpack that could easily have been mistaken for a soft toy by someone who wasn't really sure what they were looking at.'

Crosbie eyed her for a moment. Birch looked back at him, unblinking. She watched the penny drop; he knew she had a point. He raised one hand and rubbed at his forehead. Birch didn't dare look at Amy – didn't dare shatter the precarious moment. Crosbie was weighing it up, deciding whether to dismiss her, or to get on board.

'It seems to me,' she said, 'that there's only one way Beatrice could have known that Linh has a ginger cat backpack. She has to have *seen Linh*. There's no other explanation.'

Crosbie let his hand fall away from his face. Something in his expression had changed. She'd done it. She'd convinced him, in spite of himself.

'But ... a psychic? *Really*, Birch? You're going to go to McLeod and say our new key witness in this case is a *psychic*?'

Birch allowed herself to glance briefly at Amy, before turning back to Crosbie. He seemed to be squirming in his seat, as though he knew what was coming next.

'Not me,' she replied, sitting back and holding up both hands in the air. 'After all, this isn't my case. If anyone's going to tell him, Alan, it's going to have to be you.'

Diary 14/01

I learned very quickly that there *was* danger where Luke was taking me. There was danger everywhere he took me. That's because there was danger anywhere *he* was, and even when I couldn't see him, I knew I wasn't safe.

He was less kind to me the further from my parents we got. We drove for a long time. Sometimes I sat in the passenger seat of the van, and at first he'd stop and buy me sweets and fizzy drinks and let me FaceTime my family to update them on the journey. Other times I had to get into the back of the van, and fold myself into a sort of trunk he'd built in there. It was bolted to the van floor, and felt like I imagined a coffin must feel. When I was inside there, I had to be very, very quiet. I couldn't move around, or even breathe too loud, Luke said. Sometimes I stayed there for what felt like hours, and when the van was moving it was noisy and smelled of exhaust fumes. I felt sick but couldn't wretch, couldn't cough. The further we got from home, the more I had to be inside that box. I learned how to cry very quietly, and how to breathe in a long, slow way to try and keep calm.

Later, people would ask me where we drove, what borders we crossed, what checkpoints we stopped at. I didn't know, I told them. I was inside the trunk. The road signs were in languages I didn't know. Luke took my phone and wouldn't give it back. I think he threw it away. I slept on cardboard and blankets in the back of the van. It rained. I was scared. I couldn't tell them much more than that. Only that he got less and less kind, until eventually I realised he'd become cruel.

We got as far as the Netherlands. I didn't realise that was where we were; I only knew we were somewhere cold, and very flat. Luke seemed annoyed by everything I did, to the point where I didn't even want to ride in the cab of the van with him anymore, because he'd yell at me, and sometimes he'd even reach out and slap me across the face. Instead, I lay on the cardboard in the back, wrapped in a blanket, pinching my nose to keep out the exhaust smell. I wanted to go home to my parents. I knew it was a mistake to have left, to have trusted him, but it was too late. I had no way to call them. I had no way to escape.

I must have slept, because I found myself shuddered awake as the van pitched over to one side. I rolled and slammed into cold metal and cried out. Luke had accelerated suddenly, and I could feel we were still picking up speed. I tried to sit up and get my bearings. It was dark outside; I could tell by how little light filtered into the van's shell. But what light I could see was blue, and over the roar of the engine, I realised there was also a siren. We were being chased.

I can't say what I felt as I struggled to stay upright, pulling the blanket around myself to cushion my limbs as Luke threw us both left and right. I wondered if he'd driven into a wood; it felt as though he were zig-zagging through trees. I knew nothing of the police in countries other than my own, and I didn't know where we were. Were the people chasing us trustworthy? What would they do with Luke? Would they be kind to me? I guessed they were not police who could be easily bribed, otherwise Luke wouldn't be trying to outrun them. He had plenty of money on him: strange-looking cash in all different currencies, beautiful notes with silver holograms and pictures of animals.

I gave thanks for the flat roads of this strange place as Luke gunned the van this way and that. I could feel a gap opening up; the siren didn't disappear, but it did sound further away, and the blue flashing lights grew fainter. I assumed we'd keep driving, keep widening the lead, but instead, Luke slammed on the brakes without warning, and I was lifted fully into the air. I crashed into the partition between the van shell and the cab, feeling my skull crunch against the metal. Behind my eyes, I saw swimming patterns in bright colours, and I felt as though I might throw up. I wanted to curl up in my blanket and sleep, to shut out the pain. But then the van's back doors were thrown open, and Luke was standing there, a frightening silhouette against the oncoming lights. I could see the police car bearing down on us as Luke reached into the van and grabbed at my kicking legs.

'*Out!*' he yelled, and then I was hauled along the van floor, the blanket pulled up around my head. I screamed, believing for a moment that Luke's intention was to throw my body in front of the oncoming police car, perhaps to stop the chase or slow it down. Instead, he simply dragged me out on to the tarmac at his feet. I felt my head hit the back bumper, and then the ground, and gave thanks for the blanket, though the impact still hurt. By the time I had thrashed free of the fabric, Luke was back in the driver's seat, pushing his foot to the accelerator. I was surrounded by exhaust smoke, and threw my hands over my face as he spun the back tyres, spraying me with grit. He sped off, leaving me in the road.

The police were strange, and I was afraid of what they might do. I thought they'd leave me there too, and carry on after Luke, but they didn't. The police car eased to a stop beside me, every inch of my skin vibrating with the noise of the siren. They spoke to me at first in words I didn't understand, and I must have stared at them stupidly. I was crying, and my head was bleeding from where it had hit the partition inside the van. I had nothing I could offer them: only the clothes I was wearing, the dirty blanket, and my ginger cat backpack which I always kept hooked over my arm, even while sleeping. I had no money, no papers. I had nothing. I was no one.

But I realised that they might be kind. One of them was a woman, which I found surprising.

'You speak English?' she asked, bending over me. She had some sort of small light in her hand, and it made me blink, but I nodded.

'What's your name?' she asked. I liked how she spoke; her voice sounded thick, weighty.

'Linh,' I said.

'Who was that man, Linh?'

I shook my head. It made everything hurt. Beside the police car, the policeman she was with was speaking his own language into a radio. He'd turned off the siren, but I could hear others now, far away. Moving closer.

'He's Luke,' I said, hearing how tiny my own voice was. 'Luke, like in the Bible.'

I hope one day someone can tell me why I didn't scream. I hope someone can explain to me why I allowed him to take me by the arm and shove me back into the lift. On the way back down to the station concourse, he explained that we were going to walk calmly to Platform 2, where there was a footbridge. I didn't know it; I'd never come into or out of the station's back entrance. Maybe that's why I didn't argue, didn't struggle, didn't shout for help. I felt limp, like a fish, as he slid my backpack off and hooked it over his own shoulder. As the lift slid downwards, I looked again at the city lights, blurred this time with tears I tried to force myself not to cry.

I'd been waiting for this day, and dreading it, hoping it would never come. Just lately, I'd started to really *believe* it would never come. I'd been stupid.

Walking through the station was like walking through a dream. I wondered if anyone would look at us, stop us, question the strange fact of a grown-up white man wearing a fluffy cat backpack and walking arm in arm with a teenager like me. But if anyone did find it strange, they didn't show it. People made eye contact with me, but then their eyes flicked away. I wish I knew why I didn't scream.

It wasn't far to the footbridge. There weren't many people at that end of the station, and even fewer on the bridge's far side. A couple of taxis waited at a little rank by the back entrance. In one of them, I could see the driver was holding an animated phone call, shouting and gesticulating at someone far away, who couldn't see him.

We crossed the street. It was dark. A huge bridge towered above us. I saw a bus drive over it, far above me. I'd never been on this street before, and I felt like I could have been in any city, in any country, on any planet. What I mean is, I knew in that moment that I was lost, and that he was going to take me somewhere I couldn't be found.

Luke is his name, the man. That's what I told the Dutch police over and over. My parents gave him a lot of money to take me to Europe, where he said I would make my fortune. I was the eldest of four sisters. I'd seen Paris in films, and Luke had told me all of Europe was like that: tree-lined streets and riches. I believed him. I was stupid. They nodded, and said I was safe now. They lied.

He pushed me down that dark street. A few yards away, there was a small grey van. It was a different van to the one I'd seen before, but I knew without him telling me that I'd be put into the back of it. I don't know why I let it happen, this time or those other times. But I did. So many people had told me I was safe: *It's okay, you're safe now, you're safe with us.* It was never true, and it never had been. He'd come to find me once again. He always did.

It was very dark in the van, and the movement of it made me feel sick, because there was nothing I could focus my eyes on. It smelled like chemicals in there, too, and I didn't want to think about why. The feeling of being in the van was familiar and horrible, and it felt like we drove for a long time. I tried to count the turns we made: first a left, then a right, then another left, but after a while it became impossible to keep count. We drove over cobbles and my teeth rattled together against my tongue. Towards the end, I felt like we'd driven round a huge circle, so we must have gone around a roundabout. Eventually we stopped. Luke opened the van's back doors, and I stepped out into a street that could have been anywhere. There were semi-detached houses with pebble dash, and ugly little gardens under orange streetlights. I knew which one he was going to take me into, because the windows were covered over with boards.

Here are all the things I had in my backpack:
- my phone
- my charger
- my AirPods in their blue pouch with gold stars on
- my purse with my bus pass, Young Scot card, TK Maxx Treasure card, library card, photobooth pictures of me and Josie and Beth, a photo of Lang, a photo of me and my sisters when we were little, a few receipts, and £2.57 in change

- my house key on a metal keyring in the shape of a cat face with the words 'CRAZY CAT LADY'
- a packet of sanitary towels with four left inside
- a strawberry lip balm
- a nail file with a pattern of dancing avocados
- the card holder I bought in TK Maxx
- a pack of Juicy Fruit gum I hadn't opened yet
- this notebook
- two biro pens

Luke took me into the house through a dark hallway, and into the kitchen, which was small and seemed to be built quite badly at the back of the house. It was cold in there. He put on the light and it was too bright, one of those long strip kind of bulbs, and it buzzed. The kitchen had dirty white worktops with old food and dishes left out. Luke cleared a space and emptied out my backpack. He took the phone and put it in his pocket. He wound the wire of the charger around one hand, and put the plug in his fist. I thought for a second he might turn round and hit me then, but he didn't. He pocketed the AirPods and the case, and took out my purse. I asked him to give it back, or at least to give me the photographs in it, but he laughed at me. Then he made a big show of taking out the photographs and tearing them in half, to make me cry. He put my key and the keyring into his pocket with my phone, and he took the gum. Everything else he stuffed back into the bag, and then he threw it at me.

'Don't say I never give you anything,' he said.

Birch, Sunday 16 January

It was happening again, the same way it always did: one weak ceiling tile somewhere directly above the desk. A drip, tick-tick-ticking on to a pile of papers. The drip becoming a trickle. The trickle becoming a pour. A downpour. A waterfall. A flood.

The water reached her knees before anything changed. Birch was where she usually was: standing at her office door, looking out through the glass at her colleagues in the bullpen. There was Amy, throwing back her head to laugh at something, though the water around her was already deep enough to swim in. Birch rattled the door handle, and opened her mouth to shout, but no sound came. Instead, a thought came to her, somehow, seemingly from outside the world of the dream: *Enough*.

She realised that on this occasion, she could do something different. Instead of watching the water rise outside, she turned her back on the door. She waded back towards her infernal desk, now lifted from its legs and bobbing on the surface of the water, all its contents shuddering slightly, stacked folders waiting to topple. The water was thigh-deep and churning, as though moved by some invisible current. Birch put both hands on the edge of the desk, surveying its contents. Paper, paper everywhere: a hole punch, a stapler, that cow jug from her mother's house, now filled with pens. Birch's computer monitor crashed over on to its face, as though volunteering itself. Birch grabbed it, yanked it free, and waded back towards the door.

Her colleagues outside were still filing, typing, fetching coffees, the water up to their waists. Birch came to a halt around two paces back from the door. Lifting the monitor high above her head, she flung it at the glass with all the strength she could muster. It worked: the entire door shattered into pieces, seeming to disintegrate into the water below. Every head in the bullpen turned to look at her.

'Out!' she yelled, crashing out over the threshold of her office, amazed to be free for the first time in so many dreams. 'Everyone, get out! Evacuate!'

She'd woken with a start at the sound of her alarm. It was Sunday, but she needed to get up nevertheless. She hadn't been to visit Charlie in over a week. Lifting one hand to her cheek, she expected to find her hair damp, water running down her face. But there was nothing. She sat up in bed, blinking away the last echoes of the dream. Anjan was collecting her in an hour to drive her over to HMP Low Moss. She had to get up.

'Marm?'

It was Amy – the Amy from the dream – speaking. She'd waded over through the torrent to where Birch was standing, shouting, pleading with her colleagues to move. Dream Amy moved so easily through the water, it was almost creepy. Birch wondered if she was still wearing her high heels.

'What's all the fuss about?'

Birch grabbed her friend by the shoulders, amazed at how real and solid she felt. She fancied she could smell Amy's Prada perfume, black cherries and burned sugar.

'Kato,' she hissed, 'what is *wrong* with you all?' She gestured wildly at the water, still rising all around them. 'Can none of you *see* what's going on in here?'

'You're quiet,' Anjan said. They'd been on the road for almost an hour – they'd be there soon. Birch was holding a book in her lap, the latest in what she and Charlie called the Birch Family Book Club. It was just the two of them, but she liked the little in-joke of the name. They'd both read the same book at the same time; that way, if there wasn't much to talk about during visits, they could talk about their current book. This time it was *Dear Neighbour* by Jane Claire Bradley. There was a character in it, Bill, who reminded Birch of her dad. She wanted to ask Charlie if he'd also seen shades of Jamieson in this made-up contrary old man. Jamieson might be there today, himself – if he had no work on, he sometimes turned up for Sunday visits. Birch tried to focus on something other than the dream. Would Jamieson be interested in joining their little book club? Did her father read anything other than the *Sun*?

It took her a moment to realise Anjan had spoken. 'Sorry,' she said. 'I'm a little bit in my own head today.'

Anjan snorted. 'No kidding,' he said, quietly.

In the dream, Birch left Amy behind. Her friend wouldn't listen – seemingly *couldn't* listen.

'Marm,' Amy called out, as Birch half-strode, half-swam down the corridor, away from the bullpen. 'Come back! Marm?'

Birch reached the lifts. The water was chest-height now, and staying on her feet was difficult. She let herself lift off from the floor, and began to tread water as she reached out for the call button. There was a *ping*, and she heard the creak of the lift as it began its ascent from the ground floor. Too late, she remembered the advice that one should never use the lifts when evacuating a building. But that was in the case of fire, right? This wasn't a fire. And besides, it was force of habit. She'd called the lift, and now it was coming.

She and Anjan moved swiftly through the motions of the prison check-in. They both came here a lot: Birch to visit Charlie, and Anjan for work. They knew the ropes: stow all personal items in a locker in the entrance way. Over to the main desk, where the PC-mounted webcam would take an ugly photo for your temporary pass. Through the metal detector, under the watchful eye of at least one screw. Then into the waiting area, until all the visitors were checked in and assembled, and the route was moved. Once the prisoners were seated in the visit room, the screws could begin filtering their friends and family in via a series of complicated corridors and chambered halls.

'Never stops being depressing, does it?' Anjan said, as they lined up behind the first door, watching the prison guard fumble with various keys and fobs. 'Helen, you know that whatever's bothering you, you can tell me.' He gave her arm a squeeze.

She looked at his face, saw worry etched in the fine lines around his eyes. *Well*, she thought, *it involves a witness who says she's psychic, and a new weird element to my already incredibly weird dreams.*

'Seriously,' Anjan said, as though she'd spoken aloud. 'Try me.'

The lift seemed to take an age to arrive. Birch could feel the blood sloshing in her ears as panic grew inside her chest.

The water was above her shoulders; treading water was her only option now. A tiny part of her – the tiny, quiet part of her that knew this was a dream – whispered, *What if you don't wake up this time?*, and the words seemed to echo around in her skull above the water's endless, frothing din. The lift clunked closer, closer, and then finally, the call button lit up and she heard the *ping* to announce it had arrived. The doors slid open, and Birch let out a hard-edged, animal sound.

She didn't know how it was possible, but the inside of the lift was empty – empty, and completely dry.

Seeing Charlie always did something dramatic to Birch's mood, and she could never be quite sure what it would be until it happened. Some weeks, she walked into the visit room and began to fret before she'd even sat down at the table; her brother looked thin, or he looked pale, or he looked ill-slept, or like he was starting with a cold. Other times, seeing him brought a rush of nostalgia. *Hey,* she'd think, *it's my kid brother!*, and a strange churn of joy and sadness would form somewhere around her diaphragm. It was so good to see him, but so, so bad to see him here, behind high concrete walls, with his hair buzzed close to his skull. In the fourteen years he'd been missing, Charlie had become heavily tattooed, and sometimes Birch felt a kick of surprise at the sight of his inked neck and forearms.

Today, the sight of him was a tonic. As she sat down opposite him, Birch felt something heavy lift away from her. It was as though the weight of all that water, pressing hard against her ribs in the dream, had carried itself with her into the passenger seat of Anjan's Lexus and along the M8. Now, she felt like she could let it go. She looked at her brother's face, and exhaled.

'You all right, Nella?' he said, a look of mild amusement on his face. 'You look a bit waffy over there.'

She beamed at him. 'All the better for seeing you, kid,' she replied.

Beside her, Anjan was settling into a chair of his own.

'Big yin,' Charlie said, turning his attention to the man who had, briefly, been his lawyer. 'How's tricks, my pal?'

Anjan smiled. Birch liked that he liked Charlie – liked that the two men could look past all their shared history, and be so unexpectedly at ease.

'Busy,' Anjan replied. 'Always busy in January.'

Birch nodded. Crime rates always rose at Christmas, it was a known fact. Robberies were something like thirty per cent more likely to take place in December than in any other month. It showed in Anjan's current caseload.

Charlie laughed, and looked at Birch. 'Does this guy ever take a holiday?' he asked.

Birch snorted. 'Listen, honey,' she said, 'you're playing my song.'

Charlie scrunched his face. 'Oh sure, Miss Workaholic. I mind all those long, relaxed breaks *you've* taken recently, now I think about it.'

Birch placed one hand on her chest, a gesture of mock-offence. 'Excuse me,' she said, 'haven't I just had *weeks* of time off work? I've had my literal feet up, I'll have you know.'

Charlie rolled his eyes. 'Yeah,' he said, 'because you got shot, Nella. And even having been shot, you tried to go back to work and ended up getting hurt *again* on account of being – well, honestly, a fucking idiot. Hardly the same thing as going on a wee cruise, now, is it?'

Birch let herself laugh. From anyone else, the 'fucking idiot' comment might have stung, but this was Charlie. Endless verbal prodding was their thing – it was just what the two of them did.

'Whatever,' she said, adopting the old teenage tone she only ever used with her brother. 'Like you'd enjoy it if I came in here every other week with all my holiday snaps from the Algarve or somewhere. That wouldn't be much fun for you, would it, stuck in a cell?'

Charlie shrugged. 'I dunno,' he replied. 'Might beat looking at your bloody miserable face every visit. What's up with you this time, anyway? You look like you slept under a hedge.'.

Birch felt the smile fall from her face. She really thought she'd left her cares outside in the holding area. 'What do you mean?' she asked, suddenly serious.

Anjan leaned forward across the table. 'I've been trying to get her to tell me what's wrong all morning,' he said. He and Charlie exchanged a look, and then Charlie sat back in his seat, and folded his arms.

'Right then,' he said. 'Out with it, Nella. We're not talking about anything else until you tell us both what's going on in your weird little brain.'

Birch blinked. 'You can't just—'

Charlie cocked his wrist, checking an invisible watch. 'You want to run out the clock on my visit? Bit selfish, can't lie.'

Beside her, Anjan chuckled.

She sighed. '*Fine,*' she said, hearing the echo of her long-ago teenage self again. 'But you're not allowed to laugh, okay? Either of you.'

Charlie held up his hands. 'No promises,' he said.

Birch rolled her eyes. 'It's just …' She paused, unsure whether or not to lead with the dream. Anjan knew she'd been having recurring nightmares – she'd given him a short, edited version of their watery content. Charlie had no idea.

It took only a few seconds for her to realise that the dream was a subject for Dr Jane. Their next session was in less than twenty-four hours. She'd save it up for then.

'There's been a weird thing at work,' she said. 'A thing where … Christ, I don't even know where to start. I don't know what to think about it, and it's bothering me.'

Charlie raised an eyebrow. 'Let me guess,' he said. 'It involves my old friend Alan Crosbie?'

Birch let her eyes flutter closed. Crosbie had been the first officer to interview Charlie after his arrest – but she'd also told plenty of Crosbie stories in plenty of visiting hours since. She knew she shouldn't talk out of school – especially to a convicted felon, and extra-especially inside a prison, where all the walls have ears. But in recent months, she'd given up caring as much as she used to about what was right and proper. Charlie's hunger for stories from the outside world didn't help matters. He listened eagerly when she talked about her work, the weird and wonderful stuff she came across every day. Charlie had been in prison a couple of years, but before that he'd been isolated in a different way. He'd been a wanted man, a tiny cog in the huge, crushing machine of organised crime. She knew how much he enjoyed hearing her talk, acting as her sounding board, helping her lighten the load. She imagined it made him feel useful, and just lately, she'd come to understand just how important feeling useful really was.

'It does,' she replied.

Charlie clicked his fingers together, just once. He threw Anjan a knowing look. 'Called it,' he said.

Birch wondered what Anjan thought about this: her telling stories about work in front of Charlie. But when she stole a look at him herself, she saw his expression was mainly one of concern. She'd worried him, she realised, sitting so quietly in the car on the way here. He was as keen as Charlie to hear what the matter was.

'We've got this case,' she began, 'which ... I can't really give any details about, but ... it's a missing person, I'll say that. It started out as mine, but then McLeod reassigned it to Crosbie.'

Anjan was nodding. This part, he already knew.

'I was pissed off about it,' she went on, 'because ... Look, I know I always say this, but this one felt sort of personal.'

She paused, reading Charlie's face. She couldn't tell him that Winnie was involved, though she badly wanted to. Charlie had always adored Winnie – going to her house was one of his favourite activities as a child. Birch reasoned that if she mentioned Winnie's name, Charlie would worry about her. She wouldn't be able to disclose details, and he'd be left knowing Winnie was part of a criminal investigation, but not knowing how or why.

'Anyway,' she said, breezing onward, 'I didn't say anything. I just let it happen. I just let him take it off me. And then it was too late, and I've been kicking myself about it ever since.'

Charlie smirked at her. 'Well,' he said, 'I've no idea why. That Crosbie's a real stand-up guy. Can't imagine a safer pair of hands, right?'

'Right,' Birch said, allowing herself a small smile. 'If by that you mean, he's mostly phoned it in so far, then yeah. Absolutely bang-on.'

Her brother laughed, but only briefly. 'That's not all, though,' he said, 'is it?'

She shook her head. 'I've been trying not to meddle,' she said, 'but I have been keeping an eye on the case. It's rather grown arms and legs. Amy's on board now, too. And a few days ago, it ... all took a really bizarre turn.'

Charlie snorted. 'You should spend some time in this place,' he said, 'if you want to talk about *really bizarre.*'

Birch glanced around her. The prisoners were almost all deep in conversation with their visitors, but as she scanned the room, she made eye contact with a particularly fearsome-looking screw. She flicked her gaze back towards Charlie. 'Nice offer,' she said, 'but no thanks.'

Beside her, Anjan was quiet. Birch knew this was a lawyer tactic: create a silence, and the other person will usually scramble to fill it.

She closed her eyes. 'We had a ... well, I suppose she's a witness. We had a witness phone up, and keep phoning up. Next thing, she's at the reception desk at Fettes Avenue, asking to speak to someone. Saying she's got information about a case. She ended up in my office.'

Charlie raised an eyebrow. 'I don't get what's weird about—'

'She's a psychic,' Birch said, blurting out the words as though saying them fast might help her feel better about them. 'Or at least, she says she's a psychic. The testimony she's given is, she claims, based on visions she's had. Or dreams – I think she preferred the word dreams.'

Charlie was nodding, very slowly. 'Okay,' he said, drawing the word out, making it long and incredulous. 'Yeah, Nella, I'll give you this one. That *is* bizarre.'

Birch had allowed a curtain of hair to fall across her face. She realised Anjan was leaning forward, trying to peer around it.

'You must believe her story has some credibility,' he said. 'I don't think this would be bothering you so much, otherwise.'

Birch placed her hands on the table, palms down, fingers spread. It felt grounding, comforting. She looked down at her fingernails. 'I tried not to be taken in,' she said. 'And I mean, I'm not saying I *am* taken in – not by the psychic stuff. But she knew something. She told us something she couldn't possibly have known, unless …'

'Unless she saw it in her crystal ball?' Charlie scoffed.

'Or,' Anjan cut in, 'she really has witnessed something. She's involved in some way with this missing person's disappearance.'

'Exactly,' Birch replied. 'So what I'm trying to puzzle out is, how is she involved? Why is she coming forward in this way? What the hell is this woman's *deal*?'

Anjan steepled his fingers. When Birch looked up at him, she saw he was staring off into the middle distance – this was his thinking face. He never really dropped out of lawyer mode, but she could see that this new information had caused him to kick it up a gear.

'It'll be imperative,' he said, 'to get to the bottom of that particular question, ideally as quickly as you're able. I'm sure you know this, because you hesitated to call her a witness, but her testimony just isn't credible at present. The fact that she's divulged details from the case that aren't in the public domain is important, but until she can give lucid testimony, nothing she says could be used as evidence.' He sat back. She could see he was fighting against a smile. 'I'm afraid that psychic evidence is simply not admissible in court,' he said.

Birch felt like snapping at him – *Thanks, genius, I'd figured that much out on my own* – but she knew he couldn't help himself. And all he'd done was voice the very thoughts she'd been having. They vied for space in her brain with distant echoes from her flood dream, making her feel dizzy.

'Yeah,' she said, hearing an edge of weariness in her voice. 'That's it, really, in a nutshell.'

Charlie was looking at her, and she saw that his face was unexpectedly serious. She'd expected him to be amused by this new oddball Police Scotland story she'd brought him. Instead, his brow was furrowed. She felt a slight flutter of panic. Did he know about what had happened after he disappeared? Did he somehow know about the fake psychic she and her mother had given money in exchange for information about his whereabouts? No, surely not – she'd never breathed a word to him, and there was no other way he could have found out. Yet, his face looked serious.

'Of course,' he said, after a long pause, 'there's another possibility.'

Birch sat up a little straighter. She was still thinking about her past stupidity, but now she was also wondering if her felon brother could perhaps have picked up on some detail about the present cases she'd so far missed.

'Oh yeah? What are you thinking?'

Charlie shrugged, and held out one hand, as though offering her something. 'Well,' he said, 'have you considered that she might just be telling the truth. Like … have you thought that maybe she just *is* psychic?'

Diary 15/01

The Dutch police took me to the protected reception centre, and the staff there put me in the infirmary. They told me I had a severe concussion, and lacerations on my head from when Luke had slammed on the van's brakes and I'd crashed into the metal partition. 'Concussion' and 'lacerations' were English words I didn't know, and I said them over and over in my mind so I could remember them. My head did really hurt, and they had to shave off part of my hair so they could put in stitches. I felt freezing cold, and scared, but also kind of numb. I felt like too many things had happened to me too fast, and my brain couldn't keep up.

I slept a lot, in the infirmary, and tried not to have dreams. They'd taken away my backpack, and I asked for it every single day. Eventually they gave it back to me, and I was so happy that I cried. Crying made my head hurt.

After a while, I was moved out of the infirmary and into the main part of the centre. It was noisy and weird. The little kids called it The Neverland, because they'd been told they were in the Netherlands, and hadn't understood. I didn't like that name, the 'never' part. It felt like a prison I'd never get out of. I was put in a room with some girl who wouldn't speak, or couldn't. She wouldn't even look at me.

I don't know exactly how long I was there. Not long; a couple of weeks, I think. I asked to speak to my parents, to call them, or to have someone else call them for me. The staff told me it wasn't possible. They needed to make sure I was who I said I was, and they said they needed to determine my age. I told them to call my parents, and they laughed at me, like I'd said something really stupid. They didn't treat me badly, but I came to hate them.

One day I was called into a small room, and a man was sitting there. I'd never seen him before, but he spoke to me in Vietnamese as if he knew me. The staff said I should go with him. I didn't understand where, but I came to realise he was going to take me out of The Neverland. Someone fetched the backpack from my bunk, and the few things that still belonged to me. I wasn't sure that I wanted to go with the man, but I knew I didn't want to stay living alongside the girl who didn't speak to me. She cried at night and sometimes screamed as though someone was attacking her. It scared me. And I still felt numb, like I was a robot that wasn't functioning properly. I wanted that feeling to go away.

So I followed the man, who said his name was Muhammad, out of the small room and through the corridors of The Neverland. We walked through doors I'd never been allowed through before, and then suddenly, we were outside in the actual real world. It was so, so cold, and I was confused, because I didn't know what was happening. But I was happy. For a few short moments, I was happy.

I got into the passenger seat of Muhammad's car, and we drove, but not far. Maybe not even a mile. We drove until The Neverland had disappeared over the horizon, and then we stopped at the side of the road. Luke's van was parked there. He got out of it, and walked over to Muhammad's car window. He took an envelope of money – that same pretty, silvery money I'd seen before – out of his pocket, and Muhammad rolled the glass down and took it. I sat there in the passenger seat while he counted it, and Luke smoked a cigarette. They spoke back and forth a little in a language I didn't know. Then Muhammad nodded, leaned over me and popped open the box in the car's dashboard. As he tucked the money away into that space, I saw a short, black gun lying there, partly covered by a cloth. Then he slammed the box closed, and it was gone.

I got out of the car and walked to Luke's van without even being asked. The gun had scared me stupid. I knew Luke must have one, too. I couldn't believe I hadn't thought about that before. He opened one of the van's back doors, and I climbed inside. He stood for a moment, leaning into the space, grinning at me.

'You knew I was coming for you, right?' he asked.

I hadn't known, but I nodded, and his grin widened.

'Of course I was,' he said, and his voice was warm, as though it were a nice thing he was saying. 'I always will.'

I'm writing down everything I know, and everything I've seen, because I hope so hard that one day I'll get out of here. One day Luke will get arrested, and maybe I can help get him sent to prison. He should be put somewhere where he can't hurt anyone else ever again. I hope I can help make that happen.

He put me in the living room of the house. There's a fireplace in here, but it's all burned out, and there are black streaks on the walls all around, like something exploded in there. The hearth is full of old broken bottles and litter, and there's more litter and junk on the mantelpiece. The room is full of old, crap furniture: a divan bed base in two parts that's all ripped open and stained; boxes full of mouldering things I don't want to touch. It's cold; when I breathe out, I can see my breath even though I'm inside. I arrived here wearing my coat, and I've never taken it off.

There's a sofa, which is dirty and smells kind of bad, but at least it's comfortable. He gave me an old blanket. I've slept under it for a week, on that sofa, mostly with my jumper pulled up over my nose so I don't smell all the horrible stuff in the room. If I need to use the bathroom, I have to knock four times on the door. Sometimes Luke is in the house, and he takes me to the small bathroom under the stairs and stands outside the door until I'm done. If he's not in the house, I have to use the bucket in one corner of the room. I hate that bucket. I hate Luke.

He's boarded over the window, and there's a double mattress propped against the boards. It's stained with what looks like blood, one huge splotch right in the middle, like someone died on that mattress in some horrible way. I don't want to get too close to it. At night, when it's dark and I can only half see, I imagine the blood splotch coming to life and climbing out of the mattress to come and get me. I've been trying not to cry.

Some days, there were noises upstairs. I assumed Luke was up there. I assumed this was his house. It confused me, because sometimes I could hear him upstairs, so I'd knock four times on the door, louder and louder, to say I needed the bathroom, and he wouldn't respond. Sometimes I'd hear four knocks through the ceiling, the same pattern as my own. I guessed he was mocking me.

But then yesterday, he unlocked the door and came into the room with me. I was asleep on the sofa. It might have been early morning, I think, because little seams of sunlight were filtering in around the edges of the window boards. He stood in the doorway, watching me as I woke up and got my bearings. Waking up in this house is the worst thing in the world. For a few seconds, I don't remember where I am. Then I see the blood stain on the mattress, and smell the musty sofa, and I remember. It feels like dying.

'How would you like to have a cellmate?' he asked, and though my eyes were blurry, I could see he was smiling a mean smile.

I didn't say anything.

'Vietnamese parents are a fucking goldmine, kid,' he said. 'I'm going to expand my business.'

That really jerked me awake, all at once. 'My parents?' I said. 'You've talked to my parents?'

He rolled his eyes at me. 'Fucksake,' he said. 'You really are an empty-headed little cunt.'

He stepped backwards out of the room, but I could hear him moving around in the hallway. There was a scuffling sound. Then, all of a sudden, there was someone else in the room with us. A woman. A woman who looked like me.

'Here's your new friend,' he said. He'd hauled her in by the wrist, and now shoved her, hard, so she staggered further into the room. She put out a hand to steady herself, and touched the huge bloodstain on the mattress. I flinched.

'Don't make any fucking noise,' Luke said. He pointed a finger at the woman, and waited until she looked at it. 'You know what happens when you do.'

Then he slammed the door, and I heard the scrape of the bolts on the other side. After a moment, I heard the sound of the front door opening, and then he slammed that, too.

The woman and I stared at one another. She had a huge bruise on her face, and cuts around one eye that were swollen and made me feel sort of sick to look at. One of her lips had been split, and it must have happened recently, because the wound looked wet and shiny. Her hands were all busted up, and I could see she had a couple of fingernails missing.

She was wearing a hoodie that belonged to Luke; I recognised it. There was blood on it, dried on and crusty, the same colour as the terrible splotch on the mattress.

While we looked at one another, I heard the sound of Luke starting up his van, backing it out of the house's parking space, and driving away.

'*Chào chị,*' I said, hoping she'd understand – hoping beyond all hope that she'd answer back in Vietnamese. '*Tôi tên là Linh.*'

The woman blinked, then reached up and rubbed a hand over her good eye, as though she thought maybe I was a ghost, or she was hallucinating. When she moved her hand away from her face again, I saw that although she'd begun to cry, she was smiling.

That was how I met Kim.

Birch, Monday 17 January

Birch noticed that Dr Jane had made fewer notes than usual while she relayed the new and different version of her flood dream. The therapist seemed to be listening in a slightly different way than usual: not more carefully, because Birch believed that Dr Jane always listened carefully. But now the listening seemed more focused, more intent; the way Dr Jane was listening made Birch feel that perhaps this new version of the dream was more important than she'd fully realised.

'Okay,' Dr Jane said, when Birch finally came to a natural pause. 'So, first of all, I want to ask ... how do you feel about the fact that this dream – one you've experienced in almost exactly the same way so many times – has changed?'

Birch considered the question. 'I suppose it feels like progress,' she said. 'I feel like this dream has been hanging around my neck for weeks, showing me the same thing over and over again as though I'm supposed to be learning some-thing from it. And I've just been baffled by it. I'm still baffled by it – I still don't know what message my subconscious is trying to give me. But at least now it's different. Different is progress, right?'

Dr Jane cocked her head. 'I don't know,' she said. 'What makes you think it's progress?'

'Well.' Birch had become accustomed to this style of questioning; when she'd first started therapy, she'd found it irritating, like Dr Jane was a toddler deliberately responding to every statement with 'Why?'. Now she understood that Dr Jane was actually more like a chess grandmaster. Several moves ahead at all times, she wanted Birch to find her own way through the chessboard of her own thoughts.

'I guess,' Birch went on, 'it has felt like playing the same level of a computer game over and over and over again, and never doing the thing I need to do to unlock the next level.' Birch was aware her analogy was thin: her knowledge of computer games was twenty years old and based on the few occasions where Charlie had cajoled her into picking up a console. 'You know how, somewhere in the level, you have to pick up some random object or open some specific door, and only when you do that exact thing is the next level revealed to you? It feels like that. You get on to the next level and you still don't know what it's about or what to expect, but you have at least moved on. You at least get to try and do something different.'

Dr Jane was smiling. 'I think it's possible you know what I'm going to say next,' she said. 'Because I must sound like a broken record at this point.'

Birch closed her eyes. 'Yeah,' she said. 'I'm saying "I feel", but what I'm actually doing is *thinking*.' She opened her eyes again in time to see Dr Jane nod.

'Bingo,' Dr Jane said. 'The computer game is a very good analogy, very well thought out. But I asked what you *feel* about the dream being different this time. If it helps, try just one word.'

'Relief,' Birch replied, almost before Dr Jane had finished her sentence. 'I feel relief.'

Dr Jane responded almost as quickly. 'Why relief?' she asked.

Birch paused, and felt her eyes drift in the direction of the ceiling as she opened her mouth to respond.

'Don't think too much!' Dr Jane cut in, laughing. 'Keep it simple. Why relief?'

'Because I got out this time,' Birch replied. 'Because I got in the lift, and the water didn't follow me. It was like there was some sort of force field, stopping it from filling up the space. And the doors closed, and I rode down to the ground floor, and I walked out of the building.'

'You escaped.'

'Yes. But I also felt guilt, of course. Because all my colleagues were still trapped in there, with the rising water.'

'You felt guilt in the moment, while you were still dreaming?'

'Yes.'

'What about when you woke up?'

Birch shook her head. She felt the urge to connect the dots between the dream world and the waking one: to rationalise, and to embellish. *Keep it simple*, she reminded herself.

'Just relief,' she said. 'Just a huge sense of relief.'

Birch stood on the pavement with her back to the railings that ran parallel to the windows of Dr Jane's consulting room. She wondered how much it cost to rent a space within the grand Georgian walls of a New Town tenement. She wondered how much Dr Jane had to stump up to cover the cost of heating the big, airy, high-ceilinged room. The air outside was far colder than it had been inside. Birch blew out a cloud of her own breath and watched it swirl and eddy.

'I know we only have five minutes left,' she'd said, sensing Dr Jane getting ready to ease the session to a close, 'but I wanted to ask you about something, if I may.'

Dr Jane settled back into her chair a little, a *no rush* gesture. 'Of course,' she replied, 'what's on your mind?'

Birch could feel her cheeks colouring before she even began to answer. 'This is going to sound like a silly question.'

Dr Jane laughed. 'Trust me,' she said, 'in therapy, there's no such thing as a silly question.'

'Okay. I wanted to ask you what you think about psychics.'

Dr Jane tilted her head a little, and didn't immediately respond.

'See?' Now it was Birch's turn to laugh. 'Silly.'

'Not at all. Just … not what I expected. Are you thinking of seeing a psychic?'

'I'm actually going to see one after this. Not to have my fortune told, though. She's … someone who's involved in a case at work.'

Dr Jane's eyes seemed to sharpen their focus on Birch's face. 'You paused then,' she said, 'as though you weren't sure how to categorise her.'

Birch nodded. 'Yeah. Under normal circumstances, I'd call her a witness. I'd say I was going to see a witness, to take a statement. But … the things she's witnessed, she claims to have witnessed in dreams. As in, psychic ones. And truly, I just don't know what to do with that information.'

'That's an interesting way to put it. Do you mean you don't know what to do with that information logistically? As in, it's hard to know where to file this person, so to speak?'

Birch was still nodding. 'That,' she said, 'yeah. Her testimony doesn't feel like testimony. Technically she's giving evidence, but … it isn't evidence. It can't be *used* as evidence; it could never be admissible. But it's more than that, too. When I say I don't know what to do with that information, I mean I just can't figure out what to think of her.' She paused, and then remembered who she was talking to. 'Or perhaps I mean, I can't figure out how I feel about her.'

Dr Jane's smile took on a mischievous quality. 'Ah,' she said, 'I suspect *that* isn't quite right. I suspect that, if you keep it simple, like we've talked about, you probably do know how you feel about her. And maybe that's part of the problem you're having.'

Birch felt her mouth fall open slightly. She didn't know how therapy did this: Dr Jane would say something that felt immediately obvious the second it had been articulated, and yet without that articulation, Birch would never have been able to identify it.

'You're absolutely right,' she said, 'of course. I like this woman – I feel drawn to her. I *want* to believe her. That's precisely the problem I'm having.'

'The part of you that's a trained policewoman knows you need to be able to explain her testimony in court.'

'Yes – and no court in the land can do anything with psychic evidence. Anjan assured me of that only yesterday.'

'Okay,' Dr Jane said. 'But the part of you that's an intuitive human being in the world finds this woman genuine, and plausible.'

'Yes. Very plausible. But then I remember that these people … they're trained to be plausible, aren't they? They're trained to cold-read you and get into your head.'

Dr Jane was leaning forward again now; Birch could tell she'd piqued the other woman's interest. 'You think there's a possibility that she's manipulating you.'

Birch shrugged. 'I'd like to think it isn't that calculating,' she said. 'I've met and interviewed a lot of witnesses in my time. There can be a lot of reasons for someone to give testimony that … isn't quite sound.'

'Such as?'

'Well … sometimes they're being leaned on by someone else, or they're trying to protect themselves from someone or something. Sometimes they're telling a version of the truth that they think is more palatable to the authorities, or they're trying to paint themselves or someone else in a more flattering light. Sometimes they're giving a recollection that's clouded by drugs or alcohol or mental health crisis, or even just a lot of time having passed. Sometimes what they think they've seen isn't what they've actually seen. And yes, sometimes they just try to manipulate whoever's taking the testimony. But if you're asking me how this feels? It doesn't feel like any of those. It doesn't feel quite like anything I've ever come across.'

Dr Jane was quiet for a moment. Birch became acutely aware of the clock on the wall above the therapist's head; its second hand had already ticked past the time that signalled the end of the session.

'I don't know the answer to this question,' Dr Jane said, eventually, 'but I'd like you to see if you do. Are you struggling with this woman because of who she is and what she's actually saying, or are you struggling with what she represents to you?'

Birch tried to peel her eyes from the clock. 'What she represents to me?'

Dr Jane glanced up, following Birch's gaze. 'Don't worry about the time,' she said. 'This feels important. Try to be present, Helen. I'm suggesting that perhaps this person is bringing up uncomfortable feelings for you. Perhaps it's those uncomfortable feelings you're struggling with, rather than the person herself.'

Birch blinked a few times. *Try to be present, Helen.* She wasn't sure she knew how to switch gears that quickly.

'I'm sure that's true,' she said, 'but it all feels like such a tangle.'

Dr Jane looked down at the iPad that always rested across her lap. She tapped in a note that Birch wished she could crane over and look at.

'I think we should come back to this next session,' Dr Jane said, 'and see if we can't get things *un*tangled a bit. But in the meantime, it's okay if you don't know something. I realise that sounds very obvious, but it's something a lot of people struggle with. Especially in these modern times, people struggle to say the phrase "I don't know". But it's okay not to know. It's okay not to know what this woman's deal is. It's okay not to know how to feel about her. It's okay if you've never encountered anything like this before. You don't have to know everything. Indeed, it's impossible to know everything, which is pretty freeing. It means you can let things go. You can say, "Here is a thing I do not know, and guess what? That's okay."'

Birch snorted. She wanted to take Dr Jane's words as they were intended; she wanted to pull them to her, and allow them to be comforting. Instead, she couldn't help but feel nettled.

'Easier said than done,' she said, reaching for her stick.

Dr Jane laughed. 'Of course,' she replied. 'It wouldn't be therapy, otherwise.'

Birch was almost at the door when Dr Jane called out her name. This was unusual; normally, once Birch had risen from her chair, the two women didn't speak again. She turned, leaning awkwardly on the stick. Dr Jane had risen to her feet, the iPad dangling from one hand. She looked pensive.

'I don't know if this is at all helpful,' she said, 'but … I've spent a lot of time learning about the inner workings of the human mind. And let me tell you, there is so much about how we think, and about how and why our brains work the way they do, that no one has yet been able to explain.'

Birch frowned. 'Why are you telling me this?'

Dr Jane shrugged. 'I'm not saying I believe in psychic abilities,' she said. 'I'm just saying that there are over a quadrillion synapses in the human brain. We're capable of doing things with our minds every day that, if we really sat and thought about them, would seem superhuman.'

Birch looked down at the stick in her hand. She considered her dream again, the way her brain kept showing it to her – her subconscious mind insisting that her conscious mind pay attention to it, though she couldn't work out why.

She tried for a smile. 'Thanks, Doc,' she said.

Birch blew another white lungful of breath into the frosty air. Crosbie had rounded the corner and was driving slowly along the street, looking for her. She could see his head moving from side to side as he scrutinised front doors, looking for Dr Jane's nameplate. Birch stepped closer to the edge of the kerb, and held out an arm. As he pulled up alongside her, she had to force herself not to roll her eyes. He'd turned up not in his usual charcoal-grey Audi A8, but in a marked car from the fleet yard.

'Morning, Alan,' Birch said, as she dropped as gracefully as she could down into the passenger seat. 'Not your usual wheels.'

Crosbie didn't meet her eye. 'Car's in the garage,' he said. 'I just took what I was given.'

Birch bit her tongue. Turning up in a marked car was a tactical decision on his part, she was almost certain. It would intimidate Beatrice Crozier more than the Audi would have, and Crosbie had to know it would make her neighbours talk. Fresh out of a therapy session, she couldn't help but wonder if the marked car wasn't also something Crosbie had done for himself, unconsciously or otherwise.

He was about to go and do something that she guessed was a long way out of his comfort zone. Did having a police decal and blue flashing lights on the roof make him feel just that little bit more secure?

'Kato's meeting us there,' Crosbie was saying. 'She's been in Glasgow this morning.'

Birch had wondered if Crosbie might ask her about therapy, or at least make some comment about the fact that that was where she'd just been. She'd been steeling herself for some wisecrack or other. 'Oh yes?'

Crosbie nodded. He'd steered the car to the end of the street, and was sitting at the Give Way sign, indicating right. 'She's been back to see Kim Le's aunt and uncle again,' he said. 'At my urging. I really think we should try and make this mystery older man thing stick.'

He made the turn, and the Edinburgh setts rattled under the car as it picked up speed, making Birch's bad hip ache.

'It'll stick,' she said, 'if this guy is involved. If he isn't, it won't.'

Crosbie tutted. 'Meanwhile, we're going to … well, Birch, come to think of it, what are we going to do? When we get to this mad woman's house, I mean. How do you want to play it?'

Birch wanted to laugh. She couldn't believe he was asking her for advice, especially when she knew how unlikely it was that he'd actually listen.

'I guess we hear her out,' she said. 'She's a witness, right?'

He made a huffing sound. 'Of sorts,' he replied.

'Right,' Birch said, trying to sound more confident than she felt. 'So, we listen to what she has to say, and go from there.'

Beatrice Crozier lived in a small, semi-detached house in the Warristons: a neat estate of 1960s ex-Wimpey houses tucked into the space between the Royal Botanic Gardens and the Goldenacre. Birch couldn't have guessed which house was hers before they pulled up outside; Bee's looked roughly the same as all the others around it. It was the last one on the street, sitting slightly awkwardly on a rhombus-shaped plot, with a scrappy lawn and a poured concrete path leading up to the door. Plant pots lined the path; Birch had to pick her way between them with the stick as she followed Crosbie up the garden. Most of the plants had been cut back and shrunk by the January frost, but sticking out of the pots were little wooden markers on which someone – presumably Bee herself – had painted the names of herbs. *Lavender. Spearmint. Cat Mint. Lemon Balm.*

Crosbie rapped on the door, ignoring the doorbell. As he had his back to her, Birch allowed herself a small eyeroll.

She must have seen them coming, because the door opened almost immediately, and Bee appeared on the threshold. Birch had expected the smell of incense, candles burning, a lot of mirrors on the walls. But the hallway she could see behind Bee was simple. White walls, a paper lampshade, a coat rack groaning under the weight of too many coats. A simple raffia-style mat. This wasn't the house of a psychic – it was just a house. She couldn't help but feel mildly disappointed.

'Come away in,' Bee said, and stood aside as Crosbie and Birch trooped past her. Birch heard the sound of high heels on the path behind, and then Amy Kato was with them, a little breathless, and apologising for being late.

'Is arriving thirty seconds after your colleagues considered late?' Bee asked, laughing. Birch felt a bubble of tension grow and then burst as none of them laughed back.

The living room Bee showed them into was painted yellow, meaning it felt sunny even on a frigid January day. It wasn't filled with the occult tchotchkes Birch had been expecting, but it was nicely turned out. Bee had an eye for décor that was quirky but tasteful.

'You have a lovely house,' Amy said, and Birch could tell she meant it.

'Thanks,' Bee replied. 'It's wee, but it's alright for just me. I moved here out of a tiny attic flat in the Old Town. It feels like the Ritz by comparison.'

Birch smiled, and eased herself down into a chair. Crosbie, apparently too agitated to sit, set himself up in one corner of the room, where he pretended to take an interest in the titles on Bee's bookshelf.

'I've got a pot of tea on the go,' Bee said. 'You'll have some?'

'Not for me,' Crosbie said, a little too quickly.

Birch and Amy exchanged glances. It was clear they might need to do some good cop stuff to counteract whatever Crosbie was psyching himself up for.

'Sure,' Amy said. 'DI Birch?'

'Yes please. Milk and one.'

Amy, still on her feet, made to follow Bee out of the room. 'I'll help you carry,' she said.

Once they'd left, Birch shot Crosbie a look. 'Remember, Alan,' she said, 'we're here to find out what she has to say for herself. This is just a fact-finding mission.'

Crosbie didn't respond. He'd raised a hand and was drawing something out from between two of Bee's books. 'Look at this,' he hissed. He held up his hand, and showed Birch what appeared to be a box of playing cards.

She frowned. 'What?'

Crosbie held the box at arm's length, as though it had a bad smell. He flipped it over to look at the back, and for the first time, Birch saw the illustration on the front: a figure in red and white robes, one arm held aloft, hand-drawn against a bright yellow background.

'"The Rider Waite Smith Tarot Deck,"' he read, his voice tart. '"The most popular and widely used tarot deck in the world. Featuring full scenes with figures and symbols, as drawn in 1909 by Pamela Coleman Smith, with card interpretations by Arthur Edward Waite. An instructional booklet is included, explaining the tarot card meanings and how to use the cards for divination."' He chuckled. 'I can't believe anyone actually believes in this nonsense.'

Birch leaned forward slightly. She'd only ever seen tarot cards in films.

'Aha,' Bee said, elbowing back into the room with a mug of tea in each hand. 'I see you've found my deck.' She handed one of the mugs down to Birch, but she was looking at Crosbie. 'Intrigued, Detective Inspector? I'll give you a reading if you like.'

Amy had followed Bee into the room, and she and Birch exchanged glances. Crosbie snorted, throwing the cards down on to the coffee table between them. 'Absolutely not,' he said. 'I don't go in for any of this fortune-telling lark.'

'Suit yourself,' Bee replied, placing her mug down on the table next to the discarded box of cards, and settling into an armchair. 'But just so you know, I don't personally see the tarot as a fortune-telling tool. It tells you far more about yourself in the present than it could ever say about the future. It's really just Jungian psychoanalysis, only with pictures.'

Amy came to rest on the sofa beside Birch. Now they were both facing Bee across the coffee table, while Crosbie stayed skulking in his chosen corner.

'I can't say I go in for Jungian psychoanalysis, either,' he said.

'No,' Bee replied, reaching for the cards. 'I wouldn't have thought so.'

Birch tried to swallow down a smile. 'Ms Crozier,' she said.

'Bee, please.'

'Okay. Bee – before we begin, I'd like to apologise for the fact that we didn't get the chance to take a formal statement from you, the last time we met.' She forced herself not to look at Crosbie. 'We'd like to do that now, if that's alright with you?'

Bee had opened the box of cards and drawn the whole deck out into her hand. She placed the empty box back on the coffee table.

'Of course,' she said. 'Do you need to record it?'

Amy held up her phone, the recording app already open. 'If we have your consent to,' she said.

Bee nodded. 'Absolutely.'

Amy glanced at Crosbie and then Birch, both of whom responded with a tiny nod: *ready*. Amy hit the record button.

'Monday the seventeenth of January,' she said, holding the phone close to her face even though she didn't need to. 'Time: eleven forty-three am. Interview with Beatrice Crozier, Sergeant Amy Kato recording. Also present, Detective Inspectors Birch and Crosbie.' She reached out and placed the phone on the coffee table between them. 'There,' she said. 'Formalities over.'

Birch wondered if Crosbie felt annoyed that Amy had said her name before his.

Bee was shuffling the tarot cards in her hands, deftly, but without looking at them. Birch watched as glimpses of figures and shapes flashed into view, then disappeared back into the deck.

'Where would you like me to start?' Bee asked.

'Well,' Amy replied, 'there's a reason we asked for another meeting with you. Last time we spoke, you described seeing a young girl asleep on a sofa. Can you recall that scene for us again, please?'

'Yes,' Bee said, 'I've seen her a few times now. She's a young girl, a teenager, I'd guess. She's small, and thin, and she looks very vulnerable. Whenever I see her, she's lying on a sofa with a blanket pulled over her. It's always very cold: she's shivering. And sometimes, she's hugging a soft toy. A cat, I think, or maybe a teddy bear.'

Birch was nodding. She was still watching Bee's hands. 'You mentioned,' she said, 'a second person there, with this girl.'

'Oh yes,' Bee replied. 'Sometimes there are two of them. They both look young, though the girl with the soft toy is younger. She's smaller. The older girl … she's hurt. She has injuries to her face and neck. I've wondered if perhaps these two are sisters – they look alike.'

'Can you describe them further?' Amy asked.

Bee's gaze shifted away from Amy. She looked down at the cards she was shuffling. 'They're both … look, I know this isn't the right term. It's probably offensive. But it's the only non-specific term I can think of. They're both … oriental.'

Birch closed her eyes for a second.

'You mean,' Amy said, 'they're East Asian?'

Bee let out a funny sort of half laugh. 'I do,' she said. 'Yes, sorry. I do. That's a much better term. Apologies.'

'Don't worry,' Amy replied, and Birch opened her eyes again. 'That's useful information. And when you say they look alike …?'

'They both have long, dark hair,' Bee replied, 'and they're both very slim. As I say, the younger girl looks terribly small. The older one … she has blood on her clothes.'

'Does she seem badly hurt?' Birch asked.

Bee tilted her head. 'It's hard to say. She certainly looks like she's been roughed up by someone.'

Birch couldn't help but notice that Crosbie was staying very quiet. She hadn't expected it of him, and it was starting to worry her.

'Can you describe the room they're in?' Amy was asking.

'Chaotic,' Bee replied. 'It feels very full of junk. It's dirty, and dark. It's hard to see in any degree of detail.'

'Could you hazard a guess,' Amy asked, 'as to what floor the room is on? Is it small or large? What kind of building might it be in?'

Bee's eyelids fluttered closed, as though she were trying to picture the room in her mind once more. Her hands kept moving, the cards falling through them into new formations as she spoke.

'I couldn't say what floor,' she said, 'but it feels like a room in a regular house. It can't be much bigger than the room we're in now.'

'When you picture it,' Amy was saying, 'can you see any doors or windows? Any way in or out?'

Bee shook her head. 'No,' she replied. 'I can see a sofa, and a fireplace, and there's a press in one corner of the room – a sort of classic, shallow Edinburgh one. But I can't see any way out. I feel very strongly that there *is* no way out, that these two girls are trapped. And the feeling I always have is one of terrible threat, like something or someone is about to come into the room and do something terrible. I know these girls are in some horrible danger, but I'm powerless to help them or do anything about it.' Bee opened her eyes. 'And then I wake up,' she added, 'and it all fades away.'

In the quiet that followed, Amy glanced at Birch, and Birch turned her head to meet her colleague's gaze. Amy seemed unsure what to ask next. Birch opened her mouth to speak, but before she could say anything, a noise came from the corner where Crosbie was standing. All three women turned to look at him. He was clapping his hands together slowly, deliberately, cupping them slightly to make the sound louder.

'Bravo,' he said, his voice dripping with sarcasm. 'Bravo, Ms Crozier. Quite the performance.'

Amy's look had changed to one of slight panic.

Crosbie advanced across the room towards Bee. 'Now,' he said, coming to rest beside the arm of her chair, 'why don't you tell us *how* you know all of this?'

Bee's hands ceased in their shuffling. She looked up at him. 'I'm sorry?'

Crosbie gestured vaguely in the direction of Amy's phone, still on the coffee table, its red recording light blinking. 'You've given us,' he said, 'several pieces of information that aren't in the public domain. You know we're looking for two missing Vietnamese girls. You know that one is older than the other. You know that one of them was carrying a ginger cat backpack when she went missing – a backpack that looks like a soft toy. You've seen these girls, haven't you? You've been in their presence. And you're going to tell us when, and where, and how, so we can go and find them. Do you understand me?'

Bee blinked a few times. Slowly, she reached forward and laid the deck of tarot cards on the table in front of her. 'I've already told you,' she said, 'I saw this in a dream. It's a recurring dream; I've seen it several—'

'Nonsense,' Crosbie snapped. As he spoke, he reached out and backhanded the pile of tarot cards in front of Bee. They scattered on to the floor around her feet, and she let out a little cry. Beside her, Birch felt Amy jump.

'Let the record reflect—' Amy cut in, but Crosbie held up a hand.

'Let the record reflect,' he said, 'that we're being led a merry dance here, and I'm sick of it. We know you know more about this case than you're letting on, Ms Crozier. I want to know why you're hiding behind this ridiculous psychic nonsense, instead of telling us what you actually know.'

Bee was looking down at the table. Crosbie bent down closer to her, but she didn't meet his eye.

'Answer me,' he hissed. 'Do you know who's taken these girls? Who's holding them? Is it your boyfriend? Some family member? What does he *want* with them?'

'Alan,' Birch said, keeping her voice low as though she thought the microphone might not pick it up. 'You're leading the witness.'

'Shut up, Birch.'

Birch put her weight against the arm of the sofa, as though getting ready to stand. 'You're also intimidating her, in my humble opinion.'

Crosbie's eyes stayed fixed on Bee; he seemed to be staring at a spot on her cheek, as though waiting for her to turn her eyes to him. She didn't. After a moment, he blinked, and then turned his head in the direction of the phone. A line of levels bars flickered, picking up background noise.

'Let the record reflect,' he said, quietly, 'that I disagree with DI Birch's assessment of the situation.'

His voice hissed in his teeth; he was angry. But he straightened up, and took a step away from Bee.

Birch allowed herself to drop out of the tensed position she'd been in. Bee was still staring down at the table top.

'Ms Crozier,' Amy said.

Two cards remained on the table in front of Bee. The others lay across the floor, most of them face down. But the two on the table were face up, and sitting neatly, as though someone had drawn them deliberately, and placed them there.

'The Devil,' Bee said, reaching out and touching the first card with her fingertips. Birch saw that her hands were shaking. 'DI Crosbie, you've been struggling with something that feels bigger than you. Something you're not sure you can overcome – haven't you?'

Birch winced, expecting Crosbie to raise his voice again. Instead, he took another step back. He blinked, as though the step back had come as a surprise, as though he'd been physically pushed.

Bee learned over the table, inspecting the cards more closely. 'You feel a lot of shame about it,' she went on. 'The shame is like a chain around your neck. It's heavy. You can't seem to shake it.' She turned to look at him for the first time since he'd loomed towards her. 'You don't have to feel ashamed,' she said. 'But I know why you do.'

Crosbie opened his mouth, but then closed it again.

'Your other card,' Bee said, moving her hand to touch the other one, 'is the Emperor. The card of rules and strictures. You feel very bound, don't you? Duty bound, perhaps. You live by absolutes – your personal rules and laws mean a lot to you.' Her fingers hovered in the space between the two cards. 'That's why you feel so ashamed of yourself. You feel like you've broken one of your own rules. You feel like you've let yourself down.'

Birch looked at Amy, who was staring at Bee with an expression of confused wonder. Birch remembered that Amy didn't know what she knew about Crosbie's personal life. Bee hadn't come out and *said* he was a recovering alcoholic suffering from extreme self-loathing, but she may as well have.

As silence began to fill up the room, all three women turned to look at Crosbie, waiting for him to speak.

He took a long, deep breath. 'I'm sorry, Ms Crozier,' he said. 'I got a little too assertive for a moment there. Do accept my apologies.'

Birch saw, in her peripheral vision, Amy's eyes get wide. She realised hers had, too.

'Apology accepted, Detective Inspector,' Bee replied. 'You're only human. We all stumble at times. You don't always have to be like the Emperor, you know.'

Crosbie looked down at the floor. Birch could see he was still angry, but the anger was different now: sadder, and somehow further away.

'If you'll excuse me,' he said, 'I think I've had about as much of this occult nonsense as I can stand.' He looked past Birch, towards Amy. 'I trust you two can complete the interview in my absence. I'll see you back at the station.'

Birch pulled in her knees to allow Crosbie to shimmy between the sofa and the coffee table. No one spoke as he made his way through the room, stepped out into the hallway, and disappeared. They listened to the sound of the front door opening and then closing again. Crosbie's footsteps rang on the garden path. They waited, listening, until the sound of his marked car's engine had faded away.

'He's doing the right thing,' Bee said, her voice strangely distant, 'seeking treatment. I hope he's going to be okay.'

Birch wanted very badly to look at Amy, but knew she mustn't. She worried her face might give away what she knew about Crosbie. Instead, she tried to look mildly confused. 'Sorry,' she said, 'where were we?'

Amy let out a small cough. 'I think,' she said, 'that DI Crosbie did ask quite a useful question, which was, do you know who it is who's holding these girls? Have you ever … seen that person?'

Bee shook her head. 'I haven't,' she said. 'I get the strong feeling that their captor is a man, but I don't know what it is that makes me think that. Probably just my own internal bias. Violent crimes usually are carried out by men.'

Something about these words landed as a discord in Birch's mind. For the first time since the interview had begun, she remembered her prior cynicism. She remembered that Beatrice Crozier could still be a trained cold-reader – a person who knew how to say all the right things. Crosbie was right; she had to know these things somehow, and they needed to find out how.

'Do you mind if I ask,' Birch said. 'These … visions you have. How do they work? Do they always appear like dreams, when you're asleep? Do they have any triggers?'

Bee looked at her. 'Triggers?'

'You know,' Birch said, 'like … forgive me, this is a very crude example. But people say that eating cheese before bed, for example, can trigger very vivid dreams. It can even trigger sleepwalking in some people. Have you identified any possible trigger of that sort?'

Bee's mouth twisted a little. 'You think I'm making all this up,' she said.

Birch could tell that Bee wanted her to say, *No, I don't.* There was a part of her – the people-pleasing part, Dr Jane would say – that wanted her to say it, too. She found she couldn't.

'I'm not trying to catch you out,' she said. This felt like therapy, she realised, as she spoke; she was trying to say only things that were definitely true, that she definitely meant. 'I'm just curious as to how it works. I've been experiencing some recurring dreams lately myself, so I know the subconscious mind is capable of all sorts of things. I'm more wondering if you feel like the dreams are within your control. If I asked you to summon the scene with the girls again, for example, would you know how to do it?'

Bee swayed a little in her chair, rocking her head back and forth, a *How do I put this?* gesture. 'I … can't say I have control,' she said, 'because I don't really fully understand how this Knowing of mine works. I tried to explain this the last time we spoke. The only thing I'm certain of is that physical proximity helps. The closer I get to someone, the more clearly I can … this is strange wording, but the more clearly I can *know* them. Does that make sense?'

'I think so,' Birch said, but her voice wavered. She did understand, she just wasn't sure she believed.

'So, for example,' Bee went on, clearly assuming Birch *hadn't* quite understood, 'just now, when DI Crosbie walked over to me, I was suddenly able to know things about him that weren't clear to me when he first walked in. The longer he stood here, the more certain that Knowing became. I think some part of him realised that, and that's why he took a step back. We humans are more intuitive than we give ourselves credit for.'

Inwardly, Birch cursed Crosbie. She wished he'd kept his mouth shut, and she wished she'd done more to prevent his outburst. The questions he'd asked were the right ones: how *did* Beatrice Crozier know these things? Where was the information coming from? How could they turn her compelling but ultimately useless testimony into hard evidence? Birch had hoped they could take a softly-softly approach and eventually get somewhere. Now any chance of that seemed to be gone. Bee wasn't going to give them any line other than the *I'm just a bit psychic* one.

It would help, Birch thought, *if Kato weren't quite so taken in.*

'So does that mean,' Amy was saying, 'that if we put you in a car, and drove you closer to the address where these girls are being held, that you might be able to … offer more information?'

Bee nodded. 'It's certainly possible,' she said. 'In general, the closer I am to someone, the more I can know.'

'Okay,' Amy said. 'And – forgive me, I might be asking a stupid question, but – do you think if you were to get close enough to the person who's holding these young people captive, do you think you'd know them? Like, if they passed you on the street, would you be able to point that person out?'

Bee screwed up her face. 'That one's trickier,' she said. 'Some people are harder to … well, harder to know than others. Some people are an open book, but not everyone is. I mean, take the two of you, for example.'

Birch glanced at Amy. She'd been feeling some low-lying anxiety about coming to see Beatrice Crozier, and she hadn't quite been able to figure out why. She'd wanted to talk to Charlie about it, and then to Dr Jane – but neither conversation had made the anxiety disappear. She realised, right then, as Bee was speaking, what the anxiety was. It was a fear of this exact thing: of being read. Being known.

'Detective Inspector Birch,' Bee said, 'feels very knowable to me.'

Birch flinched. She couldn't help herself.

'Sorry,' Bee added, noticing. 'As I say, I can't exactly control it. I just … pick up information, I suppose, like a radio tower. But some people aren't transmitting. Sergeant Kato's frequency, I can barely pick up at all.'

Lucky Sergeant Kato, Birch wanted to say. She felt aggrieved; she'd spent a lot of her life learning how to be a closed book. It was something they taught you, when you became a police officer. Amy, meanwhile, sometimes struggled with the poker-faced part of the job. Birch felt annoyed that in the presence of this so-called psychic, Amy got to retain her privacy while she did not.

'You don't believe me, DI Birch,' Bee was saying. She was smiling an apologetic smile.

'I don't know how to feel, really,' Birch replied. 'I've been in counselling for the past six months, and it's taken me that long to get used to my therapist poking around in my brain. With you in there, too, it feels a little crowded.'

Amy laughed, and Birch felt grateful.

Bee wasn't looking at them, though: she was looking down at the floor, at the tarot cards scattered face down, mostly around her feet. She bent towards them, and her fingers hovered over one card in particular. Its back was decorated with a bright blue pattern that looked like twisted vines.

'The King of Swords,' Bee said. The card was still face down on the carpet. 'Yes, that's the one.'

Birch frowned. Bee flicked the card upright with the nail of her index finger, and then plucked it from the ground. She laid it face up on the coffee table between herself and Birch. Sure enough, the writing on the card read 'King of Swords'. Amy gasped, and then, as though realising she'd given herself away, clapped a hand over her own mouth.

'There he is,' Bee said.

Birch peered down at the card. It showed an austere-looking man sitting on a blocky grey throne. His robes were the same colour as the sky behind him, and he held a long white sword in one hand.

'You struggle,' Bee said, 'with balancing intellect and emotion.'

Birch glanced up, checking that Bee was, in fact, addressing her.

'The suit of Swords,' Bee went on, 'is the suit of the mind, of the intellect. It's the suit of logic, of rationality, and also of anxiety. It's the suit of habit, of beliefs, of values – the things that exist in our minds. Kings are meant to be the masters of their suits. But they're often a cautionary tale.'

Birch looked back down at the card. She couldn't understand how any kind of information could be gleaned from such a simple image.

'See how the king's sword is tilted?' Bee asked, as though she'd heard what Birch was thinking. 'He's struggling with the burden of keeping it upright. An upright sword in the tarot is a symbol of balance, of clarity. He's struggling to maintain that balance.'

Birch sat back. She could feel her discomfort mounting. 'And you're saying he's me?'

Bee nodded. 'The King of Swords is someone who wants to master their own mind,' she said. 'It's a struggle you're experiencing at the moment, I feel. You remember a time when you knew how things were: you understood was what right, what was wrong. Things felt simple. Now, you're struggling to come to terms with the fact that you can never master your own mind, not really. The very idea of mastery is potentially harmful. You cannot have intellect without emotion, however much you might desire it. Emotions are important, too. Pushing away what you feel isn't a sustainable path. The king will never rest easily on his throne until he realises that.'

Birch wanted to sweep the card from the table, the way Crosbie had batted away the stacked deck from in front of Bee.

If this was a cold reading, it was a good one. She felt altogether too well perceived.

'Well,' she heard herself saying, 'okay then.' She could feel, rather than see, that Amy was looking at her.

'I think,' Amy said, 'that we might have enough information to go on, for now.' She reached over and scooped up her phone from the coffee table. Birch realised with some alarm that it had recorded the entirety of her unprompted tarot reading.

'I'm sorry I couldn't give you anything more concrete,' Bee replied. If she was surprised by Amy's sudden termination of the meeting, she didn't show it. 'Anything more to go on, I mean.'

Amy was getting to her feet. Birch felt dazed, but reached down the side of the sofa arm for her stick. She had a strong desire to be outside; she realised now why Crosbie had made such a hasty exit.

'Don't worry,' Amy told Bee, 'you've been very helpful. We'll keep in touch, and I'd encourage you to do the same. Please do call us if you ... discover anything else?'

Bee nodded. 'I will.'

Birch pulled herself upright. She felt herself leaning a little more of her weight on the stick than usual. She felt like she was swaying, ever so slightly.

'DI Birch,' Bee said.

Birch realised she'd been looking into the middle distance, and forced herself to focus on the woman now standing opposite her. 'Yes?'

'I'm sorry,' she said, 'if that felt ... personal. It wasn't meant to be. The tarot is just another way of knowing things – about ourselves, and about the world. I hope I didn't cross a line.'

With some effort, Birch pasted on a grin. 'Don't worry,' she replied. 'I've had far worse things said to me in the course of this job.'

Diary 16/01

I had always told Luke that I wanted to go where I could use my English. I had always been good at English in school, and my parents were very proud of that. They said that with good English, I could do any job, I could travel all over the world. I don't know if Luke listened, or if it was just a coincidence, but I ended up here in Scotland, where it rains almost always, and that rain is freezing cold. People speak English here, but sometimes I struggle to understand. I definitely struggled in Aberdeen, which is where Luke took me.

I'd never heard of Aberdeen, but I learned it was an old, grey place, with tall buildings. Luke took me there because there were a lot of men who'd pay money for a girl like me. Men who worked hard jobs on oil rigs and on boats and driving lorries. Men with rough hands and thick black lines under their fingernails.

When Luke told my parents I'd be able to work to pay my way in Europe, I hadn't realised he meant this sort of work. I won't write about it here, the things I did – the things those men were told I would do. I don't even like to think about them. But I turned fourteen the week that I started, and that work went on for a year.

Luke gave me to a man named Joe. They worked together, he said; Joe was his friend. He'd described Muhammad as his friend, too – the man who picked me up from The Neverland. Luke had friends everywhere, and all his friends were bad men.

Luke made it clear to me that I didn't belong to Joe – I still belonged to him, Luke. That was how he put it. I was his. The money I would earn, he and Joe would split. Joe was just looking after me: giving me somewhere to live, keeping me safe. These were his words, not mine. I lived in a basement flat with Joe and several other girls: different girls, because they came and went. Some ran away. Occasionally, one was arrested and we didn't see her again. The girls were mostly white and mostly had names like Marta and Ula and Maria. I wanted to make friends with them, but Joe didn't like us fraternising. 'Fraternising' was another English word I hadn't known until then. I liked its sound, though I wasn't allowed to do it.

Luke visited sometimes. He told me I was doing well; I was making money for him and Joe, like I was supposed to. Occasionally he would bring me presents, but they were always presents that I knew were about the job I was doing: he'd get me make-up, or underwear, and I knew I was meant to use it to impress the men with the black fingernails. I was special, Luke said, because I was Asian. I got more clients than the white girls did. I liked when Luke visited, because he let me call my parents. He knew that I couldn't tell them about what was happening to me; I'd never have been able to talk to them about the things I was doing. Instead, I told them I was going to school, though I wasn't. I told them the new English words I'd learned. I told them about Scotland, how it was cold and strange but beautiful too. I told them about the huge white gulls and the friendly dogs. When they asked if I'd made friends, I'd tell them a story about one of the Martas or Ulas or Marias – sometimes a real story, but usually a fake one. My mother beamed over FaceTime, and told me I looked so grown-up. I couldn't bear to say anything that might shatter her smile. My parents had spent so much money – all their money – and they believed they'd made the right decision. I couldn't say anything. I couldn't do anything. I just had to carry on.

One night around my fifteenth birthday, there was a man – a john, as Joe called them – who was very drunk. Sometimes the men were kind to me – sometimes they didn't even want to do very much. Occasionally they did nothing, they just talked to me, or looked at me, and seemed very sad. This man was angry. Not just with me, I didn't think, but with everything – angry with the whole world. I'd got very good at the job by then, by which I mean I'd learned how to do it without being really *there*. While my body did the job, my mind did what it liked, and the men didn't usually notice. This man noticed.

'You're no even fuckin *trying*,' he said, and backhanded me across the face. My body registered the blow, but the pain of it slid off like water.

Sometimes the men didn't want to pay, or they tried to bargain with me about the price. The price, Joe said, was non-negotiable – another phrase I repeated to myself over and over in order to learn. If it wasn't paid, he'd do what he referred to as *having a word*, and this seemed to stop any trouble. Most of the men were regulars, and most of them knew Joe. They knew he was serious, and not to be crossed. But this man was new. He'd refused to pay upfront, and I expected that afterwards he'd try to haggle with me over the price. Instead, he tried to simply walk away. He'd led me down a long alleyway, and I watched for a few moments as he staggered back towards the street, weaving and unsteady. My mind had been busy wandering – thinking about anything other than this man and his terrible hands – but suddenly, as I watched him walk away, my mind decided to think of my mother. My mother, beaming at me through the screen of Luke's phone, telling me how grown-up I looked, how good my English was, how proud she was of me. My mother, believing I was safe. My mother, who gave Luke all of her money. All of her money, and it wasn't enough. I had to earn more money; I'd always have to earn more money. Money this man owed me. Money he was trying to steal.

My body took over. The man was too drunk to move quickly; he wasn't even halfway back to the lit street, the street where Joe was waiting, somewhere, in a parked car. I began to run. Within a few steps, I realised I'd kicked off the stupid high heels Joe made all his girls wear – the cobbles were freezing and greasy under my feet. The man was tall, but not broad. He was *gaunt*, in fact, another English word I'd learned. I remember my mind watching as my body lifted from the ground, jumping so that it could wrap its arms around his neck. I remember him crying out in shock, and falling forwards on to the rain-slicked ground. I remember the sound his nose made as it broke. I remember my body raining its fists down on him, landing blows wherever it could. I remember him howling, howling, howling, both of his own skinny hands held up to his bleeding face. I remember the alleyway lit up with blue flashing lights, and my own voice shouting *fuck you Luke fuck you Joe I hate you I hate you I hate you* over and over and over, until it was hoarse.

This is how stupid Luke is: he kidnapped the wrong person, and he doesn't even realise it.

That first day in the room together, Kim told me her story. She'd been working in a beauty parlour in Glasgow, and living with her aunty and uncle. She told me they were very rich: they'd come to Scotland and made their fortune, just like Luke told me I would, except in their case it wasn't a lie. Kim had come to live with them because her parents had died in a car crash. They wanted her to go to university; her uncle said it had to be Oxford or Cambridge, because they were the best.

'You can't get into Oxford or Cambridge,' Kim told me, 'unless you've been to a British high school.'

I wanted to tell her I didn't think that was true, but she's older than me, and her lip was bleeding while she spoke, so I didn't say anything.

Kim's aunty only had sons, and had always wanted a daughter, so Kim assumed she'd be spoiled. Instead, her aunty had such high hopes for her that she said she felt like she was suffocating.

'I went to high school,' Kim said, 'but I didn't get good grades. I mean, they were good, but not good enough for Oxford. I said I wanted to go to college instead, and study cosmetology. They were so disappointed. My uncle especially.'

Anyway, Kim started working in a beauty parlour when she finished school, saving up for college, because her family wouldn't pay. Not for her to do a practical degree like that; they'd wanted her to study law, or medicine. One of her workmates was a girl just like me. She'd also been found by Luke, or one of the other men he sometimes worked with. He'd lied to her, too, and lied to her family the way he'd lied to mine. Then he'd tried to sell her for money. I couldn't believe it, listening to Kim speak. The girl's name was Anh. She came from a town I'd visited, back home. Her story sounded almost exactly like mine.

Anh had got away from Luke – Kim didn't know how. She'd found work doing nails in the parlour. She and Kim were friends. Kim was happy to have a workmate who spoke Vietnamese, so they could chat easily.

'We had lots of clients, too,' Kim told me, 'and we made decent tips. White people think all Vietnamese girls do good nails. They'd ask for us in person.'

One day, Anh didn't come into work when she was supposed to. Kim tried to text her, but she didn't get a response. The other girls at the parlour hadn't heard from her, and didn't know where she'd gone. She didn't come back the next day, or the next.

'Eventually,' Kim said, 'the salon owner was contacted by someone. The police, I suppose. Anh had been detained, and was going to be deported. She had no leave to remain, or whatever they call it. They were sending her back to Vietnam.'

Kim carried on talking then, so I missed the next part. I was watching the little seam of blood that kept running down her chin from the cut in her lip. She kept wiping at it with the sleeve of her hoodie, but it kept appearing. I knew it was because she was talking, and I was making her talk, but I'd been alone in that room for several days by then, and I was just so happy she was there. But I was also thinking about Anh, and how she must have felt. Perhaps she was relieved to go home, or perhaps she was sad. I thought about how I'd feel if the police took me away without warning – if I didn't get a chance to pack my things, or say goodbye to Winnie or Beth or Josie. I'd love to see my family again, but I'd definitely feel sad. And I'd feel scared. Luke knew people all over the world. He'd followed me from the Netherlands to Scotland. He'd followed me from Aberdeen to Edinburgh. Wherever I'd gone, he'd found me. And he knew where my family lived. He could find me again, if he wanted to.

He found Kim. He'd gone into the beauty parlour, looking for Anh.

'He must have been casing the place,' Kim said, 'because he knew which table she sat at. He knew when she worked, when she had clients. He started turning up, and hanging around on the street outside the parlour. The owner said he was just some lowlife, just some guy. But I didn't like it. He gave me a bad feeling.'

I shivered as she described him. Luke, tall and broad and wearing a huge sweatshirt with the hood pulled low over his eyes. Luke, waiting in a doorway, waiting in his van, waiting, looking, watching. It was a scene from my nightmares, and it kept coming true.

'I'd started sitting at her table sometimes,' Kim said, 'and I'd seen some of her usual clients, because she was gone all of a sudden, and the owner didn't want us cancelling on people. He stood outside and watched me, sometimes for a whole shift. I was afraid to leave, even though the owner said he was probably harmless. She said I was imagining it, he wasn't watching me, he was just hanging about – or if he was watching me, it was just because he fancied me, and I should take it as a compliment. But I knew it wasn't that. Even when I left for the day, and he'd gone, I knew there was something weird about him. I walked home looking over my shoulder.'

Kim didn't want to stay at the parlour after Anh was taken away. She wanted to get out of Glasgow. Her aunty and uncle had decided that if she wasn't going to go to Oxford, she'd better marry a rich man. I almost laughed when she told me that, because it sounded like something my little sisters would say. 'Marry a rich man, so we can all be rich.' They wanted me to be like Jane in *Pride and Prejudice*, a movie they all loved. But Kim wasn't laughing.

'He was fine,' she said, 'this guy they knew, but I mean … he was old. I didn't want to get married. I was tired of my aunty telling me what to do all the time. In this country, people my age, they live alone, they live their own lives. I wanted that. And yeah, a creepy guy had started showing up at my work. And my friend was gone. I was sick of being there. I decided I could go anywhere, so one day I just left.'

I was amazed by her. She seemed so cool and confident, so much older than me, even though her eyes were red from crying and she had blood running down her chin. I wanted to hug her and never let go. I also wanted to cry, because we were stuck in this horrible room together and I didn't know how we were going to get out.

'I told them, and everything,' she said. 'I didn't just run away. I said I was going to Edinburgh. They weren't happy with me. But I didn't care. I was naive, I guess. But I never thought he'd follow me.'

'The old man?' I asked.

'No,' she said, 'Luke.'

This is how stupid Luke is: he thought Kim was Anh. He believed Anh belonged to him, like he believes I belong to him. He didn't know she'd gone home to Vietnam, and he's too stupid to realise that Anh and Kim aren't the same person.

'When he turned up at my new job in Edinburgh,' Kim said, 'I knew I'd been right. I knew this guy was big trouble. But I didn't expect what happened next.'

She didn't need to tell me; I knew. The quiet street. The grey van. A knife, or maybe just the threat of one. That dank chemical smell, and a long ride through traffic. This house. A locked door.

'He still doesn't know,' Kim said. 'He still thinks I'm Anh. He's one of those white men who thinks all Vietnamese people look alike. He has no idea. But I'm so scared in case he finds out.'

I was confused. 'How would he find out?'

She looked at me then like I was crazy. 'Don't you know why you're here?' she asked me. 'You're here because he wants to make money off you. That's all you're *for*. You know that. That's the only reason he agreed to bring you to Europe in the first place. He's going to get in touch with your family, and blackmail them for more money. You got away from him, just like Anh did. He'd made her work on the streets, too – he'd made her have sex with men, and he took the money. When she ran away, he stopped getting paid, and now he thinks he's owed. It's the same with you. He's holding you hostage so he can get money out of your family.'

I couldn't believe I'd felt hopeful when he'd mentioned my parents. It made me feel sick, thinking of him contacting them. Thinking of how worried they'd be, how much it would hurt them. They didn't have any money to give him – not any money they could spare. He'd ruin them. I couldn't help myself, then. I started to cry.

Kim shushed me, and hugged me, and I clung on.

'Not so tight,' she said. 'My ribs hurt.'

I didn't want to ask why.

'If he's trying to get in touch with Anh's parents, too,' she said, 'then eventually they're going to tell him that he's got the wrong girl. Anh got deported. She might be back home by now, or she might be being processed somewhere. But eventually she'll show up, and they'll say, "No, you're wrong, you can't have any money, because you're lying, you haven't got our daughter." And then I'll be useless to him. And then I don't know what he'll do.'

I didn't know either, but I didn't want to think about it. 'He already beat you up pretty bad,' I said. I felt a sick, guilty feeling, then; I didn't like that he'd done it, but I felt relieved that he hadn't done it to me. Not yet, anyway.

'He did everything he wanted to,' Kim said.

I hated that I knew what she meant.

Birch, Tuesday 18 January

Birch had taken an Uber home that evening, barely hearing a word of the driver's cheery prattle. It had begun to sleet, and the city passed her by in a blur of lit-up, steamed-up buses and bundled people. She'd stumbled into her frigid house and flicked on the heating. It was already completely dark; she did something she never did, and switched on the living room's big light. Usually one for mood lighting, she didn't have the energy to traipse around the room turning on table lamps. She was too busy thinking about Beatrice Crozier, and the King of Swords. Casting her stick aside, she flopped down on to the sofa.

'I'm saying "I feel", but what I'm actually doing is thinking.' She repeated the phrase she'd said only hours earlier to Dr Jane, aloud, into the empty air of the living room. Dr Jane had nodded, knowingly; this was Birch's *thing* in therapy, it was what she did. It was what she did in every aspect of life; if she could think, and avoid feeling, then she would. Therapy challenged her precisely because it forced her to stop doing that. Dr Jane pushed her to feel her feelings, a thing she hadn't ever realised she didn't know how to do.

You struggle with balancing intellect and emotion. That was what Beatrice Crozier had said. *Pushing away what you feel isn't a sustainable path. The King will never rest easily on his throne until he realises that.* Birch didn't know much about tarot, but she couldn't imagine there could be another card in that deck that would have been more on the nose. How had Bee channelled Dr Jane so perfectly? How had both of them managed to break into Birch's head and know her so well? More to the point, how had Bee known which card was the King of Swords? Such a thing could easily have been done in a side show, with a trick deck – but Birch had sat and watched Bee shuffle those cards, over and over, before they fell. She'd seen all their different symbols and colours with her own eyes.

'How is she doing it?' she demanded, aloud, to no one. 'How does she *know* this stuff?'

Birch was no closer to an answer when she arrived at Fettes Row the following morning, grateful for the quiet taxi driver who'd delivered her. For the first night in a long time, she hadn't had the flood dream, but that was probably down to the fact that she'd slept only lightly, and in short, delirious shifts. She'd woken up over and over again, bothered by questions she couldn't answer. By the time she reached the office, she realised her scattered confusion over Beatrice Crozier was solidifying into jealousy. *How nice it must be,* she thought, *to just know things, and to know them with absolute certainty.*

It was still early when Birch arrived, but Amy was already at her desk.

'Morning, sunshine.' Birch placed a paper cup of canteen coffee at her friend's elbow. 'I had a feeling you'd beat me in, so I got you this.'

'Thanks, marm.' Amy barely glanced up from her computer screen.

Birch leaned over, frowning. 'What are you on with?' she asked.

Amy sat back in her chair with a sigh. 'I've been trying to find out as much as I can about Beatrice Crozier. I thought maybe she'd have a personal website advertising her psychic services, or whatever. At least some social media. But it seems like she doesn't go in for any of that. All she has is a LinkedIn profile, and it's incredibly ordinary.'

'Hmm. That's not much to go on.'

'Right. I mean …' Amy trailed off, then threw up her hands. 'I just truly don't know what to make of all this.'

Birch hobbled a little closer to the desk so she could lean her good hip against it. 'You and me both,' she replied. 'I barely slept last night, trying to figure her out. Beatrice, I mean.'

Amy was shaking her head slowly from side to side. 'She's so plausible, isn't she? And yet … we can't make a case out of anything she's giving us. Maybe she knows where these girls are, and who's taken them. Maybe she *is* trying to tell us what's really happening, albeit in this strange, opaque way. But a part of me also thinks …'

'That it could all be absolute nonsense?'

Amy's shoulders sagged. 'Yeah. Like … she's a lead, isn't she? We have to treat this like a lead. But it could all turn out to be nothing. We could be making absolute fools of ourselves.'

Birch was nodding. She took a sip from her own cardboard coffee cup. The coffee tasted burned. 'You seemed pretty taken in yesterday.'

Amy blinked. 'Did I? Well that's good, I guess. I was trying to make up for Crosbie's bad behaviour.'

Birch winced. 'Yeah … it wasn't the greatest interview ever.'

Amy looked up at Birch through her eyelashes. 'The tarot card stuff was interesting, though. I was a bit jealous, after we left. I was the only one who didn't get the chance to be read for filth.'

Birch laughed. 'Trust me,' she said, 'it wasn't a pleasant sensation.'

Amy grinned. 'Did you feel very seen?'

'Horribly so. I'd just been at therapy, too, so it felt like a real double whammy. I can't say I'm a huge fan of other people rummaging around in my brain.'

Amy picked up her coffee and blew on it. Birch smiled at the optimism in this gesture; the canteen coffee was rarely ever hot.

'She's a funny one, Beatrice, for sure,' Amy said. 'How did she know about the cat backpack, if she hasn't really seen these girls? And who, if anyone, is she covering for?'

Birch glanced at her watch. They needed to be making a move. 'Well,' she said, shuffling her hip off the edge of Amy's desk, 'we know she dated Banjo Robin, years ago, so it's safe to assume she has terrible taste in men. Maybe it's a boyfriend? But then … if you knew your boyfriend had abducted two young Vietnamese girls, why the hell would you cover for him?'

Amy pushed her chair back. 'I guess,' she said, 'that if that's the case, she sort of isn't covering for him. She *has* told us. She's reported it, in a very weird and roundabout way.'

'True.'

Amy got to her feet, picking up her coffee cup. 'Anyway,' she said, 'into the breach, I guess?'

Birch jerked her head in the direction of the corridor that led to McLeod's office. 'You first,' she said.

McLeod kept odd hours, which nobody ever commented on, but it was especially odd to see him at the office so early on a Tuesday morning. Birch wondered if he was hoping to get away early that afternoon, to attend a function or get in a round of golf on some frosty course somewhere before nightfall. She also wondered if he was punishing them – her, Amy and Crosbie – for their decision to entertain a woman who claimed to be psychic. He'd asked for them at nine o'clock sharp, to debrief.

'I think we're being led a merry dance, guv,' Crosbie was saying. 'My suggestion is that we arrest this woman.'

Birch threw him a sharp look. 'Arrest her on what charge?' she asked.

Crosbie shrugged. 'Wasting police time would be my pick,' he said. 'Stick her in a cell for a few hours, see if that doesn't cause her to cough up what she actually knows.'

Birch looked at McLeod's face, trying to see what he made of this idea. He was reclining in his heated office chair, chin tilted back, eyes aloft. She couldn't read him.

'And if she doesn't change her story?' Amy asked.

Crosbie snorted. 'Charge her,' he said. 'I certainly feel like I've had my time wasted – I don't know about you two.'

Birch thought of Anjan. 'I'm not sure a judge would see that as sufficient grounds for arrest, Alan.'

He waved a hand as though swatting her away. 'I'd be willing to risk it.'

Amy cleared her throat. 'Sir,' she said, trying in vain to get McLeod to meet her gaze, 'I was just saying to DI Birch, I really don't know what to make of this woman, but I think it's unlikely that she's simply a time-waster. It's possible that there's absolutely no truth to anything she's saying, but I do find that hard to believe. I don't know what her motivation would be for spinning us such a complex story, *and* she's given us details that suggest she does know *something*. That's why we went to talk to her, after all.'

Claire Askew

McLeod had closed his eyes. Birch felt like throwing her now-empty coffee cup at his head.

'But,' Amy went on, 'I can't quite figure out what the best course of action is. I think we have to continue to take it seriously, but …'

She stopped talking. Birch waited to see if Crosbie would cut in, but he didn't. They all looked at McLeod.

'I think what I'm getting at, sir,' Amy added, 'is … well, we could use some guidance. What do you suggest we do in this situation?'

Slowly, McLeod levered himself into a more upright position. He looked, Birch thought, like an ungainly lizard. He looked at each of them in turn, his eyes eventually coming to rest on her.

'DI Birch,' he said, 'you're quieter than usual. I can't help but think you must have an opinion.'

Birch felt like laughing. *He doesn't know what we ought to do, either,* she thought. 'I'm quiet,' she said, 'because I'm unsure of my position at the moment. I mean, with regards to this case.'

McLeod frowned. 'I don't know what you mean by that,' he said.

She could tell that he did.

'Well, guv,' she said, 'only last week, you took me off the Linh Fortune case, and assigned it to Crosbie. Since then, I've only ever been sitting in. I'm unsure what my jurisdiction is here.'

McLeod threw her a theatrical eyeroll. 'You're a detective inspector in my team,' he said, 'that's your jurisdiction. When I ask you for your opinion, I expect you to share it.'

Birch wasn't looking at Amy, but she felt her colleague shift nervously beside her. 'Yes, guv,' she replied. She wasn't sure what else to say.

McLeod leaned forward. 'I'm serious, Birch,' he said. 'I'm not interested in hearing you whine about how I took your friend Winifred Fortune's case away from you and assigned it to somebody else.'

'I don't believe that's what I'm doing,' Birch began, but McLeod was still talking.

'It should be abundantly clear to you,' he said, 'why I did that. We've been too many rounds, you and I, in the ring of you getting too personally involved in a case and me having to drag you back into line. Add in the fact that you've been off your game lately, and … well, I did what I felt was necessary, and I stand by it.'

Amy let out a fake cough. 'Sir,' she said, 'if I could make a suggestion …'

McLeod didn't look at her, but he held up a hand to indicate she should stop speaking.

'When you say I've been "off my game",' Birch said, 'are you referring to the fact that I was signed off sick?'

McLeod used the same hand to mime a sort of half shrug. 'Same difference,' he replied.

'I just wonder,' Amy persisted, 'if it might be worth listening to what Beatrice Crozier said about physical proximity. If we—'

'With all due respect, sir,' Birch cut in, 'I don't believe it is. I think you've assumed that my being physically injured has led to some decrease in my mental capacity.'

Beside Birch, Amy sighed. When she spoke again, her voice was a little louder. 'I think if we put Beatrice Crozier into an unmarked car,' she said, 'and … well, drive her around, then that may help her feel more comfortable to disclose—'

'You haven't been as sharp as usual, Birch,' McLeod was saying. 'I'm amazed you're not willing to admit that.'

'Hang on.' Now Crosbie had chimed in. 'Can I just clarify what you're suggesting, Kato?'

Amy held up both hands. 'I'd love it if you would, Alan.' Her voice was raised.

Birch bit down, hard, on her own bottom lip. The room felt full of static. For a moment, no one spoke.

'Thank you,' Amy said, softly, to no one in particular.

Crosbie was looking at her. 'Did you just say,' he began, 'that we should take Beatrice Crozier on a ride-along, and—'

'It's a suggestion,' Amy replied. 'That's all. Since no one seems to have any better ideas.'

Crosbie let out a bitter laugh. 'I thought my idea about the arrest and the cell was an excellent one.'

Birch was still looking at McLeod. She was trying to remember Dr Jane's breathing technique. She found she couldn't; the blood sloshing in her ears was too loud.

'I'm just saying,' Amy replied, 'that we could, if we wanted to, take a softly-softly approach. After you left, Alan, Bee told us that she might be able to – how did she put it? – she might be able to *know more* if she were in closer physical proximity to the two girls. She volunteered that information. Maybe she was trying to tell us how to proceed?'

Crosbie had closed his eyes. 'You want,' he said, 'to drive her around Edinburgh in a police car in the hope that you pass some house or other and she says, "The spirits tell me they're in there"?'

'I'm saying,' Amy replied, 'it might be worth a shot.'

Crosbie opened his eyes again. 'We don't even know if these kids are still *in* Edinburgh,' he said. 'They could be anywhere by now.'

'Except,' Amy replied, 'when Bee described the room they're being held in, she mentioned an Edinburgh press in one corner.'

Crosbie gave an exaggerated wince, and *I don't know about that* gesture.

Amy was undeterred. She seemed keen to keep talking, perhaps so McLeod couldn't start berating Birch again. 'If Beatrice Crozier has information we can use,' she said, 'but she's reluctant to give it to us unless it's delivered through the lens of a psychic vision, why not give it a try? If it doesn't work, we can go to Plan B.'

'Which is?' It was McLeod who'd spoken. Amy had succeeded in drawing his attention away from Birch. Birch allowed herself to take one long breath in.

'Crosbie's idea,' Amy replied. 'Try the ride-along, then, if it turns up nothing, fine. Arrest her, and see if that works.'

Birch cleared her throat. She wasn't sure how her voice would come out when she spoke. 'You asked for my opinion, guv,' she said. 'My opinion is that we should listen to Sergeant Kato.'

McLeod eyed her with disdain. 'I asked for your opinion five minutes ago,' he snapped, 'and you declined to respond.'

Birch felt her vision glitch. Annoyance was rising in her, and she couldn't seem to get it under control. 'Oh for goodness' sake,' she said, before she could stop herself.

McLeod had turned to look at Amy, but now he rounded on Birch once again. She watched his pupils shrink. 'I beg your pardon?'

Birch swallowed, hard, but it was too late to get the words back in. 'Sorry,' she said, trying and failing to sound it, 'but that just seemed … rather petty.'

McLeod squared his shoulders. 'Did it, now? Good lord, Detective Inspector – I must say, it's very rich you sitting here telling me you haven't been off your game lately, while simultaneously being so thin-skinned.'

Birch tightened her grip on the empty coffee cup, mostly so she wouldn't launch it across the desk at him.

'*Please*,' Amy said, her voice raised again, 'can we get back to the matter at hand? Sir, I'd appreciate hearing what you think about the idea of—'

McLeod was blinking rapidly as Amy spoke, and wincing slightly, as though her voice were a buzzing fly he was trying to ignore. 'You're asking,' he cut in, his eyes still fixed on Birch, 'if you can indulge your psychic friend some more, in the hope that she eventually lets out enough rope to hang herself. Have I got that right?'

There was a pause. Birch couldn't look at her friend – the anger simmering in her chest wouldn't allow her to drop McLeod's gaze – but she wondered if Amy was silently counting to ten before replying. Amy was so much better than her at keeping her emotions in check.

'Beatrice Crozier,' Amy said, 'wants to talk. She came to us. She also made the comment about physical proximity. I think she wants to tell us more, and she might be hinting at a way we can make her feel safe enough to do that.'

McLeod brought his fist down on the desk, making all three of them jump. As his hand made contact with the table top, he finally turned his head to look at Amy. Birch let her shoulders sag, just slightly. Dr Jane's breathing technique was still evading her.

'Enough!' McLeod was angry, too, it seemed. 'I am absolutely sick and tired of pussyfooting around this woman. And why? Because she says she's seen a girl holding a soft toy.

So what? It's a cliché older than God that missing children turn up clinging to a teddy bear. She guessed at an obvious image, and you three were only too keen to join the dots between that stab in the dark and the fact that our missing person was last seen wearing a furry backpack.' He zeroed in on Crosbie. 'Honestly, Alan,' he went on, 'I would have expected you to be the voice of reason here.'

Crosbie looked wounded. 'Guv,' he said, 'I was *just* saying—'

McLeod held up a hand, the way he had earlier when Amy was speaking. He wasn't interested in hearing any more. 'That's not the point,' he snapped. 'The *point* is, everyone in this room is a police officer – or was, the last time I checked. Police officers act in response to evidence gathered. It's been what? Nine days since Linh Fortune went missing? And as far as I can see, there is yet to be a shred of actual evidence gathered in this case.' He pointed a finger at Birch's face. 'And before you chip in, Helen, I mean *hard* evidence. I'm not talking about spectral evidence, or whatever it is you think you're chasing after with this Crozier woman.' He withdrew the pointing finger, and made a slicing motion in the air with the same hand. 'I've had enough.'

Birch knew it would be a bad idea to interrupt him, though she desperately wanted to. She was alarmed by the words she felt bubbling up in her throat, the things she wished she could say. She waited for several seconds after McLeod finished speaking, before finally responding.

'Sir, I understand where you're coming from.' She still felt irritable enough that the words, though reasonable in themselves, sounded hot and unruly. She gestured towards Amy and Crosbie. 'We're none of us certain of the best way forward. But truly, I think Sergeant Kato's suggestion has merit. I think Beatrice Crozier—'

McLeod brought his hand down on the desk again, not in a fist this time, but as a flat-palmed slap. She wondered if it hurt.

'I said *enough*, Birch.'

The air between them felt thick. McLeod paused for a moment, as though weighing up what to say next. She could see from his face that it wasn't going to be good. Then he said it.

'I want you out.'

Birch blinked. 'I'm sorry?'

McLeod pointed at the door of the office, extending his arm slowly as though Birch needed extra time to understand what he meant. 'Out of this room,' he said. Dark pink spots had appeared on his cheeks. 'Honestly, I can't stand to hear another word out of your mouth.'

Birch felt a series of strange sensations as he spoke. More than anything, she was angry: angry at his heavy-handed-ness, at his inability to listen, at the way he'd spoken to her, as though she were a naughty schoolgirl. But underneath the anger was something else, something strange. Something in her head seemed to give way, snapping like a string pulled too taut. She realised the feeling was relief. She'd spent years pushing back at McLeod, challenging him – because he needed to be pushed back at, he *needed* to be challenged – but he'd never ordered her out of a room. He'd never been so openly sick of the sight of her. As she felt around for her walking stick and got to her feet, her brain replayed a scene from her most recent dream: near-submerged in roil-ing water, she'd pressed the call button for the lift. In her mind's eye, it arrived, and the doors rolled open to reveal her miraculous escape route.

'Yes, guv,' she said, her voice thick.

He knew she'd done it deliberately – spoken again after he'd told her not to – because he raised a hand to his face, and closed his eyes. 'Out,' he hissed.

Birch didn't look directly at Amy, but she could see her friend's mouth was hanging open. She did look at Crosbie, and was surprised to see the expression on his face was not the smug triumph she'd expected, but a look of quiet dismay. She shifted her gaze to the door, and with as much speed as she could muster, crossed the room and opened it. The door handle felt freezing cold to the touch, and she realised she was hot and flushed, and her heart was thudding. As she stepped out over the threshold, the sound of the rushing water from her dream echoed in her ears. She closed the door behind her and hobbled away, not pausing for fear of turning around and going back to say things she knew she shouldn't.

Outside in the Police Scotland carpark, the air was frigid. An ill wind had begun to blow, and there was sleet in it. Birch's eyes stung. She wanted to throw her head back and scream. The anger she'd felt in McLeod's office seemed to be trapped; it banged about inside her ribcage. Her hands were shaking, and she wished for the first time in many years that she had a cigarette to smoke. She closed her eyes and tried to picture Dr Jane, tried to imagine what she'd say, what she'd tell her to do right now. She couldn't even call her therapist's voice to mind. All she could hear was McLeod, saying over and over *I can't stand to hear another word out of your mouth*. She tasted something bad on her tongue – the bitter tang of adrenaline. She wondered for a moment if she might actually throw up. Instead, she spat, and when it didn't make anything better, felt embarrassed.

But there was no one around. She was alone, shivering under a lee of concrete at one edge of the car park, her walk to this spot a blur she couldn't really remember. McLeod was wrong, she thought – he often was. He was wrong so often that it made working with him frustrating and thankless. He took credit for things when they went well, and ranted and puffed and banged on the desk when they didn't. She realised how much he'd hated that meeting: three of his best officers coming to him to say they weren't really sure about something, and could he help? He didn't know how, and that bothered him. It bothered him, so he took it out on her.

She was shivering hard; she hadn't stopped to put on a coat, and now her hands were beginning to smart with cold. Nevertheless, she fished in her trouser pocket for her phone and prodded it awake. There were two missed calls there; she'd turned the phone to silent to go into McLeod's office, knowing better than to have him interrupted mid-flow by her ringtone. *Missed calls: Alyona (2)*. Birch frowned. Her hands were still shaking. Who was Alyona again? She couldn't think straight. Oh wait, yes – Alyona, her informant in Leith, with her chic flat in Sailmaker Road. Alyona, who'd said she'd keep an ear to the ground for Linh. Birch tried to make a mental note, nodding her head as though hoping to make it stick. She'd call Alyona back later. No, not later – as soon as possible. But not right now. Right now, she needed to talk to someone else.

She didn't need to think about the number; it was as though her fingertips knew it automatically, without her brain getting involved. This wasn't the first time she'd stood in this spot, in a state of some distress, and done this exact thing. As she listened to the rings – one, two, three, four – her teeth began to chatter.

Finally, an answer.

'Dad?' She even *sounded* cold. 'Something's happened. No – yes, I'm okay. Or … well, no, actually, I'm not. Not really. I need a vehicle, like, now. Any chance?'

Diary 17/01

Luke didn't come back for a long time. The house was weirdly quiet, and felt even colder than usual. Kim and I squished on to the sofa to sleep for a while, and though it felt weird, because she was a perfect stranger, it also made me cry silent, grateful tears. This was still happening, this terrible thing, but I wasn't on my own anymore.

The next morning, I had to show Kim the bucket in the corner of the room, my cheeks burning with shame.

She laughed, but it was a weird, flat laugh. 'Hey,' she said, 'at least this one's been emptied recently.'

It made my brain hurt to think that Kim had been trapped in the room upstairs the whole time I'd been trapped down here. I'd thought I was all alone with Luke. I was so happy she was with me, but also so sad.

'How long,' I asked, 'have you been here?'

Kim seemed to think about it for a long time. 'What day is it?' she asked, eventually. 'Do you know?'

'Wait,' I said, 'I'll check. I've been writing down the dates in my diary.'

She laughed properly then. 'You're keeping a diary?'

I showed it to her. I showed her all my things, the things he'd let me keep. This made her cry; he hadn't let her keep anything.

'It's my own fault,' she said, through tears. 'I was kind of unruly with him when I first got here. He didn't like that.'

'What did you do?'

She shrugged. 'I screamed a whole lot,' she replied, 'when I first arrived. I thought maybe the neighbours might hear, through the walls. And when he started hitting me to stop me screaming, I fought back. It was pretty stupid of me, but I felt like I had to try.'

I hadn't heard any screaming.

'So … when did you get here?' I asked.

Kim went quiet again, thinking. 'I guess, like … wow. I guess a month ago, give or take.'

I felt like I'd been slapped. The idea of being trapped in this room for that long was unbearable. I'd assumed Luke would only keep me here temporarily. In the past, he and I had only ever moved around – I had too many memories of feeling sick and crying in the back of his van.

'A *month.*' It came out like a whisper.

'Yeah,' she said. 'Like I say, he must be in touch with Anh's parents by now, right? It's only a matter of time until he finds out. Or maybe he already knows, and he's just waiting to punish me.'

I studied her. As well as being beat up, she was also skinny, and looked exhausted. The idea that I might still be in this horrendous room with boards on the windows in three weeks' time made me want to throw up. Kim had been in the room with me for one full day. Neither of us had eaten in that time. Luke had left an old two-litre lemonade bottle full of tap water on the mantelpiece. We took turns sipping from its battered neck.

'Maybe,' I said, 'if he finds out you're not Anh, he'll let you go.'

Kim snorted. 'Sure,' she said, 'and risk me running to the cops? Which, by the way, is exactly what I'd do, because that bastard needs to go to jail forever. He knows how much

I hate him; I've made sure he knows it. There's no way he'd let me go. When he finds out, he's going to kill me.'

Once, I'd asked Luke if he was going to kill me. It was early on, after I left Vietnam but before The Neverland, as I started to realise he wasn't a good man. He'd lied, and I was in trouble, and I was scared. He'd laughed in my face and told me I was much too valuable to kill. I'd taken that as a weird sort of compliment, because back then, I still didn't know who he was. How bad he was.

'Maybe he'll get you to …' I couldn't bring myself to name the thing itself. 'To work for him, like I used to. Like Anh did.'

Kim shook her head. She was quiet again, and I waited for her to speak.

'He's been gentle to you,' she said, 'I think. Probably because you're young. He can sell you for a very specific purpose, to very specific men. But me, I'm nothing special. He knows that. He's treated me badly, and he'd carry on treating me badly, and he'd let other men treat me badly, too. I've been thinking about it, and I think I'd rather die.'

I shook my head at her. 'You can't die,' I said. 'You mustn't.'

She sat back on the sofa and closed her eyes, as though falling asleep. 'I can't see what other choice there is,' she said.

I shuffled closer to her, then stopped. She'd flinched as I got near, and I remembered her hurt ribs. I looked at the chipboard over the window, the light in the gaps dim and grey. I could hear the spatter of snow or sleet against the wood.

'We could try to escape,' I said. 'There are two of us now.'

Kim's eyes stayed closed. She didn't reply.

I must have slept for a while. Sleep, I had learned, was a good way to forget about being hungry. I dreamed about Winnie, the day I met her. After the man in Aberdeen, the police processed me and told me I'd be put into what they called 'the care system'. I didn't trust the word 'care', not out of their mouths, not after The Neverland. I assumed I was just waiting for another man like Muhammad to come and scoop me up and take me to Luke. The room where I met Winnie felt so familiar: so like that same room in The Neverland that Muhammad had led me out of. *Oh,* I thought, *so today is the day, then. Today is the day Luke gets me back.*

When Winnie walked into the room, I didn't understand. I listened to what she said to me, but I didn't believe it. Surely this wasn't a friend of Luke's? She didn't seem like a person who could be bought with a brown envelope filled with cash. She was an older lady with neat, purplish-grey hair, and she wore a sparkly brooch in the shape of a cat, which I couldn't stop looking at. She spoke with a Scottish accent, but slowly, so I understood every word. She had crinkles around her eyes, and she seemed kind, but I was still wary. I didn't trust her on that first day, and felt like I might never trust her – she seemed too good to be true. But after a few days, I realised she really was what she said she was. I really was allowed to live in her house with her. I really was allowed to call my parents when-ever I wanted, though I still didn't tell them about Luke or Joe or the men. I really was allowed to have my own room and my own bed and enrol in school. She wasn't a friend of Luke's. She was a friend of *mine*.

Something shook me out of my dream of Winnie's house, and as I opened my eyes and remembered where I was, I felt a lurch of horror that I thought, for a moment, might simply kill me. I swallowed hard, worried I might vomit. I realised I felt warm, or the closest thing to warm I'd felt since I arrived in this place. I sat up to find that Kim had doubled the smelly blanket over, and wrapped me into it. She'd taken off Luke's bloodstained hoodie and draped it around my head like a turban.

'Hey,' I said, rubbing my eyes.

She was over by the window, doing something. She'd put the overhead light on, which must have been what woke me. She turned and looked at me.

'Nice hat,' she said, laughing. She was wearing a top that had long sleeves but a short hem. On the strip of midriff I could see, there were goosebumps.

I let the hoodie slip off my head into my hands, then I balled it up and threw it across the room for her to catch.

'I don't need it,' she said, 'honestly.'

I think I snorted at her. 'Shut up,' I said, 'it's freezing in here.'

She didn't protest further. I watched her unball the hoodie and put it back on.

'Why'd you put it on my head?'

She tapped the side of her temple. 'Wearing a hat,' she said, 'warms you up faster than anything else. I guess a jumper round your head does the same thing. Your teeth were chattering in your sleep, so I tucked you in a bit.'

I pushed the blanket aside and stood up. Hunger threatened to push me back down. I swayed for a moment, seeing if I'd faint or not.

'You okay?' she asked.

I righted myself. 'Yeah,' I replied.

Since I'd arrived, Luke had opened the door a few times and thrown things inside: packets of crisps, half a loaf of bread with stiff, stale crusts. I'd eaten them, because I'd assumed he wouldn't keep me here long. Now I knew Kim had been here a month – now Luke had been gone for over a day – I wished I'd rationed that food. The last full meal I'd eaten had been the burger in Princes Mall. I'd been trying not to think about it.

'I'm just starving,' I said, picking my way across the filthy room to where Kim stood. 'Do you think he's gone forever?'

She laughed, but it was a bitter laugh. 'We should be so lucky,' she said.

I looked around. Some of the musty boxes had been upended. 'What have you been doing?'

She shrugged. 'Seeing what's in here,' she replied. 'Seeing if he's left anything we could use to get out of here. Have you looked in any of these boxes?'

I shook my head, and she gave me a look that made me feel guilty. I'd assumed this place was temporary. Everything in the room was dirty and smelled gross. I didn't want Luke to think I'd been rummaging. I'd spent my days sleeping, and crying, and writing in this diary. I'd drawn about one thousand tiny doodles of Lang in the margins. I'd simply been waiting for this part – this trapped in a freezing, stinking house part – to somehow end, while hoping the next part wouldn't be worse.

'Sorry,' I said, in a small voice.

'It's okay,' she replied. 'You can start looking now.'

I watched as she upturned another box. It was full of mildewed sheets with rust-coloured spatters on them. I told myself the spatters were paint.

'What are you looking for?'

Kim dropped the empty cardboard box and kicked it. I could see the frustration she was feeling. The box was damp, and it crumpled around her foot as though made of cloth.

'I don't fucking know,' she said. She wasn't mad at me, I knew, but still, I recoiled slightly. 'Christ. You know what's funny? I've watched a load of videos online about how to escape when you're kidnapped. How to get out of zip ties, or what to do if your feet are duct-taped together. How to get handcuffs off without a key, that sort of thing. But no one makes videos telling you how to get out of a sealed room.'

I looked at the window boards. They'd been carefully erected. Luke had made a frame out of two-by-four planks and attached it to the bay window walls. Then he'd nailed the chipboard into it.

'You think we could bust through those?' I asked.

As if in response, my stomach growled. It was all I could do to stay upright, let alone break down a wooden wall. Kim turned her back on me, tensed, and kicked out hard at the chipboard with one foot. She rebounded against me, and we collapsed on to the floor.

'Shit,' she hissed. She was holding her side, where her bad ribs were. 'That hurt like a *bitch*.'

I helped her up. Without speaking, we hobbled over to the sofa and collapsed on to it. After a moment, Kim grabbed the blanket and threw it over us both.

'I should have tried to escape sooner,' I said. 'Now I'm so hungry, I just want to lie down.'

Kim was shaking her head. 'I tried,' she said. 'But the door upstairs was bolted, too. You can't do anything about bolts. A lock you can pick, but a bolt is a bolt. And this hoarding he's got on the windows? It's pretty tough.'

'I'm sorry,' I said again, as if it were all my fault.

She reached out a hand and brushed my cheek. 'It's okay,' she said. 'Well, no, it's not okay, it's fucking shit, but hey. At least we have each other now.'

She dropped the hand that had been touching my face. I grabbed it, and laced my fingers between hers. It made me think of my little sisters; we all held hands like that.

'And,' I said, 'there are people looking for us. We have people who care about us, right? You have your aunty and uncle. I have Winnie. They'll bring the police, and find us.'

Kim had closed her eyes again, as if she thought by doing so, she wouldn't have to hear me speak. 'It's been a month,' she said, 'and no one's come for me.'

I squeezed her hand. 'That just means he's hidden us well,' I replied, wanting so desperately to believe what I was saying. 'But they'll keep looking. Someone will come, I promise.'

I thought about the time that Luke sprang me from The Neverland. I still don't know how he did it, who Muhammad was, or who he pretended to be. He told me after he'd driven me away that no one in that place would care I was gone: they were so busy and understaffed and underfunded. Even if they cared about me, which they didn't, they had no resources to come looking for me. Not in another country. Not when I was worth so little to them.

I believed him. I was on a vast, strange continent where no one I knew lived. I had no way to contact my parents. Luke was the only person for thousands and thousands of miles who cared if I lived or died. Of course I believed him, of course I did what he told me to, of *course* I did. I hated him, and I hated what I had to do to survive, but I didn't want to die. I wasn't like Kim; I still believed I had a future. And I'd been right. Now I had Winnie. I had Josie and Beth. I had teachers who were kind and encouraged me in school. I loved school. I'd had social workers, and key workers, people who were paid money to make sure I was okay. Luke was wrong. There *were* people who cared about me. Winnie most of all. Winnie was old, but I knew she was fierce, and strong. I knew that no matter what happened, she'd search and search and search for me. Luke could have hidden me in the darkest corner in the farthest place, but eventually, someone would come. Winnie would make sure of it.

Outside, the slam of a van door. Kim's hand tightened its grip on mine, so hard it hurt my knuckles. We sat still, listening. Another door slam, then a pause. Shuffling, scuffling sounds. The jingle of keys. Luke's voice saying, 'Fucksake.' Then the many locks on the front door being fumbled open.

I lifted the blanket and peeked out. The light was still on, and the room felt too bright. Luke would come in, and see we'd emptied the boxes. I didn't like to think about what he might do. Kim's bottom lip was trembling. The cut there was still fresh, her face still bruised. A tiny part of me gave thanks that Luke was back: the hungry part of me, which believed the rest of me could take a beating if only I got to eat something.

'Please don't come in,' Kim chanted under her breath. 'Please don't come in, please don't come in.'

I huddled close to Kim, and she pulled me in. Too late, I remembered about her ribs, but if they hurt, she didn't show it. We both held our breath as the noises in the hall became noises on the stairs, and then the creak of floorboards overhead.

'Well,' Kim whispered, her voice just a breath in the shape of words, 'he's back.'

Birch, Tuesday 18 January

'Thanks for coming on another wild goose chase with me, Dad.' Birch was dialling Beatrice Crozier's number as they drove along a slushy Ferry Road in the direction of the Warristons. 'This one's even wilder than usual.'

Jamieson was still shaking his head. She'd given him a brief sense of how the meeting in McLeod's office had gone.

'Ah'm no surprised ye walked oot,' he muttered.

She laughed, though there was no mirth in it.

'Dad,' she said, 'I was *ordered* out. It wasn't my choice.'

'*Bas*tard,' Jamieson spat. 'Pittin' ye oot the room like ye're some wee lassie. Ah dinnae ken how ye work wi him, hen.'

'Yes, well,' Birch said, raising the phone to her ear, 'I might not be working with him for all that much longer. It depends how the next couple of hours go ... Yes, hello? Hi, Ms Crozier. Yes, sorry, Bee. Yes, it's DI Birch. Listen – there's no way to sugar-coat this, so I'm just going to come out with it. My detective chief inspector thinks you're messing us around and wasting police time, but I think differently, and I want to prove I'm right. I'd like to give you the opportunity to help us find our two missing girls. Yes. No – well, you're welcome, I suppose. So ... are you by any chance available – well, in the next ten minutes? Great. Superb. Yes, I'm already on my way. Okay, great.' She put the phone down. Looking at her father, she saw he was smiling. 'What's funny?'

Jamieson pulled out over the white line to nip past a bus. 'Well,' he said, 'ah just dinnae ken whit this wifey'll hink when …' He paused, lifting a hand from the steering wheel to gesture at the scruffy van they were sitting in. 'When *this* chugs up tae her front door. An' where are ye plannin' tae pit her, hen? Pretty cosy in this cab wi three o us.'

Birch sucked her teeth. 'Yeah,' she said, 'it's gonna be weird. But there was no way to use a police vehicle, I could never have got it authorised. And this has to happen now. I've had enough. The longer these girls are missing, the less chance we have of them coming back to us unhurt.'

Jamieson was nodding.

'I'm just sorry,' she added, 'to rope you in. I cannot *wait* to be able to bloody drive again.'

Jamieson grinned. 'Ah wis meant tae be helping ma pal Wullie stack roof tiles the day,' he said, pointing at the sleet-streaked windscreen, 'in this Baltic shite. Ye're daein' me a favour, ken.'

Birch laughed again, and this time, it was a little more genuine. 'Poor old Wullie,' she said.

'Forgive me, DI Birch,' Bee said, as she settled herself into the middle seat of the cab of Jamieson's van, 'but … this isn't a police-issue vehicle, is it?'

Birch tried to smile in what she hoped was a reassuring way. It was difficult; climbing into the cab herself caused her bad hip to ache. 'I thought you might notice that,' she said.

Bee gave her a mischievous look. 'Are we going under-cover?'

Birch winced. 'More going off the reservation completely,' she replied. 'I might well lose my job over this, but to be perfectly honest with you, I've stopped caring. There are two young women missing – one has been missing since December – and my commanding officer is having us all twiddle our thumbs instead of doing anything about it. So I'm doing something about it.'

Bee beamed at her. 'Choosing emotion over intellect,' she said.

'Something like that.'

'I know you don't know me,' Bee went on, 'but I'm proud of you, DI Birch.'

Birch could feel her face beginning to flush. 'You might be the only one,' she said.

Jamieson leaned forward over the steering wheel. 'She isnae,' he said. He was grinning again. He stuck out a hand for Bee to shake. 'Ah'm Jamieson Birch,' he said, jerking his head towards Birch. 'Proud da o' this wan.'

Bee took the offered hand and shook it. 'Beatrice Crozier,' she said. 'Bee. You're a policeman too, Mr Birch?'

Birch raised a hand and pressed it to her forehead. 'He most definitely is not,' she cut in. 'Like I said, we're really going off the reservation, here. I can't drive at the moment, with this bad leg, and DCI McLeod would never have authorised a police vehicle for what we're about to do. I had to improvise.'

'Fabulous,' Bee replied. She didn't seem at all fazed by what was happening, though they were now squashed into the van's cab, sitting at the curb outside her house with the engine idling. Birch wondered if she'd somehow known all along that this was coming, then forced herself to stop wondering that. 'What is it, exactly, that we're about to do?' Bee asked.

Birch took a deep breath. 'Well,' she said, 'yesterday, when we came to see you, you mentioned to my colleague DS Kato that being in physical proximity to someone can help you know more about them. This morning, DS Kato and I suggested to our boss that perhaps if we drove you around the city, you might be able to … well, get a feel for where these young people are being held. A sort of warmer, cooler, warmer kind of approach. I realise this probably sounds nuts, but for lack of any other way to—'

'It doesn't sound nuts at all,' Bee cut in. 'It was a very good idea of DS Kato's. If you don't mind me asking, why isn't she here?'

Birch was fully blushing now. She realised she ought to have known that Bee would have questions about an operation – if it could even be called that – which was so obviously not kosher. 'Because,' she replied, 'none of this is authorised. To be totally frank with you, Beatrice, I think I'm close to leaving the police force. Or being asked to leave. This is a real Hail Mary mission on my part.'

Her face felt hot. She'd said the words aloud for the first time: *I think I'm close to leaving the police force.* They'd come out more smoothly than she'd expected.

'I see,' Bee said.

'In my opinion,' Birch added, 'you're the only credible lead we have. And as I'm sure you know, the longer a young person is missing, the more serious their situation gets. The first few days are crucial, and I'm sorry to say that my team have squandered that precious time by acting altogether too slowly. It's time someone did something decisive.'

Bee gave one short, emphatic nod. 'Agreed,' she said. 'Let's do it.'

They both looked at Jamieson, whose eyes widened. 'Dinnae look at me,' he said. 'Ah dinnae ken where tae start!'

As Bee turned to look at her, Birch realised she hadn't thought this far ahead. Her main priorities had been getting to Bee's house, and convincing Bee to come on board with her as she committed career suicide. Now she'd achieved those two things, there was no more plan to fall back on. She opened her mouth, but no words would come out.

'We're looking for a two-storey house,' Bee said, 'or so I believe. The girls are in what looks like a downstairs room.'

'You're sure?'

Bee shook her head. 'Not really,' she said. 'I'm basing that on the fact that in the room there's a fireplace and a sofa. It seems logical, but it could be wrong.'

Birch sighed. 'It's all we have right now,' she said, 'and it's not a bad start, because it rules out a lot of the city centre. There aren't many two-storey houses in the New Town, and even fewer in the Old Town, where it's all tenements.'

Bee had closed her eyes. Jamieson was watching her, his eyebrows raised.

'The first dream,' Bee said, slowly, 'I was in a vehicle. I was being taken to the place where the girls are being held, I'm almost certain.'

Birch was nodding, urging her to go on, though Bee couldn't see her. 'Did you see anything on the way?'

Bee shook her head, eyes still closed. 'No,' she said, 'it was dark, and I felt nauseous. There was a bad smell. But the journey felt pretty long. Half an hour, maybe.'

Jamieson was nodding, too. 'Where did this lassie go missin' fae?' he asked. 'The wee wan, ah mean. Where wis she last seen?'

'She was out with her friends,' Birch replied, 'the day she went missing. According to Crosbie's file, they were the last people to see her. They got on a train at Waverley Station, but she stayed behind. Would you believe Crosbie is still faffing about trying to get a warrant for the CCTV?'

Bee's eyes snapped open to look at Birch.

'I'm afraid I'm not kidding,' Birch said. 'This is what I've been working with.'

Jamieson was thinking. 'So,' he said, 'if she wis abducted at Waverley, half an hour's drive is … whit? The bypass?'

'Depending on traffic,' Birch replied, 'yeah. The bypass, or somewhere just the other side of the bypass.'

'Well,' Jamieson replied, 'that's yer answer. The bypass is a big circle, is it no?'

Birch had begun to nod. 'Kinda,' she said. 'And what's more, it has plenty of suburban two-storey housing on either side of it. That's a start, right? Drive around the bypass and see if … well, if anything …'

Bee smiled a sympathetic smile. 'See if the Knowing kicks in,' she said. 'Sure. Let's try that.'

'Okay.' Birch tried to sound more confident than she felt, as Jamieson shoved the van into gear. 'Dad, let's head out along Queensferry Road, and get on by the Gyle? We can go from there.'

The van peeled out from the curb.

'Way ahead of ye, hen,' he said.

Bee seemed agitated. 'DI Birch …' she began.

Birch cocked her head to look at the other woman. It felt bizarre, being at such close quarters – even more bizarre that her father was there. It felt like something that would only happen in a dream, she realised, and the thought made her want to laugh. She wondered how she'd relay all this to Dr Jane. 'Is everything okay?'

Bee screwed up her face. 'I'm going to try my absolute best, here,' she said, 'but … you do know I'm not faking, right? This isn't all some elaborate ruse to drip-feed evidence to you, as DI Crosbie seemed to be suggesting yesterday. I'm sure it's very hard for you to believe, but I really am who I say I am.'

Birch lowered her eyes. For a moment, she wasn't sure what to say. 'Listen,' she said, eventually. 'I believe in you enough to be here, doing what's within my power to do. If you do the same, then that's all I need from you.'

Bee smiled. 'Well put,' she said. 'You're a very good police officer, you know.'

Birch didn't reply. Jamieson turned the van right out of Warriston Drive, and pulled away.

They'd driven past the East Fettes Avenue road end on their way to the bypass. They were far enough up the hill on Ferry Road that Birch couldn't see the station, but she felt its presence as they passed. A strange knot of feelings rose in her chest: she was still angry at McLeod for the things he'd said in the meeting, and the things he'd said the previous week about Linh and Winnie and *those kinds of people*. He'd been saying things to make her angry for years, but just recently, the anger was different. Birch's mother had been a fan of the expression 'I'm at the end of my tether', and Birch had never thought about what that saying really meant until right now. That was where her anger was coming from: the end of her tether. Her tolerance had run out. She was done, and being done brought a feeling of extreme weariness. She knew there were various reasons why she felt so tired: the pain in her leg, her sleep schedule being disrupted by the recurring nightmare with the flood. But she was also *weary*, and she realised that was different to being tired. It was like she'd entered a higher plane of tiredness from which she couldn't ever go back.

She also felt sad, thinking about Fettes Avenue. That building made her think about how she came to work there: how she'd worked her way up from a lowly uniform at Gayfield

Square by showing early on that she was passionate about the job. She'd been put on the CID fast track and made detective inspector in under ten years. She'd been a real blue-eyed girl, once upon a time, but somewhere along the line, the initiative and determination that had once made her stand out had become a problem. She wasn't sure how that had happened. She wished she could pinpoint the moment she fell out of love with her job, but she couldn't.

Birch gave her head a little shake. That wasn't how things worked, not in real life; there wasn't some catalyst moment that could be easily pointed to. Rather, she'd been ground down, slowly, as though she were a rock gently eroded over time by water. Eventually, something had to give way. Now the whole edifice was crumbling.

Birch realised Bee was looking at her.

'It doesn't do to dwell on things, Detective Inspector,' she said.

Birch felt her cheeks redden. It was uncanny sitting so close to someone who could apparently read your thoughts.

'Let's get through the next part, and never mind the rest,' Bee said.

Birch couldn't think of anything to say to that. She simply nodded.

The bypass was quiet; it was a Tuesday morning, getting towards coffee time. Birch wondered what Amy was doing. As Jamieson merged the van on to the dual carriageway from the Gyle slip road, she wondered how the rest of the meeting had gone. Probably not well, the way she'd riled McLeod. She found she was shaking her head again, trying to dislodge the negative thoughts. She *hadn't* riled McLeod. McLeod had got riled, then blamed her. *Keep doing that*, Dr Jane had said. *Keep reframing things, until you start to believe them.*

Easier said than done, Birch thought.

The Hermiston Gait exit was only a few dozen yards beyond the Gyle. Jamieson was leaning forward, glancing at Bee. Bee was frowning.

'Should ah … come aff here?' Jamieson asked, slowing the van.

Bee shook her head, with more confidence than Birch had expected. 'No,' she said, firmly. 'Not yet.'

Birch allowed herself to be fully taken in for a moment. If Beatrice really was psychic, how did it work? How did it feel in her body, the physical proximity thing? She recalled a childhood game, played at birthday parties: searching for something while wearing a blindfold, other kids gathered round, chanting, 'Warmer, warmer, no! Colder! Warmer, warmer, hot!' She remembered the mild, stuffy panic of the blindfold. Was that what Bee's knowing felt like?

They drove on, other vehicles passing Jamieson as he slowed at each slip road, waiting for the word from Bee. Their physical proximity, coupled with the quiet in the van, felt almost suffocating, Birch thought. Her father kept glancing at Bee, as though she were an alarm that might go off at any time.

'Don't worry,' she said, seeing him watching her. 'If anything strikes me, I'll tell you.'

Birch sat back and tried to straighten out the thoughts in her brain. She'd done the wrong thing – a stupid thing, a thing that was definitely off the books and against the rules. But she couldn't stand to sit passively by any longer while two young people remained unaccounted for. The response to Linh Fortune going missing had been glacially slow, and Birch knew why, though she'd been trying not to admit it, even to herself. Had Linh Fortune been white – had she been Winnie Fortune's biological daughter or granddaughter – Crosbie and his team would have swung into action. They'd have had McLeod's full blessing to use every resource at their disposal to bring home a vulnerable child and track down the perpetrator who'd taken her. There'd have been press conferences, and public appeals, and reporters camped out in Winnie's front garden. But Linh Fortune wasn't white. She wouldn't be considered an innocent child in the eyes of the media. She was an immigrant, trafficked into the sex trade and known to the police. She had a history of violence and trauma, and she was in the care system. There would be no groundswell of public sympathy for someone like Linh; no press conference on earth could manufacture it.

Birch's cheeks burned. They'd failed her, this poor kid, who, at seventeen, had experienced things no child – no person – should ever have to experience. They'd all failed her, Birch too, and this desperate charade was a fairly pathetic attempt to do something right. Something – for the first time since Linh's case was opened – that could actually be called *decisive*.

'Wait,' Birch said, into the silence.

Jamieson had been on high alert, and hit the brakes. An HGV behind them honked and swerved out into the outside lane.

'Shit,' Birch said. 'Sorry. I just remembered something.' She fished into her pocket, trying to extract her phone without elbowing Bee. *Missed calls: Alyona (4).*

'Whit is it, hen?' Jamieson was still driving slowly, and they were being passed by vehicle after vehicle.

Birch brandished her phone. 'I just have to make a call,' she said. 'Keep driving, Dad.'

Alyona answered after only two rings. 'Detective Inspector,' she said, in place of a greeting.

'Hi,' Birch replied. 'Sorry I'm only just calling you back. I'm having ... kind of a strange morning. What have you got for me?'

'Some information,' Alyona replied, 'about a guy who's shopping around for pimps in Edinburgh.'

Birch frowned. 'When you say "shopping around" ...?'

Alyona paused for a moment, as though trying to think of a better choice of words. 'This man,' she said, 'he has two girls he wants to put on to the street. Vietnamese girls, which made me think of your case. Sounds like trafficking to me. And he's looking for someone to ... take care of them for him.'

'Oh my god,' Birch said. 'Two Vietnamese girls – you're sure?'

'This is what I was told.'

Birch glanced over at Bee. Alyona's voice on the other end of the phone was clearly audible in the van's crowded cab. Birch wondered if the other woman was reading her racing thoughts in that moment – if she even needed to.

'So, who's the guy? What do you know about him?'

'Not a lot,' Alyona replied. 'I'm sorry. He's a white guy, apparently. Thirties, maybe. And he's based in Dalkeith.'

Birch's eyes widened.

Beside her, Bee let out a strange, shushing breath. 'Yes,' she said, softly. 'Yes, of course. Dalkeith.'

They were approaching Sheriffhall Junction.

'Dad!' Birch snapped, without really meaning to. 'You need to come off here!'

Jamieson indicated left, and moved the van on to the slip road.

Bee was speaking. 'In the first dream,' she said, 'I was in the back of a van. A van like this one, I suspect – it felt small, and confined. I was disorientated, but … there was a roundabout. A large one. I felt like I was thrown around in a circle.'

'Sheriffhall.' Birch had let the phone drift away from her face, but Alyona was still on the line.

'Detective Inspector?'

Birch gave her head a little shake, and lifted the phone to her ear again. 'Sorry, Alyona,' she said, 'I have to go. I can't tell you how helpful this is, though, truly.'

When she replied, Alyona sounded vaguely amused. *Yeah,* Birch thought, *this is all pretty weird.*

'If I hear anything else …'

'Yes,' Birch replied, 'please call me. Anything at all you learn about this man, any detail, however small – please let me know.'

'I'll do that.'

Jamieson was dithering as Birch hung up the call. Someone else honked a horn.

'Which lane?' he asked. Ahead of them, the carriageway split from two lanes into four.

Bee had closed her eyes. Her forehead was furrowed.

'Well,' Birch said, 'if you felt thrown around in a circle, the driver can't have come off at the first or second exit. He must have gone all the way around, or nearly. So he went into Dalkeith on the old road.'

Bee was nodding, but not saying anything.

'Bear right, Dad,' Birch said. Her father did as he was told. Bee still had her eyes closed, and she was frowning, as though whatever she was seeing behind her eyelids was troubling her. Birch couldn't help but feel another tinge of uncertainty. Alyona could have said anything on that call. If Bee were faking this, she'd have gone along with it, whatever it was. Birch gave her head a shake. It was too late for these doubts now. They were doing this thing, and there was no going back.

The lights changed, and cars shoaled out into the roundabout, Jamieson's van among them.

Bee still had her eyes closed. 'Yes,' she said, as they navigated the long curve of the lane, 'this is it. This was what it felt like.'

Jamieson indicated left and merged on to Old Dalkeith Road. 'Jist tell me,' he said to Bee, 'where tae steer, an ah'll dae it.'

They approached the King's Gate with its quaint sandstone gatehouse.

'There's a long curve here,' Bee said, just as Jamieson began to turn the wheel for the corner. 'Then we drop down. Downhill.'

Jamieson nodded, though Bee couldn't see him. The pair of them put Birch in mind of a rally car duo: the driver only ever as good as his navigator, and the two of them connected by – she wanted to laugh, as the thought occurred to her – an almost psychic-seeming link.

As they dropped down into the outskirts of Dalkeith, Bee began to become agitated – she lifted her hands into the air in front of her, as though she might be about to start conducting music. Her eyes were still squeezed shut. 'He made a turn,' she said. 'Not yet, not yet. A right.'

They were approaching a mini roundabout. Jamieson indicated, then turned.

'Yes,' Bee said.

They climbed a slow rise, came to traffic lights, and stopped.

Bee opened her eyes. 'This is the way,' she said, looking at Birch. Her face was wide open; there was no artifice in it. 'I can't tell you how I know, but it is. I know it is.'

Birch's policewoman brain wanted to scream. *I don't know how I know, but I know?* That's not an answer. It's not admissible in court. It's not *good enough*. But she'd tried being a policewoman, and that approach hadn't worked.

She nodded, putting herself in Bee's hands. 'Where next?' she asked, as the light changed.

'Straight on,' Bee replied.

Jamieson cleared the crossroads, and they drove on, past the library, a pub, a queue of people waiting for a bus.

'Somewhere down here,' Bee said, closing her eyes again, 'there's a left. The street is narrow, I think, because when he turned in, he slowed right down.'

They passed another set of traffic lights, and then a left turn appeared ahead of them: a residential street, hemmed in with parked cars. Jamieson looked at Bee, but her eyes were squeezed tightly shut.

'Here, Dad,' Birch said. 'I think it's here.'

Jamieson made the turn, and sure enough, he had to slow the van right down in order to make his way between the cars.

'This is it,' Bee said. 'We're almost there now.'

They were approaching a place where the road widened, and a side street opened up.

'Straight on?' Jamieson asked.

Bee's eyes were still closed. Birch noticed that her eyelids had begun to flicker, as though she were dreaming.

'Straight on,' Bee echoed.

It was a classic Scottish residential street: along one side, three-storey tenement blocks with stair doors and little yards surrounded by chain-link fencing. Along the other side, larger quarter-houses with gardens front and back, kids' toys on the lawns and cats sitting on windowsills. In summer there'd be weans out on the pavements on their bikes, Birch knew, or scrawling hopscotch grids in the road with chalk. The residents would no doubt say this wasn't the sort of place where criminals lived – not the sort of person who'd abduct a teenage girl, at least. But Birch knew better. If her decade-and-more of policework had taught her anything, it was this: the worst and most inhumane things could happen absolutely anywhere. If anything, crime could thrive in the plausible deniability built by people wanting to assume their area was good. *No, I can't have seen what I thought I saw. I must have been mistaken. That kind of thing doesn't happen around here.*

Bee's eyes flew open. 'Broom Park,' she exclaimed, the name seeming to occur to her in the same second that she said it. 'The street's called Broom Park.'

Birch clawed for her phone. As she swiped to the Maps app, she realised her hands were shaking.

'We must be close,' Bee said, bending forward towards the windscreen as though physically willing the van to drive faster. 'I can see the house, now. It's an end terrace, right where the road runs out. There are concrete steps in front … and a high garden wall.' She clapped her hands together, just once. 'Number 39! I can see the front door!'

Birch waited while her phone found the address. Sure enough, it was just a few streets away. 'Dad,' she said, 'you're going to get to a bend in a minute. There's a right turn off it. Then another right turn, on to a road that turns into a dead end. Number 39 is the last house on that road.' She brandished her phone. 'We're two minutes away, according to this.'

Bee was still talking. 'Jesus,' she said, 'it's a hiding place, alright. There's a big sweep of tarmac outside, like a turning circle, of sorts. But then it's just waste ground. All overgrown.'

Birch was nodding. 'Only one approach,' she said. 'That figures. That's the sort of house drug-dealers like, too. They can always see you coming.'

Jamieson made the first right turn.

'I don't like that idea,' Bee said.

Birch frowned. 'What idea?'

'That he might see us coming.'

Birch laughed, but the laughter jangled with nerves. 'Fortunately for us,' she said, 'we'll be turning up in a noisy, rusty old van, rather than a nice, quiet unmarked police car.'

Jamieson snorted. 'Less o the lip,' he said. 'This van's ma pride an joy, ya wee besom.' He made the second right turn.

'He's a really bad guy, this guy,' Bee said. 'He's a really bad, mean bastard.'

Amy had been right, Birch thought. Whatever this was – whatever Bee was doing – putting her in physical proximity to the perp's address was working.

'Can you describe him for me?' she asked.

Bee nodded. Her eyes had widened, and she looked genuinely afraid. 'He's tall,' she said, 'and broad. Blond hair, with a fade. He has tattoos on his hands.'

'Age?'

'Not old. No older than forty.'

Jamieson had slowed the van right down. They were running out of street; the waste ground Bee had described was beginning to appear above a rise in the road.

'Dad,' Birch said, 'start looking around. Try to look lost.'

Jamieson nodded, and immediately hunched over the steering wheel, peering at the houses as they passed. Birch turned back to Bee. She could feel her years of police training taking over, as though she were switching to autopilot.

'How many people in the house?' she asked.

'Three,' Bee replied, seemingly without thinking. 'The two girls, and … him.'

'He's armed?' Birch asked, though she knew the answer.

Bee nodded.

'I can't be specific,' she said, 'but yes.'

The terrace came into view, and they got their first look at the farthest outlying house. Birch recognised it immediately as a building that had been made to look mothballed: mothballed, but not derelict, not anything anyone might feel the need to call the police about. There was hoarding over the windows, but no graffiti. No weeds. No litter. The high garden wall marked the end house out from its neighbours, but on the other side of it, Birch could just make out the top edge of a skip, placed in the front garden. She whistled. This guy was smart. To anyone who didn't know what they were looking at, this was a house under construction – a fixer-upper. To her, it was a house that someone had carefully fortified. As they drew level with it, she clocked the discreet home CCTV system tucked along the roofline, almost invisible against the guttering.

'Oh god,' Bee said, as they passed the front of the house. 'Oh god, it's so horrible in there. Those poor kids.'

'Let's carry on past,' Birch said, nodding to her father. The cracked tarmac of the turning circle Bee had described was ahead of them. 'I suggest we drive as far as we can, and then turn round. I doubt we'll be out of range of the cameras, but still. Dad, get your phone out once you've stopped. Make it look like you're looking at a map.'

'Oan it,' Jamieson said. The loose road surface scattered under the van's tyres as he swung the wheel to turn around.

Bee had put both hands over her face. Her shoulders were shaking.

'Tell me what's happening,' Birch said. 'Tell me what you're seeing.'

Bee's voice, when it came, was muffled, but Birch could hear the fear in it.

'I can see them so clearly now,' she said. 'Those poor girls.' She uncovered her face, and looked over at the house. Its gable end was about twenty yards away, a camera lens winking from the eaves. 'They're so scared.' She looked at Birch, and her eyes were wet. 'I think they think no one's coming for them.'

Birch felt her jaw tighten. She reached down and unbuckled her seatbelt. 'Let's prove them wrong,' she said.

Diary 18/01

Kim and I listened until we were sure Luke was safely upstairs. Then, without speaking, we both dived out from under the blanket and began stuffing all his garbage back into the boxes Kim had emptied out. The damp, crinkly cardboard felt gross in my hands, and Kim swore under her breath as the first box she picked up tore and gave way.

'I can't remember where they all were,' I whispered.

Kim bundled two boxes together in her arms, and hoisted them into a corner. 'Hopefully,' she said, 'Luke can't either.'

He stayed upstairs for a long time. We retreated to the sofa, and sat looking up at the ceiling, listening to the floorboards creak above our heads.

'Where do you think he went?' I asked Kim.

Kim's head was cocked to one side; she was listening to Luke moving around upstairs.

'I wondered,' she said, 'if he might have gone to get someone else. I assumed that was why he moved me out of that bedroom. To make space for another girl.'

I felt my heart get faster when I thought about that. Like Kim, I turned my face upwards, in the direction of the noises upstairs. But the longer we sat there, the more certain I became that only Luke was up there, moving around.

'It's just him,' I said, after a while.

'Yeah,' Kim replied.

I didn't know how to feel about the idea of another person coming into the house. I didn't like the thought of someone else being stuck up there alone, like Kim had been. But she was right – why else would he have moved her? I remembered my growling stomach, the light-headedness making my vision swim. Would another person mean even less food? I felt so faint that my efforts to replace the boxes had made patterns dance across my retinas. But I also felt a tiny pang of something sick and guilty, the thinnest and most miserable shred of hope. If Luke went and got another girl, a third girl, things might get better for me and Kim. The house might become more like Joe's house had been in Aberdeen – maybe that was what he was trying to create. I'd hated Joe's house at the time, but it had been a hundred times better than this place. I didn't want to go back to working with men, the men with the black fingernails and alcohol on their breath. But if I had to do it, I thought, I'd do it. I'd get to be outside again, that way.

Kim was pointing upwards. The footsteps were on the move, now; we listened as they began to move down the stairs. I looked over at the boxes. I couldn't remember how they'd looked before, though I'd been in this room with them for days and days.

'You think he'll notice?' I whispered. Kim didn't reply.

The footsteps faded; whoever was walking around had made it to the bottom of the stairs. I reached for Kim's hand. For a few moments, silence.

Suddenly, the sound of a phone ringing: the speakerphone *brr brr* of a call being connected. Then the ringing stopped, and a distant voice said, 'Hey, man.'

'Fucking hey to you too.' Luke sounded pleased with himself. His voice was loud; he must have been standing right outside the door. I squeezed Kim's hand.

The man on the other end of the phone said something I couldn't properly hear.

'Superb,' Luke said. 'You won't regret it, pal.'

I glanced at Kim, but she was looking intently at the door, listening.

The other man spoke. Again, I couldn't hear the words he was saying, but I heard him laugh.

'Yeah,' Luke replied. 'Sorry, man, I've fucked her up pretty bad. Bitch just wound me up, you know how it is. She'll need a bit of time for her face to heal. But the other one's good to go – the little one.'

More muffled responses from the far-off man.

Now it was Luke who laughed. 'Seventeen,' he said, 'but she looks way younger. Seriously, you can charge whatever you like. Tell them she's fourteen. Tell them she's a virgin. You stand to make a bloody fortune, trust me. We both do.'

We didn't hear the rest of the call; he left, still talking to the man on the other end. There was a part of me that had always allowed itself to relax when Luke wasn't in the room, but it was a tiny part. The rest of me was in turmoil, racing through lots of different feelings. He was talking about me. He was talking to another man like Joe. I was going to be sold again. I felt sick. I felt enraged. But I also felt a strange kind of relief. At least I knew now what his plan was. At least I knew roughly what might happen next. At least I knew that at some point, I'd get to leave this room. I'd get to see the sky again. And if I was outside, under the sky, on my own feet, then maybe I could run. I didn't know where I'd go – I didn't know if there was a single place on earth that Luke wouldn't find me. But perhaps I could try to escape. Perhaps I could get back to Winnie, and she could help me.

Kim curled up next to me. 'I was right,' she said, and I could see there were tears running down her face. 'I just want to die. I want to die right now.'

I didn't say anything back. I was thinking about how pointless it would be to die this way: nailed into a freezing-cold room, hurting yourself in some way to make yourself bleed out, or maybe just fainting from hunger and never waking up. I realised I felt annoyed with Kim for the first time since I'd met her. I couldn't stand the idea of her dying, because she was my friend, but also because if she died, then Luke would win. At the same time, I knew she was right, and that things were hopeless. Luke *always* won – he always, always came out on top. I closed my eyes and thought about my sisters back home. My parents. If I tried to run away from Luke, would anyone ever find me? Would they ever know what had happened to me? How far would I get before he found out where I was, and brought me back to this terrible room? Perhaps Kim was right, and dying was the better option. The thought was so depressing that I couldn't even cry.

Kim and I must have slept, I don't know for how long. It felt like a long time; waking up was breathless and difficult, like trying to swim up from the bottom of a freezing-cold pond. When I opened my eyes, I could see daylight filtering into the room between the pieces of chipboard. Kim was still curled up beside me, her eyes closed, the bruises on her face turning a yellowy brown. The room was dim as always, but I realised with a horrifying start that Luke was standing over us. He smelled like food, and the outdoors, and the stench made my stomach turn over. He had his phone in his hand, and in the faint glow cast by the lit screen, I could see he was grinning.

'How are you doing *Cục Nợ*?'

I hated that he called me this. It was meant to be cute, but coming from his mouth it meant something foul. I tried not to show my disgust on my face; I'd learned it wasn't a good idea.

'I'm hungry,' I said, my voice a dry croak.

His grin widened, and he took a strange, tottering step. He seemed drunk, or high. Possibly both. He was pleased with himself. 'I thought you might be.'

With the hand that wasn't holding the phone, he was hiding something behind his back. I didn't like that; in the past, he'd held a knife there, waiting to frighten me.

'Please,' I whispered. I didn't really know what I was asking for.

Swaying, he swung the hidden hand around until it was in front of him. Dangling from his fingers was a bucket of fried chicken. My mouth fell open. That had been the food I'd smelled. I forced myself to resist the urge to fly at him, scratching like a cat, to wrestle the bucket from his grasp.

He straightened his arm and held out the bucket so that it hovered over my head. 'Got you a treat,' he said, tripping over the words.

It was a trap, I was sure of it, but I didn't know what kind.

'Thank you,' I said, and it sounded like a question.

He laughed an ugly laugh. Then, in one deliberate motion, he flicked his wrist and upturned the bucket, showering me with crumbs and grease and pieces of chicken. They disappeared into the folds of the blanket and down the gaps in the sofa. Some rolled away on to the filthy floor. I couldn't help myself; I began to scramble for them, hating the idea that they might spend too long touching anything in that disgusting room. My thrashing limbs shook Kim awake.

'Don't you girls eat too much,' Luke said, already backing out of the room. 'Don't want you two getting fat. You'll have clients to see soon.'

The chicken was cold, every piece furry with dust and grime. Nevertheless, Kim and I both had our mouths full before he'd finished bolting the door. We might be going to be sold to men, but it wasn't going to happen today. We might decide we'd rather die, but it wouldn't be now. We'd survive another day. At least one more.

Birch, Tuesday 18 January

Bee jumped as Jamieson flailed out an arm across the van's cab, grabbing his daughter by the shoulder.

'Ye cannae be daein' this, Helen,' he said. 'No efter last time.'

Birch's hand was on the van door handle; she was ready to lever herself out on to the street. She stopped, as startled as Bee was by her father's outburst.

'De ye even huv a plan, hen?'

Birch opened her mouth to speak, but found she didn't have any words to say.

'Ah thought as much,' Jamieson said. He withdrew his arm, giving Birch a hard look.

Bee was also looking at her. 'He's right,' she said. 'I'm sure you know this, but the man in that house is extremely dangerous. If he overpowered you, it could—'

Birch held up her hands. 'I know,' she said, trying not to sound irritable, and failing. 'I know. But we can't just sit here and do nothing. Not now we've found the place. Every minute we stay here, the more suspicious we look.'

Bee tilted her head. 'Why not call for back-up?' she asked. 'Isn't that … forgive me, most of what I know about the police is from TV shows. But isn't that what you do in a situation like this?'

Birch was staring out of the windscreen, studying the house. 'Ordinarily,' she replied, 'yeah. But in this case, if I called and asked for the cavalry, McLeod would never authorise it. We don't have proof, you see. As far as he's concerned, this could just be some random address.'

Bee looked crestfallen. 'I promise you,' she said, 'those young people are in that house. I know it. I am one hundred per cent certain.'

'Okay,' Birch replied. 'But even if he took your word for it – which he won't – that's still a big gamble for McLeod. We're talking about an armed perp, so we'd need a full tactical division, plus ambulances for the kids. If we busted the door down and the place was empty, that's a hell of a lot of resources wasted.'

Bee looked down at her hands.

'I'm not saying I don't believe you,' Birch went on. 'You only need to take one look at that house to know it's the address of an absolute scumbag. I'm just saying McLeod won't believe you. And he certainly won't believe me.' She turned back towards the house. 'Besides,' she said, 'surrounding this place with police-issue rifles could open a can of worms we really don't want. We don't know how entrenched he is in there. He could have ammo, food supplies, the lot.' She reached down and touched her bad hip, remembering. 'It would immediately become a hostage situation, with very vulnerable hostages. I've been there, and done that, and I never want to have to do it again.'

'That,' Jamieson put in, 'is exactly whit ah wis hinkin.'

Bee nodded, and went quiet. For a moment, none of them spoke.

'In which case,' Bee said eventually, 'what do you suggest?'

Jamieson reached out towards Birch again, only this time, he was pointing at the van's glovebox. 'Go an keek in there fer me, hen,' he said. 'Ah might huv an idea.'

Birch clicked open the glove box. It appeared to be full of litter: empty crisp packets, half-crushed Coke cans, old

parking ticket stubs. Underneath it all, she could see one corner of the van's battered service manual.

'Jeez,' she said, 'I feel like we need scene of crime officers
in here.'

'Wheesht!' Jamieson said. He snapped his fingers in the
direction of the open glove box. 'Hae a wee dig aboot in there.
See whit ye can find.'

Wincing, Birch plunged one hand into the detritus, and felt
around. Her fingertips brushed something cool and smooth.
She reached a little further, got hold of the object, and drew
it out.

'Dad! Holy shit.'

Resting on Birch's palm was a gravity knife, almost as long
as her hand-span, even with its blade tucked in and locked.
Jamieson reached for it.

'This is an extremely illegal item I'm holding,' Birch said.
When her father simply rolled his eyes, she held out the knife
so he could take it from her. 'I don't even want to think about
why you have it. When all of this is over, I'll be confiscating it,
for sure.'

Jamieson snorted. 'We'll see,' he said. He released the knife's
mechanism, and the blade shot out, making a whipping sound
in the close air of the van.

Bee jumped. 'Whatever this idea of yours is,' she said, 'I'm
afraid to say I don't think it's very good. The man in there is
a psychopath.'

Birch raised an eyebrow. 'I agree,' she said. 'Where did you
get that thing?'

Jamieson grinned. 'German SS knife,' he said, turning the
blade so they could see how sharp and thick it was. 'Ah won
it fae a gadge in the Gunner wan night, playin poker. That wis
years ago.'

Birch closed her eyes. 'You mean to tell me,' she said, 'you've been driving around Edinburgh with a *Nazi* knife in your van … for several *years*?'

Jamieson was shaking his head. 'C'moan,' he said. 'Nivver mind that. Dae ye no want tae hear ma idea?'

Birch threw up her hands. 'Honestly,' she said, 'if it involves knocking on the front door and then stabbing our perp, then no.'

With a practised hand, Jamieson flicked the knife blade back into its casing. 'Och, huv a wee bit faith in yer auld man, Helen,' he said. He pointed through the windscreen. 'See that van?'

Birch and Bee looked up, following the line of his finger. Outside the house, a dark grey van was parked up. It had no decals, but could easily have been a trades van. Birch made a mental note of the number plate.

'That's *his* van,' Bee said, sounding certain. 'That's the van he brought the kids here in.'

'Ah guessed as much,' Jamieson said. 'So, mah plan is … we daunder over there an stick this wee beauty in wan o the tyres.' He brandished the knife. 'Then Bee, away an chap oan the door. "Eh, 'scuse me pal, some cunt's slashed yer tyre, wid ye fuckin believe it?" He comes oot tae huv a look, an Helen an I run in an get the weans oot.'

Bee was looking at the knife in Jamieson's hand. She didn't speak.

'Oh yeah,' Birch said, 'great idea – we leave Bee stuck outside with the armed perp on her own. Sure, why not?'

'We'd be quick,' Jamieson shot back. 'We could be in an oot, *bam*.'

'Not necessarily, Dad. What if the kids are restrained? What if there are code locks on the internal doors, or combination locks? We don't even know where in the house they are.'

Jamieson lowered his hands, and the knife.

'I do,' Bee said, softly. 'If I went in, I could go right to them.'

Birch shook her head. 'No,' she said, 'it's a no-go. It's too risky.'

Bee turned to look at Jamieson. Birch felt something unspoken pass between them. In that moment, she truly believed in Bee; this woman really was psychic.

Jamieson looked over at her, and grinned. 'Looks like ye're outvoted,' he said.

The loose, frosty tarmac crunched under Birch's boots as she and Bee crossed the turning circle. They were headed for the house's blind gable end – Birch hoped that if they tucked in close to the wall, they'd be directly under the mount of the CCTV camera, and therefore out of its range. Birch felt very conscious of her walking stick, how conspicuous it made her. For all she knew, the perp could have been watching them for several minutes already.

'I don't like this,' she said. She and Bee were walking close together, huddled against the cold wind. 'I do not like it at all.'

Bee had her arms folded, hugging herself. 'I'll admit,' she said, 'I'm happier with this version than the version where *I* went to the door to lure him out. But I'm worried about your dad. What if the guy attacks him? What if he overpowers him?'

Birch snorted. 'That's the one part of this plan,' she said, 'that I am *not* worried about. My da's an old gadge, but he's been in a lot of bar fights. He knows how to hold his own. My main worry is, he uses that ridiculous knife on the guy. Even if he doesn't, I should technically still be arresting him for possession of a prohibited weapon.'

They reached the house's gable end, and Birch turned her back to it, pressing herself close to the pebbledash. Bee copied her.

'The minute you see one of these kids,' Birch said, 'you yell for me, okay? As soon as we know they're definitely there, I call in the cavalry.' She reached down and touched her jacket pocket; the number was already keyed in, ready to dial.

'They're definitely there,' Bee said, 'I already know it. But yes – I'll tell you.'

Birch looked at the other woman. The wind was blowing her long hair up and around her face, which seemed drained of colour. It was clear how frightened she was. But she was also tough; Birch could see it in her eyes.

'I'm about to give Dad the high sign,' she said. 'You can still back out of this, if you want to. You're a civilian. You don't have to get involved.'

Bee attempted a wan smile. 'Your dad's a civilian, too,' she said.

Birch grimaced. 'Yeah,' she said, 'but he's a nutter.'

To her surprise, Bee reached out and touched her arm. 'He's desperate,' she said, 'to show you how much he loves you. He's making up for his past mistakes. I truly believe he'd do anything for you.'

Birch blinked. She was trying to get her game face on. The last thing she needed was someone rummaging around in her psyche again. 'I'm saying,' she said, 'that this is your last chance to walk away.'

Bee shook her head. 'No chance,' she said. 'I know how scary it is in there for those girls. They've been in there far too long. Let's get them out.'

Birch nodded, just once. Then she raised her hand over her head, and waited until she saw Jamieson – still in the driver's seat of the van – flick a brief thumbs-up. As he pushed open the driver's door, she lowered her arm. She cursed herself for storming out of Fettes Avenue without even so much as a coat: only her thin suit jacket with its crap pockets. She had no baton, no cuffs, and no radio on her. It felt wrong, feeling the adrenaline build and not having the familiar weight of those items to reassure her.

The two women watched as Jamieson sauntered across the turning circle, his hands in his pockets. Birch marvelled at how well he seemed to fit into these surroundings, before remembering that Jamieson may as well have been at home; his house on Boswall Parkway was a quarter-house flat, not at all unlike the ones they'd just driven past.

He didn't look over at them as he passed the gable end and disappeared out of sight. Birch glanced over at Bee, then gave her a wave to indicate that they ought to move along the line of the wall. Together they crept a few feet, until Birch was right at the house's corner. Had she wanted to, she could have bent her neck and peered round to watch what Jamieson was doing, but she didn't dare.

They were close enough to hear the whoosh of the blade as Jamieson unlocked the knife. A second later, there came the fat thud of the metal biting into the grey van's front driver's side tyre.

Birch flinched at the sound, which seemed deafening. 'Fucksake,' she hissed. 'He could be watching all of this happen. We could be walking into a trap.'

Out of the corner of her eye, she saw Bee shaking her head. 'No,' she whispered back, 'it's okay. He's asleep.'

Birch turned and looked directly at the other woman. 'You're sure?'

Bee closed her eyes for a few seconds, a gesture Birch couldn't help but find slightly theatrical. Then she opened them again. 'Yes,' she said. 'Absolutely sure. He's been drink-ing, and now he's asleep.'

Birch heard the creak of hinges as Jamieson pushed open the high garden gate set into the rendered breezeblock wall. A couple of seconds later, he knocked on the front door.

Birch held her breath. Nothing happened.

'Like I said,' Bee whispered, 'he's asleep.'

They heard Jamieson knock again, louder this time.

Bee stiffened. 'He's heard,' she hissed. 'He's up.'

Birch pushed her shoulders back, and felt them click. She wanted to whirl round to grab Bee by the shoulders and shake her. *How do you know that?* she wanted to demand. *How?* But there were other things to think about now.

'God, I hope you've got that knife well hidden, Dad,' she said, so far under her breath that she didn't think Bee could hear. 'Don't go being a hero.'

There was a scraping sound; on the other side of the front door, locks were being undone. This seemed to go on for a long while.

'Awful lot of security,' Birch whispered, 'for an empty house.'

Finally, she heard a familiar sound: the rattle of a door with its safety chain still on, opening.

'Hiya, pal,' Jamieson said. His tone was perfect: jovial, slightly concerned. 'Och, did ah wake ye? Sorry.'

From inside the house, there came a response Birch couldn't hear.

'Ah wis jist passin',' Jamieson replied, 'an … well, yon grey van, is that yours, aye?'

This time, the response was audible. 'What about it?'

'Well, ah'm afraid tae say,' Jamieson replied, 'some cunt seems tae huv slashed wan o yer tyres, pal.'

There was a pause. Birch imagined the other man looking Jamieson up and down, trying to decide if the old man was a threat. *He is,* she thought, *he's a fucking danger,* but a young, stupid man might not realise it. Sure enough, she heard the sound of the safety chain sliding out of its catch.

'Fuck*sake*.' That was the man in the house.

'Aye, ah ken,' Jamieson replied, blithely. 'Kids the day, eh? Wee bams.'

As the hinges of the garden gate squealed, Birch glanced backwards at Bee. Looking at the other woman, the utter stupidity of the plan hit her like a car at speed. There were so many things that could go wrong here, but it was too late. She could see Bee was ready: as ready as a scared civilian with not a single hour of training could possibly ever be.

'There, see?' Jamieson said. 'Driver's side front. If ye get doon an hae a look, it's gubbed.'

Birch leaned forward and risked a look round the corner of the wall. Jamieson had done his job beautifully; he'd led the perp round the side of the van, blocking his line of sight to the house, then stationed himself at the van's rear corner. Even if the perp looked up, he'd see only the old man.

Birch held her breath, and made a dash for it. She could feel Bee at her back, shuffling on the balls of her feet to avoid making noise. The gate hinges were going to creak, there was no way to prevent them. Birch simply shoulder-barged the gate, waved Bee through, and then let it slam shut behind her.

'The fuck?' That was the perp's voice. The front door of the house was ajar.

'In!' Birch hissed, and Bee leapt up the two steps and over the threshold.

'Hey now,' Jamieson was saying behind her. 'Calm doon, pal ...'

She couldn't look back; there wasn't time. Birch followed Bee in through the front door, crashing it closed behind her. Breathing hard, she looked at the series of elaborate locks fitted to the inside. They all required keys she didn't have … but there was the safety chain, and a single bolt. They would hold the door for a short time. She shot the bolt, and slipped the safety chain on.

Outside, the perp was raging. 'The *fuck* is this?' he yelled. Though she could hear him steaming up the path, she still jumped when he made contact with the other side of the door. 'Who's in there? Who's in my *fucking* house?'

Birch turned and looked at Bee. In the dim light of the hallway, the other woman's eyes were big as saucers.

'Here,' Bee whispered. She was standing outside a door that led off the hall, pointing. 'The girls are in here.'

Birch looked at the door. It was fastened with four bolts, much thicker than the one on the front door. The perp was battering against that door already, so hard that Birch could feel the reverberations through the soles of her feet. She hadn't seen him yet, but he must be a big man. He wouldn't be kept out for long.

'You get in there,' she whispered to Bee.

The other woman's eyes widened. 'Where are *you* going?'

Bee had already begun fumbling at the bolts with shaking hands.

'I'm going to check the other rooms,' Birch said. 'I'll be fast.' She turned her back on the other woman, and sped up the stairs. She still had her walking stick in one hand, and her hip burned with pain as she went; she allowed herself the fleeting thought that her physio hadn't prepared her for an impromptu raid on a suspect's house. But her pain didn't matter. The perp was hollering outside the door, and Birch could hear a loud cracking sound she didn't like as he slammed his body against it. She hoped her father had had the good sense to get away, as she'd told him he ought to.

Top of the stairs and turn right. Another door with four bolts: two into the jamb, one into the lintel, one into the floor. She pulled each one back, her fingers smarting; they were heavy, and stiff, but she was in. She pushed open the door and staggered into the room.

At first, the room seemed empty. The hoarding over the window made it almost completely dark; only a couple of thin seams of light filtered in. The room wasn't large; it was a classic spare bedroom, with a wall of scruffy fitted wardrobes, and a narrow single bed. Even in the dim light, Birch could see the bed was filthy, piled with a nest of old ripped sheets. She was breathing hard.

Suddenly, her heart caught in her chest. As her eyes adjusted to the gloom, she saw that the wardrobe doors were fitted with padlocks. She crossed the small space, looking around as she went. She'd been wrong; this wasn't a classic spare bedroom at all. This was something else.

A cracking sound from the front door had turned into a metallic splitting sound. The door was giving way. They were running out of time.

Suddenly, there were footsteps on the stairs: several sets of them, and the sound of panicked whispers. Then Bee was in the room, panting, casting around for Birch.

'Over here,' Birch hissed. Her eyes had adjusted to the darkness, and she could see that behind Bee, in the space on the other side of the room's threshold, were two young women. Their faces were indistinct, but they both had long black hair. Both were crying.

'Helen.' The terror in Bee's voice was a high, discordant note. 'They're here. The girls are here. We've found them.'

Birch straightened up. The pain in her hip made her teeth grind together. 'Girls,' she said, holding out an arm to the two girls and stepping back, 'get in here. Get down behind the bed.'

The two young women complied, stumbling through the room. In the blur as they passed her, Birch saw how pale they looked, how thin their arms were. Their fear was palpable, and it turned Birch's skin cold. They knew the man who was breaking in. They knew what he was capable of.

Then something happened that Birch hadn't expected. The taller, thinner girl placed her hands on the smaller girl's shoulders. Birch felt a brief flash of shame, realising she didn't know which of the girls was Linh, and which was Kim. She watched as the taller girl pushed the smaller one down, whispering something to her that Birch couldn't understand. Then the tall girl straightened up.

'I don't want to hide,' she said, looking at Bee. 'I want to fight. I want to help.'

Birch held out a hand, and opened her mouth to tell the young woman no, she needed to get down, and stay down.

But Bee spoke first. 'Okay,' she said. 'Help me barricade the door. Helen, if you're going to call the cavalry, now's the time.'

Before Birch had even absorbed the words, Bee had slammed the bedroom door, and the two women began flinging the filthy sheets off the bed and on to the floor. Birch reached into her pocket and drew out her phone with a shaking hand. When she unlocked it, there was the number. She hit 'dial'.

Downstairs, a metallic smatter: the safety chain had given way. Only the bolt remained. Bee and the tall girl upended the mattress and shoved it hard against the door. Under the boarded window, beside the radiator, the smaller girl was sobbing.

Amy picked up. 'Marm, are you okay? Are you—'

'Kato,' Birch cut in. 'Stop talking and listen. I've found our girls. Both of them. Bee was right about everything. But now we're in a tight spot and we need the cavalry. I mean armed, tactical – fuck it, airborne if you've got it. And I need them right now. I'm at—'

'Thirty-nine Broom Park,' Amy said, 'Dalkeith. We're already on our way. But Helen – are you hurt? Are the kids hurt?'

Birch blinked. 'How did you know?' As she asked the question, she realised she knew the answer. 'Did my dad call?'

'He did,' Amy said. 'As soon as you went through the front door, he told me. But never mind that. I'm organising ambulances. I need you to tell me if anyone's injured, and how badly.'

Birch looked around. By the door, Bee and the tall girl were propping the bed base against the mattress. Outside the front door, the perp was roaring. She realised she had no idea how to answer Amy's question.

'I'm fine,' she said, 'but our perp is outside the door – and I mean *right* outside the door. We've got maybe seconds before he's back in the house. I don't know what state the girls are in. They're walking and moving about, but you and I both know that doesn't mean shit. The main issue is, we're barricaded in a room with a very angry scumbag outside. He's mad enough to take the house down brick by brick if he has to, and I'm led to believe he's armed. So if you'd be so good as to send a whole lot of guys with guns down here, asap?'

'Armed support is en route,' Amy replied. 'We're flooring it over there, fast as we can. Just hold him off for another five minutes, would you?'

Birch watched as Bee put her shoulder to the back of the bed base, pushing her whole weight against it.

'Right you are, Kato. I've got to go and help keep this bastard at bay.' She hung up before her friend could respond.

Downstairs, the battering at the front door had stopped. The house felt frighteningly silent without it. Was the perp inside, checking through the rooms? Was he outside on the landing, listening?

Birch looked back towards the locked wardrobes. She had an idea of what was in there, if she could only …

'Kim,' she said. The taller of the two girls turned around, her head cocked in surprise at hearing her own name. 'I need you to help me.'

'What do you need?'

Birch gestured at the wardrobes. 'You know what's in there?'

'Yeah, I know alright. He kept me in this room for a while. All his weapons are in those cupboards. Guns, big knives. Even a sword, I think.' Kim spat out a bitter laugh. 'That's probably why he wants to get back in here so badly.'

Bee was still pushing against the makeshift barricade they'd erected. The other girl – Linh, Birch realised, this was Winnie's Linh! She was even wearing the furry backpack, like Bee had said! – had moved from where she'd been crouched behind the bed and was trying to help, though she seemed very weak.

'I thought so,' Birch replied. 'Okay. Here's what we're going to do.'

Diary 18/01

Kim was talking to me about dying – about how she'd do it. There was broken glass in the fireplace; that was one way.

'It would hurt,' I said. I had to curl my fingers into my palms and squeeze, the thought of it was so awful. 'Cutting yourself like that, it would hurt so bad.'

Kim shrugged. 'At first,' she said, 'yeah. But then I guess it would ease off. Everything would just fade away.'

The cold chicken I'd wolfed down was sitting heavy in my stomach. 'You can't,' I said, and I realised how much like a child I sounded. 'You can't die.'

Kim was shaking her head. She'd been crying, but now she'd stopped. There were salty, silvery tracks on her face. 'At least it's a choice,' she said. 'A choice I'd be making.'

I was shaking my head, though I knew what she meant. I wanted to tell her it wasn't that bad. I'd done Luke's bidding, and Joe's bidding, and the bidding of the men who gave them money. I'd survived it. I'd hated it, but I wasn't sure it was worse than dying. I opened my mouth to say so, but then I realised how nonsensical it would sound. I didn't know what dying felt like, after all.

Kim looked like she might say something else, but then she stiffened. Outside, there were footsteps on the path. Then, at the front door, a knock.

We both looked upwards. Luke was inside, I was sure of it. After he'd dumped the chicken on us, he'd gone back upstairs, and we hadn't heard him come down. Besides,

Luke wouldn't knock on his own door. I looked at Kim, not daring to speak.

'It's the man,' she hissed. 'It's the man he was talking to on the phone. He's come to get us.'

I felt my pulse speed up. I felt everything at once: relief that the man was here already, that Kim hadn't had the chance to hurt herself, that soon – maybe in just a few minutes – I'd get to be out of this room. But I also felt terror. Who was this man? Would he hurt us? Would he be cruel? And how did I even know he'd take us outside? Maybe this was why Luke had moved Kim out of the upstairs room. Maybe we'd stay here with the man. Maybe the room would be where we'd see clients. Maybe we'd never escape. I didn't know if Kim was thinking the same things I was, but I saw she'd started to cry again.

Luke hadn't heard the knock, or if he had, he hadn't moved. No sound came from the upper floor. After a moment, the person on the other side of the door knocked again, louder this time.

Upstairs, I heard a muffled grunt, then the sound of the floorboards. Luke had heard. He was crossing the landing. He was coming down the stairs. Kim put both hands over her mouth to stifle her sobs. Remembering her sore ribs, I draped an arm around her shoulders. We listened as Luke unlocked the front door's many locks. Outside, a man's voice.

'Hiya, pal. Och, did ah wake ye? Sorry.'

Kim and I exchanged glances. This wasn't Luke's man from the phone call, coming for us. This was an unsuspecting stranger.

'The fuck do you want?' That was Luke.

'Ah wis jist passin',' the stranger said, 'an ... well, yon grey van, is that yours, aye?'

'What about it?' I could hear the irritation in Luke's voice.

Kim nudged me. 'Should we scream?' she hissed.

I didn't know how to respond. I wanted to listen to the exchange; we didn't know yet who this other man was.

'Well, ah'm afraid tae say,' the stranger said, 'some cunt seems tae huv slashed wan o yer tyres, pal.'

I could feel Kim's body tensing up next to me, ready for … something. I didn't know what. I realised I was doing the same thing.

'Fuck*sake*,' Luke spat.

'Aye, ah ken,' I heard the stranger say. 'Kids the day, eh? Wee bams.'

Their voices faded. The stranger had obviously moved back, away from the house and into the street, and Luke had followed. I hadn't heard him close the door behind him.

Kim balled her fists. 'We have to scream,' she said. 'Now, while the front door's open. That guy will hear. Someone will hear.'

I didn't respond. I felt frozen, unsure what to do for the best. If we screamed and the man didn't hear, or didn't care, and didn't do anything, Luke would beat us afterwards for sure, the way he'd been beating Kim since she arrived. She was already badly hurt. I wasn't sure if we should risk it. Kim was pulling a big breath in now, ready to do it.

But before she could, there was a new noise outside the door. I heard the sound of the garden gate, then footsteps, scuffling, hurried. Someone came back into the house – it didn't sound like Luke. It sounded like someone in a hurry. Then it sounded like two people.

'In!' A woman's voice. I realised I hadn't heard a woman's voice – beside Kim's – for days. The front door closed, and I could hear someone rattling the locks.

'Who's in there?' Luke's voice was advancing back towards us now, but still outside. 'Who's in my *fucking* house?'

In the hallway, I heard whispering. I felt a new, strange kind of fear; I had absolutely no idea what was happening. Kim and I clung to each other as Luke threw himself against the outside of the front door. He started yelling, and only some of the noises he made were words. I'd seen him angry plenty of times, but now he sounded almost animal. I could hear him pounding against the door, and I wondered how good the locks were.

Over the noise, the sound of footsteps heading up the stairs.

'No!' Kim shouted. 'Here! We're in here!'

She needn't have spoken. Someone was still in the hallway; as Luke raged outside the house, we could hear the sound of the locks on our own terrible door being undone. After what felt like an eternity, the clattering of bolts stopped, and the door was carefully pushed open.

'Don't hurt us,' Kim shouted. 'Please!'

I don't know who I expected to walk through that door. Because I'd heard women's voices, I think I thought it would be Winnie. A tiny, stupid part of me thought that Winnie had somehow found us, had tricked Luke, and was coming to save me. But the woman who came through the door was someone I'd never seen before, and she looked afraid. Her face was very, very pale. For a second, I thought perhaps I was asleep – I'd fallen asleep and was dreaming that Luke had been locked out of the house by a ghost.

'You're here,' the woman said. She spoke as though she knew us both. 'Girls – you're here. I've found you.'

Kim was on her feet. 'I don't know who the fuck you are, lady,' she said, 'but you have to get us out of here.'

The woman reached out her hands, but Kim didn't go to her. Slowly, I got to my feet, looking around for my backpack.

It was on the dirty floor by the sofa – it was dirty now, too, from being in this room – and I snatched it up.

'I'm here with the police,' the woman said. 'We're going to help you.'

Outside, Luke was throwing his entire weight against the door. I could hear it straining against its hinges. Kim had moved closer to the strange ghost-woman now, and I followed her.

'Are you real?' I asked, and the woman looked at me. I saw she had tears in her eyes. 'Are you really actually real?'

'Yes,' the woman whispered, widening the span of her arms so that now she was holding one hand out to Kim and one towards me. 'I'm real, I'm here. My name is Bee. I've been looking for you. I'm so happy I've found you. I'm so happy you're both okay.'

I drew level with Kim. I wanted to go to this woman. I wanted to throw myself into her arms. But Kim was keeping just out of her reach, so I did the same.

'I don't know how you call this *okay*,' Kim said. She gestured towards the door, towards the sound of Luke, only feet away and howling. 'We're trapped here.'

Bee glanced behind her. 'Is there a back door?'

Kim threw up her hands. 'I've no idea,' she said.

I shook my head. 'There isn't,' I replied, and my chest filled with cold dread. 'I've been in the kitchen, and there's no other door.' I pointed towards the noise and fury of Luke. 'Only that one.'

Outside, another yell, and then an impact against the door that made a splintering sound.

'Okay,' Bee said, backing out of the room, 'upstairs, then. That's our only choice right now.'

We followed her. I pulled the backpack on to my back, so my hands were free. I'd never been up the stairs in this house, but Kim jostled me in front of her so she could bring up the rear, and I sprinted after Bee as fast as my weak legs could go. At the top of the stairs, we stopped, and Bee looked around. We were on a small landing, with three doors off it. Two were open, one closed. One, I could see, was the bathroom. Bee stepped over the threshold of the other open door.

'Over here,' someone said – another woman. I looked past Bee into the dark room beyond, to see who was speaking.

'Helen,' Bee said, 'they're here. The girls are here. We've found them.'

Kim was hanging back. She seemed unwilling to step into that room, though I didn't know why. I could see the other woman now, though her face was hard to make out in the dim light. She seemed to be leaning on a silver stick, like an old person, but her voice sounded young.

'Girls,' she said, and she held out her arm towards us, 'get in here. Get down behind the bed.'

I didn't know there was a bed, but I staggered into the room, too scared and confused to do anything other than what I was told. I could feel Kim following me, shepherding me along. I realised this must be the room Luke had kept her in. She knew it – she knew where we were going.

There was a window; I could see that now, as my eyes got used to the darkness. It was boarded over like the one downstairs, but a little light crept in at the sides. And yes, there was a small bed. I felt Kim put her hands on my shoulders, and gently move me into the strip of floor between the bed and the chipboard hoarding. I wanted her to crouch down with me, so I could cling on to her. Instead, she turned away, and faced the woman with the walking stick.

'I don't want to hide,' I heard her say. 'I want to fight. I want to help.'

The woman with the walking stick didn't reply, but Bee did. 'Okay,' she said. 'Help me barricade the door. Helen, if you're going to call the cavalry, now's the time.'

Cavalry. I'd heard that word in English before, but not known what it meant. I watched as Bee and Kim pulled the sheets off the bed I was crouching behind. I realised they were going to move it, put it against the door so Luke couldn't get in. I could hear him still slamming his body against the front door downstairs, and there were terrible metallic noises that sounded like locks giving way. I knew he'd soon be inside. I realised I was crying, hard and loudly.

The woman with the walking stick was on the phone, talking fast. I could tell she was scared; her voice sounded spiky. She was begging them – someone, anyone – to come and help, to come as fast as they could. I wondered why, if she was a policewoman, she was here on her own, with only Bee. I wondered why she was hurt, and walking on a stick. Why had they sent these two women to find us? Why hadn't they sent men with handcuffs and police dogs and guns?

The woman had stopped talking on the phone. She was standing watching Kim and Bee as they moved the bed to cover the door.

'Kim,' she said, and Kim turned around.

'What do you need?' Kim asked.

'You know what's in there?' She was pointing at the wardrobes on the other side of the room. I turned to look at Bee, who was pushing herself against the door now, making her own body part of the barricade to keep Luke out. I realised I had to help – I was more scared than I'd ever been, but I had to help. I uncurled myself from the floor and went to stand next to Bee. As I passed Kim, I heard her say the word 'guns'.

I reached out my hands and pressed them, palms flat, against the barricade. I was only a few inches away from Bee now, closer than I'd been since she came into the house. I could smell her perfume, and I could see in her face that she was very scared. She looked at me in a strange way, then – a way no one had ever looked at me before.

'Linh,' she said, quietly. 'You poor thing. You've been through such a lot.'

I wanted to ask her how she knew my name. How she knew anything about me. I wanted to ask her why she was here – she didn't seem like a policewoman. Maybe she was a key worker, or someone like that, but why she'd be here, now, in Luke's house, holding a bed base against a door so he couldn't get in and kill us, I didn't know. On the other side of the room, Kim and the policewoman were prising open one of the wardrobe doors. I heard Kim cry out as she forced her fingers into the tiny gap she'd managed to open up.

'I know,' the policewoman said, 'I know that hurts, I'm sorry. But just a little wider. Just a little—'

Downstairs, I heard the terrible clatter of the front door as it finally gave way. Before it had even swung inward fully and hit the wall behind, I could hear Luke's feet on the stairs.

'Fucksake,' the policewoman was saying. 'Come on, come on …'

Bee reached out a hand and touched my shoulder. I realised I was sobbing again.

'Be brave,' she said.

Luke had reached the landing now.

'You fucking *bitches*,' he yelled. I didn't know who he meant – Kim and I, for escaping, or these two strange women, for coming into his house. Perhaps he meant all of us.

'There!'

I turned my head. Kim had clawed the wardrobe door open far enough that the policewoman had been able to push the end of her metal walking stick into the gap. Now she was pushing against it, her cheeks puffed out, using her weight to turn it into a lever.

Luke kicked the door to the room from the other side; I felt the force of it reverberate through the barricade we'd made, and then through my whole body. Bee let out a sharp noise, but the barricade held.

'I'm gonna fucking *kill* you,' Luke growled, and another impact came. As it did, I heard a strange, loud pinging noise, and saw the glint of the padlock as it sprang from the wardrobe door and ricocheted off into the corner of the room.

'Hold on,' the policewoman shouted. 'Just a few seconds …'

But we didn't have a few seconds. Luke had thrown his whole weight against the door, and I felt it in my hungry, aching bones as it gave way. The force of it sent Bee and I flying; I ended up in a pile on the floor near Kim's feet. When I looked up, I saw she was holding a long, thin metal cylinder in both hands. It took me a moment to realise it was a gun.

'Hands up!' the policewoman shouted. 'Police!'

If Luke heard her, he didn't show it. He was still thrashing around in the doorway, flinging the bedframe out of his path. He was roaring. He looked like a wild animal. I felt certain he was going to kill us all.

'Put your hands where I can see them!' the policewoman said.

Luke came to a stop. He was panting, feral with rage. I cowered, terrified that he'd look at me, but he didn't. He was looking at the gun the policewoman was pointing at him: another long, thin one, the same as the one Kim was holding. Bee was slowly climbing back to her feet, only a few inches away from him. Her back was pressed to the wall, but her eyes were fixed on Luke.

'Don't threaten me,' Luke hissed, 'in my own fucking house.'

'Hands up,' the policewoman said. 'I won't ask you again.'

Luke smirked at her. 'Yeah?' he said, and I saw one hand dart behind his back. Then, suddenly, there was a gun in it: a different kind of gun, a small one. *A revolver*, I thought, remembering the word from some distant English lesson. It must have been in his waistband, or in his back pocket. He pointed it at Bee. She was so close to him that the barrel nearly brushed her forehead. 'How about you shut the fuck up, you pig bitch?'

I held my breath. Beside me, I could feel Kim shaking all over, and I prayed that her legs wouldn't give way.

'Put the weapon down,' the policewoman said. There was a new edge in her voice that I recognised as true fear. 'Don't do anything stupid, please.'

'Fuck you,' Luke hissed. 'I'll kill all you cunts, don't think I won't.'

A strange and awful silence settled in the room. Luke was pointing his gun at Bee, but looking at the policewoman. I'd been looking at Kim, trying to see her face, though it was difficult from where I was. But then Bee spoke, and everyone's eyes turned to look at her.

'Oh, Luke,' she said. Her voice was strange; it wasn't angry, and it wasn't scared, not like the policewoman's voice was. It took me a second to realise it, but her voice was sad. She was *sad* for him – for *Luke*. 'You were just the sweetest little boy,' she said.

'Bee.' That was the policewoman, her voice a warning.

But Bee carried on. 'You didn't deserve it, you know,' she said, in the same soft, sad voice. 'No child deserves that sort of cruelty.'

Luke's eyes had gone wide. I realised I'd never seen him look anything other than cocky before. Now he looked confused, though still very angry.

'Shut up,' he hissed, and he shook the gun in Bee's face. 'Shut the *fuck* up, before I make you shut up.'

Bee shook her head, as though refusing the demands of a person pointing a gun at her was something normal and easy. 'You grew up with that cruelty,' she said, 'so that was all you ever knew how to do, wasn't it? Be cruel. That's all you've ever done.'

Luke had pushed his lips together, but he was breathing through them, fast and hard. Flecks of spit were spattering his chin.

'But you can stop that now,' Bee was saying. 'You can make a choice to do something *not* cruel, just this once. You can let these little girls go. You can let us go.'

Luke's eyes boggled at her. For just a second, I thought maybe he'd drop his arm, and the gun, and say, *Yes, you're right*, and let us walk free. Instead, he lifted his hand slightly and pressed the barrel of the gun directly into Bee's forehead.

'Nice try,' he said.

Then the bang.

III.

Birch, Tuesday 18 January

'So there I am,' Birch said, 'stood there with nothing between me and an armed trafficker but some old furniture, trying to shove my bloody cane into this wardrobe because I think it might have guns in it, but I don't actually know. I've got two vulnerable young people and a terrified civilian in my care, and honestly, not a single idea in my head. I tell you, I thought it was curtains. I was thinking, "This is it, idiot. This is how you die. This is how we all die." Happily, the malnourished twenty-one-year-old standing next to me had a bit more nous.'

Rema was grinning. 'It must have been so satisfying,' she said, 'for her to shoot that bastard. I can't imagine how I'd feel if I'd been held for over a month in those conditions, and then someone gave me the chance to level a shotgun at my captor. I'm amazed she didn't blow his entire head off.'

'Listen,' Birch said, 'initially I didn't know what had gone on. For the first few seconds, I thought it was him who'd fired. I thought he'd murdered Beatrice, my poor civilian. It wasn't until he fell on the floor that I realised he was the one with a hole in him. And my next thought was, "Wait, did I do that? Because I don't remember pulling the trigger." But no, it wasn't me. It was the kid standing next to me. Literally everyone else in that room was more effective than I was, when it came down to it.'

Rema raised an eyebrow. 'I'm not saying I agree with that assessment,' she said, 'but … I'm really proud of that girl. Little Linh, too.'

Birch laughed. 'Yeah,' she said. 'Linh was up on her feet before I'd figured out what had happened. I don't think the perp had even hit the floor before Linh was on him. She absolutely malkied the guy – I mean, really rained blows down on him. I have to admit I didn't make a great deal of effort to stop her. I could hear the cavalry outside by then and I just thought, you know, good on you, kid.'

'Maybe you should persuade her to join the force,' Rema replied. 'She'll be eighteen next year.'

Birch winced. 'I think the poor girl's been through enough trauma for one lifetime,' she said, 'without inflicting a career in Police Scotland on her as well.'

Rema took a sip of her lukewarm coffee. 'True,' she said. 'So, what shape is our perp in?'

Birch shrugged. 'He'll live,' she replied. 'Kim's aim wasn't up to much – she hit him in the thigh. But it was enough to knock him on his ass and get him to drop his weapon.'

'Hey,' Rema said, 'I've had police marksman training and I probably couldn't hit a barn door – certainly not with a random shotgun someone had just handed me. That kid's a hero.'

Birch raised her coffee cup. 'Amen to that,' she said.

Rema raised hers to meet Birch's, and they knocked the cardboard rims together.

'Cheers,' Rema said. 'How's your dad doing?'

Birch grinned. 'His pride's a bit bruised,' she replied. 'I think he wishes he'd been able to take the perp down single-handed, and save us all.'

Rema dipped her head to one side. 'I mean,' she said, 'he kind of *did* save you all, by calling for help. From what I hear, armed division were mobilised a good few minutes before you called them yourself. He gave them a really important head start.'

'I've told him that,' Birch said, 'but his male ego has taken a bit of a battering. In his mind, he saw the guy had a gun so he ran away, and that makes him a coward.'

'Er, excuse me,' Rema said. 'How is that anything other than just damn good sense?'

Birch held up her free hand in a *beats me* gesture. 'Hey,' she said, 'as someone who was shot not that long ago, I completely agree. Getting the hell out of dodge and calling the professionals was exactly the right thing to do. Hopefully he'll see that, with time.'

The two women fell silent. Birch's hip ached. They were sitting on hard plastic chairs in a corridor of the Edinburgh Royal Infirmary, outside Linh Fortune's hospital room. Winnie had arrived, and they were giving the pair some time alone.

Rema jerked her head backwards, in the direction of the room behind them. 'She's a lucky girl, this one,' she said. 'I believe the papers will write it up as "found safe and well".'

Birch nodded. 'As safe and well as you can be,' she said, 'when you've just added a new heap of trauma to all the trauma you've already experienced. But yeah, she got off lightly in comparison to Kim. That arsehole really did a number on her.'

Rema looked off down the corridor, as though she thought Kim might appear there. Her room was the next door down, on the opposite side of the corridor to Linh's.

'Such a brave girl, though.'

Birch let out a low whistle. 'You're telling me,' she said. 'It was dark in that room, so I didn't see until we got outside how beat-up she was. And he'd been holding her for such a long time. She's just skin and bone, the wee scrap. And yet I think she was ready to break me in half and use *me* as a weapon if it meant she got to level that scumbag.'

Rema snorted. 'Sounds like the best use for you, in the situation,' she said.

Birch laughed. 'Harsh,' she said, 'but probably fair.'

Rema took another sip of coffee. 'This stuff,' she said, 'might be even worse than our Fettes coffee.'

Birch raised her cup, and peered into it, as though inspecting the grainy liquid inside. 'I dunno,' she said, 'that's a pretty bold claim.'

Rema smiled. 'I need a second opinion,' she said. 'Where's Sergeant Kato?'

Birch jerked her head in the direction of Kim's room. 'She's in with the Le family,' she said, 'overseeing the reunion.'

Rema's smile faded. 'Oh, that's going to be a tough one. I can't imagine there's much love lost between Kim and the aunt and uncle.'

Birch nodded. 'Yeah. It must be tricky to be the girl who goes missing, and no one reports it for several weeks.'

'It's especially gutting,' Rema said, 'that the person who finally thought to raise it was her *boss*. And even then, she only contacted us because of the crank phone calls.'

Birch raised her eyebrows. 'I've just realised, that's like if I went missing, and McLeod was the only one to raise the alarm. Can you *imagine*?'

Rema cackled. 'Wouldn't take him a month, though,' she said. 'He'd notice way sooner than that if you were gone. There'd be no one letting him know how full of shit he is.'

Birch laughed, but her heart wasn't in it. 'You're right,' she said. 'He'd notice – but he wouldn't raise the alarm at all. He'd just sit back and enjoy the quiet life he's always wanted.'

Rema downed the last of the coffee, then made a face. 'Ew,' she said. 'This stuff has *sediment*. Anyway – is Kim's boss going to press charges, about the phone calls?'

Birch glanced in the direction of Kim's door once again. 'I don't know yet,' she said. 'Kim's uncle has admitted it was him. Apparently it was the second thing he said to Amy, after "Is Kim okay?". Confessed to the whole thing.'

'Hey, that shows his priorities are right,' Rema replied. 'Is Kim okay? Also, I did some threatening behaviour, sorry. That is the correct way round for those two statements. It shows remorse, too.'

'It does. I mean, I get it. I hope Carol gets it, too. I don't think anyone realised Kim was actually missing – if they had, I suspect they would all have behaved differently. I think everyone in her life just thought she was dodging them.'

Rema lifted her empty coffee cup and took aim at a nearby recycling bin. 'Poor kid,' she said, letting the cup fly. It landed dead centre, and disappeared into the bin.

'Nice shot,' Birch said.

There was a scrape and a click, and the door behind them eased open. Both women turned, and then rose to their feet as Winnie Fortune let herself out of the hospital room, and closed the door softly behind her.

'Winnie,' Birch said. The older woman's face was wet, her eyes red. 'Are you okay? Do you need a hug?'

Without speaking, Winnie nodded, and Birch opened her arms to her mother's old friend. She clung on as Winnie cooried into her, and sobbed.

'Och, Helen,' she said. 'I don't know how to thank you, hen. Truly, I think you saved her life.'

Birch gave Winnie a squeeze, then released her from the embrace. 'The person you need to thank,' she said, 'isn't me. It's a woman named Beatrice Crozier. She provided information that led us to the whereabouts of Linh and the other young woman.'

Winnie pulled a handkerchief out of her sleeve, and dabbed at her eyes. 'Can I talk to her?' she asked. 'This Beatrice Crozier. If that's the case, then I'd like to thank her. Though I'm sure you're also being far too modest, Helen.'

Rema leaned forward slightly. 'I can confirm,' she put in, 'that she is. As usual.'

Birch batted a hand at Rema. 'I assure you,' she said, 'I'm not. As for Beatrice … I'm sure we could get a message to her. Speaking to her directly might be a bit of a problem at present.'

Winnie cocked her head. 'Why? Is she hurt?'

Birch winced. 'She's … in police custody,' she replied. 'I believe DI Crosbie is interviewing her as we speak.'

Winnie frowned. 'Has she done something wrong?'

Birch shook her head – perhaps, she realised, a little too vigorously. 'No,' she said, 'not as far as I'm concerned. But DI Crosbie is … keen to understand how she came to obtain the information she gave us.'

Winnie let out a little huffing sound. 'DI Crosbie,' she said, 'is worse than useless. If it were up to him, Linh would still be trapped in that house. Crosbie ought to be interrogating that man! Luke Stanford, or whatever he calls himself.'

Birch placed a hand on Winnie's shoulder. 'I'm happy to say,' she replied, 'that Luke Stanford is also in police custody, though he needs to recover from his injuries before we can interrogate him. Stanford is one of his many aliases … we're working on figuring out his actual name. But if he's who we think he is, then we believe that Interpol are also interested in speaking to him. I feel confident that his days of international jet-setting are now officially over.'

Rema chuckled. 'I think his days of going *anywhere* are now officially over,' she said.

'Good,' Winnie retorted. For just a moment, Birch thought the older woman might actually spit, right there on the floor of the hospital corridor. 'That man is a menace to society. You know I'm a good Christian woman, Helen, and I never say this about anyone. But I hope he goes straight to hell.'

Birch's eyes widened. For Winnie, this was as strong as strong language got.

'Or, failing that,' Rema said, 'HMP Barlinnie.'

Winnie dabbed at her eyes again, composing herself. 'That,' she said, 'will do in the meantime, yes.'

Birch smiled. 'How's Linh doing?'

Winnie's eyes dampened once again. 'Och, she's a wee fighter,' she said. 'I can't believe how strong she is. She's sitting there in a hospital bed with tubes coming out of her, looking so thin and pale and tired, I can barely stand it. And yet she's laughing and smiling, and asking after the cat and her school friends. She's a wee marvel, she truly is.'

'The tubes are nothing serious, Winnie,' Rema said. 'Linh is very dehydrated, and she hasn't had much to eat in the nine days she's been gone. But other than that, the doctors say she's in great health. Like you say, she's strong.'

Winnie blew her nose into the handkerchief. 'She's had to be strong,' she replied, 'with all she's been through. She's had to learn to be strong, in a way no child ever should. It's too much, it really is. So I've made a decision: enough is enough. First thing tomorrow, I'm going to contact her family in Vietnam, and see if they won't let me adopt her.'

Rema threw Birch a look. 'That's a hard road, Winnie,' she said. 'Are you sure?'

Winnie was nodding. 'I'm sure I don't want that child to suffer any more hardships,' she said. 'And I know that if she turns eighteen and nothing's changed, there'll be a whole world of new horrors she'll have to endure. I know that she'll lose her status as an unaccompanied minor, and become a *migrant*, to use the horrible term the tabloids love so much. She'll go from being a bright wee girl with her life ahead of her, to being seen as a problem and a criminal. They'll want to deport her home, but there'll be all sorts of red tape and nonsense, no doubt. She'll be put in one of their so-called migrant hostels, or worse, a detention centre. Some people spend *years* in those places, sitting in a cage like an animal while their papers get pushed around! I won't have it. I'm sure her family will feel the same. I'm going to tell them, I'll never consider myself her parent – she *has* parents, and I'd never try to replace them. But I'd like to be her legal guardian, for as long as she wants to stay in this country, so that no one can take away her dignity ever again. Not on my watch. And if she decides she wants to go home, then she can. If she decides she wants to go to university, then she can. The way I see it, I'll be helping her choose her own future, rather than watching while it's stolen away from her.'

Birch looked at Rema. She was relieved to see she wasn't the only one whose eyes were suddenly wet.

'You're a damn good woman, Winifred Fortune,' Birch said. 'I only wish my mother was still here to support you through what you're about to do.'

Winnie looked up at her, and smiled a tearful smile. 'Oh, Joan's here, hen,' she said, reaching out and touching Birch's arm. 'She's standing here, right in front of me.'

Birch paused outside McLeod's office door for a moment, screwing up the courage to knock. She thought of all the times she'd steamed up to this door, full to the brim with some hunch or theory or plan she wanted approval for, ready to spill over with enthusiasm or ire while McLeod wore his hangdog, barely-listening face. She thought of all the times she'd cajoled him, all the times she'd convinced him, all the times she'd pissed him off. She thought of the time on Operation Kendall when he'd called her a 'damn fine officer', right there in front of her, and in front of other people. It had been all she could do to stop her jaw from uncoupling and hitting the floor. Then she thought of their conversation a few days prior: her, tired and confused and bothered by dreams of deep water; him, saying, *We can't make it too easy for these kinds of people to settle here*. She thought of him only hours ago, glaring at her with true fury in his eyes and saying, *I can't stand to hear another word out of your mouth*. It was that memory, so fresh and strange, that made her finally raise her hand, and knock.

'Come in.'

She pushed the door ajar, and poked her head through the gap. 'Guv,' she said, 'do you have a minute?'

He didn't appear to be doing anything; his chair was tilted back and turned towards the window. The sky outside was dark, and the streetlights threw a strange glow into the room.

'What can I do for you, Birch?' he asked.

She opened the door a little wider and stepped inside. She knew it would look ominous to close the door again; it would betray the fact that this wasn't simply her nipping by for a chat. But this needed to be a closed-door conversation. She pushed the door to gently, then dipped the handle. It clicked shut.

'I've been at the hospital,' she said, turning back to face him. 'I've only just got back. How are things progressing?'

He wasn't looking at her – not directly. She could feel him looking at a spot on the back wall of the office, somewhere slightly above the top of her head.

'Beatrice Crozier is still in custody,' he replied, 'if that's what you're asking.'

'Partly,' she said. 'Is Crosbie getting anywhere, do we know?'

He gave his head a small shake. 'Not the last I heard.'

McLeod was livid. He didn't need to say anything, or do anything; she'd known him long enough to be able to simply read it from the atmosphere in the room. She'd done what he'd told her not to – again – but he couldn't do anything about it, because whether or not he liked her methods, she'd brought in the bad guy. She'd found the vulnerable young people the bad guy had abducted. She'd raised questions McLeod couldn't answer, and caused problems he didn't know how to solve. The case had been solved, as far as they knew, by a psychic. That was going to be embarrassing, in the press and in the bar and at McLeod's golf games. His poker face was good, but not good enough. He was livid. Of course he was.

'How are our young people doing?' he asked.

Birch took a step towards his desk. It felt, as it so often did, like a wall between them. 'Linh Fortune is in great shape,' she said. 'Hungry and dehydrated, but otherwise fine. Asking to go home already.'

McLeod gave a brief nod.

'Kim Le,' she went on, 'has had a worse time of it, I'm afraid. The doctors say she has several broken ribs, and there's evidence of sexual assault. Her face is pretty beaten up, too. I think she'll be in hospital a while longer.'

Again, McLeod nodded. 'And our perp?'

'Also in the hospital,' she said, 'getting his leg fixed up. We'll start in on him tomorrow, see if we can't get him in the mood to talk. But in the meantime, you might need to take a phone call or two from Interpol.'

She could have sworn she saw him sit up a little straighter.

'Yes,' he said, 'of course. It seems our Mr Stanford had his fingers in an awful lot of pies. Quite the entrepreneur.'

'Indeed,' Birch said. 'We're looking at all sorts of charges, here. Trafficking, kidnapping, rape, GBH – and that's only for starters. There'll be weapon and probably drug charges too, and conspiracy to – well. Conspiracy to do a whole variety of things, depending on our success finding possible accomplices.'

'Some rap sheet,' McLeod replied. 'Let's make it stick, shall we? And no more heroics, please, Birch.'

'Yes, guv.' She forced herself to take another step forward.

McLeod eyed her, sternly. 'I mean it, Helen. This case is already a PR nightmare, so frankly, I'd appreciate it if you'd—'

She reached out and dropped a folded piece of paper on to the desk in front of him. She'd been holding it tightly, and could see where her fingers had warped and dampened it. McLeod stopped speaking, and looked down at it.

'You don't have to worry about me anymore,' she said, gesturing towards the paper, 'because that's my letter of resignation.'

McLeod's eyebrows shot into his hairline. Whatever he'd expected, it wasn't this. 'Helen,' he said. 'You're not serious?'

Birch took another step, but this time, she was backing towards the door. 'I've never been so serious in my life,' she replied. 'It's been an honour and a privilege to spend the last decade and more serving as a police officer, but I'm afraid I simply cannot do it any longer.'

McLeod had picked up the letter and was holding it, still folded, in both hands. 'Do you mind,' he said, 'if I ask the reason why?'

She stood up straight, recalling what Winnie had said earlier, at the hospital, about seeing her mother in her.

'I suggest that you read the letter, sir,' she replied. 'You'll find that I've compiled a list.'

Epilogue
Bee

DI Crosbie called me back for interview several times. I hired a lawyer, which was easier than I expected. Apparently, there are plenty of people willing to represent you if you phone them up and say, 'I'm psychic, and it's got me into some hot water with the police.' They just need to know you'll be able to pay. I was happy to pay. I didn't know how to give the police what they wanted. They kept asking me to recite what I knew, over and over again, obviously hoping my story would change. Or perhaps they were hoping a crack would appear, the light of some new and better version of events glittering in the space behind it. It was never going to happen, because what I was telling them was the truth. The truth doesn't change; it's fixed. They're police officers. They know that. They just didn't like the truths I had to offer. They wanted different truths, tidier truths.

I'm fifty-one, I told them. Ever since I was a little girl, I've lived with this thing I call the Knowing. It manifests in a variety of ways. When I was younger, I saw ghosts. In high school, I realised that sometimes I knew things about people that they hadn't actually told me. It was a gradual process, coming to understand that I wasn't like everyone else. I knew things because I knew them. I didn't know *how* I knew them, but I knew them, and I was never wrong. I told them how, on the eve of the new millennium, I'd looked at a photograph of my father and seen how he would die. It took him ten years to do it, but die he did – in exactly the way I'd seen. I didn't know how I knew, but I knew.

I told them the dream I'd had about Rosie Cole was a new thing; I didn't remember ever having had the Knowing manifest itself in a dream before. After Rosie was found, it didn't happen again for a long time, and I assumed it was a one-off, a strange blip in my already strange psyche. That, or perhaps I'd beaten down that part of the Knowing with the huge cudgel that was my shame over the case of Rosie Cole. Her assailant was sent down for life, without any hope of early release. One of the charges was child molestation. I'd known, and said nothing. Done nothing.

I told them that the first time I dreamed of Linh, I felt a terrible, creeping dread. The dream was vague, and strange: I was in the back of a van, being driven somewhere by someone I was afraid of. It was dark, there was a bad smell, and I felt nauseated. It could have been just a dream like any other. But I knew it wasn't, because I knew. And then the dreams kept coming: Linh shivering on the sofa, cuddling her ginger cat backpack. Linh and Kim sleeping top to toe, wrapped up in a grubby blanket for warmth. The terrible threat pacing the floor in the room upstairs from them. I couldn't stop those dreams. I knew they were real. I knew that somewhere, these things were happening, and I was watching them. I couldn't sit by and do nothing all over again. I had to speak up. I owed it to Rosie.

I told them how scared I'd been, the day DI Birch and Jamieson picked me up in the van. As we got closer and closer to 39 Broom Park, I could feel the Knowing getting stronger, the things I'd seen coming into sharper focus, like photo negatives dropped into solution. I knew that at some point, we'd cross a threshold of proximity to that place, and the whole terrible story would fall into my head. When it did, and I knew everything that had happened in that house, there was no question of walking away. If anyone was going through that front door, it was me. I wanted to undo the bolts myself. I wanted to know what it meant to turn the Knowing into doing.

I told them how I listened as DI Birch charged up the stairs. I didn't watch her go; I was already fumbling with the bolts on the living room door, pulling them back as fast as I could with shaking hands. By the time I'd opened the door, Luke Stanford had begun trying to batter his way in. I thought, at first, that the room was empty: a grimy nightmare crack-den room with a blown-out fireplace and a bad smell. But I knew, because I knew, that the girls were in there. I just had to convince them they'd be safe with me.

They were on the sofa, cowering together in a little ball of limbs. Kim had curled her whole frame around Linh, and when she turned her battered face up to look at me, I saw she was ready to fight tooth and nail for this girl she'd met only days before. I saw what a fierce creature she was, and I understood why Luke had wanted to hurt her so badly. He hated that she was strong, and refused to be cowed in spite of all his violence.

'I'm here with the police,' I said, and saw the spark of hope in both their faces at the sound of that word, *police*. 'We're going to help you.'

That seemed a stupid thing to say when Luke was outside slamming his body against the only door we could possibly have walked out through. I told them – DI Crosbie and his friends – how the Knowing seemed to leave me, then, right when I needed it most. Did I know if we'd get out of that house? If Luke would get in? If he'd kill me, or them, or DI Birch, or all of us? No, I didn't know. Perhaps, for those

few minutes, there was no Knowing. Our fate hung in the
balance of whatever decides. I don't remember running up
the stairs. I don't remember hearing the phone call DI Birch
made. I remember making the barricade, but only in flashes.
Mainly, I remember pleading, pleading in my head: *Tell me
how this ends. I need to know.* And I didn't know. In those few
moments, I got the thing I'd prayed and begged and mith-
ered for so many times: the Knowing had gone away. It felt
like I'd stepped on a landmine, like a whole essential part of
me had been blown away.

The lawyer's name was Caroline, and she did whatever it
is that lawyers do. The police couldn't charge me with anything – certainly not with wasting police time, the charge DI
Crosbie kept dangling over my head. If anything, Caroline
said, the police were wasting *my* time, having me repeat the
same testimony over and over without any obvious justi-
fication. They let me go for the final time late one freezing
February night. The pavements were lethal with ice, but the
roads were gritted. It was quiet, with no one around, and nothing in the world more frightening than the things the Knowing
had decided I needed to see. I walked home alone through the
dark, in the middle of the road, scuffing the soles of my feet
on the grit. The stars above my head guttered and flashed,
and I thought about silver coins in the bottom of a well. When
I got home, I found a letter on the doormat, written to me by a
woman named Winifred Fortune. DI Birch was no longer DI
Birch by then – the time the police had spent trying to make
some charge or other stick to me had been longer than her
notice period, so she'd got free of them before I had. But DI
Birch, as I'll always think of her, had given Winifred Fortune
my details, and urged her to get in touch. I knew these things
before I'd even opened the envelope.

Winnie asked me to go to her home for dinner. She wanted to thank me in person for the things I'd done to help find Linh. I didn't want to be thanked, and I didn't really want to talk about the Knowing, but in her letter, Winnie told me Linh had asked to see me, too, and there was no way I'd refuse that girl. I couldn't imagine what it must be like to be only seventeen, and to have been through as much as she had. There was no way on earth I was going to refuse her something that was in my power to give.

Winnie Fortune's house wasn't huge, but it was old-fashioned and well-built, with big, high-ceilinged rooms. As I took off my coat in the hall, I could feel the presence of the children who'd lived there, like a tribe of ghosts standing patiently just out of my line of sight. Their stories were waiting to be known, if I cared to know them, and what they'd tell of this place was goodness and learning and safety and care. Winnie Fortune herself was a closed book, the way some people are – or perhaps she was so open that there was simply nothing about her that was left to be known. She'd given away as much of herself as she possibly could, and I marvelled at her generosity.

'Come away in,' Winnie said, leading me down the hall towards a bright, narrow kitchen, its door ajar. 'The girls are just in the dining room, here.'

The kitchen smelled of something delicious, but I turned right as Winnie directed, through a different door. The dining room immediately reminded me of my mother; along one wall was a sideboard with matching china plates not all that different from her precious Hedgerow set. The room was so warm and trig and welcoming, with flowers on the table and cork-bottomed placemats laid out at four neat intervals. Linh and Kim were already seated, their chairs close together, the two of them laughing and chatting in their own language.

I felt like an interloper, my arrival in the room breaking open the happy bubble of their talk. But as I moved into the room, they both stood, and though neither one of them had seen me since that day in the miserable house – their captor yelling and puffing and pushing a handgun into my face – they came over and held out their arms to hug me. Kim first, and then Linh.

'You both look so different!' I said, and it was true. Kim's face had been bruised and bloodied that day in the house, and she'd looked dangerously thin. Now her bruising had all but disappeared, and the cut on her mouth was fading into a scar. Though still very slim, she'd put on weight, and her eyes looked bright as she grinned at her younger friend, who came in for a hug and held on tight. Linh was very petite, but she seemed taller than I'd remembered her, and older. In the house, she'd seemed like a child. Now, I could see she was a young woman, almost grown-up, with a graceful bearing that spoke to the incredible strength I knew she possessed.

'You look great,' I said, as we sat. I wanted to say it over and over again.

'Winnie's been feeding us up,' Kim said. 'I come here, like, four times a week for my tea. I just can't get enough. She is *such* a good cook. I've even brought my flatmates over a few times.'

As if on cue, Winnie appeared in the room with a patterned casserole dish in her oven-gloved hands. 'Don't over-egg the pudding, young lady,' she said. 'I don't want Beatrice's expectations to be too high.'

'It's hotpot tonight,' Linh said, nodding in the direction of the casserole dish. 'I promise, it's delicious.'

Winnie made a *tsk* sound. 'It's just good, simple food,' she said, 'like my mother used to make. You can't beat the classics, that's what I say.'

'It'll be the best hotpot you ever eat,' Kim said, already reaching for a plate. 'Really – I guarantee you.'

I didn't need to taste the food to know that Kim was right. Just the smell as Winnie lifted the lid of the dish was enough. The food was so good that for a while, the four of us ate in silence, only speaking occasionally to inform Winnie of how much we were enjoying ourselves.

'Linh just got her prelim results back,' Kim said, after a while.

Linh groaned. 'Stop,' she said, nudging her friend in the arm. 'It's just prelims, it's not a big *deal*.'

'It *is* a big deal, babe. You're really freaking smart, okay?'

'Whatever.'

'No, not whatever. I'm gonna tell Bee about it, because I'm proud of you, and I think she'll be proud of you, too.'

Linh rolled her eyes, but didn't protest further.

'She got an A in English,' Kim said, leaning forward over the table towards me as though to underline the importance of what she was telling me. 'An A! I didn't get an A in English, and I've lived here since I was twelve.'

Linh blushed. 'I just *like* English,' she said, 'so it isn't hard. It doesn't feel like studying if you like doing it.'

Kim put down her fork and used her free hand to make a *blah blah blah* motion. 'Yeah, yeah. Stop being modest. Your brain is brilliant – the end.'

I couldn't stop smiling. I hated how they'd been thrown together, but I loved the adorable double act these girls had become.

'What about after your exams?' I asked. 'Are you thinking about uni?'

Linh smiled a shy smile, and I knew – because I knew – that I was asking about something special, something she held close and warmed herself by. The glowing coal of a quiet dream.

'Edinburgh,' Kim said, her mouth half-full of food, 'has the oldest English literature department in the world. Did you know that?'

I felt my eyebrows lift. 'I do now.'

Kim pushed her fork around the plate, scraping up gravy. 'She thinks she's not smart enough for that, but I think she should apply.'

Linh rolled her eyes again. 'You're talking about me like I'm not sitting *right here.*'

Kim stuck out her tongue. 'Sorry, babe. I'll stop it if you promise to put Edinburgh on your UCAS form.'

Linh looked at me from under her eyelashes. 'I'd *like* to,' she said. 'Edinburgh would be amazing. It's got such a good library, and I mean, I've looked at the syllabus. It looks great. I could stay near my friends, and Winnie, and Kim of course.'

Kim snorted. 'Apparently I don't count as one of her friends.'

'Shh.' Linh nudged her again. 'You know what I *mean.*' She looked back at me. 'I just … I feel like I ought to be realistic, you know? I'm just really not sure if I'd get in.'

I put down my knife and fork, and looked at her across the table. The Knowing felt so strong in that moment that I thought it might lift me up bodily and levitate me out of my chair. I wondered then if maybe all those years of struggle with the Knowing had actually been leading me here, to this room, and this moment, when I could use it to say something I knew had the power to change someone else's life for the better.

'Trust me, sweetness,' I said, placing a hand down flat on the tablecloth, 'you're going to get in. I know it.'

Acknowledgements

I must start by thanking the absolutely brilliant, patient, kind and understanding Charlotte Seymour, who has stuck with me through thick and thin in recent times – Charlotte, I appreciate you so much. Thanks too to the team at Johnson & Alcock for all their support.

I am grateful to Phoebe Morgan for her considered and extremely thoughtful editing – Phoebe, you helped me make this book so much stronger. And I must mention the wider team at Hodder & Stoughton – a great number of you have worked on the DI Birch series over the years and I won't forget your many contributions.

Thank you to Dominic Stevenson, whose work with care experienced young people has changed countless lives for the better. Dom, thank you for giving me the idea for this book, and so much of your time to talk about the issues within it – I hope this mention makes up for the lack of UFOs! Esa Aldegheri, Rachel Farrier and Marjorie Lofti: thank you for all the work you have done and continue to do to support refugees, asylum seekers, migrants and all displaced folk, and thank you for the opportunities you've given me over the years to be involved in that work and the conversations around it.

Somehow, I managed to write this book in the midst of a year that felt like an endurance test. There are not enough thanks in the world for the friends who helped me through it in myriad large and small ways. Alice Tarbuck, Stella Birrell

(#wife4lyfe!), Debz Butler, Jane Bradley, Kerry Ryan, Leon Crosby, Sasha de Buyl – thank you. I love you all.

Thank you to my wee brother Nick for always being there for big, weird conversations over many cups of tea – and for letting me crash on the sofa so often! Team Askew as a whole has outdone itself this year in terms of showing up to offer strength and support – as always, Mam and Fath, without you, I am nothing.

A special mention must go to Geoff Byers, for always asking me how the writing is going, for understanding about procrastination, and for teaching me it's okay to say "I don't know." Everyone else should forgive the in-joke, but: "how many grand slams have you won, Andrew?"

Finally: heartfelt thanks go to Beverley Johnson and Malcolm Jones, whose voices I followed out of the dark woods – and of course, to Al Smith, who walked the path with me.

Have you read all of Claire Askew's acclaimed crime novels?

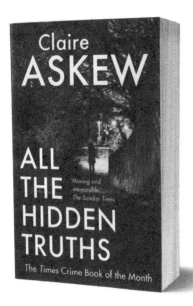

Winner of the McIlvanney
Prize for Scottish Crime
Debut of the Year

Shortlisted for the
CWA Golden Dagger

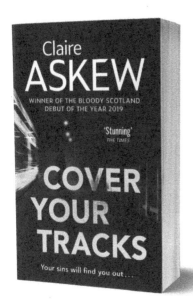

'It's as good as Rankin!'
*The Peterborough
Telegraph*

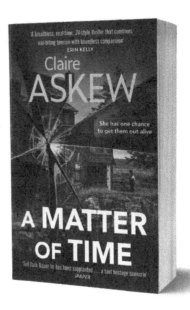

'A master of the suspenseful
police procedural'
Sunday Times Crime Club